THE *Walls* WE BREAK

KATELYN TAYLOR

PLAYLIST

<u>**Vi's Playlist**</u>
Start Listening Here! – https://spoti.fi/3WbZU9a
Breathe by Taylor Swift, Colbie Caillat
I Hope You Dance by Lee Ann Womack
Love Song by Sara Bareilles
Everywhere by Michelle Branch
She's So High by Tal Bachman
Breathe by Michelle Branch
Fallin' For You by Colbie Caillat
Rainbow by Kacey Musgraves
Slow Dancing by Aly & AJ
Ship To Wreck by Florence+The Machine
Snow On The Beach by Taylor Swift (Ft. Lana Del Rey)
This Love by Taylor Swift
A Thousand Years by Christina Perri

<u>**Declan's Playlist**</u>
Start Listening Here! – https://spoti.fi/3VQCqqh
Talkin' Tennessee by Morgan Wallen
One Of Them Girls by Lee Brice
Dangerous by Morgan Wallen
Sweet Home Alabama by Lynyrd Skynyrd
Singles You Up by Jordan Davis
She's With Me by High Valley
You Proof by Morgan Wallen

Take It From Me by Jordan Davis
More Surprised Than Me by Morgan Wallen
Beautiful Crazy by Luke Combs
She's Everything by Brad Paisley
Slow Dance In A Parking Lot by Jordan Davis
Do I Make You Wanna by Billy Currington

DEDICATION

To all of the survivors. You are stronger than your circumstances. Just breathe and you will find the light at the end of the tunnel. Or a sexy pro football player. Preferably both.

TRIGGER WARNING

Please be aware that The Walls We Break does touch on and display certain scenarios and actions that could be potentially triggering for some readers. If you are uncomfortable with any of these triggers please be cautious about continuing on as your mental health is always first priority. Potential triggers include, domestic violence (physical, psychological, neglect), trauma, PTSD, attempted sexual assault.

Contents

PROLOGUE

VIOLET

Six Years Ago

The smell of copper is thick and heady, practically suffocating me inside this shrinking room. My limbs are heavy and my vision blurred.

Get up, Violet. You need to get up.

I hear the distant voice inside my head, begging me, pleading with me to muster up the strength to stand, to move. Just a few more minutes. I need just a few more minutes. To process, to hurt, I'm not really sure. I just need more. Just a few more minutes and then I'll get up.

My head aches as the events play back over in my mind, a single tear running down my cheek before I'm able to stop it in time. How did everything come to this? How was my life able to be irrevocably changed in less than four hundred and eighty seconds? The hurt extends past the physical ache that is wrapped around each part of my body like a vice. It's deep, internal, and, by far, more painful.

Get up, Violet. You need to get up, now.

Blowing out a choppy breath that makes my chest burn, I slowly rest my palms against the hard carpeted floor beneath me before applying pressure. My face tightens as my ribs scream in pain at the forced movement.

You can do this. One step at a time.

Taking as deep of breaths as I can through my rapidly swelling nose, I'm somehow finally able to get onto my feet. My balance wavers for a moment before I quickly place my hands on my desk for balance. I squeeze my eyes shut for a moment to get my bearings before I look down at the object in front of me.

How could two little lines change so much?

One little plus sign and the life I thought I knew imploded on itself.

The pain inside me begins to ebb, or maybe that's just me willing it to do so. Either way, I somehow find the strength to stand a little taller, a little straighter before I reach for my purse and make my way out the door.

I don't know what to do or where to go. Everything has changed now. I feel my walls slowly forming as I try to stand, building themselves to immeasurable heights as I begin taking small steps towards the door, becoming unbreakably strong by the second.

Each step hurts and has me ready to crumble into a heap. I can't let myself do that, though. I have to keep moving.

It's not just me anymore.

CHAPTER ONE

DECLAN

PRESENT DAY

"Well, I gotta say, Jim, the most surprising announcement made this year for me was the last-minute trade of Declan Daniels to the Seattle Crusaders."

"Yeah, drafted by the Knoxville Bucks his junior year at Brighton University, he has been with the team for six years and has had an incredible career in that time."

"I heard that the trade was made by Daniels' request," a third commentator chimes in.

"Really?" The other two ask simultaneously, instantly perking up at the juicy rumor that is no doubt floating around the sports community right now.

Granted, it's not a rumor. I did request the trade, but no one but myself, Coach Paxton, and Coach Aberton needs the details. That's one thing they don't tell you when you are a little kid dreaming of making it big one day as a pro baller. They don't warn you that anything that happens in your life, private or not, becomes public knowledge. Almost like the public has the right to know what kind of protein shake I drink for breakfast, who I am dating or that one annoying as fuck reporter who had the balls to ask me if I was a boxer or briefs kind of man.

I shake my head as I turn off the radio and put the car into park. It's late and nearly pitch-black outside. I landed in Seattle a few hours ago, and after I dropped my stuff off at my new condo, I got into the truck that I had ordered and just drove. I've only been to Seattle for away games and when that did happen, I only saw the hotel room and the stadium. Things are different now, though. This is my new home. My new team. My new city.

To be fair, not everything is new. I used to play with a few guys on the Crusaders in college. Actually, we were all super tight. Sebastian Caldwell is the Crusaders' star tight end– has been for seven seasons now. He can be a prick sometimes, but he's a good guy. Then there is Slater Santos, the fastest running back in the NFL, or at least he likes to say so. Slater and I used to be attached at the hip, but when we both got drafted our junior year to opposite ends of the country, we all lost touch.

It'll be good to play with those guys again, not that I didn't love the Bucks. I practically grew up with the team. My dad was the starting Middle Backer for the Knoxville Bucks for over eight years and left behind a legacy when he retired after a nasty shoulder break when he was thirty. It was almost surreal when I got the news. I was being drafted by the Knoxville Bucks.

It's been an amazing six years. I wouldn't trade it for anything, but I'd be lying if I said that I wasn't a little concerned about what the future held for me. I'm not old or anything; I'm only twenty seven. But in the NFL, with a career as long as I have had in the position I am in, guys don't usually make it much longer. I know my time is running out to make a name for myself, a name away from Knoxville. I don't wanna be known as Rodney Daniels' son when I retire, which is why I had to get out of there, and what better place than with my college best friends?

I haven't caught up with the guys yet. It'll be great to see them again, but I didn't anticipate this heavy sense of loneliness to wash over me when I got here. I had never focused too much on relationships in the past. I'm too busy, and I see how a majority of the times this type of job puts a strain on even the most solid relationships. I never wanted to do that to myself or a girl, so I kept it casual.

Besides, if you aren't into cleat chasers, then it is pretty fucking impossible to find a woman as an NFL player. As soon as they find out what you do, dollar signs flash in their eyes, and they latch onto you like a starving piranha. Our QB back in Knoxville got wrapped up with one of those. Stupid fucker got her pregnant and married her. Now he is taking every advertising opportunity and commercial that he can get his hands on to support his wife's shoe shopping addiction.

I shake my head at the thought. Yeah, I'll pass on that. I came to Seattle to make my own name, reconnect with old friends and have something that is just mine, and that is damn sure what I'm gonna do.

Chapter Two

Vi

I let out the yawn that's been begging to be released for the last hour before I sigh softly. It's been an exceptionally long day, and I'm practically fantasizing about my bed at this point. That's what I get for taking an extra night shift at the diner after working all day at the shop.

Glancing at the clock, I blow out a sigh of relief. Only five more minutes. *Thank god.* Looking around the diner, I see that my last table of the night has just cleared out. I move over to collect the dishes when I hear our cook Frankie come out from the kitchen.

"Hey, Vi. I gotta get going. You need anything before I go?"

I look over at him and smile as I shake my head.

"Nope, I'm good. Have a good night, Frankie."

"You too," he calls out over his shoulder as he heads out the back.

I walk to the back of house and load the dishes into the dishwasher before getting a mop bucket started. It has been nonstop raining today, which means the floor is streaked with mud and water. A typical day in the Pacific Northwest. Once the bucket is filled, I roll it to the front and begin work on the stained floor.

My well loved Converse squeak across the floor as I slowly make my way around the room. They are bright red and by far my favorite pair. Sure, they clash with the robin egg blue sixties diner dress that is the uniform but who said you had to wear boring shoes? No one. Ever.

Glancing down at my shoes, my eyes catch on the same inky marking they normally do. Across the top of my right toe says, 'Just Breathe.' I remember the day I wrote it. I was drowning, suffocating. My mom always told me that a deep breath can fix near everything or at least help. Now, it's a constant reminder when I wear these shoes that no matter what is going on, all I need to do is breathe. Kinda weird, I know, but if you've been there, then you get it.

Unfortunately, the worst sound that I could ever imagine chimes through the small restaurant not two minutes later, the door. I blow a piece of chocolate brown hair out of my face as I groan under my breath. When I glance up, I see a man in a hoodie and aviator glasses step in through the door. He looks around the room, obviously taking notice of the empty booths before stepping further inside.

Take the hint buddy, go away.

I walk up to the front counter doing my best to screw in my customer service face, even if the only thing I want to do is go home and be done with this day. Smiling, I come face to face with the late-night customer just as he takes off his glasses and lowers his hood.

Woah.

This guy is drop dead gorgeous. Can a guy be gorgeous? Because if so, that's the perfect way to describe him.

He has short chestnut brown hair that is slightly longer on top. His jaw is sharp with a short, well trimmed beard that makes him that much sexier. The guy is huge too. He is built like a freaking brick house with wide shoulders and arms as thick as my thighs. Seriously, I don't even know how he made it through our tiny doorway. His lips are pink and full and look way too soft to be on a man who looks like this.

What really catches me off guard though are his almost glowing golden amber eyes. They are so vibrant and intense they are almost wolfish. I've never seen anything like them and yet I've never been so entranced by anything in my entire life. His larger than life presence is taking up every inch of the previously empty diner.

"Hey. Sorry. Are y'all closed?" His deep voice rumbles with a thick southern drawl as he looks around the room.

I blink hard for a second before I realize that he just asked me a question and yet I'm still just standing here like an idiot, blatantly checking him out. My cheeks flame as I quickly look away and glance over to the clock before looking back at him.

Get it together, Vi.

"We are in three minutes. Our cook already went home."

"Oh, alright. I was actually just looking for dessert."

He looks genuinely bummed out and likely more upset than some-one should be about missing out on a late-night treat. I know that

I should kick him out anyways so that I can finish closing, but for some reason, I feel kinda bad for the guy. Though he is undoubtedly the most attractive man I have ever seen in my life, I still notice the dark shadows under his eyes and the exhaustion that is heavily written across his face. It looks like he is having a bad day. I know I have had my fair share of those and would have loved it if just one person could have cut me a break.

"We have some pie," I say gesturing to our display case. "We are kind of famous for our apple pie."

His eyes brighten just a bit more, as if that were possible, the sight instantly causing me to suck in a sharp breath. Damn. Those eyes are something else.

"Warm?" He questions.

I roll my eyes and smile. "Of course. Eating cold apple pie is like a sin."

The small grin he gives me in response causes my stomach to dip and my heart to thump out of rhythm for a second. I quickly glance down at my feet, doing my best to collect myself.

Dang, it's been a long time since a guy has thrown me off kilter like this. But if anyone would have the capability to do so, of course it would be this walking talking magazine ad of a man.

"So, is that a yes on the pie?" I ask softly as I flick my eyes up to meet his.

"Yes. Two please, ma'am," he says, his grin stretching into a full smile that showcases a set of perfectly straight white teeth as he takes a seat at the counter.

I set my hands on my hips as I raise a brow at him.

"Excuse you. I think I should have at least another ten years before I'm referred to as a ma'am," I say with a wrinkled nose and a suppressed smile.

The man lets out a rough laugh as he nods his head in agreement.

I quickly grab two plates and dish up a piece of pie to each before I heat them up and add a scoop of vanilla ice cream on top. Once I'm done, I push the warm desserts towards him which earns me another one of those full smiles. Seriously, who has teeth *that* white?

"Thank you," he says as he peeks at my name tag. "Violet."

"Vi," I correct with a small smile.

"Vi," he says slowly as if he is rolling the word over his tongue before he nods his approval. "I like that."

I feel my cheeks begin to heat as I give him a quick nod and turn to wipe down the inside of the microwave again before closing the door and moving around the counter to finish mopping. When I pass him, I notice that he is staring down at the second plate with a far off look in his eyes. I should probably just keep my head down and let him eat his food in peace, but my big freaking mouth is running before I can even try to stop it.

"Hey, are you okay?" I ask softly.

He startles for a moment like he forgot where he was before he turns to look at me with a strained smile.

"Rough day."

"Not a whiskey man?" I joke as I gesture to the pie that he seems to be drowning his sorrows in.

He lets out a rough laugh as he scrubs his large hand against the edge of his jaw. "Not tonight. I'm not someone who likes to get drunk on their birthday."

"It's your birthday?"

The man nods with a sad smile as he glances at the other piece of pie again.

"Is that why you got two pieces? Double the celebration?" I tease lightly, hoping to break the suddenly thick tension.

His vivid eyes clash with my hazel ones as he seems to be contemplating something before he speaks.

"It's my brother's birthday too. He can't celebrate it anymore. I always get an extra of whatever I'm having for him."

My smile falls as a heavy feeling settles into my stomach. I know firsthand how painful it is to lose someone close to you. I never had any siblings but losing any family members hurts like hell.

"Your twin?" I ask softly.

He nods as he pokes at his plate. An idea comes to my mind as I hold my hand up to stop him from digging in.

"One second. Don't take a bite yet."

Before he can say anything, I hurry into the back and go into the office where I remember we have a few left over birthday candles from when we celebrated Miranda, our owner's birthday. I grab a couple and a lighter before coming out to the front. The man raises a brow in question as I push a candle into each slice of pie.

I begin to sing happy birthday to the best of my ability, which isn't that great, honestly. I have to admit I'm not exactly Beyonce, but it's the thought that counts, right? When I get to the name part of the song, I pause and look at him expectantly.

He gives me a sweet smile as he looks at me.

"Declan."

"And your brother's name?"

A flicker of something flashes across his face at my question. He swallows for a moment before tilting his head to the side, looking at me almost like he is trying to assess me. Like he is seeing me for the first time.

"Donny."

I nod before filling in their names and finishing the song. He looks at me for half a beat before he looks down at his candle, closes his eyes and blows it out before moving to blow out his brother's. His eyes are still closed for a few seconds, and when he finally opens them and looks up at me, I notice that they are a little glassy.

"Thank you," he whispers hoarsely, his accent making his voice come out thick as he speaks.

I nod softly and give him a sympathetic smile.

"You hungry?" He asks, pushing Donny's plate slightly towards me.

"Oh, no. I shouldn't," I say.

"Donny won't mind. Hell, if he was here, he'd love to brag about how he gave the pretty woman his pie. Probably say he was more of a gentleman than me," he chuckles softly before looking up to me with a sad smile.

I hesitate for a moment before I reach to my side and grab a fork before leaning my elbows against the counter and taking a small bite. We sit there for a few minutes, eating in comfortable silence before he speaks again.

"What do your shoes say?" He says as he glances over the counter where my right toe is just barely visible. For some reason, I feel suddenly embarrassed about my little daily affirmation and shuffle the foot behind myself.

"Nothing," I shrug casually. He watches me for a moment before he gives me an accepting nod.

"So, do you work most nights?"

I look up to see him watching me with a timid grin, his large shoulders slightly hunched over. For someone that looks like he came right out of a commercial, I would expect him to be a little more cocky, full of himself. Instead, he almost seems shy, sort of sweet.

I shrug. "Usually just a couple nights a week, been working more often lately, though. We are pretty short staffed at the moment."

Declan nods. "I was a bus boy in high school. Worked a lot of late nights then."

"Oh yeah?"

"Well, not tons. I was fired after about a month. Turns out I'm a pretty shitty bus boy."

A surprised laugh bubbles out of me, and I shake my head as I lean against the counter.

"Well, it takes true talent to work in a diner. Guess you just didn't have what it takes."

He barks out a surprised laugh as he nods. "Guess not. I had my plate full as it was anyways."

"With what?"

"Football mainly."

My smile slips and I wrinkle my nose as I push away from the counter, pretending to busy myself with stacking napkins. And my interest is officially lost. Too bad. He was the first guy in a long time that had me even looking twice.

"What was that look?" He asks curiously.

"Nothing," I shrug.

He is quiet for a moment before he speaks again. "You don't like football?"

I don't like football *players*. Whether they just played in high school or not is irrelevant. They are all the same and definitely not the type of company I want to keep, even if it is just for a few minutes on a weeknight at work.

"Not really," I say simply.

"Really? How can you live in Crusader country and not like football?"

He isn't wrong. Living in Seattle, it's kind of assumed that everyone is a huge fan of the local NFL team. We are known for being the loudest and wildest fans in the league. Not my thing, though. I smile tightly and shrug. Declan looks at me curiously before he nods to himself as he takes a bite of his pie.

"Sorry to disappoint," I say, trying to ease the weird tension in the air.

He shakes his head as he chews.

"Just...surprised. Most women love football players."

I scoff and roll my eyes before I nod and glance up at the clock.

"Gotta get home to the husband?" He fishes.

I give him a pointed look that tells him he isn't as sly as he thinks. His grin is filled with embarrassment at clearly being caught but it doesn't waver as he watches me patiently.

"Not exactly."

"Cryptic. I knew there was something interesting about you."

I laugh and shake my head. "There is nothing interesting about me, trust me. Maybe you just aren't being direct enough."

"Fair enough. Are you married?"

I hold up my naked left hand and wiggle my fingers. An almost satisfied looking grin spreads across his face as he leans back into his seat.

"Boyfriend?"

I shake my head, doing my best to hide my smile. Normally when I get overly chatty customers, especially men, I'm able to put them in their place pretty easily. For some reason though, this man has me absolutely tongue tied and my face flaming hot.

"Good," he says with a nod and that dang smile.

I raise an eyebrow in question, but he doesn't say any more. Instead, he ducks his head and I swear I see his cheeks pink up, just a bit. This guy is too freaking cute for his own good. Maybe for my own good, too.

Declan takes his last bite of pie before pushing the plate away as he rubs his lean stomach with an appreciative groan. I don't miss that as he does that, his hoodie sleeves pull up slightly, revealing dark tattoos, twisting around his forearm like ivy. I wonder how far up it goes? *No. Vi, stop ogling the poor guy like he is the first sign of water that you've seen in days.*

I grab the plates off the counter and bring them to the sink in the back.

When I come back out, he is standing with his hands in his pockets at the counter. Holy crap on a cracker. This guy isn't just big, he is huge. I didn't really notice at first, but now being only a few feet away, I see that he dwarfs my 5'3" frame. He has well over a foot on me and probably a hundred pounds of pure muscle as well.

"So, what do I owe you for the amazing pie?"

I blink out of my thoughts and crane my neck up to look at him. He is watching me with that same soft smile that I can now recognize has a tint of nervousness to it. What on earth would this man have to be nervous of? Ever?

"$9.98."

He nods and pulls out a hundred dollar bill before dropping it onto the counter. My eyes bug out as I look up at him.

"I'm sorry, I don't think that I can break that this late at night."

He shrugs. "Keep it. The company was well worth it."

I cock my head to the side and furrow my brows. Did he just call me a...

His eyes widen as he realizes his implication and raises his hands quickly. "Shit no, that isn't what I meant." He curses under his breath before he looks up at me with apologetic eyes. "I was trying to be charming, guess that didn't work out too well."

I laugh and shake my head. "Not terribly, no."

He lets out a rough sigh and gives me a strained smile. "Okay then. I'm just going to come out and say it. I would really like to take you out sometime."

My eyes widen in surprise as my stomach clenches while those eyes burrow into me. I've known this guy for all of ten minutes, and he's asking me out? I can't tell if it's flattering or creepy. Again, instead of wearing a cocky smile like any other man that looks like him would, he smiles at me genuinely, patiently waiting for my answer. He seems to be a really nice guy and obviously he is hot as hell but...

"I'm sorry. I can't."

His shoulders deflate just slightly as he rubs the back of his neck.

"So, there is someone else?"

"Something like that," I say softly.

He nods as he looks to the floor before giving me a small smile and a shrug.

"Well, it was real nice to meet you, Vi. If you ever change your mind, let me know," he says as he hands me a napkin with his name and number on it.

I take it from him and smile so that I don't hurt his feelings any more than I already have. I already know that I have no intention in ever calling him, though. I think he sees it on my face too because he sighs quietly after a moment before turning toward the door.

"Have a goodnight, Declan," I call out just as he steps out the door. Amber eyes snag my gaze one more time as he offers me a smile that makes my stomach flip before he slips off into the night.

I try to shake off the encounter as I finish closing up and head home, but he seems to be the type of man that is hard to forget. When I pull up to my apartment complex, I blow out a heavy breath before getting out of my car and trudging up the stairs. Once I unlock my door, I step inside to see Judy, my seventy-five-year-old neighbor and for all intents and purposes, adopted grandmother, sitting on my couch knitting.

I give her a sleepy smile as I set down my purse and slip off my shoes.

"How was your night, Sweet Pea?" She asks as she begins packing away her things into her bag.

"Good, we were pretty slow. I had a last-minute customer, though. Sorry for being late."

"You're fine. Tucker went to bed around 7:30 after he had me watch his Mickey Mouse DVD about a million times," she groans in mock irritation.

I laugh and nod. "Sounds about right. That kid is obsessed."

"Same time tomorrow?"

"If you don't mind?" I grimace. "The extra money has really been helping us out a lot lately."

"Sweet Pea, you are twenty four years old. You work yourself too hard between the shop, the diner, and taking care of Tucker. You can only take on so much before you crack."

"I'm just trying to do the best I can, Judy," I say with a determined smile that I can feel falter slightly.

"I know. That is all you can do. I just hope you don't have to live like this forever. I mean, when was the last time you went out and had some fun?"

"I went out dancing with Mindi when she was in town a couple of months ago."

She rolls her eyes and folds her arms. "Okay, when was the last time you went out and had some fun with a *man*."

So long I couldn't even tell you.

"Mhmm. That's what I thought," she says accusingly, like she could actually read my sad thoughts.

"I'm a little busy, Judy. I don't have time to date," I deflect.

"Oh, that's fucking bullshit, and we both know it."

Judy is the sweet grandmother that Tucker and I never had, but when she is passionate about something, her mouth starts running like a sailor. She is the feistiest woman I have ever met. It is one of the many things that I love about her.

I sigh heavily as I walk over to the kitchen and get some water.

"Alright, it's late. I will get off my soap box for now, but I'm serious. You deserve happiness." She looks down the hallway towards the bedrooms before looking back at me. "You both do."

"We are happy," I say with a smile that is just a tiny bit forced.

She pats my hand lovingly like she sees right through me before she ambles out the door and across the hall to her apartment. Once the door is shut, I walk through our apartment and quietly peek my head inside Tucker's room.

He is nestled in his bed with his blankets tucked all the way up to his chin. His messy golden hair is hanging in his eyes, and I remind myself that I need to give him a haircut tomorrow. That kid's hair grows like nobody's business, and I never seem to be able to keep up. I never seem to be able to keep up with much these days.

Watching him sleep is still one of my favorite things to do, even if he is four now. He always seems so content and happy. I hope he feels that way when he is awake too.

Not wanting to wake him, I slowly slip out of his room before I step into my own. I peel off my dress and grab a baggy t-shirt and a pair of pajama pants. That dress is way too fitted for my taste. Maybe it would be fine if I didn't still have most of the baby weight. I know I'm not fat or anything, but my stomach isn't totally flat, my hips have a little extra, and my ass is definitely fuller than it ever was growing up. I've finally started coming around to embracing my body, though. My mom always used to preach about how the most beautiful thing that a woman can wear is confidence, and she honestly couldn't be more right.

Tossing the dress into the laundry hamper, I crawl into bed and plug my phone in. Blowing out a soft breath I glance at the clock and see that it's already 11:15PM, that means I have six hours until I have to open the shop up.

Rolling onto my side I notice something white on the ground that must have fallen out of my dress pocket. Furrowing my brows, I slide out of bed and bend down to pick it up, quickly reading it with a smile.

Declan – 206-556-XXXX

He was so gorgeous, and I really think he was a genuinely nice guy. Can't say I've had much experience with those before, but from what I could tell, he seemed sweet. He had me *almost* considering the idea of going out with him. Just for a moment I wanted to imagine a scenario where I would have said yes. I can't entertain those thoughts for too long, though.

I close my eyes and try to settle my mind. Despite my best efforts though, I can't get Judy's words out of my head. It's been so long since I've even really noticed a man outside of what he was ordering. Today's interaction made that painfully obvious.

I didn't do or say anything outright embarrassing but if he could have heard the thoughts running through my head I would have combusted from embarrassment for sure. It's a good thing that I turned him down. I've got way too much going on in my life. I already have one guy who is my whole world, I don't have room for anything or anyone else.

Besides, I just don't think I could ever get involved with anyone seriously. Not with Tuck's heart on the line. I'd never admit it but sometimes I think his heart isn't the only one I'm worried about.

Chapter Three

VI

My alarm goes off entirely too soon the next morning, and I groan as I turn it off, blinking my eyes blearily before tossing the covers to the side and stumbling my way to the bathroom. The warm shower helps me wake up fully, and soon, I am drying my hair and brushing on a light layer of mascara. I pull on a pair of jeans and a flowy white shirt with my pink pair of Converse.

I'm kind of an addict. I loved them growing up but wasn't nearly as hooked on them as I am now. Glancing at the pile of shoes in my closet, I chuckle. I literally have every color of the rainbow in Converse. Sure, they are all really worn in by now, but I take really good care of them so you would never know that I've had most of these pairs for the last eight years. Besides, a little worn in just means it has character.

Once I'm fully dressed, I walk into Tucker's room and kiss his head. "Tuck, baby. It's time to get up."

He groans, and I think he murmurs, 'no, thank you' as he rolls over. I laugh softly as I rub his back, trying to coax him into waking up. At least he's polite.

When he realizes that I'm not leaving, he sighs and slowly sits up, sleepily rubbing his eyes. I walk over to his dresser and pick out his outfit for the day as he stretches before crawling out of bed.

"Did you have fun with Grandma Judy last night?"

"Uh huh! She let me watch Mickey Mouse all night."

"So I heard," I smirk.

I walk over to him and help him into his clothes, even though he can dress himself I always like to help. He is my baby, and I am so not ready for him to not need me anymore. Once he is dressed, I follow him into the bathroom where I set out his toothbrush and begin putting toothpaste on it for him.

While he is getting ready, I head to the kitchen. I pour the last of the milk and some cereal in a bowl for Tuck as I turn to make his lunch. Glancing inside the fridge, moving around the contents, I frown. *Mental note: Buy more jelly when I get paid next.* I start making a peanut butter sandwich for Tuck before pulling out his favorite Mickey Mouse cookie cutter. I place it over the sandwich before smiling down as I cut off the excess and wrap the sandwich up. We may not always have a lot, but I always try to make things special when I can. I toss in an apple and a cheese stick before zipping up the lunch box.

I look over to see Tuck finishing his cereal before he hops out of his seat and walks the bowl over to the sink. He isn't tall enough to rinse the dishes, but he can set them in the sink. He is always trying to help me out even when I don't ask. He is the sweetest kid in the entire world, I guarantee it. I still don't know how I got so lucky.

A few minutes later and we are out the door and on our way to his daycare. Once we get inside, he gives me a quick hug and a kiss before he runs into the room to play with his friends. I give the owner, Claudia, a wave before I head back out to my car and drive to work.

When I pull up to the shop, I park my car out front before grabbing my purse and keys. Above the shop is a huge sign that reads Blooming-Deals. Margret, the owner of the flower shop, thinks that she is quite the wordsmith, but I personally think that the name is tacky. If it were my store, I would name it something more simple, timeless.

That's the dream, one day at least. Margret has been hinting at retirement for a couple of years now and talks about me taking over. I'm not sure when or if that day will ever happen, so for now I just smile, nod and bide my time as her manager.

I love working with flowers. It's a passion that I didn't know I had until the last five years. Some think that my job consists of putting some random flowers together and wrapping them up in a little bit of pretty paper, but I don't see it that way. Every flower has its own meaning and origin. Combined or alone, I do my best to make every bouquet beautifully unique and meaningful.

Kind of like greeting cards, each flower or bouquet can be used for different reasons. People can give them as a thank you, congratulations, condolences and my favorite, just because. Those ones aren't very common, but when someone comes in to pick up something 'just because,' it practically makes my whole day. Sometimes we get walk-ins and those are fun too, but our big money makers are events like weddings, graduations, and funerals.

I'm the Monday-Friday opener, and the next person won't come in until later this afternoon. Even though I am still dead tired from working at the diner last night, I love my peaceful mornings in the shop. I get to work on arrangements by myself without distractions as I blast my music in the back and get lost in it all.

After I get the shop opened, I reach over to grab my phone and put on my 2000's pop playlist. When *Low by Flo Rida* comes on, I immediately begin bopping my head and shaking my hips as I look over my to-do list for today. An hour or so goes by when I hear the jingle of the bell up front. I quickly pause the music before I walk out to the counter with a smile in place as I wipe off the pollen that is stuck to my shirt.

"Good morning, how are you today?" I greet.

"A whole lot better now," a familiar voice rumbles.

My eyes flick up to the man that is standing at the register before they widen.

Declan.

"Hi," I say as I look around the shop to see if anyone else is in here. *Just us.*

"Are you following me or something?" I ask skeptically after a moment.

He laughs lightly and shakes his head. "Just lucky, I guess."

I look at him for a moment to see if I can sense any malicious intent or maybe pick up on any creep vibes that I didn't catch before. But just like last night, all I see is a warm almost timid smile, bright inviting amber eyes and a handsome package to wrap it all up in.

"How can I help you?" I ask, deciding that this is just some crazy coincidence.

His cheeks flush as he rubs the back of his neck and looks down at me. "Uh, I was just looking for some flowers."

"Well, you're in a store filled with them, so I would say that you're on the right track," I tease.

He throws me a flirty grin and winks. "Thanks smartass."

I laugh and smile. "Occasion?"

"Just because," he shrugs softly.

My heart stutters, and I try to contain the swoony smile that is begging to spread across my face. Was he somehow able to read my thoughts not even two minutes ago or something? He continues to smile at me kindly, and I can't help but think about how he looks so different than our usual walk-ins.

They are typically frantic or somber looking, searching for some flowers to make amends or give condolences that their words cannot make. It isn't like everyone tells me their life story when they buy flowers, but more often than not, people feel some need to tell me that they majorly screwed up and are buying apology flowers. I have a few regulars for that occasion, specifically.

"Quickest way to a girl's heart," I sing lightly.

"Really?" He asks curiously.

"Oh yeah, you wouldn't believe what a surprise bouquet of flowers does to a girl. They are a highly underutilized gesture in my opinion. Flowers are basically magic."

"I never thought about it like that before but makes sense. My mama always goes crazy when dad brings home flowers," he laughs.

I nod and smile. "Is this for a girlfriend? Wife?"

He gives me a small smirk and shakes his head.

"I'm single. Considering I asked you out last night, I thought that would be obvious."

"Not as obvious as you may think," I mutter under my breath.

His brows dip as his smile fades into a frown.

Oops. I guess he heard me.

"I'm not that kind of guy."

I force a smile and push away the ugly feelings that are currently warring inside of me.

"Good, that kind of guy is the worst."

He nods his agreement as he watches me carefully. I can't help but look back at him, almost instantly getting lost in those enchanting eyes of his. My god, did he get more good looking overnight or something?

"So, what kind of flowers were you thinking?" I ask, trying to pull my attention away from his heavy gaze.

"Uh, the pretty kind, I guess," he says as he scratches the back of his neck almost awkwardly.

I laugh and shake my head. I wish I could say it's the first time that I've heard that, but I would be lying. Valentine's day is filled with at least two dozen men saying the exact same thing.

"Okay, well obviously you can't go wrong with roses. We have some rose bouquets right over there. Or we have some variety bouquets over there if you want a little of everything," I say gesturing to our display cases.

"I want something unique, one of a kind."

I grin. "Those are my favorite. Here, come on back and you can pick some flowers that you like, and then I'll put them into a bouquet for you."

He smiles as he walks around the counter. "You do this for all of your customers?"

"Only the cute ones," I tease.

Where did that come from?

I don't flirt with strangers, like ever. I guess there is a first time for everything. What is this man doing to me?

A wide smile breaks out across his perfectly tanned face, and I find myself smiling as I lead the way to the back room. When we get to the prep table, I push aside what I was working on and gesture around us.

"See anything you like?"

His eyes are firmly trained on me for several seconds as he smirks before looking around the room. I have several buckets of different kinds of flowers that are out for the wedding I was working on, and to the side, you can see inside our walk-in that has the rest of our inventory inside. Declan looks totally overwhelmed with wide eyes, and I can't help but laugh as this mountain of man takes up this tiny back room and seems so uncomfortable and unsure. Like I said before, too cute for his own good.

"What's one of your favorites?" He asks.

"Hydrangeas, hands down. If I owned a house, I would have a hydrangea bush planted every couple of feet along the front yard. Expensive but gorgeous."

I pull out a couple of white hydrangeas to show him what they look like.

"They come in white, blue, green, purple and pink."

"The white is nice...right?" He asks cautiously, like there could actually be a wrong answer.

I smile and nod. "Very nice. Classic beauty."

He nods and smiles almost like he is proud of himself as he looks around.

"What else?"

I move to the cooler to grab some other options before bringing them out to show him. To my surprise he picks purple and pink dahlias to go along with them, which are my second favorite flower and not a usual choice from customers.

"So, you have two jobs?" He asks.

I glance up at him as I play with different ways to arrange the flowers.

"Mhmm."

"That must be exhausting."

I shrug. "It isn't so bad. The diner is pretty simple, and it is easy money, which is nice. My piece of crap car just blew up the radiator a few weeks ago, obviously that wasn't a cheap fix, so I'm grateful that I have a way to pay for emergencies like that."

"What kind of car do you have?"

I grimace. "A '93 Ford Fiesta."

He cringes and shakes his head before laughing softly.

"What?" I ask.

"Nothing. I was gonna try to make you feel better and tell you your car isn't so bad, but that's pretty bad."

"Thanks, jerk." I say as I toss a stem at him.

He chuckles before taking a half a step closer to me and nudges my shoulder causing me to smirk. I do my best to bite back the huge smile that wants to break through and despite knowing better, I wish that he would brush against me again.

"It's better than no car," I counter.

He nods. "True."

"What do you drive, Mr. high and mighty?"

"A pickup."

"Probably new, huh?"

He shrugs, and I nod because despite only seeing him twice now, he looks like a man that has money. His clothes are casual, yet they look expensive, and his hair looks like it was done by a professional. I mean, the obscene tip he gave me last night kind of gave it away too. Looking away from him quickly, I continue playing with the bouquet, trying to find the right balance of the flowers before I turn it to face him.

"Alright now you just need a filler. You could go with some traditional laurel greens or maybe some baby's breath?"

He wrinkles his nose and lifts an eyebrow. "They named a flower baby's breath?"

"It's just a nickname," I chuckle.

"Why?"

My smile slowly drops as my brows furrow.

"I actually don't know."

We both bust out laughing and goosebumps breakout across my skin at the sound of his deep baritone laugh. He continues laughing while his eyes remain on me, causing my stomach to flip when a dimple pokes out on his left side. Our chuckling slowly subsides, yet we are both still grinning at each other like total idiots. Pulling my eyes away from him, I grab the baby's breath to show him what it looks like.

"It's really pretty in bouquets though, very understated."

I grab the bouquet and put some baby's breath through the empty spaces so he can see roughly how it will look. Once I like the arrangement, I hold it up to show him.

"What do you think?"

He smiles at the bouquet briefly before his eyes sear into mine.

"Beautiful."

I bite back my smile and nod as I start binding it together. Once it is secured, I put some pretty green paper around it before tying it off. When I hand it to him, he takes it into his large hands, inspecting it before grinning. I smile and nod before we make our way to the front so that I can ring him up.

"Hold on though, before you go, I need to get a picture of this. It's one of my favorites in a long time."

"Really? Okay, sure." He holds the flowers up awkwardly so that they are facing me. When I snap the picture, I notice that I can see his smiling face in the background. I can always crop him out.

Or not.

"Thanks," I smile as I pocket my phone.

He nods as he pulls out his wallet. "Thank you. This was really fun. I mean, I know you did all of the work, but I like to think that I helped."

"You were actually zero help. You were basically a handsome mannequin," I joke as I ring up his bouquet.

His smile widens and turns devilish as he leans his elbows onto the counter. "You think I'm handsome?"

Feeling ridiculously embarrassed, I try to pretend like I am not affected by his knowing smile and hauntingly beautiful eyes. I strategically avoid making eye contact as I pretend to mess with the register.

"Oh, don't act like you don't know. I'm sure you have a line of women out the door throwing themselves at you."

He turns around to look at the empty shop with a frown.

"Guess I'm having an off week."

I bark out a surprised laugh and nod. "$40.27."

He smiles and hands me his card. Declan's fingers graze against mine as I take it from him, and I can't stop the tingling feeling that races up my arm from the contact. My eyes flick up to meet his, and I see that he is currently smiling at me like it's his favorite thing to do. I pull away quickly and hand him his card and receipt, making sure not to touch him this time.

"Thanks for all of your help, Vi."

"My pleasure," I smile.

He picks up the flowers and gives me one more devastating smile before he walks out the door. Blowing out a wistful sigh, I turn on my heel to get back to work but only make it two steps when the door opens again. I turn around to greet the next customer and falter when I see Declan walking back inside with the bouquet in his hands. My brows dip and my lips purse.

"Is everything okay?" I ask.

"Yeah, just came by to drop these off," he says as he hands me the bouquet with a simple nod.

"Uh, what?" I laugh awkwardly as I slowly take them from him.

He gives me that bashful smile that I have already become accustomed to as he looks down at me.

"I came in this morning to buy flowers for *you*. It was a total surprise that you worked here. So, here you go. I hope you like them."

I am speechless. My mouth is parted slightly as I look back and forth between the flowers and him. To my horror, my eyes even get a little misty.

"What's wrong?" He asks quickly, his smile falling instantly as panic takes over his face. "You don't have to take them. I don't want you to cry! Shit," he swears under his breath as he rubs the back of his neck. "I just wanted to do something that would make you smile."

I stare at him for a few moments as I listen to him ramble on before I speak.

"No one has ever given me flowers before," I whisper as I stare at the bouquet for a few seconds before I look back up to him.

The panicked look on his face fades as his eyes soften before he gives me a sincere smile.

"You deserve them."

My stomach flips as I see the sincerity across his face. Who *is* this guy?

"Why?" I blurt out. "I mean, you don't know me. We are virtual strangers."

He shrugs as he tucks his hands into his jeans and glances at his shoes before looking up at me through his thick dark lashes.

"I haven't been able to get you out of my head since last night. I was going to take a chance and stop by the diner tonight with the flowers and...I don't know. I didn't really get any farther than that yet," he chuckles nervously.

"Thank you," I say softly. "I really love them."

Declan's face fills with relief and he gives me an easy smile. "You're welcome. I would still really like to take you out."

I give him a sad smile and shake my head. As much as I would love to say yes, a little boy with hazel eyes pops into my head and reminds me that I have more than my pathetic sex life, or lack thereof, to think about.

"I'm sorry. I just can't."

He nods and frowns like he expected that but doesn't like it. The way he pouts reminds me of Tucker, and it cracks the shield I have over my heart, just a little bit.

"I understand. I'm sorry if I ever made you uncomfortable," he says softly.

I smile and shake my head quickly. "No, not at all. I just...can't."

"Fair enough. You have my number," he nods with a half smile before walking out the door.

I look down at the flowers in my hand and sigh. It really is one of my favorite bouquets in a long time. Makes sense considering I designed it myself. Last night I thought he was just flirting since he was there, but what man goes out of his way to buy flowers for a woman he doesn't even know? A woman who rejected him the night before.

Maybe he thinks that I am a challenge of sorts? That doesn't seem right, though. He doesn't seem like the player type. Declan seems too sweet, a little shy even which is a really admirable quality compared to most men out there.

Walking over to the back room, I grab a vase and fill it with water before I place Declan's flowers in it. I set the vase to the side in the back so that I can look at them while I work. I lower myself to the flowers and inhale the sweet smell slowly before I smile.

I pick up where I left off on my work, sneaking glances at my flowers every couple of minutes. I just can't get over the fact that someone gave me flowers. It shouldn't be that weird for me. I live and breathe flowers. I have seen thousands of people buy them to give others but there is something different about receiving them personally.

My day goes by pretty quick after that. Since it is June, we have been pretty busy with wedding season which makes the days fly by. Margret comes in to take over for me at 3PM. She doesn't like working full shifts anymore, and I don't mind the hours, but I'm thankful that I don't have to pull an open to close after working at the diner last night. Once I catch her up on what still needs to be done, I'm in my car and on my way to pick up Tucker.

"Hey, Vi," Claudia greets as I walk in the door.

"Hey, where is Tucker?"

"He's in the bathroom. He will be right back." She looks around and takes a step closer, lowering her voice. "I actually wanted to talk to you. Tucker has been asking the other kids questions about their parents, specifically their dads. One of the kids started teasing him. I shut it down quick, but Tucker was pretty upset."

I sigh heavily and run a hand through my hair. "Alright, thanks for telling me. Looks like we will be having an uncomfortable conversation tonight."

She gives me a sympathetic smile and squeezes my shoulder. Just then, Tucker comes out of the bathroom and looks over to see me.

"Hi, sweetie," I say as I crouch down and hold my arms out to him.

He instantly runs to me and throws his arms around my neck, holding me tightly. My little guy loves to try to act tough especially in front of others, but he is as soft as they come on the inside. He has the biggest heart in the whole world, and I know that his big tender heart will probably get broken a lot going through life. God help me for when that day inevitably comes. I hear him sniffle and decide we both just need to get home.

I lift him up as I stand and sling my purse over my other shoulder while he clings to me. Claudia mouths, 'good luck' to me as we pass her. I dip my head and smile as I walk us to the car. Once I get him settled into his car seat, I hop into my seat as we make our way home. We drive in silence the whole way, and my stomach is in complete knots over the fact that my little guy is hurting.

When we get home, Tucker sits on the couch and pulls his knees up to his chest. I plop down next to him, waiting for him to speak first. After a few moments, he finally caves.

"Tanner said that if I don't know my daddy, it means I did something bad, and he doesn't want me," he says quietly.

My body fills with rage instantly. I have never wanted to hit a kid before, but I'm pretty damn tempted right now. Taking a long deep breath, I close my eyes and do my best to rein in my emotions before I open them and look down at him.

"Tuck, you know that isn't true, right? Tanner was just being mean."

"Why doesn't my daddy want me?" He asks, tears brimming his little hazel eyes.

"Baby," I whisper as I blink back tears of my own. "It has nothing to do with you. He just wasn't ready to be a daddy. Trust me, it's his loss. You are the most amazing kid in the whole world. Anyone who doesn't know you is missing out."

He sniffles and nuzzles into my side. I kiss the top of his head and squeeze him tight before turning on the worn-out Mickey Mouse DVD and hold him for what seems like hours. It's the shittiest feeling in the world as a mother when you can't protect your child from hurting. It feels even worse when that hurt is caused by the other parent. Maybe if I wouldn't have fallen for the wrong dirtbag, this wouldn't have happened, but then I wouldn't have Tuck and that is something I could never wish for.

Chapter Four

VI

The next day, I have both arms filled with hot plates as I maneuver around the counter and out to the anxious family in the lobby when the diner door opens.

"Go ahead and sit anywhere," I say with my back still turned as I begin carefully setting down the plates at the table.

"Do you guys need anything else?" I ask with a smile.

The woman at the table smiles and shakes her head just as one of her kids knocks over an entire soda in her lap. Her eyes widen in shock before she blows out a heavy breath.

"Napkins, please."

I nod quickly and turn on my heel to rush over to the counter to grab extra napkins when I slam into the wall. Wait, not a wall. Glancing up, my stomach flips when I see Declan standing in the middle of the diner, a kind smile on his face and those amber eyes setting every single nerve ending in my body on fire.

Shaking my head, I quickly take a step away from him.

"Sorry," I blink as I hurry over to the counter and scoop up as many napkins as I can before rushing back to the soaking wet woman.

When I turn back around, I see that Declan has taken up residence in the corner booth and is currently looking over the menu. Glancing around, I see that all of my other tables are taken care of for now. Taking in a small breath, I pull out my notepad and walk over to Declan's booth with the same customer service smile that I give everyone. I definitely don't smile bigger just because this sexy as sin man is watching me walk towards him with a satisfied smile and hungry eyes.

When I get to his table, I smile but don't say anything. The smell of his cologne mingling in the air around us has my mind suddenly blank

Declan watches me with a patient smile before he chuckles lightly. Shaking my head subtly, I lift my pen and notepad as I speak.

"What can I get you?"

Declan's dimpled smile stays in place as he speaks, never taking his eyes off me.

"I'll take the chicken fried steak, please."

I jot it down as I nod. "Anything to drink?"

"Water, thank you," he says as he leans his forearms against the table.

I glance down, getting a full view of the tattoos I got only glimpses of the other night. Tonight, Declan is wearing a black fitted t-shirt that looks like it was made for him as it sculpts against his wide chest and thick biceps. The black designs vary as they wrap around his corded arms. I find my eyes tracing up those arms, craving to explore the full extent of them until I am stopped in my pursuit by black cotton. Shame.

Flicking my eyes back up to Declan I see that he is watching me with an amused smile before his eyes rake over me appreciatively. My cheeks burn with embarrassment, but I do my best not to flee right then and there, even if that is what I would love to do more than anything right now.

When his eyes come back up to me, I feel like it's an appropriate time to get the hell out of here.

"I'll get that rung in right now," I say with a head nod to which he just smiles and nods as I turn to go.

I feel his eyes on me the whole time, and when I get to the register upfront, I quickly tap in his order before quickly glancing across the lobby to see that Declan is still staring at me. I didn't have to look to know that, though. I could feel it all the way from across the room. It's a heavy feeling that has my skin pricking with heat and my stomach continuously flipping. Not sure if that's a good or a bad thing. I'm going to go with bad, yeah, very bad.

Doing my best to put the drop dead gorgeous man in the corner out of my mind, I quickly spin on my heel to get back to my other tables, but in doing so, I feel the breeze of my dress lifting up. I quickly push down the material behind me, but it's already done. I glance over my shoulder to see Declan's eyes have moved from my face to my ass where the dress was definitely not covering it two seconds ago.

I rush off to the kitchen, pushing the building embarrassment inside me aside as I grab table twenty four's fries. Thankfully, I was able to drop off Declan's food while he was texting, so at least we didn't have another drawn out stare off. I definitely did not enjoy that. Right? Right.

I'm carrying a stack of blueberry pancakes over to the man around the corner of the diner when a deep southern voice calls out, not too loud but just loud enough for me to hear.

"Favorite color." Declan says.

I stop in my tracks and pause. Cocking my head towards him I raise my eyebrow at him.

"What?"

"Favorite color," he nods, like that is all the explanation I need.

Furrowing my brows, I shake my head at him slightly.

"Are you asking me my favorite color?"

Declan nods with a patient smile.

"Why?" I ask suspiciously.

He shrugs. "I would've guessed red from those shoes you were wearing the other night but now you're wearing bright green shoes. And then at the shop you had on pink ones. Also, the flowers you like come in a ton of colors so that wasn't going to narrow things down much either. So, favorite color?"

Glancing down at my Converse, I look back up to him skeptically before answering.

"Rainbow."

Declan looks surprised before he smiles and shakes his head.

"That's a cop out. You can't pick them all."

"Says who?" I challenge.

Declan lifts a large hand and rubs his beard seemingly in thought before he lifts it up and runs it through his hair and chuckles.

"Shit, I don't know."

I smirk as I shake my head softly and drop off the pancakes to the customer. A half hour later, the diner has cleared out except for a few tables, Declan being one of them, and I am wiping down the tabletops when he speaks a few booths over.

"Favorite food?"

Smiling to myself, I lower my head before I school my expression and look up at him.

"Are you going to do this all night?"

Declan grins and shrugs as he rests his forearms against the table and leans forward, seemingly eager to see if I will respond. Tossing the rag on the table, I cross my arms as I think about just blowing him off and walking back to the kitchen. Despite that thought, I still answer him.

"Mexican. No, wait. Italian. No, a good steak," I finally decide.

Nodding Declan chuckles.

"All solid options."

"What about you?" I throw back.

"Sweetheart, I'm 6'3, 275lbs. I'll eat just about anything."

A surprised laugh bubbles out of me as my cheeks flush, causing Declan's dimple to pop out as he leans back into his seat. We don't say anything more for the rest of the night. When he is the last person in here, he stands up, pulls out an insane amount of cash and drops it on the table before looking up at me.

"Have a good night, Vi. I'll see you soon."

"You will?" I ask.

His eyes rake over me from top to bottom before he softly bites the inside of his lip and nods with a chuckle.

"Oh, yeah. Real soon."

It's been two weeks of the same thing. Every day that I have a shift at the diner, he is there. I'm starting to wonder if he somehow got a copy of the schedule or if he comes every night to see if I'm here or not. Again, is he charming or creepy? I still haven't quite decided.

He comes in, sits at the corner booth if it's not taken, and waits for me to take his order. He always asks me how my day is going before ordering. Occasionally when I pass by, he will ask me random questions that catch me off guard every time.

Last night, he asked me if I could be any animal, what one would I be. Who thinks about this kind of stuff, let alone asks a basic stranger? Normal people want to know your full name, where you grew up or how many siblings you have but not Declan. He only ever seems to ask the strange questions.

I secretly kinda love it.

If it was anyone else practically stalking me at my job and asking me random questions, I would have probably already called the cops. There is something about him that is sort of calming, though. I feel it in my gut that he isn't a threat to me. Though, to be fair, it wouldn't be the first time my gut was wrong. Still, there is something about him that puts me at ease. Maybe it's his dimpled smile and perfect teeth, maybe it's those wolfish amber eyes that track me like I'm his sole focus or maybe it's that deep southern drawl that makes my thighs clench with every syllable. In any case, I don't think Declan is a true threat to me, at least, I don't think so.

Since he has been coming to the diner religiously, he hasn't asked me out again. I don't know why that simple fact has me feeling a twinge of disappointment. It's not like I could say yes even if he did, nor would I want to. Right? Right.

It's Friday night, and my feet are practically celebrating that it's almost the weekend. This week kicked my ass, and I'm looking forward to nothing more than hanging out with Tuck and relaxing. Maybe we will go to the park and get some ice cream since it's been so nice lately. With all the tips I've been getting lately, thanks to Declan, we can definitely splurge a little.

Like clockwork, the door chimes as it opens and in walks Declan. His eyes meet mine instantly and my stomach flip flops as he holds his phone up to his ear, giving me a wink as he heads for the corner booth. The butterflies currently swarming my stomach and flying up to my chest won't stop no matter how much I will them to. I hate that I look forward to seeing him so much every shift. The most dangerous thing a woman can do is depend on a man, for anything. Yet here I am, being all heart eyed and giddy for a man who is so very clearly out of my league for so many different reasons it isn't even funny. Not to mention he used to play football. Sweet or not, I know his type.

It's surprisingly dead for a Friday night so as soon as I finish bringing out my orders and re-stocking the caddies on the empty tables, I head over to Declan.

"I know," he says into the phone, looking out the window as he does. "I miss you too. I can't wait to see you. Alright, I love you. Bye," Declan says before hanging up and turning to face me.

My previous smile slips as my heart clenches inside my chest. I thought he was single? He told me he was. Obviously, he lied. I knew it. There is no way that a-

"My mama," he says with a knowing grin.

His mom.

He was telling his mom that he loves and misses her while my mind immediately jumped to the idea that he had a girlfriend. Can someone spell trust issues?

Get it together, Vi.

Pushing down the burning embarrassment overwhelming me, I slap on a smile as I nod and pull out my notepad, even though I know he only ever orders one of three items off the menu.

"What will it be tonight?" I ask.

"Steak, please."

"Medium rare with steamed veggies and a baked potato?" I confirm.

"You know me so well, Vi," he says teasingly.

I scoff and roll my eyes but can't fight my smile as I pocket my blank notepad.

"No, I don't. You're just predictable."

"Is that a good thing?" Declan asks.

"Not quite sure."

He shrugs as he settles his arms on the table like he always does. The neckline of his shirt stretches as he does, giving me yet another glimpse of the dark ink decorating his skin. God, what I wouldn't do to see the entire piece. Just once. I would never admit it out loud, but Declan has appeared in a dream or two of mine. All of them being extremely explicit and extremely fucking hot. I can't remember the last time I had a dirty dream about anyone but since this man showed up it seems to be all I can dream about.

I go about the rest of my shift like usual. Declan asks me what superpower I would want to have if I could have anything, to which I answered flying, obviously. Then when the place is empty except for me, him, and our cook, he stands up from his booth but instead of walking out the door, he walks right up to me.

I take a step back on instinct, but he only follows me. I've joked about the way that he watches me makes me feel like a hunted prey, but I'm not joking anymore. He is stalking towards me like a predator who has cornered a scared rabbit. His strides are even and sure, his body wide and his eyes trained on me steadily.

When my ass bumps into the front counter, I know that he has me trapped, and so does he. My heart is beating out of my chest as my blood begins to thrum inside my veins. Declan stops just before his chest can brush against me. All of the air in the room seems to evaporate in an instant, and I'm left breathing deeply, desperate for an ounce of fresh oxygen.

Declan watches me for a second before he cocks his head to the side softly and reaches out, lifting his giant hand before gently brushing a piece of hair that fell out of my ponytail long ago, and tucking it behind my ear. When he pulls his hand away, he lets his fingers graze against my cheek, causing a smattering of goosebumps to race down my neck and out to my arms.

He must see it, or he is replaying a joke in his head because a low chuckle rumbles through his chest as he bends down until our faces are only a few inches away from each other. The overwhelming scent of his cologne is intoxicating, and though the rational part of my brain is telling me to get away from this man quick, the irrational side tells me to lean in a little closer.

"Are you ready for me to ask you out again yet?" Declan drawls lowly, his lips ghosting over mine, not close enough to touch but enough for his breath to make my lips tingle.

"What?" I rasp.

"Are you ready for me to ask again, sweetheart?" He repeats patiently with a soft smirk.

It takes me a few moments for his words to register in my head before I clear my throat.

"I-I can't."

"Hm," he says as he leans in just a hair closer.

I can't help but arch into him slightly. There are less than a few millimeters separating me from this man's perfectly full lips. Well, that and my stubbornness but I feel that weakening by the second.

"Almost," Declan rumbles as his eyes trace over my face before standing up and taking a step back.

I blink a few times, doing my best to clear this lust fog that he has somehow settled over me before I shake my head and look at him.

"I'll see you Monday, Vi," he says with a confident smirk before he turns and heads out the door.

Before I can respond, he is already gone. I'm left standing there like a fish out of water, my mouth opening and shutting as I try to figure out what the hell just happened. What did he mean by almost? Almost what? And Monday? That bastard has to have a copy of my schedule, or maybe he has just figured out that I have weekends off by now. Either way, I should probably be more than a little unnerved, but if the wetness of my panties is anything to go off of, then unnerved is the last thing that I'm feeling right now.

Chapter Five

Declan

I pull my hoodie over my head just a little more and push my aviators in place as I step through the grocery store doors. I'm not always easily recognized, but when I am, it's chaos, and all I want is to grab a few things and get home. Coach rode my ass at practice today, and my tub is practically calling my name.

So far Seattle is proving to be a little more low key than Knoxville was. Back in Knoxville, it felt like everyone knew me. Granted, I grew up there and it's a hell of a lot smaller than Seattle, so maybe that's got something to do with it. Either way, I'm really fucking grateful for the little bit of privacy I've been getting lately.

As I step down one aisle, I instantly make eye contact with a man. Even through my glasses and baggy sweatshirt I can see the recognition in his eyes followed by the gaping mouth as he slaps his buddy on the arm. Quickly, I duck to the next aisle hoping to avoid any attention, when a tiny body crashes into me.

"Whoa there," I say as I grab the shoulders of a little boy who can't be older than five.

"Sorry," he says as he looks up at me with big hazel eyes.

"No worries, big man." I look around for his parents but don't see anyone around us. "Where are your parents?"

"My mommy said I couldn't have these gummy bears. She wanted me to put them back, so I ran. I don't have to put them back if she can't catch me, right?" He asks with a devilish smirk.

I let out a rough chuckle and shake my head as I take my glasses off and squat next to him.

"I don't know about that. We should probably look for your mama. I'm sure she's worried about you."

"You talk funny," he says with furrowed brows.

Chuckling, I shake my head as I answer him.

"Well, I'm not from around here. If you were in my town, everyone would say you talk funny."

"Where's that?"

"Tennessee."

"Is that far away?" He asks.

I nod. "About the other side of the whole country."

His eyes turn the size of saucers at that, which makes me smirk as I look around us again, still not finding anyone who looks like they lost a kid.

"What's your name?" The kid asks.

"I'm Declan. What's yours?"

He opens his mouth to answer when I hear a panicked voice shout, "Tucker?!"

I glance up to see the stunning woman that I can't get out of my head rushing towards us. That is until she sees me and freezes mid step.

Vi.

"Hi Mommy, this is my new friend-"

"Declan," she mutters under her breath.

Her large hazel eyes widen slightly as I stand up and give her a slow smile, taking her in. She is wearing a teal shirt under a black leather jacket with a black pair of low-rise Converse and a pair of tight blue jeans that I'm sure do wonders for her amazing ass. I should know, I've had the pleasure of watching that ass bounce all around in that hip hugging uniform over the last few weeks. The woman is fucking edible and I'd bet every dime that I have she doesn't know it.

Good, makes her all the more sweet.

A soft throat clears, and my eyes dart up to meet Vi's narrowed ones. I feel my cheeks heat at the fact that I was just caught and am about to apologize when I realize something that I almost overlooked.

Mommy? She is a mom? I don't know why it surprises me, but it does. All the moms I know are much older than I would peg Vi and they definitely don't look like *that*. Is that why she has now rejected me at every chance?

I'm normally a pretty confident guy, except when I'm around her, apparently. For some unknown reason I'm a wreck around Vi. I say the wrong things, I clam up and I find that all of my normal confidence and smoothness goes right out the window. Hell, the smoothest I've been able to be around her was last night when I almost kissed her. And even then, I was sweating bullets.

It doesn't help that she's the first woman to reject me in...well, ever. I'm not exactly a player, but I've dated my fair share of women, all who didn't take much more than a few smiles and compliments to have them practically begging me to take them home. Not Vi, though.

"Yeah!" Tucker exclaims. "How did you know his name?" He asks his mom, shaking me out of my thoughts.

Vi turns a disapproving gaze towards Tucker as she places her hands on her hips in a total mom move that has me smirking.

Somebody's busted.

"Because I know everything. You're in trouble. You know you can't run away like that in a busy store. Someone could have taken you, you scared me half to death, Tuck!"

"But I just really wanted the gummies," he pouts as he holds the bag tighter.

Vi sighs as she shakes her head.

"I already told you, baby, we are going to grab ice cream after this. You can have one or the other but not both."

Blowing out a disappointed breath, he kicks the floor before he sets the bag of gummies on the shelf and walks over to her, his arms extended. She rolls her eyes before she bends down and hugs him tightly. My chest warms as I watch them. I've always been really close to my mama, even more so since Donny. It's probably weird that I'm just standing here staring at them. I should just go and get on with my shopping, but I can't seem to move.

You can see the love between the two of them is strong, and it causes a small smile to slip across my face. This woman has grabbed my attention from the moment I set eyes on her. After spending just a few minutes with her, I was hooked. Now seeing her like this adds so many more layers that I'm fucking desperate to peel back.

"Don't do that again, promise?" She asks as she pulls away from him, scanning his body like she is checking for injuries. Tucker sighs and nods as Vi stands back up, her beautiful eyes coming up to land on me.

"Crazy seeing you here, Vi. I think the universe is trying to tell us something," I say as I take a step closer to her, doing my best to pull some of that charm out from last night.

She gives me an amused smirk as she pulls Tucker into her side, probably so he won't dart off again before she takes a healthy step back.

"What might that be?" She asks coolly.

"I don't know, but I intend to find out," I smirk.

She lets out a surprised laugh before she can push it down. I fucking love that sound. I've made her laugh a few times now and each time she almost seemed surprised to be doing so. My guess would be that she isn't used to laughing all that much, and that's a damn shame for humanity because her smile is breathtaking, and her laugh is beautiful.

"I don't think so," she says with a headshake and a cocked brow.

I give a light laugh, trying to disguise the disappointment I feel at being rejected by this woman four out of four times. She can't cut me a damn break.

My eyes drop to the basket in her hands and frown when I notice an off-brand jar of jelly and a couple boxes of inexpensive pasta. I find my mind instantly wondering if they struggle financially. I mean, she works two jobs so you wouldn't think so, but at the same time, who works two full time jobs if they aren't struggling, right? More importantly, why does the thought of them struggling cause a weird ache in my chest?

I look back up to her and see that she's watching me. She seems almost uncomfortable as she shuffles the basket slightly behind her, like she's embarrassed of it. Trying to divert her attention, I give her my most flirtatious smile before I take a half a step closer to her.

"Dinner," I say softly, glancing down to Tucker before looking back at her.

It comes out like a statement which is exactly how I intended. Asking didn't work the last few times so I'm taking a different approach. With anyone else I would have backed off after the first time, but she isn't like anyone else. There is something about her that has me all twisted up and I'm really fucking curious to find out what it is. She raises her eyebrows like I must be crazy. Maybe I am.

"Say goodbye to Declan, Tucker. We gotta get home," she says, her eyes suddenly looking anywhere but me.

"Bye, Declan!" He says with a huge gap toothed grin that has me smiling despite his mom's obvious brush off.

"See you later, big man."

He smiles at me as he walks off towards the checkout counter with his mom right on his tail. She only graces me with a side eyed glance and the barest trace of a smile. I find myself grinning as I watch her walk away like a fucking dumbass.

Once they are out of sight, I glance down the aisle and see the abandoned pack of gummy bears that Tucker put back. Without second guessing it, I grab them and run through the store to grab the few things that I came in for before I turn back and jog to the self-checkout.

I ring up my stuff and pay for it quickly as my eyes scan over the people at the checkouts. I don't see them anymore, they probably already left. When I glance out the store front windows, I suddenly see a swish of chocolate brown hair in the parking lot with a little hand tugging on hers. My lips quirk up as I hurry out the store and head right for them. When she opens the door to her piece of shit Fiesta for Tucker, I shout out at them.

"Hey, wait up!"

They both glance at me with curious looks, heads cocked slightly. Woah, the likeness between these two is wild. When I catch up to them, Vi looks like she's lost all patience with me for the night and seems ready to tell me off. Instead of walking up to her, I brush by and crouch down to eye level with Tucker.

"Hey, big man. The lady inside rang these up for me by accident. I don't like them too much, and I don't want them to go to waste. Do you think you could take them off my hands?" I pause before adding, "As long as it's okay with mom?"

I turn to see Vi's eyes narrowed into thin slits at me. I'm not sure if it's because she is just sick of me or if it really is over the gummy bears. Either way, she still looks adorable.

Tucker's eyes go wide with excitement as he glances up to his mom, seemingly seeking permission. Vi's eyes narrow at me for a moment before she glances down at Tucker and sighs, nodding her head. Tucker whoops in celebration before he grabs the bag eagerly, trying to tear into it right here and now.

"Easy. I think you should probably have dinner first," I say as I glance to Vi, who gives me a subtle nod.

He sighs exaggeratingly, but the excitement in his eyes doesn't leave.

"Thank you, Declan."

"Thank you. You're really helping me out, big man."

He nods proudly, like he feels like he made a difference. This kid is fucking hilarious. I stand up and smile at Vi as she stares at me like she is trying to figure me out. Without saying a word, I wink at her and walk off towards my car on the other side of the parking lot.

"Hey," Vi shouts.

I look over my shoulder to see her standing there with narrowed eyes, her hands on her hips.

"Tomorrow, 8 o'clock. Sunlight Apartments, Unit 3A. Don't be late."

My eyes widen in shock before I smile bigger than I have in a damn long time.

"Can't wait," I call out before I turn back around.

I try to pretend that I missed the blush that took over her creamy complexion. She probably thinks I didn't see it, but I did. It was the cutest damn thing that I've seen. That's probably the only thing about her that's cute, though. The woman is a living wet dream. You can tell she doesn't see herself that way, but I plan on changing that. Real soon.

Chapter Six

Vi

"Why did I tell him yes?" I groan as I run my fingers through my hair.

"Uh, because you said he was the hottest guy you've ever seen," Mindi says with a smirk.

I glance down at my phone to see her spread out across her bed.

I mean, she's not wrong. The guy is sexy as sin, he could get anyone he could ever want. So why the hell would he want to go out with a single mom who moonlights as a waitress?

I should cancel. Despite how sweet and kind he has come across, I know his type. Everyone has a pretty façade, but the insides rarely match. It never ends well. So why have I spent the last forty-five minutes emptying out my wardrobe to find a semi decent outfit that still fits?

"I know that look," Mindi scolds. "Shake that shit off. You are *not* backing out."

I shoot her an irritated glare. Sometimes I hate how well she knows me. Pulling at the little black dress that I found in the back of my closet, I frown at my bedroom mirror.

"Will you stoppp? You look hot. If we weren't states away, I'd bang the shit out of you," Mindi calls out.

That gets a laugh out of me. "Thanks, I guess. I haven't worn this thing since pre-Tucker. It definitely fits a little tighter than I remember."

"All the better. Show off the goods. You have an amazing rack, highlight those bad boys."

I snort as I shake my head, debating on if I should change despite Mindi's praises. I glance at the mountain of clothes piled on my bed, wondering if I should try something else back on.

"No," Mindi answers like she can read my mind. "You are hot. The dress is hot. Your makeup is flawless. Your hair is effortlessly beautiful. Chill the hell out and take a deep breath, babe."

I take a deep breath through my nose and blow it out before looking at her and nodding.

She smiles at me approvingly.

"Good. No one wants to fuck a woman who looks like she is chronically constipated."

My mouth drops open. "Okay, thanks. Love you too. I think I've had enough of your pep talk."

She cackles on the phone as she blows me a kiss.

"Just trying to loosen you up before your date does."

"Mindi!"

"Love you, bitch! Tell me everything tomorrow! Byeeee," she says as she hangs up.

Shaking my head, I glance down at my feet. Shit, I forgot about shoes.

I dig through my closet until I am torn between a pair of heels and a pair of flats. They honestly both look uncomfortable. Do you think he will care if I just wear my Converse? I'm all for looking pretty but I also really like being comfortable.

"Whatcha doing, Mommy?" Tucker asks as he bounces in to sit on my bed.

"Just choosing a pair of shoes, baby."

"I like the pointy ones," he says pointing to my heels. "They look like the ones the silly guy at the fair wore."

I chuckle as I lean down and kiss his forehead, picturing the clown on stilts that gave Tucker a sticker at the fair last year. He isn't too off. I haven't worn heels in forever. I'll probably walk with as much grace as a clown in three feet high stilts. Still, they will hands down look better with the dress than flats so I slip them onto my feet.

Yep, ridiculously uncomfortable.

"Alright, baby. Bedtime." I say as I lead Tuck into the bathroom so that he can brush his teeth.

"Aw, can I stay up just a little longer, Mommy? Pleaseee?" He begs with those big puppy dog eyes that tug at my heart every time.

I smile and shake my head. "Sorry, sweetie. It's past your bedtime anyways, and Mommy is meeting a friend."

"Is it Auntie Mindi?" Tuck asks as he picks up his toothbrush and begins scrubbing his teeth.

"No, just another friend."

His brows furrow as he talks over the brush.

"You don't have other friends."

I huff at that as I cross my arms over my chest.

"Gee, thanks kid. Now you're really going to bed."

He grumbles a little but doesn't give me too much of a hard time. I read him a quick story and kiss his forehead before turning on his night light and closing his bedroom door.

My eyes skate around the hall and I can't help but smile. I'm proud of how far we've come, we just moved from a one-bedroom apartment to a two. Tucker was so excited to have his own room, and it made me happy that I could do that for him. Granted, our apartment is not lavishly furnished by any means. Most of it I bought second hand online or picked up at thrift stores or garage sales, but everything is clean and well taken care of. Besides, why would I pay nearly ten times the price just to get it brand new when Tucker is bound to spill grape juice on it in the first twenty four hours of owning it? No, especially with kids, gently used things are your best friend.

Judy is knitting on the couch and looks up when we come into the living room, gasping when she sees me.

"Violet Ann, I didn't know you owned a dress?"

I roll my eyes at her attempt at humor.

"First, we both know that my middle name isn't Ann, so I don't understand why you insist on calling me that. Second, do I look okay?" I ask as I run my hands down the front of my dress.

"Sweet Pea, I'm just giving you a hard time. You look spectacular. His jaw will hit the floor. I guarantee it!"

I smile uneasily as I look at the clock, it's 7:58PM. He should be here any minute. At first, I didn't think much of this, but now my stomach is filled with butterflies, and I can't stay still. I'm not sure what I am so nervous about, probably the fact that I haven't been out on a date in close to six years.

As if I conjured him, I hear a heavy knock against the front door. My stomach drops as my eyes widen anxiously. I glance over at Judy as she shoos me towards the door. Taking in a deep breath, I walk across the room and pull the door open.

When I see Declan filling up my entire doorway, my breath catches. He is wearing a black sport coat and slacks with a white button down shirt. Declan's hair is perfectly in place, his beard perfectly trimmed, and his bright white smile is aimed right at me. True to Judy's word, his jaw is slightly unhinged as his eyes rake over me.

"Wow," he says softly. "You're stunning."

A blush creeps up my neck, and I duck my head to try to ease the redness. I glance around the room nervously, wondering what he sees when he looks inside. Does he see a single mom, struggling to make ends meet with mismatched furniture in a worn in apartment? I really hope not. I do the best I can, and it's always been enough for us, but I'm not sure if the same can be said for him.

Carefully, I dart my eyes over to Declan to see if I can catch any look of disgust or disappointment, but instead, he seems to have not taken his eyes off me, a warm smile across his face. Judy clears her throat as she looks at us with a devilish smirk.

"With the way Vi talked about you I was half expecting you to show up with a horde of paparazzi. She did say your face belonged on a magazine."

My eyes go wide as I glare at Judy. Declan lets out a rough laugh and shakes his head.

"Next time, maybe."

I send Judy one more poisonous look before turning to Declan with a raised eyebrow.

"Next time? Don't you think you're getting a little ahead of yourself there?"

His eyes trail over my bare legs in a slow perusal before they flick back up to my face.

"Nah, I got a good feeling about this."

My heart skips at his words, and my skin warms at the look in his eyes.

Oh, damn, alright then.

"Declan, this rude woman who can't keep things to herself is Judy," I say, switching topics as I gesture to my people-watching neighbor.

He nods and smiles at her, and I swear to you, Judy blushes. I don't blame her one bit though. Even just a few seconds of Declan's attention will force you to reach for the closest thing to fan yourself with.

"It's a pleasure to meet you, Ma'am."

"Oh, I think the pleasure will be all Vi's tonight," she says with a sly grin.

"Judy!" I screech.

Declan laughs while he puts his hands in his pockets, clearly amused.

Kill me now.

"Thank you for watching Tuck again, we won't be too late," I say as I grab my purse and urge Declan to step out the door.

She shoos me away like I'm being a burden. "Be late, by all means. Hell, if you don't come home at all, I'll take it as a good sign," she says with waggle of her eyebrows.

Dead. Literally dead. I don't know if it will be her or me, but someone is dying tonight.

I sigh before I wave over my shoulder to Judy as Declan softly ushers us out the door. When it closes, I blow out a deep breath.

"I am so sorry. That was incredibly painful for me. I can't imagine how you are feeling."

Declan laughs as he lets me walk down the stairs first.

"She's hilarious, I wish I could have seen Tucker again. He seems like a great kid."

I give him a tight smile as I nod. Just because he has technically met Tucker does not mean I want him to be spending time with my son. I barely know this guy, and even if he was Jesus himself, I'd feel way too uneasy about introducing someone to my son so soon. I'm already a nervous wreck worried about getting to know this guy just on my own.

"Yeah, he is," I say lamely.

Declan smiles at me though I don't miss the flash of what looks like disappointment on his face. Something clenches inside my chest that he would actually want to see Tuck again. Even if it's a bad idea, it's sweet.

When we make our way down the stairs, he resumes his spot next to me with his hand hovering just over my lower back. A few times his hand brushes the back of my dress, and the simple touch sends a tingling sensation running up and down my spine.

Declan walks us over to a new looking black pickup truck before he opens the door for me. I smile in appreciation before I scoot inside. As he walks around to get into his side, I try to think about the last time that a guy has held the door open for me. Then, I realize that I don't think a guy ever has.

When he fires up the truck, he smiles at me softly before backing out of the small parking lot and turning onto the empty street.

"This is nice," I comment as my eyes skate over the inside of the truck.

"Thanks. I just bought it."

I glance around at the sleek interior and all of the fancy gadgets on his touch screen. You can tell it cost a pretty penny, but it isn't flashy by any means. I really like that he isn't the type of person to flaunt his obvious wealth. Though his clothes are nice, he dresses like an average guy, almost inconspicuous, but I don't know how he expects a man of his size and his good looks to be inconspicuous.

"So, where are we going?" I ask as he drives us into the city.

"You'll see," he says with a shy smile.

I think he's just as nervous as I am. His leg has been bouncing non-stop since we got into the truck and his knuckles are gripping the steering wheel for dear life. Everything about this man is so disarming, so approachable. That's probably what makes him the most danger-ous.

CHAPTER SEVEN

VI

After a short drive, Declan pulls into a parking lot and shuts the truck off. He turns to me and smiles before he gets out and walks around to my side. I try to look around to see where we are, but everything is so dark that I can't actually make anything out.

Declan opens my door and offers his hand to help me out. I take it as I slide out and can't help but love the way his large hand engulfs mine. Even in my heels, I still have to crane my neck to look up at him.

"Do you trust me?" He asks.

"Not really, no. I don't even know you," I answer honestly.

He laughs and nods, his thumb caressing the back of my hand gently almost like he is afraid he will spook me. Declan reaches into his pocket and pulls out a bandana as he gestures to put it over my eyes. I laugh nervously as I watch him.

"Uh, didn't you know you are supposed to wait to reveal your kink until at least the third date?"

His eyes flare with what looks like desire before he chuckles and squeezes my hand tighter for a moment. "Not what this is for, but I'll keep that in mind. I have a surprise for you. Is this okay?"

I bite my lip as I watch him. This night is quickly shaping up to be a bad horror movie. If I was in my pajamas on the couch right now watching this play out, I would be screaming at the girl to run. She agreed to a date with a total stranger, he picked her up at her apartment where he knows her and her young child live alone, he wants to blindfold her and take her into the dark and she doesn't even know his last name.

"What's your last name?" I blurt out quickly.

"Daniels," he says with a small smile as he watches me carefully.

"Declan Daniels?" I repeat.

He nods quietly as his eyes continue to trace over my face, looking for what, I'm not really sure.

"That's kind of a mouthful don't you think?"

He chuckles and nods. "Blame my mama."

I laugh before giving him the okay to blindfold me. It is probably dumb that I take comfort in knowing his last name. I shouldn't feel so comfortable with this guy who is a perfect stranger. I am letting my guard down in a potentially dangerous situation, which is just too stupid to even comment on. For some weird reason though, I have never felt safer in my whole life.

Once the blindfold is secured, he takes my hands in his and starts slowly walking us forward. My heels click against the pavement until they sink into something soft. Grass?

I wobble for a minute when one of Declan's hands grip my waist to steady me. The spot that he is touching, sears through my dress and sends sparks skittering across my skin. His other hand traces over my goosebump covered arm before grabbing my hand.

"Are you cold?" He asks, concern lacing his voice.

"N-no. I am okay. Sorry."

"Don't be," he draws as the hand resting on my hip flexes against me once before he slowly pulls away.

After another minute or so we stop walking. Declan seems to be just standing there, holding my hands.

"Is something wrong?" I ask blindly.

"No," he says softly. "You just look really beautiful tonight."

"Thank you. You look very handsome. At least, from what I can remember," I tease.

His husky laugh wraps around me as he reaches behind me to untie the blindfold. "You ready?"

I give an anxious head nod as my heart thuds in my chest. When the blindfold is peeled away, it takes me a moment for my eyes to adjust to my surroundings. The first thing that I see is a table set for two sitting on the grass overlooking the water. I glance around and notice we are standing on the edge of Green Lake Park, just beside the lake. There are two candlesticks in the middle of the table and silver domed dishes on either side. In between the candles is a simple bouquet of Hydrangeas and Dahlias. I look up to Declan, my mouth parted in shock.

"I got them from another flower shop. I wanted to actually surprise you this time, but they didn't do nearly as good of a job as you did."

"This is for us?" I ask in disbelief.

He nods as he leads me over to the table and pulls out my chair for me. I blush and sit as he pushes it in before sitting in his own. Is this real life? Like seriously, please no one pinch me, ever.

"How did you do all of this?" I ask as I look down at the table before glancing all around us.

He just smiles and shrugs before he takes the dome lids away for us. The dishes look to be expertly plated with steak, asparagus and a scoop of mashed potatoes.

"I hope steak is okay. I wasn't really sure what to choose, but I know you said it was your favorite. If you don't want it though, I could always-"

I cover his hand with mine across the table to stop him from going off on a nervous ramble. Though I have to admit, I kind of like his ramblings.

"This is amazing," I say with a soft smile.

Tension I didn't notice before in his shoulder's release at my words, and he practically sags in his chair with relief. His fingers move under my hand until our hands are intertwined.

"Good."

We eat in silence for a minute or so, enjoying the meal and the beautiful summer night, not once unlacing our fingers. I tried to pull away just for a second, and he only tightened his grip on my hand. Good thing I'm left handed, I guess.

"I'm still in shock. This isn't real life. This kind of stuff only happens in books or movies," I say after a while.

Declan smiles as he takes a sip of the delicious wine he poured us.

"That's the reaction I was going for. I wanted to take you out for a nice night, but something told me you weren't the type of girl that enjoyed over the top restaurants."

I snort and shake my head. "Pay a hundred dollars per plate and leave hungry? No, thank you."

He grins. "Couldn't agree more."

"So where are you from Declan Daniels? With an accent like that you definitely aren't a born and raised Washingtonian."

"Nope, I'm a southern boy. Born and raised in Knoxville, Tennessee. My parents are still there. My sister, Danielle, is living in New York."

"That's really cool. I've always wanted to visit New York. What took her out there?"

"School at first. Then she got her law degree and joined Greene & Associates out there. She is hoping to make partner in the next year or so."

"Wow, that's amazing. So, what brings you all the way to Seattle from Knoxville?" I ask.

He shrugs simply as he picks at his food. "Work."

I nod. "What do you do?"

"Followed in my father's footsteps."

Okayyy? I knew he was a little reserved, but I didn't know that I would be carrying the entire conversation. I raise an eyebrow that tells him to elaborate which causes him to chuckle softly.

"My dad runs a football program for young players. He helps train them in the off season and gives them the best chance to get scouted and improve their skills. I help out wherever I can, but he runs the show."

Football.

Suddenly I'm not as interested in his background anymore. I knew he played in high school, but I didn't know it was a part of his life still. It's probably wrong of me to dislike an entire sport just because of one player I encountered, but I do, I hate it. I nod politely but don't ask any follow up questions as I push the mashed potatoes around my plate.

"What about you? Are you from here?"

I nod and smile.

"Siblings?"

I shake my head.

"Where do your parents live?"

Now I'm being the difficult one. I give him a forced smile as I fold my hands into my lap.

"They died when I was nineteen. Car accident."

He frowns. "I'm so sorry. That's a really hard thing to go through at any age."

I shrug. "It's life. I have too much to be thankful for to focus on what I don't have."

Declan smiles softly and nods. "I like that. What about Grandma Judy? Is she really Tucker's grandma or?"

"No, she's just our neighbor. But she has lived in the building as long as we have, and we hit it off instantly. As you could tell, she is a bit of a spitfire, but she is the sweetest with Tuck."

"I like her," he grins.

His smile slips a bit as his face becomes serious. I already know in the pit of my stomach the next question he is going to ask. It is my least favorite question that everyone, apparently even Tuck now, asks.

"And his father?"

"Not in the picture," I say simply as I take a sip of wine.

He nods as he watches me carefully. It looks like he wants to pry more but probably realizes that would be horrible first date etiquette. Sensing that the mood needs to change, he smiles at me and eases back into his seat.

"So how old is Tucker?"

I smile. Tucker is one of my favorite things to talk about, and I will gladly take the distraction.

"He is four, will be five in August."

"That's cool. Starting Kindergarten?"

"Yes," I sigh. "I'm so nervous. He is a sensitive kid and is already struggling with other kids picking on him. I'm really worried about what school will be like for him."

"He seems pretty tough to me, and he has you to look up to. I know I don't know you very well but from what I've seen, you've got to be one of the most hardworking and independent women that I have ever met."

I swallow roughly and nod. "Thank you, that actually means a lot."

Declan grabs my hand across the table again and gently brushes his thumb across my wrist. My pulse skitters at his touch, and I can't help but hope he never lets go.

"Why me?" I ask softly.

His brows dip. "What?"

"You have been pretty persistent, despite me turning you down several times. Why keep trying? Why me?"

It's an innocent enough question, and most might play it off, but I need to know. Does he see me as a pretty face? A challenge? I want to know what goes on underneath that handsome exterior. I would be lying if I said that I didn't have a ton of baggage, most of that being insecure about not being enough for, well, anything.

"Can I be honest?" He asks.

"Please."

He blows out a soft breath as he glances out past me before his bright eyes meet mine.

"There is just something about you. You caught my attention instantly because you're obviously gorgeous, but you were different too. After you turned me down at the diner, I was bummed but could tell you had made up your mind. But that night, I couldn't stop thinking about you. I wanted to see you again, even if you would never give me a chance. I wanted to be near you." He shrugs and ducks his head nervously. "I feel different around you, even if I'm just sitting in the diner booth, watching you work. I like it."

I'm not sure what would have been the right answer, but that was better. That was so much better.

"Wow," I say softly. "That's pretty deep for a first date. Most men would be terrified to be that vulnerable with a woman."

"Oh, I'm definitely nervous. You are an intimidating woman, Vi," he chuckles.

"What?" I gasp in mock horror. "I am a delight. I don't know what you are talking about."

He chuckles before rolling his eyes and giving me a cheeky grin. We fall into easy conversation throughout the night. I tell him about how I dropped out of college when I got pregnant with Tucker and got a job at the flower shop. At the time, I didn't really care where I worked, I just needed money, but I soon fell in love with it. I also told him about my dream to have my own shop one day, whether I take over Margret's or open my own.

"What's holding you back?" He asks.

"Money," I laugh. "Isn't that what is holding everyone back? Or at least most people. Opening up a shop is incredibly expensive to start from scratch like that, and I don't really believe Margret when she says she is going to retire. I swear that woman will die with a pair of shears in one hand and a flower in the other. Can't say I blame her."

He frowns but nods understandingly. "Well, I hope you're able to get your dream one day. You're incredibly talented, and I see the way your face lights up when you talk about it. You're really passionate."

"Thank you," I say with a soft smile.

We finished dinner at least an hour ago and have just been laughing and talking ever since. He is really easy to talk to and seems to always know what to say to make me smile or laugh.

"Ready for our next stop?" He asks.

My eyes bug out. "You have more? What other tricks do you have up your sleeve?"

"Well, if I tell you now, then how am I gonna secure a second date?" He teases as he stands up and offers me his hand.

"I think the odds are in your favor," I say with a flirty smirk.

Declan winks at me before he intertwines our fingers as we slowly walk back to the car.

"Wait. Don't we need to clean all of that up or something?" I ask, gesturing to our dinner set up.

He pulls me along gently and shakes his head. "I've got it covered."

"Looks like you thought of everything Mr. Daniels."

"I try," he grins.

Chapter Eight

VI

We drive for another fifteen minutes or so before my mouth drops open and I turn to Declan excitedly.

"Oh my gosh! Are you serious? I didn't even know they had these things anymore!"

He smiles and nods as he pulls into the entrance and hands some cash to the attendant booth.

"Me neither. There are only a few left in Washington."

Smiling, I look out the window as Declan drives his truck through the narrow grass aisles of the drive-in movie theater before choosing a spot towards the back. It's not like we aren't going to get a great view no matter where we are in this giant truck, and he was probably thinking about other people in smaller cars. I don't know why I assume that about him, he just seems like the kind of man that would consider that kind of thing. Maybe it's the whole southern hospitality thing.

When Declan parks and shuts off the truck, he glances over to me and smiles.

"Want anything? Popcorn? Drinks? Candy?"

"Oh, I'm so full from dinner. I don't think I could eat another bite."

Declan shrugs as he opens his door and steps out.

"There's always room for popcorn. I'm pretty sure people have a second stomach just for it."

I let out a laugh and shake my head.

"I think that might just be you."

"Sweetheart, I'm a man, I have three stomachs," he says as he slaps his large hand against his ripped stomach. Or at least what I'm guessing is a ripped stomach. From the few times I have brushed up against him or ran straight into him, there wasn't a soft thing about the man.

I laugh again and shake my head as he smirks and heads over to the concession stand. Turning towards the huge movie theater screen I see that the featured movie tonight is Scream. Oh my gosh, I can't believe it. One of the first days that Declan started coming into the diner he had asked me what my favorite movie was, and I had told him Scream. I can't believe he remembered.

I've loved horror movies ever since I was a child. It was always my dad's and my thing. My mom was always terrified of them and refused to watch them with him, so when I got old enough, he started letting me watch them with him. It became a weekly thing for us that we would binge our favorite horror movies, but my dad's top pick was always Scream, mine too.

My eyes begin to mist over as my mind whirls with countless movie nights. God, I miss them both like hell.

Declan pops back into the cab a few moments later, a charming smile on his face that quickly fades when he gets a good look at me. Concern instantly overtakes his features as he quickly sets down the popcorn and other snacks he grabbed before reaching over and taking one of my hands.

"Vi, what's wrong?"

I quickly blink the building tears back and give him my most convincing.

"Nothing," my voice strains before I clear my throat and nod. "I can't believe you remembered," I say as I gesture towards the screen.

His face softens as he glances from the screen and back to me.

"I remember everything you tell me."

I bite my lower lip in an attempt to suppress my wide smile as I nod.

"Somehow, I don't doubt that."

"C'mon, like my mama always said, nothing makes a woman's tears dry up faster than some chocolate," he says as he hands me a small tub of dips ice cream and then a box of Reese's pieces.

I laugh and shake my head as he sets the rest of his haul down onto the floorboard before sliding in and shutting the door. I know the man was joking about having three stomachs but Jesus. He has a large bucket of popcorn, a hot dog, a small box of nachos and a pack of licorice.

I give him a wide-eyed look and he just shrugs before his cheeks pink up a bit as he grabs a few pieces of popcorn.

The movie starts a few minutes later, and a wave of nostalgia instantly hits me. It takes Declan all of three minutes to do the whole fake stretch thing before settling his arm over my shoulders. I'd call him out for being so cheesy if I wasn't blushing like crazy over having this man wrap himself around me.

I haven't been on a date in over six years but it's easy to say this is the best date I have ever been on, probably the best date anyone has ever been on, hands down. Glancing over at Declan, I see that he is already watching me with a soft smile. My blush deepens, but I do my best to push it to the side.

"Thank you. This has been the best night that I've had in probably ever, honestly."

Declan's smile widens. "The pleasure is all mine. Thank you for giving me a chance."

I nod before leaning over the middle seat and kissing his cheek. His body goes still as soon as my lips brush his skin. I slowly pull away but not too far as he turns to face me. I look up to see his brilliant amber eyes burrowing into me. My tongue wets my lips slowly, catching his attention as his eyes snap down to the movement.

Gently, he raises his hand to cup my jaw as his thumb brushes against my cheek. I lean into his touch and smile softly. He uses his hold on me to bring me closer until his velvety lips brush against mine. Declan groans softly before he lifts his other hand to hold the other side of my face and pulls me into him deeper.

His tongue swipes at the seam of my lips and I part them allowing him access as he dives in and slowly strokes my tongue. Declan's lips move so carefully, so perfectly. I know that it isn't just the fact that this is the first form of intimacy that I have shared with a man in almost six years. No, this is without a doubt the best and most intense kiss that I have ever had in my life.

Suddenly, something in the kiss changes. Declan gently nips at my lower lip, as if he is testing the waters, and I whimper softly in response. Our mouths begin moving quicker, more frantic. He nips at me again, a little harder this time causing me to let out an even louder moan.

Slowly, Declan pulls back until he can fully see me. Embarrassment shoots through me. Why did I have to make that freaking sound? Now things are weird.

Instead of laughing or acting weirded out, his wolfish eyes seem to almost glow in the darkened cab before he lowers his hands, gripping my thighs as he drags me across the center console and into his lap. My dress rides up my thighs, just barely exposing my black panties but before I can go to pull my dress down, Declan is hiking my dress up, exposing my panties fully before his eyes lock onto mine.

"If you don't want this, I need you to speak now, because you've been killing me in this dress all fucking night," he says, his voice laced with need and desperation.

I bite my lower lip and nod softly, clearly giving him all the permission he needs before he slips a finger under my panties and right inside me.

My head tilts backwards as he pushes deeper.

"Damn, baby. You are fucking soaked," he practically growls as he slips another finger inside.

"Oh my god," I gasp as my hands dig into his shoulders, holding on for dear life as he quite literally fucks me with his fingers.

I'm not a virgin, I mean, obviously. I have a kid, I've had sex and done nearly everything in between, but it's been years since a man has even looked at me twice, let alone touched me. I almost forgot how good it could be. Or maybe it's never been this good and it's just Declan. Either way, I'm already trembling right on the edge, and he has barely even started.

The movie plays in the background though I'm too wrapped up in Declan to pay too close attention, but the familiar dialogue fills the cab around us.

"You should never say, 'who's there?' Don't you watch scary movies? It's a death wish. You might as well come out here to investigate a strange noise or something."

I glance around quickly to see if anyone is close enough to see what we are doing. Then his finger curls inside me, and I suddenly don't give a shit. My hips move on their own, working with his fingers as he brings me closer and closer to the edge. I feel the strap of my dress slip down my shoulder, partially exposing one of my breasts, but I'm too lost in this right now to be shy. Declan apparently isn't too lost not to notice, though. His eyes hone in on the newly exposed skin as he brings his other hand up and tugs the fabric away from my breast before lowering his mouth down, running his tongue across my pebbled nipple.

Sparks light up inside me at the motion and have me desperate for more.

"More," I gasp. "Please, please."

A deep chuckle leaves Declan's chest as he does it again. A zing of pleasure rips through me again, and I know that I won't last much longer if he keeps that up.

"Go ahead, baby. Cum on my fingers, I've been dying to know what you taste like since the moment I laid eyes on you."

I clench around his fingers at his words, earning me a low growl as Declan continues licking and sucking on my nipple. When his teeth graze against me, I'm a goner. I shatter apart into a million pieces on top of him and cry out way too loud considering we literally have cars on either side of us not four feet away from us. All of that doesn't stop me from crying out his name as I cum harder than I have in my entire life. My vision blurs as my orgasm washes over me like a tidal wave and pleasure rips through me from the top of my head to the tips of my toes.

And this is just his fingers. What could the man do with something else?

As I'm at the height of my orgasm, I suddenly feel a sharp sting and look down to see that Declan has sunk his teeth into the side of my breast, hunger and desire thick in his golden eyes. Shit, he really is like a wolf.

When I finally come down, Declan presses gentle kisses to the indentations left behind from his teeth as he slowly eases his fingers out of me. His breathing is labored as his chest moves up and down like he is the one that just experienced the most intense orgasm in history. His eyes are firmly glued to mine, his face full of want and something else that I'm not quite sure how to read as he lifts his fingers into his mouth and sucks.

My pussy clenches at the sight as he leisurely licks and sucks on his fingers like they are covered in the most delicious treat he has ever had. My god. I don't think I've ever seen anything so erotic in all my life.

"You are perfect," he murmurs as he licks his fingers clean.

I blink at him before I swallow. How am I supposed to respond to that? Perfect? Me? Hardly. But with the way this man looks at me he has me almost believing it. Almost.

Now that the lust haze has faded, I feel almost awkward. Do I get off him now? Do I need to get him off? I probably should, right? It's only fair.

Nervously, I reach down between us and rub my hand against the hard on that is currently tenting his slacks. I haven't touched a man in so long, is it stupid if I say I don't really know what to do in this moment? Declan seems to catch on to my nervousness because he grabs my wrist with one hand and cups my face with the other.

"That's not how this thing is gonna work, baby. You don't have to do anything just because I made you feel good."

"But I want to," I say softly.

He smiles as his thumb strokes over my cheek.

"I want you to too, but not in the cab of my truck in a public parking lot. When you touch me, I'm gonna need a whole lot more time with you than we have."

Disappointment and also excitement fill me at the same time. Declan brings me in for a very chaste but sweet kiss before pulling back and setting me back into my seat, He winks at me before we glance up to see that the movie is over, and people are beginning to leave.

Declan's large hand reaches over and rests on my knee before squeezing gently. We smile at each other like we have a secret even if the whole damn place knew what we were up to. Putting the truck in drive, Declan slowly pulls out of the drive-in as he makes his way back to my place, never taking his hand off my knee once.

When we pull up to my apartment complex Declan rushes out of his side to get my door.

"Thank you," I smile.

He only nods before wrapping his arm around my shoulder as he steers us towards the stairs. We pause just outside of my door before I step out of his hold to face him. I'm definitely disappointed that the night is already over, I wish it didn't have to be. Declan is really amazing. I like him more than I thought I would. More than I probably *should*.

"I had an incredible night," he says as he tucks a piece of hair behind my ear.

"Me too."

He smiles as his fingers gently brush the side of my face.

"Does that mean I get another date?"

"I think the odds are slightly in your favor."

He smirks as he bends down until his nose is brushing against mine, his hand now palming the side of my face.

"Only slightly?"

I try to think of something witty to say but when his breath is fanning across my lips like this my mind goes totally blank and all I can think about is feeling his soft pillowy lips against mine just one more time.

His lips close the distance between us, and I arch into him as his tongue licks the seam between my lips. Our mouths move together in perfect sync, like we've been doing it all our lives, which I know sounds totally corny but there is no other way to describe how perfect it feels to be kissed by him.

His other hand goes to my hip to pull me in closer as the kiss turns more heated when my front door suddenly swings open, and Judy leans against the door frame with a cheshire grin on her face.

"Well, hi, kids," she greets with a mischievous smirk.

"Hi, Grandma Judy," Declan greets like he's known her his whole life.

"Have a nice time?" She asks me while continuing to smile at Declan.

"Yes, we did," I answer.

"Good, it's about time you had some fun. I'm going to head home. I will see you tomorrow night?"

"Thank you, Judy," I nod as I hug her.

She moves past me and stops in front of Declan, pointing one of her knitting needles at him like they are deadly weapons.

"Violet is a special woman. You better treat her right, or I will whoop your ass."

"You have my word, Ma'am," he says very seriously.

"Good boy."

She pats his cheek lovingly before she slips out the door and across the hall without another word.

"Again, sorry," I cringe as I turn to face Declan.

He chuckles softly as he brushes his lips against mine once more.

"Don't be. I like her."

I swallow and nod as he continues to stare down at me, not fully standing back up as he continues to cup my face.

"So, I can see you again?"

I bite my lower lip and nod, which causes him to smile.

"Can I have your number?"

Oh my gosh. Did I really just have the best night of my life with a man that doesn't even have my phone number?

"Of course," I say as he hands me his phone. I quickly enter my number in it before handing it back to him.

He looks down at the screen and smiles before nodding.

"I'll text you. Lock this up, okay?" He says as he gestures towards the door.

Smiling, I lean up and press my lips against his once more before taking a step into my apartment.

"Goodnight."

"Goodnight, Vi," he smiles before turning and walking down the stairs.

When I close the door, I lean my back against it before slowly sliding down to my butt, a wide smile on my face that I couldn't brush off even if I tried.

Chapter Nine

Declan

I wake up to the sound of my phone ringing. I groan before smacking my hand around my side table until I reach it. Clicking accept, I put it up to my ear with my eyes still closed.

"Yeah?"

"Is that anyway to answer the phone, Declan Daniels?" My mother scolds.

I wipe the sleep from my eyes and let out a sigh. "Sorry, Mama. I just woke up. What's going on?"

"Oh nothing. I just heard from a little bird that you had a date last night."

"Mhmm. And would that bird happen to be about 6'2", fifty eight years old, and your husband?"

"Maybeee," she draws out.

I called my dad yesterday before I picked Vi up. We have always been extremely close, and I just needed help getting out of my own head. To say I was nervous was an understatement. It isn't like I haven't gone out on dates before, but it hasn't been since high school. I'll admit I had my playboy days in college. Then when I was drafted into the NFL, I didn't even have to try. Women were throwing themselves at me just because I was a pro ball player.

It was fun for a couple of years, but the shine has definitely worn off. When I come home to this fancy condo with a nice view and the finest furniture, it just feels empty, lonely. Shortly after moving to Seattle, I realized that being alone fucking sucks. Back in Knoxville, I had my parents just ten minutes away when I was bored or wanted to be around people that knew me as more than a good football player. Out here, I just have the team, which I'm thankful enough to have some of my best friends as a part of that team but still, it's not the same.

From the moment that I met Vi, I knew that she was different, and damn was I right. She is fucking incredible, beautiful, smart, talented, and strong as hell. She's an amazing mother and all of that wrapped up into one package scares the living shit out of me. What's worse is that I already like her, a lot. She is all I think about day in and out for three weeks. I called my dad and asked him if there was something wrong with me. He just laughed at me.

"Sounds like she is exactly what you need then."

I don't doubt that. The bigger question I find myself asking is if I am what *she* needs.

Vi hasn't really told me about Tucker's dad; I haven't really asked much. She doesn't have to tell me anything for me to know that he walked out on them, though. You can see it in Vi's green flecked eyes when she mentions him, the hurt is still there. Though, I don't think that she is actually hurting over him, but instead she hurts because he walked away from Tucker.

"Why don't you just say what you called to say, Mama? I have practice in an hour."

"No need to be testy. I'm just curious. Your father said you sounded quite smitten."

Yeah. Because my retired NFL linebacker father uses the word smitten.

"I like her," I admit as I run a hand through my hair.

My mama squeals, and I groan. She has been all over my case for years, hoping I would settle down. I haven't had the slightest desire to though, until recently.

"What's her name? What does she look like? Can I have her number? Please, please! I promise I won't say anything embarrassing. I just wanna get to know your girlfrien-"

"She isn't my girlfriend. We went out once and just getting her to agree to that was hard enough."

I don't share that it was the best date of my life, and Vi said that she felt the same. I also don't share that she seemed to let her guard down last night somewhere between the dinner and the cake. Who knows if Vi and I will even work out, though? I definitely don't need my mama butting in and scaring her away before I have the chance to make her mine. Because from the first moment that I laid eyes on Vi, I knew I wanted her to be mine.

"How so? You're such a handsome boy and a very talented football player. Not to mention what a sweetheart you grew up to be."

Yeah, I also don't bring up the fact that I misled her about my job. From the first time I met Vi, I learned that she seems to have some type of grudge against football, and I'm assuming football players are lumped in with that. When she didn't recognize me at the diner, I was relieved to just be a person while I grieved the loss of my twin on our birthday. Then when I told her my full name on our date and she still didn't recognize me, I was intrigued.

I'm not trying to be cocky or anything, but I'm pretty well known to most people that keep up with NFL players. I'm one of the highest paid middle linebackers in the league. I've been to the Super Bowl twice, and I even did some publicity stuff a couple of years ago when I was with the Bucks.

I *do* help my dad with the football program in the off season, so that part is true. But my job is a professional football player. I already worry that I made a mistake by omitting that piece of information, though. All it would take is for her to google my name and then the cat is out of the bag. I like just being Declan with her, though. I like that she isn't interested in me for the fame or the money. She likes me for me, it's refreshing.

"She's different, Mama."

She hmphs, and I can practically hear her cross her arms.

"Well, will we meet her when we come to your first pre-season game?"

Blowing out an irritated breath I wipe my hand down my face.

"I don't know. It's brand new. I'll let you know when there is some-thing to know, okay?"

I am feeling way too overwhelmed in my thoughts for 6AM to indulge my mother right now. Plus, a small part of me wants to hide away Vi from the world, keep her to myself. I see how special she is, but I'm not sure how I feel about others knowing just yet. I want time with her, to see how she feels about us before I release the parental hounds or worse, my sister.

"Fine," she sighs. "Well, I love you and I hope you are enjoying yourself out there."

"It ain't home, but it's pretty cool. Slater insists on giving me 'the full Seattle experience' one of these days."

She laughs, and I can practically see her light up from all the way on the west coast. It's no secret that my mama has had the hots for Slater since she met him. Unfortunately, Slater knows it too and flirts with her every chance he can get just to get under my skin. I don't know how my dad can just laugh it off. I knew Slater back in his bachelor days, I wouldn't let him within fifty feet of my wife if I had one.

"I love that boy. Give him a kiss for me!"

I snort. "Yeah, I'll be sure to do that, Mama."

"Love you, baby."

"Love you, Mama."

I hang up the phone, toss it across the bed as I lay there and think about last night. Fuck. It was a damn good night. By far the best I have had in a long time, maybe ever. She is an incredible woman, the most incredible that I've ever met, hands down.

I don't know Vi extremely well yet, but from what I can tell, she works herself into the ground, which bothers the fuck out of me. From the conversations that we have had, it seems she is at work more than she is anywhere else, and quite frankly, what does she have to show for it? An unreliable piece of shit car that could break down on her and Tucker at any minute and a minimalistic apartment in a sketchy neighborhood. How can someone work so hard and have so little to show for it?

Reaching for my phone, I type out a quick text to Vi before I can stop myself. I told myself that I was going to play it cool, make her wait a little. Who the hell am I kidding though? I was ready to text her the moment I left her apartment so seven hours later isn't so bad.

Chapter Ten

Declan

Getting out of bed, I go through my morning routine before heading to practice. I'm just walking into the locker room when someone calls out to me.

"Mikeyyyy!"

I turn around to see Slater jogging up to me before practically jumping on top of me in what is a very Slater way of greeting people. The guy is the life of the party everywhere he goes, even if there is no party.

"Slater, get the fuck off me, dumbass."

He cackles before his tattooed hand slaps my back as we walk to the locker room together. I'll never forget the day Slater got his first tattoo. It was the summer after our freshman year and before we both were heading home, we wanted to get some ink. I went with a piece on my bicep that eventually grew to cover the length of my arm, while Slater went for a rose over the top of his hand. I honestly don't know what he was thinking.

Slater cried like a little bitch, not that he would admit it to anyone, and now whenever he gets new ink, he always uses numbing cream, and I never stop giving him shit for it. It was our thing for a while there until he came up to Seattle. Almost like a therapy for us. Then we split ways, and both kept at it, and now we are more tattoos than skin, at least that's what mama says.

"Ah, don't be that way Mikey Mike. You know you missed me."

I roll my eyes and chuckle at the crazy bastard as I start putting my gear on.

"Hey, I tried to call you last night. We haven't actually hung out since I left Brighton U. I've missed you fucker!"

Just two weeks into Slater and my junior year, he got a call from his mom's boss. She collapsed at work and was taken into the hospital. After some tests were run, they found out that she had breast cancer, stage three. Since she was up here in Seattle, and we were in college in California, he knew he couldn't stay at Brighton. He was lucky enough to talk to the University of Seattle's head coach and somehow smooth talk his way into a full ride scholarship and starting spot on the team. I still don't know how he did it.

Slater got scooped up and drafted that spring, and it's now been two years since Slater's mama has been officially cancer free. I feel bad that I haven't made time for him or Seb since I got up here. Life has been crazy busy though, and honestly, I've been in a weird haze ever since I met Vi.

"Sorry, man. I was out," I say as I pull on my practice jersey.

He gives me a knowing grin and winks. "Found a jersey chaser, huh?"

I let out a dry laugh and shake my head. "Not exactly."

His brow arches as he waits for me to continue. If he thinks I'm gonna sit here and locker room talk my girl, he has another thing coming. *My girl.* Shit, I like the sound of that.

Shrugging my shoulders, I grab my helmet and head out of the locker room. Slater runs behind me to keep up, obviously not letting it go as his eyes practically drill a hole into my head.

"She doesn't know that I play," I clip out, keeping my eyes straight ahead as I walk.

His eyes widen as he laughs. "What? Does the girl live under a rock?"

"No," I snap feeling oddly defensive. "She just doesn't like football. She told me that the first time we met. Something must have happened because she seems to really hate it. She didn't recognize me, and I didn't volunteer the information. It's really nice to just go out with a woman and be a regular guy once in a while."

"That is the stupidest shit I have ever heard!" Chad Brownstone, our star QB, chimes in. "The best part of being a pro player is to have all of the bitches begging to jump on your dick. You can get those girls to do anything you want. Why the fuck would you want to be a regular guy?"

I internally groan as he pushes his way in between Slater and me. Chad is the epitome of a jock asshole, or as my sister likes to refer to them as, jockholes. He's cocky, narcissistic, and always only looking out for himself, which should make him a shit quarterback, but the guy has got a ton of raw talent. Too bad I can't stand the prick.

There is no point in responding to him, all he wants is to get a rise out of me. I don't know why, but I have been on his shit list ever since I showed up. I'm not even an offensive player, so it isn't like his dislike comes from an insecurity thing. For whatever reason, he always seems insistent on fucking with me. I'm not typically a confrontational guy. I like to go with the flow usually, but he pushes me a little every day and someday–probably soon–I know that I'm gonna snap.

Maybe that's his goal.

"All I'm saying is that you probably only have one or two more seasons in you before they bring in someone younger and better, *if* you don't get taken out by injury first. Might as well live it up while you can, Daniels," Chad calls out as he slaps my back a little harder than can be considered friendly before he jogs ahead of us.

My fists are clenched and my jaw tight as I watch the prick round the corner and step onto the field. I look over to Slater and notice that he has an equally displeased look on his face.

"I fucking hate that guy," I mutter.

"Don't we all, man, but he's QB1."

"Yeah, yeah."

Slater and I jog onto the field where we run through our warm-ups before practice starts. I love football. When I'm sad, mad, happy or anything in between, football is exactly what I need. I know that I won't be able to play forever, as a middle linebacker, or the 'Mike,' it takes a toll on your body. Considering I have already been playing in the NFL for six years, some would say I have already had a long and successful career. It will suck when my career is over so I just try to enjoy it while I can.

Practice is a hard but good one. We are all busting our asses, perfecting our game as the pre-season gets closer. Once practice is over, I take a quick shower before I change back into my street clothes and grab my stuff. As I walk out of the building, my phone buzzes. When I pull it out, I see Vi's name across the screen, and my stomach dips in anticipation as I open the text that I sent her this morning and her response.

Me: I had a great time last night. I can't wait to see you again.
Vi: Me too. It was the best.

I smile as I type out my response.

Me: What was your favorite part?

Her response comes in quicker than I would have expected.

Vi: The movie, definitely.

Me: No way? Me too. Especially when we weren't paying any attention to it.

Vi: Oh my god. I meant the actual movie.

I can't help but chuckle as I slide into the cab of my truck as my phone vibrates again.

Vi: But that was nice too.

Me: Just nice, huh? Message received. I'll be sure to step up my game next time.

Vi: Again with the assuming. Who said I wanted to go out with you again?

Chuckling to myself, I scratch my hand along my beard as I type out my response.

Me: You did, sweetheart.

Vi: Well, what did you expect me to say? Who can think when they have someone like you crowding them like that?

Me: So, is that a no to another date?

Vi: ...It's not a no.

I smirk.

Me: So, how does this week sound?

Vi: Busy. I work at both places every day this week and then this weekend we have errands we need to run.

Disappointment fills me as my smile falls.

Me: Next week? Saturday?

I see the bubbles show up and disappear before they show up and disappear once more. After several minutes of staring at my phone like a psycho, I decide to set it to the side and drive home. When I pull up to my parking garage, I shut the truck down and reach over to see that she responded.

Vi: Saturday.

Smiling probably bigger than I should considering it took her so long to agree, I settle back into my seat and close my eyes. Fuck, this girl has got me all twisted up. She's a whole hell of a lot different than the other women that I've dated in the past. I think that's what I like best about her, though. She's hard to get a read on sometimes, clearly a ball buster and no doubt comes with more baggage than I can imagine. For some reason, all of that just makes me like her more.

CHAPTER ELEVEN

VI

Declan: Favorite pizza?

Wiping the sleep from my eyes, I can't help but laugh. I thought the random questions would end after we went out but over the last week we have been texting and talking on the phone non-stop, and every day, Declan asks me several questions about myself. I thought it was weird at first but it's actually kind of fun. I feel like I've known him for months as opposed to weeks.

Me: Chicken Bacon Ranch. Mindi and I practically lived on that stuff in college.

Declan: Never had it, but now I wish I had.

Me: Favorite band of all time?

Declan: Lynyrd Skynyrd. I think if I would have said anyone else, I'd have my southern man card taken away.

I bite my bottom lip as I shake my head and smile.

Me: Can't have that now, can we?

Declan: No, ma'am.

Me:...Watch it.

Declan: I'm really looking forward to our date tonight. I'll pick you up around eight again, sound good?

Me: Perfect. What are we doing? How should I dress?

Declan: No spoilers. Dress warm.

I huff a laugh as I toss my phone on my bed and get ready for the day. Over the last week, I've not only learned a ton of random facts about Declan but a little bit more about him as a person. He was born and raised in Knoxville and only left for college out in California before going back home to work at his father's organization. His whole family is involved in one way or another, and it all brings them even closer. I may hate football, but I love that it's something they all bond over.

Declan asks about Tucker every day. He asks how his day has gone, what his favorites are, and pretty much everything else in between. It makes my chest tight every time he asks about Tuck. Partly because I think it's so sweet that he seems to have a genuine interest in not just me but Tuck too. The other part is that it makes me extremely nervous how seamlessly this man seems to be fitting into my life, how he seems to get how Tucker is always my first priority, and instead of being intimidated or upset with that, he is understanding and agreeing.

I step into the kitchen and pull out the Mickey Mouse waffle maker that I got at a garage sale last summer before I start making breakfast. It's become a sort of tradition that every Saturday morning Tuck and I make Mickey Mouse waffles for breakfast. It's his favorite part of the week and honestly mine too. I hate to think that not too long from now, he will be too cool for this. I wish he would just stay my little guy forever. What I wouldn't give to make time slow down, just a little. He's growing like a weed right before my eyes, and every day, he looks less and less like the baby wrapped in a little blue blanket and more like a young man.

Blinking back the building tears behind my eyes, I groan before sniffing and pushing them back. God. I've been so emotional lately. I'm supposed to start my period any day now, and I'm definitely not looking forward to that, but maybe once I get it, I'll start blubbering for no damn reason.

We end up having a very low-key day. Tuck and I build a Lego city about six times, we do a few loads at the laundry mat and made a short trip to the park across the street before we headed home so that I could make Tuck some dinner. For my date tonight, I decided to go a little more casual and comfortable. So, I chose a taupe cardigan, a white t-shirt and a pair of dark wash jeans. Tucker chose my shoes again, but this time I made him pick out of my Converse selection. He ended up picking a pair of beige ones, so it doesn't look too strange and is way more comfortable than the heels from last week.

Tucker is already asleep in bed and Judy is knitting on the couch when Declan knocks on the door. I do a little happy dance before I quickly check myself and grab my purse. I don't miss Judy side eyeing me with a smirk as I open the door.

As soon as I swing the door open, my breath catches. Declan is leaning up against the door frame with a dimpled grin, his amber eyes practically glowing in the dimly lit hallway. He's wearing a dark brown leather jacket just a few shades lighter than his hair with a white t-shirt underneath, blue jeans and a pair of worn in looking brown cowboy boots. I didn't know until now how drop dead sexy the combo is. It's flawless in that sexy biker cowboy bend me over in the stables kind of vibe.

"Sweetheart, I'm a proper gentleman. I'd take you to a bed the first time I have my way with you. The stables are for horny teenagers or ranch hands touching what they shouldn't."

All the color drains from my face as I look from Declan's teasing grin to Judy's stunned expression before she lets out a cackle and begins slapping her knee.

"I did not say that out loud," I whisper, mostly to myself, partially to the universe because that did NOT just happen.

"Violet Ann you sure as shit did," Judy hoots as tears literally start leaking from her eyes.

"I didn't know your middle name was Ann?" Declan smiles, clearly not affected by my overwhelming embarrassment.

"It's not," I say at the same time Judy says, "It sure is."

I roll my eyes at her as I push Declan out into the hall deeper as I grab the door handle.

"We'll be back later unless he changes his mind," I call out as I shut the door.

I'm pinned up against the wall next to my door in an instant as Declan crowds the space between us, his wide hands palming my hips as his right thigh sneaks between my thigh while his nose brushes against mine.

"Never," he says before pressing his lips against mine.

My stomach flips at the feeling as he deepens the kiss, his tongue darting out to stroke against mine as I raise my arms to go up around his neck. My hand tangles into the longest part of his hair as his grip on my hips tightens. I slightly raise my hips against his leg, causing a growl to erupt from his chest as he breaks the kiss quickly, resting his forehead against mine as his chest rapidly rises and falls.

"Hi," he rasps huskily.

"Hi," I squeak back, my voice cracking slightly making Declan's eyes twinkle before he leans down and presses a quick kiss against my lips as he straightens himself to his full height and offers me his hand.

I lace our fingers and can't help but smile as a tingling sensation races up my arm from the contact, leaving a wake of goosebumps in its path. We catch up on what we've been up to today, even if we have been texting literally since we both woke up.

Before long, we are pulling up to Discovery Park, a popular beach front park on Puget Sound. Instead of heading to the parking lot, though, Declan keeps driving until we are parked on the beach. I raise an eyebrow at Declan as he shuts the truck off.

"I don't think you are allowed to park on this beach," I say as I point to the sign indicating you need a permit to do so.

He rolls his eyes before giving me a smirk.

"Rules are meant to be broken every once in a while."

I laugh and shake my head. "Whatever. If the cops come, I'm totally ratting you out."

He covers his chest like he's wounded.

"Ouch, I didn't take you for a snitch."

I shrug, not able to hold back my teasing smile.

"It's called self-preservation, buddy. Every man for themselves, or in this case, woman."

Declan laughs and shakes his head before leaning in and brushing his lips across mine once more.

"Alright, do me a favor and don't look, okay?"

"What? Didn't have time to have a friend set up an elaborate lakeside meal?"

"Nope. Got something different planned tonight. No peeking," he warns with a fake scowl that quickly melts into a dimpled grin before he steps out of the truck.

I shake my head and turn to see what he is grabbing from the back of the truck when he shouts.

"Hey, hey! What did I say? No peeking, woman!"

"Okay, okay, sorry!" I chuckle as I face forward.

Looking down, I watch as the slow rolling waves rush against the gravelly sand before slowly receding only to come back up again. Washington nature is beautiful in a lot of ways, but the beaches are less than stellar. Most of them are more rock than actual sand and the water is so cold no one would willingly go swimming in it, summertime or not. Okay, maybe that's just me. I know a lot of people do but I think they are insane because the Sound never gets warmer than low fifties.

Only a few minutes go by before Declan comes around to my side of the door, offering me his hand with a secretive smile. I eye him warily as he shuts the door behind me and leads us around the back of his truck. My mouth drops slightly as I take in the bed of Declan's truck.

His tailgate is down, and a fluffy comforter is lining the bed. There are at least twelve pillows lining the back along with a few battery powered candles lining the edges. A box of pizza, a six pack of beer, and a laptop open with the movie *Halloween* ready to play is laying in the middle of everything. Turning to face Declan, I shake my head as I look at him.

"How are you even real? Like, c'mon. This is literally straight out of a movie."

"Do you like it?" He asks softly, tucking a piece of hair behind my ear, a hint of nervousness creeping across his face.

"Like it? It's amazing, Declan. I just am not sure what I did to deserve all of this," I say gesturing around us.

Declan's face frowns slightly before softening back into a smile.

"If you can't answer that yourself then I'm not doing my job well enough. Don't worry. I'll step it up."

I laugh as I push his chest softly, no surprise the mountain of a man doesn't waver an inch.

"No, please don't. I don't want to get used to this treatment when I wake up."

He gives me a shake of his head and a wink before his hands come to my waist, and he lifts me effortlessly, sitting me down into the bed of his truck before he joins me. We wiggle back until we are resting against the pillows before Declan grabs another blanket from behind us and lays it across our laps. He lifts his left arm up slightly, I'm not sure if it's an invitation, but I don't really care. Despite it being summer and the blankets, it's cold as hell out here so I push the building butterflies inside me away as I scoot against him. I glance up to see Declan watching me with almost surprise before his arm comes around me and holds me close. My face ends up resting on his firm chest as he hits play.

Chapter Twelve

VI

We watch the movie for a little while and have a few slices of chicken bacon ranch pizza and some beer. Well, I did. Declan ate basically three quarters of the whole pizza, you know, three stomachs and all. Throughout the movie and despite us being practically wrapped up together, his hands haven't wandered even an inch and he hasn't done anything more than a quick kiss to the top of my head here and there. I can't help but feel a twinge of disappointment sinking in. I mean, I'm not looking for a hookup or anything, but then again, this man gave me the first orgasm given by someone other than myself in over six years, and I definitely wouldn't mind a repeat of one of those.

As if he can read my mind, I feel the air around us suddenly shift before Declan reaches a hand down to cup my jaw before tilting my face up to look at him. His amber eyes flick over my face for a moment, something heavy and complex playing across his face as he shakes his head softly.

"You are so fucking beautiful," he whispers reverently, almost like he can't even believe it.

I go to tell him that he is crazy, I'm average at best when his mouth covers me, effectively shutting me up. His body slowly wraps around me until I am underneath him while he trails kisses down my neck and across my collarbone. I arch my back into him as he wraps his hands underneath me, pulling me flush against him where I feel his hard cock against my thigh.

A small moan escapes my lips, and I see a devilish smirk cross his face as he kisses a trail down my chest to my cleavage. His fingers slide underneath my shirt and behind my back, teasing the hooks of my bra as he does.

"I haven't been able to stop thinking about these since last week," he murmurs before he slowly starts lifting my top and bra off.

I press myself against him tightly so that he has better access and let out a low moan at the feel of his fingers against my bare skin. He moves quickly and soon he is peeling the scrap of material away from me. My nipples pebble in the cold air, and I can't suppress a shiver when his hot breath skates across my newly exposed skin.

While still maintaining eye contact, he takes a nipple into his mouth, deftly swirling his tongue around rhythmically. I groan and bury my fingers into his thick dark hair while he expertly works me. One of his hands begins to slide across my stomach and then brushes against the seam on my thigh. Declan pulls his mouth away to capture my lips.

"I've been dying for another taste of you. Lay back, baby, let me take care of you."

Heat rushes through me as Declan slowly and somehow smoothly maneuvers his way down my body until his mouth is hovering just over my jean clad thighs. Softly, he taps the side of my ass.

"Up."

I don't even hesitate. I arch my back and lean up as Declan quickly unbuttons my jeans before sliding them down my legs, my panties going with them. He tosses them to the side before his eyes come down to meet the newly exposed skin. Unease suddenly seeps into me with the fact that I am completely naked in front of this man. I cover my arms over my stretch marks across my stomach casually, hoping that he doesn't notice. His eyes darken as they flick up to my eyes before trailing over my naked body.

Slowly, his hands rest over mine before gently prying them away from my stomach and onto my sides. I cringe, waiting to see the flash of disappointment when he sees that I'm not perfectly toned with flawless skin like I'm sure he's used to. Instead, he keeps his eyes on me as he lowers his mouth to my stretch marks, peppering each silver line with adoring kisses before he gets to the lowest one and lightly runs his tongue along it. I feel my pussy instantly get wet at that as he continues making his way lower as he speaks against my skin.

"Don't ever try to hide yourself from me. You're beautiful, Vi. Stunning. You have the body of a fucking goddess."

Continuing his descent, he presses a soft kiss against the seam where my thigh meets my pussy, his beard brushing against the sensitive skin, causing my legs to tingle as he does. His warm lips trail a path leading in more and more until he is in the middle. With his eyes still firmly on me, he flattens his tongue and gives me one long stroke through me.

My eyes instantly roll into the back of my head as Declan lets out something that sounds like a combination of a growl and a groan. The gentle softness he currently had suddenly evaporates into thin air. His large hands grip my thighs, spreading me wide open for him as he buries his face into me and feasts like a starved animal. His beard rubs against my thighs again. The feeling is a mix between pain and pleasure that has me craving more. His tongue licks and flicks in all the right places as one of his hands snakes down and slips a finger inside me.

"Declan," I moan softly.

His pace quickens causing my legs to tremble. How the hell am I supposed to not cum instantly when I have this god of a man between my thighs, licking and sucking me like I'm a melting ice cream cone?

I don't want to cum yet, though. I want to make him feel good too.

"Declan," I say, though it comes out as more of a strangled moan before I clear my throat. "Declan, stop."

His head instantly pops up, his brows furrowing with concern.

"What's wrong, baby?" He asks.

"I-I need to make you feel good too. You got me off last time, but you didn't get to," I say softly, my cheeks heating with embarrassment.

He smirks at me and shakes his head.

"Baby, this isn't a tit for tat thing. I *want* to eat your pussy. It's the most delicious fucking thing I've ever tasted in my whole life. I wanna fucking drown in your sweet cum. Don't worry about me. Just lay back and let me devour you."

"But," I say a little louder. "What if I want to make you feel good too?"

Ugh. I'm so freaking awkward I hate it! I've never been good at this kind of thing. I know what I want, but vocalizing it? Yeah, not my strong suit.

Declan looks at me for a second as if he is trying to see if I am being honest or not. He gives me a quick nod before he slides up to lay on his back next to me.

"Come sit on my face, baby girl."

My eyes widen and I freeze. "What?"

"Sit on my face, Vi. You can make me feel good while I eat your pussy until you cum all over my face."

Nervously, I crawl over him backwards before lowering myself to hover just over his face. A sexy chuckle comes from beneath me as Declan's hands grip my hips.

"How am I supposed to suffocate in this beautiful pussy with you way up there? C'mere," he says before he yanks my hips down, dropping me right onto his face.

I try to wiggle away so that I don't accidently kill him or something but his hold on me is unrelenting as he resumes his work, expertly twirling and twisting his tongue against me. I let out a soft moan as my hips begin to slowly move against him, earning me a pleased groan in response.

Looking down, I see that his jeans are as tented as a thick pair of denim can be, it looks almost painful. My hands quake slightly as I reach for his belt buckle as I carefully undo it. I haven't been with a man in so long. What if I do it wrong? Declan clearly has learned a thing or two over the years which obviously means he has been with plenty of women. What if I don't do it right? What if I don't compare.

A long lick and a quick nip shakes me out of my thoughts, causing me to clench in pleasure. Fuck it. Finishing undoing his jeans, I slip my hand inside to pull out his cock.

Holy shit.

I can barely wrap my entire hand around him. How the hell am I supposed to fit that thing in my mouth? Declan must sense my hesitation because he pulls up for a second to speak.

"You don't have to, baby. You're in control here."

His words put me at ease and give me the little comfort I needed. Pulling him out the rest of the way, my eyes round as I look at him, but I don't hesitate this time as I lower myself down and run my tongue over the length of him.

"Fuck!" He hisses. "Just like that."

I repeat the moment a few more times earning equally as enthusiastic responses each time before I take his tip inside my mouth. At that, Declan yanks me back down on him as he eats me faster and more desperately than before. I match his pace, bobbing my head up and down as I take him deeper and deeper each time.

His cock is velvety and thick. As my tongue licks him from base to tip, I open my throat up and hollow my cheeks as I suck him deeper.

One of Declan's hands reaches up and slaps the side of my ass cheek as he groans in what sounds like pleasure.

"Shit, yes, baby. Shove my cock down your sweet little throat like a good girl."

Declan's tongue begins flicking over my clit which sends my legs shaking. Without thinking twice on it, I rub my pussy against his face, riding his tongue like it is his cock. Continuing to lick and suck on my clit, Declan slips a thick finger inside me. I clench around him instantly as I let out a muffled moan before I lower my head to take him deeper.

We are a mix of muffled moans, hands, and tongues, and I wish we never had to stop. Reaching down I cup his balls as I begin massaging them while I suck him faster. Declan's hips begin thrusting up and down as he works farther and farther down my throat as he does.

I feel his balls begin to tighten in my hand and know he is right on the edge. Opening my throat up, I take a deep breath before lowering myself and taking him in fully. His tongue presses harder against my clit as his finger hooks up and rubs my g-spot furiously, sending me right over the edge. His legs quake and tense as his hot cum shoots down my throat, both of us riding out our orgasms simultaneously as I swallow him whole.

Slowly, I ease off him and go to stand but only make it so far before Declan yanks me back down until I land on top of him.

"That was the hottest fucking thing I've ever experienced in my life," he says before placing a kiss to the side of my head.

"Yeah," I breathe out ineloquently. My head still spinning. I can't believe that just happened. I also can't believe how bad I don't want to stop there.

I glance over to tell Declan that exactly when red and blue lights suddenly flash in the night around us. Our eyes both widen to the size of saucers as we quickly scramble to get dressed. I am just able to yank my shirt on and pull my jeans over my legs, sans panties because who the fuck can find them in the pitch black like this when we hear an officer shout at us.

"Alright, kids. Break it up."

Declan is the first to get out of the truck, walking around the cab as he makes his way up to the parking lot where the police officer is currently parked. I'm sliding out of the bed just a few seconds after him, but I can hear the moment he sees Declan for the first time from all the way over here.

"Oh, uh, not kids then," the cop laughs to himself. "You guys can't be out this late and you shouldn't be parked on the beach without a pass and all that aside you definitely shouldn't be doing whatever you were in the bed of that truck."

I cringe as I slowly make my way over to them. Ugh. I hate being in trouble. Even in school, I was always a stickler for the rules. My stomach is instantly twisted into knots as I pray to god this won't end up as anything more than a warning. I swear, if we go to jail for public indecency, I will never forgive Declan. I mean, maybe I will, one day. If he goes down on me like that again. Shit, no. Stay focused, Vi. Stay out of jail. Stay out of jail.

I hear soft murmuring between Declan and the officer, and Declan pulls out his wallet and hands him what looks like his ID. Declan tosses a worried look over his shoulder at me as their whispering becomes quicker. By the time I reach them, the officer is handing Declan's ID back to him and nodding.

"Alright, you guys need to get cleaned up and head home now or I'll have to take you in."

"Thank you so much, Officer. We are on our way now," Declan says as he reaches down to hold my hand while he shakes the officers.

He nods at us both before strolling back to his patrol car.

"C'mon," Declan says, as he leads up back over to the truck.

"What happened? Are we in trouble?"

"No," he shakes his head. "But I think we are going to cut tonight early. I'm sorry, sweetheart," he says as he begins gathering up pillows and tossing them in the backseat of his truck. I can't believe I didn't even see them earlier.

I grab the laptop and the blankets before putting them in the back as well. When we are all cleaned up, Declan opens my door for me before jogging around to the driver's seat and pulling off the beach and onto the road. He waves to the officer, who gives us a single wave back, before leaving the beach as well. My heart is still hammering inside my chest as I turn to face him.

"What did you say? Did you get fined or something?"

Declan shakes his head. "Nah, he was really cool. Told us that you can't park on the beach without a permit and people aren't allowed to hangout here after dusk for safety reasons. Obviously, he suggested we keep 'intimate' activities at home."

"Oh my god," I groan as I slink back into my seat. "Do you think he saw me? Riding you?" I blush as the words leave my mouth, and I notice that Declan's cheek pink up slightly before rubbing a hand through his beard and shrugging.

"I don't know. It was probably one hell of a view for him if he did."

My mouth drops, and I grab a pillow and smack his arm. He tries to dodge it as he laughs causing me to chuckle along with him. Suddenly, the embarrassment and fear I felt from being caught become funny and maybe even a little exciting? We laugh literally the entire way back to my apartment, never stopping for more than a few seconds to breathe as we do.

It was a great night.

Chapter Thirteen

Declan

It's been over a week since we were almost busted for public indecency in the bed of my truck. Shit, if the cop hadn't recognized me and agreed to keep it on the down low because of the upcoming season, I have no doubt we would have gotten slapped with some fines and maybe even a night at county as a scare tactic. Thank god that didn't happen. I could see how terrified Vi was.

She didn't have time to get together last week, which was disappointing, but I get it. I haven't been able to stop texting or calling her despite her being busy, though. She also must not be that busy because she always finds the time to get back to me. I can't wipe the shit eating grin off my face at that fact alone.

It's Monday, and I just finished practice for the day. I'm changing into my street clothes when Sebastian comes up to me. I'm a big guy, but this guy is a fucking tall. At 6'6 and over 250 pounds, he was drafted by the Crusaders right out of college. Next to Slater, Sebastian is probably one of my closest friends, even if we all grew apart over the years.

Last week, I went over to Sebastian and Erica's house and had dinner and played with their kids. They have twin three year old girls, Daphne and Rosalie, who are fucking adorable. It's funny to see Seb like that, all domestic and family-man like. It suits him, though. He and Erica went through some shit to get where they are, and I couldn't be happier for them.

I wonder if Tucker would get along with the girls? Is that weird? The fact that I'm already wanting to introduce Tuck and Vi to my friends? I mean, I think first I need to be officially introduced to Tucker, and who knows when that will be. It all just feels right, though. As much as I wanna keep her to myself and my career under wraps, I wanna share everything with her. I wanna show her off. Fuck. I gotta tell her the truth.

Soon.

"Hey, Seb. What's up man?"

"Not much. Want to grab a beer? Erica and the girls are visiting her mom, and the house is boring as fuck right now."

I'm fucking tired from today's practice, and I really don't wanna, but I feel for the guy. Boring is code for lonely, and I can personally attest to how much it sucks, especially since I found someone who I love spending my time with.

"Sure, man. Where were you thinking?"

"McCleary's?"

I let a small smile slip from my face. McCleary's happens to be right across the street from Blooming-Deals.

"Sure, mind if I make a few quick stops?" I ask.

He shrugs as he runs a hand through his shoulder length brown hair and starts walking towards the parking lot. Seb and I are alike in a lot of ways. We don't talk much. We don't feel the need to. Slater is definitely the more outgoing one out of our group. Well, him and Trevor but no one has really talked to him much over the last couple of years.

"You guys going to score some pussy?" Brownstone calls out to us.

Seb rolls his eyes but keeps walking. I glance behind me and shake my head.

"Nah."

"You guys are fucking lame as hell. Caldwell, when are you going to let me at that fine piece of ass you got at home? I'll take her off your hands for the night so you can get some new pussy," he laughs waggling his eyebrows.

I see Seb's hands tighten into fists, and he swings around to face Chad. I get in Seb's face and push on his chest, quickly trying to de-escalate the situation.

"He isn't worth it, Seb. Let it go. Think of Erica and the girls. The fucker isn't worth you ruining your career over," I say urgently. Seb's breathing is labored as he glares daggers at Chad over my head.

"Come on man, let's get out of here," I urge him.

Seb's eyes flick to me, and he gives me a sharp nod before he turns back around and storms out of the locker room. I hear Chad cackling like a fucking hyena from behind us, and for some reason, it grates me more than usual.

"What the fuck is your problem, man? Why do you have to be such a fucking asshole? Who says shit like that to a teammate about their *wife*? It's disrespectful as fuck," I spit, disgust clear on my face.

He takes a few steps towards me, puffing out his chest and standing up straight. It isn't any use though since I have a solid three inches and sixty pounds on the guy.

"None of your fucking business, Daniels. Be thankful you don't have a wife, or I'd have to go after her just to prove a point." He takes a menacing step closer to me and lowers his voice.

"Listen up, this is my fucking team. I run this shit, you hear? If I want, I can make your life a living fucking hell. Shit, I may even get you kicked off this team just like that," he snaps. "So, I'd watch how you talk to me from now on."

I raise an unimpressed eyebrow, waiting for him to spew more shit. He seems to notice that I'm not at all rattled as I cross my large arms across my chest. His comment about going after my wife hit me a bit more than it should have but fuck if I'll let him see it.

Images of him trying to go after Vi flashes through my mind making me feel downright murderous. I take a deep breath, trying to keep my temper in check before I blow it out and turn around. I hear Chad talk some kind of shit to other guys in the locker room, but I don't waste another second on the douche.

When I get outside, I find Seb smoking a cigarette angrily against the wall.

"You know, Coach will have your balls if he sees you smoking," I remind.

He grunts before tossing it on the ground and stepping on it. We walk to my truck and get inside before taking off. Since Seb lives just down the road, he probably just took an Uber or more likely ran to practice.

"What did that little fuck have to say when I left?" He grumbles.

I scoff. "Nothing worth repeating. I know that he is damn good on the field, but I wish the coaches were as sick of his shit as everyone else."

"Same."

After a couple of minutes, we pull up to Sally's Sweet Treats, a bakery that Vi said has her favorite red velvet cupcakes in the city.

I throw the truck in park before I hop out. Seb lifts his eyebrows in question, but I just smirk. I order Vi's treat and am back in the truck in a few minutes, on our way towards McCleary's and Blooming-Deals.

"What's with the sugar craving?" Seb asks as we park.

"It's not for me. It's for my girl."

His eyebrows shoot up in surprise as he gets out of his side.

"When did this happen?"

I shrug as I get out. "We met a couple of weeks ago. We've been spending some time together. I really like her," I say feeling weirdly self-conscious. We don't usually talk about shit like this, and it makes me feel awkward. Shit, everything about Vi makes me feel awkward.

"She works right over there. I'm just going to drop this off. I'll meet you inside."

When I cross the street, I notice that I have a shadow. I give Seb an exasperated look, and the cheeky fucker smirks at me.

Blowing out a breath, I shake my head as I open the door and step inside. Instantly, I see my girl smiling at a customer before they walk out the door, gawking at us. When she sees me, a beautiful smile takes over her face that makes my heart trip up. Damn, this girl has got me twisted up into knots.

"Hey, baby," I say with an easy smile.

She blushes slightly as she looks over at Seb, no doubt feeling awkward about us having an audience. Vi walks around the counter and right up to me, wrapping her arms around my neck in a hug. When she pulls away, I grab the back of her neck and dip down for a quick kiss. Her cheeks flush brighter, and I can't help but love that I'm the reason for it.

"What are you doing here?" She asks.

"Was in the neighborhood. I know you got a shift at the diner tonight, so I thought I'd surprise you," I say as I pull the cupcake box from behind my back.

Vi smiles sweetly as she opens the box, her eyes lighting up when she sees what is inside.

"Thank you," she beams. "This is so sweet."

"I hope so. That's the goal when they put all that sugar in it," I wink.

"Oh my god! That was fucking bad," Seb laughs.

I shoot him a glare before turning back to Vi with a smile. She looks at him and steps past me, holding out her hand to him.

"Hi, I'm Vi."

"Seb," he responds as he shakes her hand politely.

She smiles and nods. "I assume you are a friend of Declan's?"

"Only on his good days," I joke.

Vi laughs lightly as she looks at both of us. "Gosh, do you only keep friends that are a certain height, Declan? You two look like giants walking around us mere mortals."

"Comes with the job," Seb shrugs.

I shoot him a panicked look. Shit. I didn't tell him that Vi doesn't know about what I do, and I would really like to keep it that way at least for now.

"Job? Oh, do you guys work at the organization together? Did you used to play football too?" Vi asks.

Seb's face is full of confusion as he looks at her and glances at me. Just before it looks like he is about to answer, I jump in quickly.

"Yeah, but then he got old and slow, so he helps out with the camps," I say hoping it sounds as smooth as it did in my head.

Vi seems to accept it as she smiles and nods. "Well, thank you for stopping by, and for the cupcake."

Her big hazel eyes look up at me, happiness shining in them, sending my heart racing just looking into them.

"Of course," I say softly as I take a step forward. "I missed you. Think we could spend some time together this weekend? Friday?"

Her smile turns to a frown. "I wish. Judy has plans with some friends of hers, so I don't have a sitter after I get off here. I already had to give my diner shift away so that I can be home in time. We are probably just gonna have some dinner and hangout at the house."

I nod, though I don't do a great job at hiding my disappointment. This woman's like a drug. I never seem to get enough of her. I know better than to ask if I can join them, she wants to wait before I'm around Tuck and I respect that.

"Maybe," she starts almost nervously, "You could come by for dessert? Watch a movie? You have to like Mickey Mouse. Unfortunately, it's nonnegotiable for Tuck."

My face practically splits in two and my heart flips in my chest. She wants me to meet him? Officially? I mean, maybe she doesn't. Maybe she's just being nice. Either way, I'll fucking take it!

"I'll be there. Any requests?"

She shrugs. "Whatever. Tuck is a sucker for anything chocolate."

"You got it," I smile.

She smiles back at me, her cheeks an extra dark shade of pink as she ducks her head and holds onto the box tightly. I love how bashful she can be sometimes. I get the same way around her, as strange as it is.

"Well, we should probably let you get back to work. I'll call you."

"Okay, nice to meet you, Seb," she says as I pull her in for a quick kiss.

"You too," he says as his eyes dart between us curiously.

I smile at her before we walk out the door and across the street. We don't say a word until we are seated in a back booth, away from prying eyes and ears. Once our beers are placed in front of us, he leans forward with his elbows resting on the table.

"Alright, talk."

I sigh and wipe a hand down my face. "She doesn't know I play ball."

He snorts before taking a sip. "No shit. Why?"

Shrugging I spin my glass on the table. "She doesn't like football for whatever reason, sounds like she downright hates it. When we met, she didn't recognize me. I was just a regular guy to her, and it was really nice. Then she learned my name and didn't recognize it, and I thought why ruin it, right?"

"Wrong. All it takes is one google search and your cover is blown. Take it from me man, honesty is key, with everyone."

"I know," I groan. "I need to tell her. I hate keeping secrets from her. I just feel stuck at this point. The more we see each other the more real things get. The deeper things get. Man, she has this kid, I've only met him once, but she tells me about him all the time. He's funny as hell. I'm really into her. I don't wanna fuck this up."

His eyebrows shoot up to his hairline at that. "Wait. She's got a kid? That's what you guys were talking about? You sure you are ready for everything that entails?"

I nod instantly, knowing without a doubt that I want it all with her, with both of them.

Seb grunts as he nods slowly. "If you really like this chick, tell her sooner rather than later."

"Yeah," I sigh. "Maybe I could do it out at dinner sometime. Break it to her in a neutral environment. She seems like the type of a woman that would wanna avoid making a scene so maybe in public is my best chance for her to hear me out."

He lets out another snort and shakes his head. "You're planning on manipulating the girl into being okay with dating an NFL player? Are you fucking stupid?"

"What?" I scowl. "I think it would go over better than talking at her apartment where she could flip and kick me out."

"Whatever you say, man."

Chapter Fourteen

Declan

After a quick stop at Sally's Sweet Treats I'm knocking on Unit 3A at Sunlight Apartments. My palms are a little clammy and the fluttering in my stomach that is usually only there before kickoff is heavy. Shit. If I didn't know any better, I'd say that I'm more nervous to be here than the first time I knocked on this door, and that can't be possible because I felt like I was ready to damn near puke. That was until Vi opened the door and knocked the wind right out of me.

Now here I am again, still desperate as hell to impress this amazing woman but also a four year old who is her entire world. No pressure.

The door is thrown open wide and I'm met with a familiar gap toothed grin.

"Declan!" He shouts excitedly before wrapping his arms around my leg.

Damn, I didn't think he would even remember me, let alone hug me. I squat down to be on his level, setting the box in my hand to the floor as I pat his back.

"What's up, big man? You been behaving for your mama?"

"Uh huh!"

"Yeah, right," Vi mutters as she comes over to the doorway. "If he was behaving, he wouldn't answer the door not knowing who it could be."

I chuckle as I nod and look at Tucker.

"She's right, big man. You never know who it could be. Probably best if you let your mama answer doors."

"Okay, fineee," he draws out before he darts off down the hallway.

I chuckle as I stand up and grab the big white box I brought with me. Vi shakes her head and sighs as she looks up at me.

"Hi," she smiles.

"Hey, beautiful. How was work?" I ask as I give her a brief kiss and step inside.

"Good. It was pretty slow, so I just worked on some display bouquets. It was fun. Oh, let me show you this one. I had to take a picture of it. It's one of my favorites," she smiles as she quickly grabs her phone and starts scrolling.

A second later, she flips her cracked iPhone around to show me the picture of a pretty bouquet with red, orange and white flowers. Couldn't tell you what they are called but it looks real nice, and it's got some of that breath of a baby stuff in it.

I grin as I set the box down onto the dining room table and wrap my arms around her lower back, checking to make sure the coast is clear before I steal a quick kiss. When we break away I rest my forehead against hers.

"You're so talented, sweetheart."

"Oh my gosh, stop. It's nothing," she shrugs modestly.

I shake my head. "I mean it, you blow me away."

"I remember, and we almost went to jail for it," she smirks.

My eyebrows hit my hairline as my smile drops into an open mouthed gape.

"Violet Ann, get your mind out of the gutter."

"Ugh not you too! Only Judy can call me that, mainly because I can't get her to stop."

Chuckling at her, I see when she notices the box. She steps to the side and curiously opens it, her eyes widening when she sees it before she shakes her head and laughs.

"You didn't."

"Ordered it right after Seb and I left you on Monday. Triple layer chocolate cake with chocolate filling and chocolate frosting. Oh, and they threw some chocolate shavings on there too."

"Tuck is going to flip. First gummy bears and now chocolate cake? I'll be sure to send you his dentist bill."

I laugh and go to respond when a high pitched screech interrupts me.

"IS THAT FOR MEEEE?!" Tucker screams.

He barrels towards the table and almost makes it to the cake before Vi catches him around the waist and shakes her head.

"Easy, Tuck. It's for everyone. First, what do you say to Declan for bringing it?"

His big hazel eyes turn to look at me, some of his blond hair falling into them as he looks up.

"Thank you, Declan!"

I smile and nod. "You're welcome, big man. How about you help me dish up?"

"Okay!"

"I can do it," Vi says.

Shaking my head, I rest my hand on her arm and smile.

"I got this. You've been on your feet all day. Just relax."

She smiles softly at me before nodding and taking a seat at the table. I turn to Tucker, sticking my hand out for a high five that he meets eagerly before we take the cake to the kitchen to slice.

Chapter Fifteen

Vi

I'm sitting at the dining room table as I watch Declan who nods at Tucker's whispered words in the kitchen before he stands up and turns around to face the fridge. Shit. I didn't even think about needing milk for whatever Declan brought. I think we have a little left but not a lot.

Thankfully, when he grabs the jug of milk, it looks to be about half full before he grabs three glasses and fills them. Tucker helps him carry the glasses and sliced cake pieces to the table. I can't help but smile as I watch them work together. It makes my heart clench seeing Tuck look so happy, and it does other things to me seeing Declan so sweet with my baby.

I was hesitant about inviting him over. As soon as the words left my mouth, for a moment, I wanted to take them back. We've only been seeing each other for two months. Isn't that too soon to let them meet? Then again, they kinda already did meet, briefly at least. It was clearly enough for both of them though because Declan religiously asks about Tucker every day without any prompt from me, and Tucker has asked a few times about the super tall guy that bought him gummy bears. Maybe it was a bad idea to let Declan officially meet Tucker so soon, but he just seems to fit into my life so perfectly, curiosity got the best of me, I guess.

We each eat one piece of cake, though I definitely noticed that Tuck's is twice the size of Declan and mine. I gave Declan the side eye when I saw it and he just smiled and ducked his head like he was the child getting scolded.

Tuck keeps us plenty entertained as he rambles on about Mickey Mouse and animals. Two things that have absolutely nothing to do with each other, but he is equally obsessed with both.

"Mommy says that one day she will take me fishing since I don't have a daddy to take me," Tuck says a few minutes in, seemingly out of nowhere.

Both Declan and I stop eating as the air suddenly becomes heavy and tense, at least to us. Tuck happily continues chowing down seemingly oblivious to the awkward statement he just made. I glance to the side to see Declan watching both Tucker and I with something resembling sympathy. It makes me uncomfortable and frankly embarrassed.

I know what people may assume about me. If only they knew the full story. With Tucker bringing up his dad more and more lately, I think it is really starting to bother him, and it breaks my heart that it's the one thing in the world that I'll never be able to give him.

The room is quiet for a little before Declan clears his throat. Here he goes, running for the hills. Who wants to deal with a single mom and a son who is desperate for a dad? I don't care how amazing he is, that is terrifying to anyone.

Well, the night was nice while it lasted.

"Do you wanna go fishing with me sometime, Tucker?"

Wait. What?

"Your mama can come too, it would be fun," he adds on as his eyes flick to me, seemingly checking for permission before they focus back on Tuck.

"You have a boat?" Tuck asks with surprised eyes.

"No, but we can lease one."

"Lease?" He questions.

Declan's lips tip up into a smile. "Borrow one."

Another wide grin spreads across Tucker's face and he nods eagerly.

"Yes! Yes, please! Can we, Mommy? Please! Please! I'll clean my room, and you won't even need to ask!"

"You should clean your room without me asking anyways," I say with a raised brow.

He gives me a look that screams 'let's be real here.' Both of them are now watching me, not so patiently, waiting for an answer, and I am officially put on the spot. Shit.

"We will talk about it," I say diplomatically. Tucker nods before he yawns. "Alright, time for bed, buddy. Say goodnight."

Tucker scoots out of his chair as I get up to stand next to him and take him to bed.

"Goodnight, Declan. Thanks for the cake!"

"Night, big man."

I look over to Declan and give him a small smile. "I'll be right back."

He nods as he stays at the table, watching me with a smile. When we get to Tucker's room, I get him settled under his blankets and turn on his night light before kissing his forehead and closing his door. As I walk back out into the living room, I see Declan is in the kitchen doing the dishes.

"Oh, please. You don't need to do those. I'll take care of them."

"I'm already done," he smiles.

"I thought you said you were a bad bus boy?" I ask as I cross my arms over my chest

He smirks and rolls his eyes. "That was like ten years ago. I've picked up a thing or two since then."

I smile and nod as he dries his hands off and leans against the kitchen counter.

"I'm sorry if I overstepped about the whole fishing thing. I felt bad for Tucker. My dad was real busy when I was his age, us kids didn't get to do a lot of that stuff growing up. It sucks. I just wanted to make him happy."

"Why?" I ask curiously.

Declan pauses for a second, seemingly asking himself the same question before he answers.

"Because he deserves it. He's a good kid. Just because his dad ain't around doesn't mean that he shouldn't get to do fun things like that."

I run my fingers through my hair and move to sit down on the couch. Declan wordlessly follows and sits next to me, leaving a respectable amount of space in between us.

"Look, these last couple of months have been amazing, but I think things are getting a little too heavy a little too fast." His brows draw together as his knee begins to bounce. "I like you Declan, but it obviously isn't just me," I say as I gesture to the hallway where Tuck is now sleeping.

"We are a package deal, and I just don't know if I'm ready to bring a man into Tucker's life fully. If he got attached to you and things didn't work out..." I trail off and shake my head. "He couldn't handle it. I'm not sure if I could either if I'm being honest. It's why I told you I couldn't go out with you in the first place. I have to look out for what is best for Tucker. He comes first, always."

Declan nods and looks down to his bouncing knee before he turns to face me.

"As he should. I'll admit, when I first met you, I had no clue that you were a mom. It surprised the hell out of me. Not in a bad way, though. If you think you can scare me off because you put your kid's needs before everything else, you're dead wrong. It makes me like you that much more. You're an incredible woman, and he is an incredible kid. I wanna spend more time with you, both of you. I like you both. I..." He pauses and looks away for a moment before he looks back to me, his amber eyes intense with emotion. "I wanna keep seeing where this goes. Us."

His words have me pausing. They do something to me. Something that I didn't think was possible. My walls are trembling, not much, but I feel the tremor. I feel the first crack in my previously sturdy barrier, and it's all because of the man in front of me. I'm honestly not sure how to feel about it. My instincts tell me this is dangerous, that I need to run far and fast from this man who has the capability to ruin everything I've fought for over the last six years. Yet here I am. Desperately wanting to give in, to tell him yes.

"What if it doesn't work out?" I whisper more to myself than anything.

He gives me a meaningful look as he reaches out and his thumb grazes my cheek softly.

"We'll never know if we don't try."

I don't know who moves first but the next thing I know Declan's soft lips are pressed against mine, gently pressing against me like he is savoring me. A stark contrast from the man he was in the truck. I gotta say, I think I like both.

When he pulls back, he rests his forehead against mine for a moment before he kisses the tip of my nose and smiles softly.

"I should probably get going. I know you got work in the morning, and if we don't stop now, I'll do something stupid like fuck you right here on this couch."

I flush at his words, a small albeit slightly slutty side of me desperate for him to make good on his words. But the rational, sensible mom side of me agrees with him, and unfortunately, she wins tonight. I nod as I stand with him. We walk to the front door before he turns to me and smiles.

"I had a real nice night. Thanks for having me."

I nod as I lean on my tiptoes to kiss him gently. He holds my face tenderly like I am the most precious thing in the world. He continues the kiss for a few more moments before pulling away.

"Thank you, for everything," I whisper into his ear.

His large arms wrap around me tightly as his head rests in the crook of my neck. I feel so small in his arms, so protected, so important. This is weird, right? I shouldn't feel all of this. Not this fast. Maybe I should have dated a little more the last couple of years. Then I wouldn't be going crazy over the first guy to take me out.

"I'll see you soon," he smiles as he pulls away. He places one more soft kiss on my forehead as he steps out the door, turning to me before he leaves. "Make sure you lock this behind me."

I nod and smile which earns me a dimpled grin and a wink in return before he walks down the hallway. I lock the door and lean against it with a goofy smile on my face. He is going to break my heart, probably Tuck's too. How could he not? I feel way too much too fast. Is it so bad that I want to see how it plays out, though? Even if this ends in heartbreak, I can tell it's going to be a hell of a ride.

Chapter Sixteen

Declan

I'm in the parking lot of the practice stadium, ready to go inside for practice but stuck on the phone with my mama. We talked just the other day after Vi had me over for dessert with Tucker. I knew I wasn't going to be able to keep too much of our relationship under wraps for long. Suzannah Daniels has ways of getting information one way or another, and it's typically best if she hears it directly from you. So, we spent about an hour on the phone talking about Vi, about Tucker, and about the insane feelings I've been having for this woman so quickly.

Mama was so excited she damn near jumped on a plane that night to come out and meet them. I had to beg and plead that she would stay put and not scare off this girl before I have a chance to make her mine officially. Then, I texted my dad just in case to make sure that he would keep mama on the ground.

When Tucker told me so casually last night that he hasn't gotten to go fishing because he doesn't have a dad, it broke my damn heart. It also filled me with a confusing amount of rage. I wish I could track down the deadbeat piece of shit and kick his fucking teeth in.

I can't tell you why I feel such a primal need to protect and care for Vi and even Tucker. I have only known her for a few weeks and met him only once. Still, I know with every fiber in my being I would do just about anything to put a smile on either of their faces.

I don't know when they split, or how long, if ever, the guy was in Tucker's life. But one thing is for damn sure, he fucked up. Tucker is the coolest little guy, and he is missing out. I wasn't lying last night when I told Vi that I like them both, that I wanna give us a shot. I do, more than I probably should. Her being a mom doesn't intimidate me like I expected it to. Instead, it makes me appreciate the woman she is, the mom she is. Maybe that is just the mama's boy in me, though.

"Declan, c'mon. You gotta at least let me talk to her! I've been patient! Y'all have been seeing each other for going on three months now. A mama has a right to meet the woman who has stolen her son's heart."

"First off," I sigh, "Patient is the last thing you have been since you found out about her, mama. Second, it's only been two and a half months. Third, who said anything about anyone stealing anyone's heart?"

"You did," she sasses.

I let out a humorless chuckle as I rub at my temple. This woman.

"Oh yeah? When?"

"The second you spoke about her. I could hear it in your voice, baby. You're head over heels for this girl."

I scrub my hand over my mouth before running my fingers through my beard. I ain't gonna deny it. Not saying it's true, but it's definitely not *not* true. I know that what I feel for Vi is big and consuming. I can hardly go a few hours without something reminding me of her in one way or another. Not like it's a bad thing. She is one of my favorite things to think about. Fuck. Maybe I'm worse off than I thought.

"Well at least tell me that you're planning on bringing her to the auction at the end of the month?"

"No, Mama. I wasn't planning on taking the girl I just started dating across the country to Knoxville so that we can go to a football program's gala where everyone in the room but her knows that I am a pro ball player."

She scoffs on the phone. "Well, there is an easy fix to that. Pull your head out of your ass and tell her the truth."

"Mama, you just swore," I say stunned, she only uses 'foul' language very rarely.

"Well, you're being an idiot. You're gonna blow it with this girl and then your heart will be broken, and I won't be any closer to grandbabies."

I roll my eyes and shake my head at her antics.

"Mama, I don't think Vi would go, whether she knew the truth or not. We are just getting started. I don't know if a cross country trip is what would be best right now."

"Declan, tell me a woman that wouldn't love an all expenses paid trip to a place she's never been and to a dress up gala surrounded by rich and famous people?"

Violet. All of that sounds like everything she would hate.

I've learned real quick that money is just not something we talk about. Like when I opened her fridge and saw how bare it was, I almost said something but what the hell could I say that wouldn't embarrass her and make her feel like she isn't doing enough when she's doing everything? She kills herself to provide for them, seemingly never catching a break. Who knows how many nights she has stressed over keeping food on the table or making sure that the heat stays on?

"I don't think so, mama."

She sighs heavily. "Sweetie, this is a part of your life, football is a part of your life. It's practically been your whole life for as long as you've been able to walk. You can't only show some parts of yourself and withhold the others? You're gonna doom this relationship before it even begins."

I roll my eyes and am ready to bang my head into the steering wheel when my door is tossed open. Slater peeks his head in, and smiles at me until he sees that I'm on the phone. I give him a look as I mouth 'my mom,' which causes him to smile widely before he yanks the phone from my grasp and puts it on speaker.

"Hey, Mama Daniels, it's your favorite wide receiver/secret lover," Slater smirks.

I smack him over the back of his head as my mother's laugh echoes through the speaker.

"Oh Slater, you are too funny. We sure miss you, sugar. You're coming to our gala at the end of the month, right?"

"Do you think I would miss out on a chance to see my best girl all dressed up? Not a chance. I'll be there, make sure you save me a dance."

She giggles, I shit you not, giggles, like a schoolgirl as she responds.

"Great. Now make sure my son brings his new girlfriend."

"She's not my girlfriend yet," I say as Slater says, "I'm on it."

I shake my head as I hang up. "Bye, Mama."

Blowing out a breath, I lean my head against the headrest before Slater speaks.

"So, you gonna bring your girl to Tennessee? You know Mama Daniels won't rest until you do."

I blow out a breath and shake my head again. He's right. Fuck.

CHAPTER SEVENTEEN

VI

I go back and forth on what to do about the whole fishing thing. Mainly because both men have been working me over from both sides. Finally, after Tucker has officially worn my patience thin, I text Declan.

Me: So, Tucker is pretty insistent to go fishing now. He won't stop talking about it. Does your offer still stand?

His response comes almost instantly.

Declan: Of course. How does next Saturday morning work for you?

Me: Actually, good. How early are we talking?

Declan: You ever heard the early bird gets the worm?

Me: Yeah. I'm that bird every damn day, and I would kill to sleep in for once.

Declan: Fair enough. I can pick you guys up at seven?

Me: ...That is still pretty early.

Declan: It will be worth it.

Me: Will there be coffee?

Declan: Of course. Growing up with my mother and sister, I learned young not to speak to a woman in the morning if they haven't had their caffeine.

Me: They taught you well. Caramel iced coffee with extra caramel and whip, please!

Declan: That's more sugar than caffeine.

Me: Sugar high, caffeine high, what's the difference?

Declan: You got it, beautiful. I can't wait to see you.

On Saturday, I wake up too early for my liking but the prospect of spending the day with Declan has me moving a little faster than I normally would. Only a little, though.

After I get out of the shower, I slip on my swimsuit before throwing a pair of jeans and a white t-shirt over the top before sliding on my daisy covered Converse that my parents gave me for my eighteenth birthday. I brush out my hair and fluff it the best as I can before rubbing on some tinted moisturizer and some waterproof mascara that I had in the back of the medicine cabinet.

Walking into Tucker's room, I push the door open before rubbing his back a few times.

"Tuck, it's time to get up. Don't you want to go fishing," I sing softly.

His eyes spring open before he practically leaps out of bed. For the first time in probably ever, he races to the bathroom and begins brushing his teeth without me even having to hassle him. I chuckle to myself as I set out a pair of shorts and a shirt for him to wear. He is still bouncing on the balls of his feet as he comes into the room and quickly gets dressed.

As I move to the kitchen to finish packing a bag for us with a few snacks that we have around the house as well as some change of clothes and sunscreen, Tucker is rambling on about how excited he is to go fishing and how he can't wait to see Declan.

Tuck seems to already be getting a little attached to Declan, and it's honestly making me nervous. Maybe this is a bad idea. Then again, if I ever want to date anyone, they have to know that Tuck will always be number one. They have to know that a relationship with him is just as important as a relationship with me. Declan seems to already get that which makes a sense of ease settle through me.

At 7:00AM on the nose, a heavy knock comes from our door. Tuck takes off running, swinging the door open wide as he bounces in place.

"Declan!"

"Tucker, what have we talked about?" I say exasperated.

"But it's just Declan! He's not a stranger."

Declan's deep laugh carries through the house as he ruffles Tucker's messy head.

"Mind your mama, big man."

"Okayyy. Can we go see the fishes yet?"

Declan smiles before turning to face me. His eyes lock onto mine and butterflies rush through me as his eyes scan me from head to toe. He is wearing a pair of black board shorts with white stripes down the sides and a white t-shirt that wraps tightly around his large tattooed arms and wide chest. I hadn't fully realized it before, but Declan is really in shape, like he is completely ripped.

Without even realizing I'm doing so I sink my teeth into my bottom lip as my eyes rake over him. When they come up to meet his face, I notice him staring at me with a hungry look, his eyes darker than I've ever seen. A thrill runs through me that I made him look like that. That he is staring at *me* like I am his last meal, and he is starving.

Tucker runs back over to the table where he is eating his breakfast as Declan walks deeper into the apartment towards me. When he stands in front of me, he peeks over his shoulder to glance at Tucker before he looks at me. I think he is unsure if he can be affectionate with me in front of Tucker, which melts me to see how considerate he is of Tuck and my feelings.

I give him a small nod and wrap my arms around his neck to hug him as his arms snake firmly around my waist.

"Thank you," I whisper into his ear.

His arms tighten slightly before he releases me with a soft smile.

"Almost forgot," he says as he hands me an iced coffee that I didn't even realize he was holding.

"You're an angel," I groan as I take a sip.

He smiles at me before turning to Tucker. "So, are you guys ready?"

"Yes," I smile as I grab our bag.

Declan automatically grabs it from me, letting his fingers linger against mine before slinging the bag over his shoulder. He smirks as we walk over to the dining room table.

"You ready, Tuck?" I ask.

He nods eagerly and takes his cereal bowl to the sink before he slips on his shoes and practically pulls my arm out of its socket as we head out the door. When we get down to the parking lot, I go over to my car to get Tuck's car seat. I know that technically he would be fine with just a booster seat at his age and height, but this is my baby we are talking about. I'm not risking anything where he is concerned. Though, he is getting a little big for it. Maybe we will transition after his birthday.

Once I have the seat undone it's only in my hand for a moment before Declan swoops in and carries it over to his truck. Declan unlocks his truck and opens the door to the backseat as he begins attempting to install the car seat. I lean against the door with an amused smirk on my face as I watch him struggle for a solid four minutes, at least.

Visibly frustrated, Declan finally steps back and runs a hand through his hair as his eyes narrow at the car seat like it is public enemy number one. Standing up on my tip toes, I kiss his cheek and pat his back.

"Watch and learn, buddy," I say as I slide in front of him and fasten the car seat in ten seconds flat. When I am finished, I turn around and smile while he frowns at me.

"That is the stupidest thing I've ever seen," he grumbles.

I laugh lightly as I grab Tuck and lift him up into his seat. As I buckle him in, I can feel Declan's gaze watching me intently. I think it's sweet that he wants to know how to put his car seat in properly and how to buckle Tuck in. Declan seems like the kind of guy who does everything perfectly, so his interest is probably more about him being irritated that he isn't good at something than about knowing how to install a car seat. Still, it's sweet.

We shut the door and Declan walks me around the truck and opens my door, helping me in before he goes around to his side.

"Why did you open Mommy's door, Declan?" Tuck asks.

Declan looks up into the rear-view mirror and smiles at him.

"Because she's a lady. You should try to open a door for anyone, really. It's polite."

"Really?" Tucker asks surprised before he looks over to me. "I'm sorry I don't open your door, Mommy."

I smile and turn around to face him as I pat his leg.

"That's okay sweetie. You're my kid, so the rules are a little different."

"But I wanna be poh-light like Declan," Tucker says, mimicking Declan's accent.

I glance over to Declan, and I'm pretty sure I just witnessed his heart melt all over the floorboard of his truck. I know mine sure as hell did. Declan's cheeks pink up just a touch, and he nods before he clears his throat.

"Thanks, big man."

Declan starts up the truck and backs out before we head down the road. I can't help but sneak peeks at him as he drives. When his amber eyes meet mine, my heart seizes for a second before it finds its rhythm again. I feel like a giddy teenager as I sit in the passenger seat with my hands in my lap, trying to resist not running them all over him. Except now, instead of parents supervising us, we have a four year old.

When we pull up to a boating dock uptown, Declan gets out of the truck and helps Tucker out of his seat before they both come around and get my door. I see Tucker look up to Declan for a second, seemingly for approval, as Declan gives him a short nod and a wink.

"Thank you, sir," I say to Tucker.

He beams up at me, pride filling in his sweet hazel eyes.

"You're welcome, Mommy!"

Declan grabs the bag I packed and a bag of his own before he intertwines our hands and walks us down the dock. We stop at a large white yacht with tinted windows surrounding the sides. It's huge and looks to have two decks. Is that a hot tub on top? Who comes up with this kind of stuff?

"Is this our boat?" Tucker shouts excitedly as he bounces on his toes.

Declan laughs. "Well, only for the day."

"This is so cool! This must cost a bajillion dollars! Isn't this cool, Mommy?"

I'm honestly a little stunned. I was expecting like a rowboat or something. Definitely nothing so lavish. I cock a brow and tilt my head at him.

"What did you say you did for a living again? Are you a secret prince or something?"

Declan waggles his eyebrows and winks causing a laugh to bubble out of me. Movement catches my attention out of the corner of my eye as I see a man waiting for us at the end of the ramp to the boat.

"Mr. Daniels?" He asks with a smile as he puts his hand out to shake Declan's hand.

"How you doing?" Declan greets as we follow behind him.

"Very good, sir. I'm Darryl, I will be your captain today. It looks like it's going to be a beautiful day."

"Perfect. This is Vi and Tucker," he says introducing us.

Darryl smiles as he shakes my hand and waves to Tucker.

"You have a beautiful family," he says before he gestures for us to board.

"Oh, we aren't-" I start.

"Thanks," Declan says easily with a wide smile.

He slips his arm around my shoulder casually before he smirks at me conspiringly and guides Tucker and I onto the boat. I guess it's easier to let the guy assume what he wants. Probably easier than giving him the rundown of our relationship. Is that what this is? Are we in a relationship? I mean, I hope we are, but it isn't like it's a subject that has been brought up and there is no way that I'll be the first one to broach the topic of labels or expectations.

When we step inside the boat, I'm a little taken back. Everything is crisp, clean and plush. The kitchenette has granite countertops, all of the seats are white leather with black embroidery and a full-sized black dining room table is set off to the side with six chairs surrounding it. This thing looks even more spacious on the inside than it did on the outside, and suddenly, I'm feeling extremely out of my element.

Tucker is bouncing off the walls, opening every cabinet in sight and shouting excitedly about how cool the boat is. I cringe as he slams a door a little too hard, dollar signs instantly beginning to flash inside my head.

"Tuck! Careful, please!"

Declan steps inside behind me with an easy smile as he watches Tucker race around. Leaning down to speak in my ear.

"He's fine. I'm glad he likes it."

I turn towards him and put my arms around his neck to pull him down into a hug. "You know, I think a rowboat would have more than sufficed."

He pulls back and shakes his head grinning. "No way, and miss that reaction?" He says as he points to Tucker.

"Please don't spoil him. I can't afford to keep up with you," I joke lightly.

"No promises," he winks before he slips past me and goes over to Tuck so that they can check out the inside of the boat together.

Soon, the engine rumbles to life beneath us and we begin slowly moving through the water. I step out to the back deck and watch the wakes we leave behind as we push deeper into Puget Sound. The wind tosses my hair from side to side as I close my eyes and take a deep breath before slowly letting it out.

"Pretty beautiful, huh?" Declan's deep voice rumbles from behind me as his thick arms wrap around my waist.

I gasp for a moment before I turn around to face him, giving him a soft smile as I do.

"You scared me."

Declan smiles before his arms tighten around me a little more.

"So, what do you think? Do you like the boat?"

My laugh comes out a little hollow as I shake my head.

"This isn't a boat, Declan. This is a freaking floating mansion. It's kind of a lot, honestly. I get that you are trying to impress me and show off or whatever but this kind of display of money makes me a little uncomfortable."

Declan looks at me for a few moments, seemingly in thought when he cocks his head to the side.

"Why?"

"Because I just..." I break off with a sigh as I whisper, "It's just not what we're used to, you know? This isn't my life," I say as I gesture around us.

"I mean, but it is, right? You and Tucker are here right now, aren't you?"

"On your dime," I point out, probably a little sharper than I meant. "I don't want you to think I'm a gold digger, Declan. I'm far more interested in the size of a man's heart, not his bank account."

"I know," he says gently, almost like he is trying to talk a crazy person off the ledge. I guess that makes me the crazy person. "That's why you, of all people, deserve to be spoiled, Vi."

I open my mouth to argue, but Declan crowds me, his lips hovering just above mine as he speaks.

"I'm sorry. I wasn't trying to show off or anything. My family is well off, and this is just how I was raised. I didn't think about how it could look to someone who wasn't raised like that. I just wanted us to have a good day together."

Great. Now I'm the asshole.

"I'm sorry. Money is a hard subject for me sometimes. It isn't your fault. I was projecting. I want us to have a good day too."

He smiles softly, tucking a piece of hair behind my ear before gently spinning me around so that I'm facing the water. His arms wrap around my waist tightly as his chin rests in the crook of my neck. We stay like that for several minutes, mesmerized by the soft wake we leave in our path as we push out deeper into the water.

It takes me by surprise how unbelievably natural it feels to be so affectionate with him so soon. There is no awkward tension or cautious fumblings like most people have when they first start spending time with someone. Everything about Declan is smooth, calm and honestly, pretty perfect.

"Where is Tucker?" I ask as I look around the back deck. I haven't seen him in a little while. Who knows what kind of trouble he has gotten himself into.

"He's upstairs with the captain. Darryl is letting him steer," Declan says.

"So, this may be our last few moments?" I joke.

I feel Declan's lips tip up into a smirk against the sensitive skin of my neck. His lips slowly glide across my skin until they settle on the shell of my ear.

"Guess we should make the most of it," he whispers.

A shudder escapes my lips before I turn around to face him. One of his hands cups my face gently like I'm a porcelain doll before he tilts up slightly. Leaning in close, his full lips brush across mine tenderly. The instant we touch, my heart flip flops as my stomach somersaults. Declan groans softly into the kiss before pulling me closer. I loop my arms around his neck and press my body flush against his.

My heart is beating so hard that I don't doubt he can feel it through my chest. I've never felt a thrill like this from just kissing a man before. Hell, I've never felt a thrill like this from just being around a man before. Period.

There is just something about Declan that almost seems to draw me in. I recognize that I'm dropping my walls entirely too fast, and I'm practically serving myself up on a platter for heartbreak. Something completely naïve in me tells me that he is different, though. That I can trust him. That I can trust *this*, whatever *this* is.

His lips trail away from mine as they move across my cheek and down my neck. When he reaches my ear, he places another gentle kiss before he speaks softly to me.

"I've been wanting to do that since the moment I walked out of your apartment last week."

I can't help but let out a wide grin. "You've been thinking about me all week?"

He scoffs as he threads his fingers through my hair. "Couldn't stop if I tried."

"I like that," I say before I give him a chaste kiss and turn back to face the water.

I hear a content sigh from behind me and feel Declan's body press against me again as his hands rest on the railing on either side of me. My head tilts back slightly to rest against his shoulder casually like this is just something we do every day.

CHAPTER EIGHTEEN

VI

O nce the boat stops moving and we anchor, I decide it's time to check on Tuck. When I step into the cockpit, I see him sitting on a bench behind the wheel with a captain's hat on.

"Mommy, did you see! I drove the boat all by myself! I did good, huh?"

"You did so good, sweetie," I smile.

"I think we could have a future captain on our hands," Darryl says with an amused smirk.

Tucker's eyes widen with excitement as he looks up to me. I chuckle and grab his hand.

"Why don't we head downstairs? Declan is getting our fishing poles ready."

"Do I get my own?" He asks as we make our way to the back deck.

"You bet. Are you excited?"

"Uh huh! This is the funnest thing ever!"

"Good, I'm glad," I say as I rub his back with a soft smile.

When we get outside, I see three seats have been placed around the back deck and three poles are set up and sitting inside the pole holders on the ledge of the railing. Tucker runs right over to Declan and begins ambushing him with rapid fire questions. To my surprise, Declan seems to know quite a bit about fishing and explains to Tucker what everything is called and how to cast a line.

"Nice, big man! That was perfect!" Declan exclaims when Tucker's hook plops into the water.

His smile is huge as he looks up to Declan and then over to me. Declan quickly casts his line and comes over to help me with mine.

"Gosh, I haven't done this since I was a little older than Tuck," I say once we are settled into our seats.

"Yeah, it's been a while for me too," Declan agrees as he reaches over to hold my hand. It seems like he can never stop touching me, whether he realizes it or not. You won't be hearing any complaints from me, though.

"Really? You seem pretty well versed."

He shrugs. "I didn't always get tons of time with my dad growing up but when I did it was definitely quality. Donny was really into fishing, so he was always more interested in it than me. I was usually just along for the ride, but I remember a lot," he says with a far-off look, his eyes never leaving the water.

The air is quiet around us for a bit before Declan speaks again, a little softer this time.

"We were seventeen when he died. We did everything together, maybe it was just a twin thing or maybe it was an us thing, but we were inseparable all our lives. One night he wanted to go to a party that someone was having on their dad's boat. I had football camp in the morning, so I didn't wanna go but he went anyway. I guess he drank too much, that's what people said. He ended up falling overboard, and no one realized it until it was too late."

My mouth parts in shock and goosebumps prick against my skin at the raw vulnerability in his voice. Wordlessly, I stand up and walk over to him, sliding into his lap. He doesn't say anything, but he does wrap his arms around me tightly and hauls me into him as close as possible. I slip my arms around him and hold him for a little while, doing my best to take some of his hurt away, as if that was possible.

"It's been ten years, and I still miss him like crazy. Kinda feels like I'm missing a piece of me, you know? He never got to graduate high school, go to college, or even fall in love. I can't help but wonder what would have happened if that night would have ended up differently. If I would have been there, having his back like I always did. I guess I didn't when it counted most, though," he says as he roughly swallows.

"Hey," I say softly as I turn his face towards me. "You could never have known. It was an accident. A horribly heartbreaking accident. I have played the what if game before, it does all harm and no good."

Declan nods as he looks at me before giving me a sad smile.

"You know, I have always hated my birthday. Well, ever since Donny passed, but this year was probably the best one in a very long time. I met an incredible woman and ate the best piece of apple pie that I've ever had."

I smile at his words and squeeze his shoulder. "You're pretty great yourself."

Declan kisses the side of my head as he holds me just a little tighter. Any tighter and I think he is going to crack one of my ribs.

"My family got really close after Donny passed," he continues. "Before it seemed like we were always off doing our own things. When a tragedy happens families either band together or fall apart. We were fortunate enough to be the band together kind. My dad stopped traveling, Danielle took a year off from college to come home, and now I'm that guy that talks to his parents and sister on the phone at least once a week."

"That's really wonderful," I smile. "My parents were boring 9-5 workers, which was perfect. We were really close too. Every Sunday was spent at church in the morning and then my mom would make a roast dinner. She grew up in the south, so her traditions lived on even in the Pacific Northwest. Life always felt so full with them."

I blink my eyes rapidly as I begin to feel the familiar sting of building tears. Even after six years, I still miss them a lot. I probably always will. Declan reaches over and grabs my hand, squeezing it lightly. I force a watery smile and squeeze back.

"I really wish Tuck could have known them. They would have spoiled him rotten. My mom would have made him cookies every time she saw him, and my dad would have done all the stuff with him that he did with me. Fishing, camping, learning to ride a bike. It makes me sad that he will never have grandparents."

"What about your parent's folks?"

"Dad was a late in life baby. Both of his parents had passed by the time that I was twelve. My mom was an orphan, she bounced around in group homes until she was eighteen. She met my dad freshman year of college and fell in love."

Declan twists his mouth in a frown and nods. His eyes glance over to Tuck, who is currently playing with the worms we brought for bait. Declan scoots a little closer to me, lowering his voice.

"And his father's parents?"

I grimace. "They made it perfectly clear that they want nothing to do with me or Tucker."

Declan shakes his head and looks down, like he is trying to hide his emotions. I can see it written all over his face, though. He looks angry on my behalf. I cup his face and give him a grateful smile.

"It's okay, really. They're not good people. I wouldn't want Tucker to be exposed to them anyways. We have Judy and my best friend, Mindi, comes to visit a couple of times a year. She took a job in LA after she graduated college but when she visits, Tucker always has the best time. She is the stereotypical cool aunt who loads him up with sugar, buys him anything he asks for and stays up late watching cartoons with him."

Declan smiles. "Sounds like you have some good people in your corner."

I glance at him before I settle on his deep golden eyes.

"Can never have enough," I say softly.

He smirks and leans in to kiss me before Tucker yelps. We both straighten, and Declan quickly places me on my feet before he rushes over to Tuck.

"What's wrong, big man?"

"My pole is moving!" Tucker shouts as his pole bows and wiggles in its holder. Declan grabs it and begins to reel it in.

"It's because you got a fish! Come here and hold it, I'll help you."

Tucker smiles excitedly and scrambles over to grab the top part of the pole while Declan continues to hold on to the bottom.

"Alright, start reeling it in. Yeah, just like that!" Declan instructs.

After a minute or so of fighting, they reel in...

"Is that a shoe?" I ask as I walk over to them.

Tucker wrinkles his nose while he looks at the sneaker hooked on to his pole as Declan lets out a laugh.

"Women's size six. Want it?" He teases.

"I would, but I'm a seven," I shrug with mock disappointment.

"You are way older than seven, Mommy," Tucker chimes in.

I scowl at him. "We were talking about shoe size, but thanks for that one, bud."

"You're welcome," he smiles, completely oblivious to my sarcasm.

Declan re-baits Tucker's line and casts it back out before placing it into the holder. After an hour or so of Tucker and Declan playing hide and go seek through the boat and absolutely no bites on the poles, they come running up to me.

"Mommy, we're hungry!" Tucker announces.

"Oh yeah? I packed you some snacks in our bag, sweetie."

"I actually had lunch set up for us if you're hungry, Vi," Declan says.

"Oh, okay," I say as I stand up from my lounge chair. "What can I help with?" I ask.

He smiles and shakes his head. "Not a thing. Enjoy the sun. You guys like burgers?"

"Burgers while we fish?" I ask playfully.

He shrugs. "It was a backup plan in case we didn't catch any fish, which I'm glad for since we aren't having great luck."

I smile. "Well, we both love burgers. Are you sure I can't help?"

"Nah, I got it."

"Can I help?" Tucker asks.

Declan grins at him and sticks out his hand for a high five. "If you wanna."

Tucker nods excitedly and races into the kitchen. Declan chuckles before glancing inside the boat and looking back to me before he walks over to me, capturing my lips in a passionate kiss that ends entirely too quickly.

"What was that for?" I ask, dazed as he pulls back, grinning down at me.

"Because those pretty lips were just begging to be sucked on."

My face flushes as I bite my lip. "Okay, Casanova. You better get in there before my kid burns down the boat."

Declan winks at me as he walks away, causing my stomach to flip. Damn, that man has a mouth on him. Damn if I don't love it, though.

Twenty minutes later, lunch is ready, and we sit down at the dining room table to eat cheeseburgers and potato salad. We laugh as Declan tells us stories of him fishing growing up while Tuck spouts off question after question at Declan. Since the guys cooked, I offered to do the dishes while they went off to soak up some sun. Once I put the last dish away, I feel Tucker tugging on the bottom of my shirt.

"Mommy. Declan said we can go swimming. Can we go now, pleaseeee?"

I dry my hands and laugh softly. "Sure, buddy. Let's go put on your swimsuit."

I grab our bag and Tucker's hand as we make our way to the bathroom. Taking a deep breath, I peel off my shirt and jeans and put our clothes back into the bag and help Tucker put his arm floaties on before we make our way back out to the deck. When we step outside, I see Declan standing near the railing in just his board shorts, and I have to physically stop myself from swallowing my tongue.

Before, I thought only male models or gym rats actually had fully defined six packs, but obviously that isn't true because Declan is the most in shape man that I have ever seen. His tan skin shines in the sunlight, and I can't help but drink him in. My eyes stare at his muscular shoulders and move down to his firm pecs, across his rippled stomach and finally to the defined v that disappears to somewhere I definitely want to explore later.

I'm also greeted with what I have been wondering, and dreaming about, for weeks now. From Declan's collarbone down to the bottom of his pecs and both his arms, he is covered in tattoos. You can tell that they were done at different times, probably by different artists but somehow they all flow together. They are all black but different shades. It gives them so much dimension and depth that I find my eyes tracing over the same tattoos over and over again. Why are tattoos so hot? Weren't we taught that tattooed men were scary? That we should stay away from them? All I can think about is how that tattooed arm will look wrapped around my naked skin.

I don't make much effort of hiding my perusal so I shouldn't be surprised when my eyes come up to his face and I see a cocky grin spread across his lips. His eyes skate down my semi-naked body as well, and when his golden gaze flicks back up to my face, I see the heat that they hold.

I do my best to fight the urge to cover myself. I have a little more of everything everywhere and stretch marks from being pregnant. His heavy gaze makes me feel sexier standing here in front of him than I probably have ever felt in my entire life. The attraction between us is palpable, and I wonder how we are going to survive an entire day like this without giving in to it.

Suddenly, Tucker runs from behind me and over to the edge by Declan, a wide smile on his face. Declan looks down at him with a matching one.

"You guys ready?"

"Uh huh!" Tuck shouts.

Declan smiles down at him and gestures with his head. He climbs down the side ladder and dips into the water before sharply inhaling.

The Pacific Northwest isn't exactly known for warm water, but today it's in the mid-nineties, so cold water or not, people will swim.

I turn to Tucker and smile. He is looking a little paler than before as he stares at the water, frozen in place.

"Are you okay, sweetie?" I ask him softly.

"It's deep, huh?"

"Well, it is the ocean, honey," I say with a smile.

"I don't know, Mommy…"

"That's okay. We don't have to go in."

He looks at the water hesitantly like he isn't sure. Declan swims over to us lazily with a smile.

"Everything okay up there?"

I grimace and shake my head. Declan's brows furrow as he pulls himself up onto the deck.

"What's going on, big man?" He asks as he squats next to Tucker.

"It's kinda scary," he says softly while he tugs on his arm floaties.

"Yeah, it's pretty big. How about we stay on the boat today. Maybe we can try swimming another time in a pool or something to start?"

Tuck chews on his bottom lip just like I do when he is nervous as looks out at the water hesitantly.

"I wanna be brave like you."

"Ah, big man, don't worry about it. Your mom says that you haven't really swam before. Starting off in the ocean is a big deal."

Tuck looks over at Declan seemingly contemplating his options.

"Will you stay with me?"

"Of course."

Tuck gets a look of determination across his face as he nods tersely and walks towards Declan. Declan throws a questioning look at me, and I give him a look that tells him to just go with it. Quickly, Declan slips back into the water and holds his arms out for Tuck. I hear him take a deep breath before he literally jumps in and practically cannonballs on top of Declan's head.

They both go under for half a second before Tuck emerges and then Declan. Both of them yelp and gasp from the cold water before they burst into laughter. Tuck stays latched around Declan's neck like a monkey, but Declan doesn't seem to mind one bit.

I dip my toe in the water and widen my eyes at Declan. Okay, maybe I was wrong. I don't care if it's ninety outside. No way am I getting in there.

"What's wrong, Mommy? It isn't scary," Tuck calls out about twenty feet away from the boat.

"Yeah, mama!" Declan taunts with a mischievous smirk.

"I'm good over here," I say as I slowly lower myself to the edge before dangling my legs into the water.

I watch as Declan and Tuck seem to be whispering something to each other as they flick their gazes over to me. *This can't be good.* Declan swims over to me with Tuck in his arms, both of them wearing playful smirks that have me narrowing my eyes in suspicion.

"What are you doing?" I ask.

Instead of replying, Declan pushes Tuck towards the boat where he can hold on to the side before he grabs my thighs and yanks me into the water. The icy water wraps around me as I'm plunged under, all of the breath in my lungs instantly stolen. When I break through the surface, I let out a screech and hear Declan and Tucker laughing hysterically.

I splash Declan with a look of mock irritation, when really, I am fighting a smile of my own. It soon turns into an all-out splash war with Tuck and Declan teaming up on me.

Betrayed by my own child, I don't believe it.

I knew I was practically powerless to Declan's charms, but it seems he has been able to turn my own son against me. I don't even try to hide the smile that spreads across my face at the sight of them laughing and playing together.

CHAPTER NINETEEN

VI

After a little while, all of our teeth are chattering despite the sweltering heat outside, so we decide to get back on the boat. We spend the rest of the day soaking up the sun and playing some board games we found inside.

Just before sunset, Tucker passes out, and Declan carries him to a bed in one of the cabins. When he comes back out, I'm sipping a glass of wine laying down on one of the plush loungers.

"Hey, gorgeous," he smiles as he bends down and kisses me before squeezing next to me on the lounger.

I scoot over to make room for him, which isn't an easy task since the guy is a freaking tank. Once he is on his back, he drapes one of my legs across him and settles us so that I'm basically on top of him.

"Let me know if I'm crushing you," I say as he wraps his arm around me.

"Baby, you would have to weigh another hundred and fifty pounds before you could even come close to crushing me."

I blush at how casually he calls me baby as I settle my face against his firm chest that is now unfortunately covered in a cotton t-shirt. We look out over the water in comfortable silence as the sun begins to dip lower in the horizon, painting the sky a beautiful orange and yellow combination.

"I think Tucker is having a good time," he says with a smile.

"Oh, he is having the time of his life." I glance up to him and press a chaste kiss against his lips.

"Thank you again for today."

"Of course. Thank you guys for coming. He's a real good kid. You did a good job with him, especially all on your own."

Tears begin to gather in the corners of my eyes, and I do my best to fight them back.

"Thank you," I rasp. "You have no idea how much that means to me, really. I wish I could give him more, though. I hope I can one day. But we are happy, we have everything we need and try to make the best out of every day."

"What more do you wanna give him?" He asks, sounding genuinely interested.

"Everything," I laugh almost pitifully. "I wish that my fridge was always filled with healthy filling food. I wish that I could afford to buy him the newest toy or new clothes. Almost everything he has is hand me downs, which is fine, and Tucker has never known the difference, but he is getting older now. I worry he will be that kid in school that gets teased for not having a ton of money, ya know? Kids are stupid and cruel for the dumbest reasons."

"You work your ass off, Vi. That is obvious to anyone. Tucker is going to be just fine."

"I hope so," I sigh as Declan's fingers start running through my hair.

"What about Tucker's dad? I know you said that he isn't in the picture, but he at least helps out right? Like child support or something?"

I frown and look up to him. "No. It's, um, a long story."

He squeezes me tightly and his eyes urge me to continue. Only Mindi and Judy know the full truth. Others know partial truths. There is something about Declan that makes me feel like I can open up to him, I just don't know if I am ready to share *everything*. So, I settle for a partial truth.

"He didn't want to be a dad. When I got pregnant, he showed his true colors, and I realized that it was for the best. I-I guess it wasn't that long of a story," I shrug softly.

"But he is still responsible, whether he wants to be a dad or not is irrelevant. He can't just leave you two to fend for yourself! He can't-"

Declan clenches his jaw and shakes his head for a minute before he looks down at me as pushes the hair away from my face.

"You are one in a million, Vi. I've never met a woman like you. On one hand, I'm so pissed that someone would give you and Tucker up so easily, but on the other, I'm so relieved. If that guy wasn't a complete fucking idiot, I wouldn't be holding you in my arms right now, and that would be a shame because it's become my favorite thing."

My stomach dips at his words and the sincerity that is shining in his bright eyes makes it hard to breathe. We sit in silence for a few seconds, enjoying the view and the comfortable silence that settles around us. It's terrifying how perfect all of this feels, how right it all feels. I just shared some of my most private information, leaving me raw and exposed and yet all I feel is safe and supported.

"I'm kind of scared," I whisper, making sure to keep my head against his chest as I speak.

"Of what?"

I pause for a moment.

"You."

His hand reaches down to cup my jaw before he tips my chin up slightly until our eyes meet.

"Me too, but I like you too much to question it."

I bite my lip and nod my agreement, earning a swoon worthy grin before his mouth descends onto mine. I don't know how long we sit there, getting lost in each other before light footsteps sound as a small voice calls out.

"Mommy? Where are you?" Tucker calls out.

"Out here, big man," Declan calls.

Tucker ambles out to us, sleepily rubbing his eyes.

"Have a good nap, sweetie?" I ask. Tucker nods and I look around to notice that we are almost pulling up to the docks. "Oh my gosh. I didn't even realize we were moving."

Declan turns to me and whispers into my ear, "You were a little preoccupied."

I smack his arms and roll my eyes with a smile on my face.

"Hey, Mommy! No hitting!" Tucker scolds.

"Yeah, mama," Declan teases.

I scoff as I stand up. "Whatever, I won't be ganged up on, *again*," I say in mock offense.

I hear their joint laughter coming from behind me as I go inside to slip on my clothes over my suit. Within a few minutes, we are saying goodbye to Darryl, and he tells us he would be happy to have us out again sometime. He even lets Tucker keep the little captain hat he had worn earlier.

When we get in the car and take off towards home, I turn around in my seat.

"So, what did you think of fishing, Tuck?"

"It was boring. But the boat was so cool! Today was the funnest ever!"

"I had a great time too. Thanks for letting me come," Declan says with a soft smile.

"You're welcome!" Tucker smiles.

I laugh softly and shake my hand as I settle back into my seat and reach my hand across the center console for Declan's hand. He glances down and smiles before lacing our fingers together and bringing the back of my hand up to his lips. Our hands rest in his lap the rest of the way home, all three of us enjoying the peaceful silence.

When we pull up to our apartment complex, Declan parks his truck before getting Tucker's door and then mine.

"Thank you," I smile.

"Of course," he smiles.

Declan undoes Tucker's car seat before walking over to where my car is parked a few spaces over. I quickly unlock it for him but decide to not put him through the hell of re-installing it as I quickly step in and strap it together.

When I'm done, I turn to see that he is shooting a glare at the car seat, like it has personally offended him. I can't help but let a small chuckle slip out, causing his glare to melt off his face as he smirks at me before grabbing my hand. I also notice that on the other side of him, Tucker's little hand reaches for him as we walk across the parking lot.

I see Declan's nervous eyes find mine, he seems to be checking to see if this is okay or what he should do. I smile at him and squeeze his hand in reassurance. It looks like I'm not the only one that feels comfortable with Declan crazy fast.

We make it up to our apartment quickly, and I unlock the door and gesture for Tucker to say goodbye.

"Say thank you to Declan for taking us out today, Tucker."

"Thank you, Declan."

Tuck gives him a hurried hug before he rushes inside to no doubt squeeze in cartoons before bed. Declan briefly hugs him back and then turns to me when Tuck is gone.

"He's such a sweet kid," he says almost reverently.

"Yeah. He has the biggest heart. I think it's pretty obvious he's kinda crazy about you."

"Hopefully, he isn't the only one," he smiles as he takes a step towards me and wraps his arms around my waist.

"Definitely not," I whisper before his lips touch mine.

Declan moves leisurely like we have all the time in the world. His soft lips move against mine like they were always meant to. I can't remember a kiss ever being so breathtaking, and it seems like every single one with Declan is this way.

When we break apart, he rests his forehead against mine before kissing the tip of my nose. I giggle and loop my arms around his neck.

"When can I see you again?" He asks.

"I had to pick up a Saturday and Sunday shift at the diner this weekend." He looks disappointed as he looks down at the ground. "But I only have a night shift at the diner on Saturday, and I get off at six on Friday," I respond with a smirk.

His amber eyes spark with excitement and a smile stretches across his face. "Any chance you could get away for the night?"

I bite my lip contemplating how I could make that work, when the door across the hall opens and Judy pops her head out into the hallway.

"Sure, she can. Tuck and I will have a sleepover!"

"Judy!" I screech. "Have you been spying on us?"

"Of course. What other kind of entertainment am I supposed to get at my age in this dump? I need to live vicariously through you."

"Holy shit," I murmur shaking my head.

Declan just laughs seemingly amused and not at all creeped out like he should be. He raises his eyebrows in question, and I laugh and shake my head.

"Judy," I grit with a forced smile. "Would you mind if Tuck slept over Friday night?"

"Well, I would love that, Sweet Pea! I'll see you kids then," she winks before stepping back into her apartment.

"I'm so fucking sorry," I groan as I bump my head against his upper chest.

Declan rubs his hands slowly up and down my back.

"It's fine, baby. I like her, she's hilarious. And she's a part of your family, and I love that she has been there for you and Tuck."

I smile. "Me too. Thank you, so much."

"For what?"

"For getting it, all of it. For understanding that Tucker comes first. That I'm not one of those moms that could ever toss their kid to the side for a relationship. Er, I mean, uh, if that is what this is. If not, that is totally coo-"

He holds a finger up to my lips to stop my rambling and smiles as he brushes it softly against my lower lip.

"This is definitely a relationship, the start of a damn good one by the looks of it. And of course, I get it. I wouldn't like you if you weren't that type of mama."

I smile giddily up at him and lift onto my toes to reach his lips. His hand cups my jaw bringing him closer to me and I sigh as his tongue gently strokes mine. Everything with him is sensual, calculated and fucking perfect. This man gives me butterflies and fireworks all at the same time. It's terrifying to feel so much so fast, but I'm trying to focus on not running from a good thing but embracing it.

"I better get out of here before Judy starts taking our picture for her private collection," he whispers with a laugh.

"Ew," I say as I smack his chest playfully.

His laughter vibrates through his body before he steals one more kiss, gently brushing his thumb across my cheek.

"Friday?" He asks.

"Friday," I nod.

His lips brush my forehead before he steps away. "Sweet dreams, baby."

"Goodnight," I smile as I step through the door, watching him wait for me to get inside and lock the door before he leaves.

Chapter Twenty

VI

I take a deep breath as I look at my reflection in my bedroom mirror. My chocolate hair is in loose curls, and my makeup is done minimally per usual. Declan didn't say what we were doing tonight, or where we would be staying, I'm just assuming that we will be going to his house.

I pull at my black sleeveless blouse as I adjust myself. My high-rise dark wash jeans rest just over my belly button and the silk top leaves only a half an inch of exposed skin at the hem. I paired the outfit with my white Converse. I swear, every time I go to get dressed for a date with him it becomes a game of 'what to wear.' I know this is at least my seventh outfit, and I'm going with it.

Declan and I have been seeing each other for almost three months now, but it already feels like so much longer. I think he feels the same way, at least I hope so. I have never been the type to fall hard and fast, in fact it took Tucker's dad six months just to get me to agree to go on a date with him. He was a total player with a nasty reputation, and I wasn't interested. Then he started showing me a secret sweet side, I thought it was just for me. I thought maybe he was just insecure about giving that part of himself to others, he made me feel special...until he didn't.

I push the past far out of my mind and focus on tonight. Declan is nothing like that piece of shit. When I first met Declan, I waited for the alarm bells to go off in my head, but they never did. It kinda surprised me. I mean, Declan is drop dead sexy and from my experience that equals womanizer.

Women all around the world would kill to have a night with him if they had a chance. That alone was enough to put me off. Then he opened his adorable mouth, and I realized that I had him all wrong.

I like that he isn't a show boater or a one-upper. I like that he isn't afraid to be vulnerable and say exactly what's on his mind. I like that he sometimes rambles when he starts to get nervous.

I just like him.

A lot.

A knock sounds through the apartment, snapping me out of my thoughts. I grab the small bag that I packed with some basic overnight stuff before walking down the hall to open the door. When I open it, I see Declan leaning his shoulder against the doorway with a lazy smile on his face that only grows wider when he sees me.

His eyes spark as they take me in from head to toe. When he makes his way back up to my face, he takes one large step towards me and grips the back of my neck, pulling me in for a heated possessive kiss. I gasp in surprise for a moment before I melt into him.

All too soon, he breaks the kiss and lets out a ragged breath.

"I swear to god, I think you get more beautiful every time I see you," he murmurs against my lips.

"I'm not so sure about that, but by all means, flattery will get you everywhere," I tease.

He smirks and tilts my chin up to capture my lips once more before pulling away, his eyes scanning the room.

"Where's Tucker?"

He almost looks excited to see Tuck, and it does something wonderful to my heart. I can tell he isn't bullshitting me or saying what he thinks I want to hear when it comes to my son. He genuinely likes Tucker, cares for him. We talk about him at least in passing every night. Declan is always checking in to see how he is doing and what he is up to. Turns me into a pile of goo every damn time.

"He's already at Judy's. I didn't tell him I was staying the night with you," I say almost awkwardly.

"Oh. Uh, is this something we should be keeping from him?" He asks as he rubs the back of his neck.

"No," I rush. "Well, kind of, I guess. I don't know. I've never dated since Tuck was born so I just don't know how much I want him to know. I just figured telling him that I'm spending the night with you might raise too many questions."

Declan nods understandingly. "I get it. Whatever you're comfortable with."

I give him an appreciative smile and kiss his cheek.

"Thank you," I say softly.

He nods and smiles before picking up my bag.

"This all?"

"Well, I figured I wouldn't move my entire closet just yet," I joke as we walk to the door.

Declan shrugs as I lock the apartment before he grabs my hand.

"I wouldn't mind."

I stop mid-step, and my eyes widen. I was just joking, there is no way we are even close to that point. Not so soon, right?

He seems to realize that I have stopped walking and looks back as he takes in my expression. The panic must be written across my face because his eyes widen quickly.

"Sorry! I didn't mean that you should move in. Not that you can't if you wanted to. I mean, if you wanna. But if not, then forget I said anything. Uh, shit." He runs a hand through his hair nervously as his eyes bounce around anxiously.

"I just meant if you wanted to keep some things at my place I wouldn't mind, because I would like you to come over as much as you can. Only if you are comfortable with that. I'm not trying to pressure you or anything. There are no expectations. I just-"

"Declan," I interrupt. His eyes swing up to me, so many emotions swimming in them all at once. I take a step closer to him and squeeze his hand while I smile. "Shut up."

He blows out a breath and nods. "Good call."

I laugh lightly as we walk down the stairs and out to his truck. When we start down the road, I notice that we are heading towards downtown. It's just now beginning to hit me that I don't even know where he lives. I assumed he was well off but from the looks of where we are headed, I'd say he is slightly more than well off.

When we pull into a parking garage underneath a ritzy glass condo complex, my suspicions are confirmed as I raise my eyebrows. He parks with ease and catches my stunned look.

"What's wrong?"

"You don't seriously live here, right? We're just visiting a really really rich friend of yours or something?"

He lets out a soft chuckle and gets out of the truck. That wasn't an answer! What the actual fuck?

I slowly slide out of the truck as Declan opens my door for me. He grabs my hand and laces our fingers together before making our way inside to a perfectly polished lobby. I keep giving him questioning looks but he does a really good job of avoiding eye contact. The front desk man smiles widely at us and nods.

"Good evening, Mr. Daniels," the man greets.

"How's it going, George?" Declan asks as we move to the elevator.

"Very well, sir. Thank you."

Once we are inside the chrome elevator, he hits the eight button and pulls out a key card and swipes it in a reader before the doors close and takes us up to what I assume is the eighth floor. Who has to put a key card in just to use the elevator?

The moment the doors open my jaw hits the ground. We step right inside his condo entryway from the elevator, there isn't even a hallway or anything! As my eyes sweep through the place, I notice that everything is sleek, modern and huge. No exaggeration, it is at least three times the size of my apartment, which I guess isn't overly ridiculous since my place is slightly larger than a shoe box, but still.

Declan hangs back with his hands in his pockets as I step tentatively across the shiny white marble floors. The walls are a neutral taupe color, and all of his furniture is different variations of whites, light browns, and blacks. Once I'm through the foyer, I step into what looks like the living room with two couches set up in perfect view of the obscenely huge TV and fireplace sitting front and center.

I turn my head to see a large mahogany dining room table that has six plush white chairs situated on each side. I also see a kitchen that seems like it is better suited to be inside a restaurant instead of a condo. The cabinets are the same color as the dining room table with crisp white and taupe colored granite countertops and stainless-steel appliances everywhere.

Spinning on my heel, I stare up at Declan with widened eyes, and my eyebrows up to my hairline.

"This place is out of control. How can you afford something like this working for a youth football training organization?" I ask incredulously.

It's kind of a rude question, but I don't really care. I suddenly feel like I barely know the man in front of me. I mean, I guess I don't know him all that well really, but that isn't the point.

Declan nods his head towards the balcony to my left.

"Wanna talk out there?"

"Are you going to answer my questions?" I ask, still stunned as I make my way across the room and through the glass doors.

Being this high up we pretty much look over all of Second Avenue. Everything looks so small up here as the city lights twinkle in the night sky. It's something else up here. A view I definitely never thought I would see, that's for sure.

I feel Declan standing a few inches next to me as I look over the balcony edge. When I glance to the side, I see that he is watching me with a complicated expression. Screw this.

"What the hell is going on Declan? Who are you really?"

He doesn't speak for a moment, just watching me. It looks like he is having an internal debate for a minute or so. Finally, he lets out a breath and sighs before reaching out carefully and placing his hand on top of mine. I let him for now, but he definitely needs to start talking.

"My name is Declan Daniels. My father is Rodney Daniels. He was a linebacker for the Knoxville Bucks for over eight years. As you can imagine, he made quite a bit of money with such a long NFL career for a linebacker. Instead of blowing it like most, he set up trust funds for us kids. The organization is a little bigger than I let on. It's a multi-million dollar business that thousands of athletes around the country participate in to be in the best possible shape for college and NFL scouts."

I blink slowly as I watch him. He looks like he is about to say more, but I cut him off.

"So, you are like, a millionaire?"

He shrugs with an indifferent look on his face. My brows dip.

"Why didn't you tell me?"

"Why would I?" He counters. "I wanted you to like me, not my money."

I roll my eyes and scoff, shaking my head. "Seriously? I don't want a damn cent from you. What, did you pick up the dowdy waitress because you thought she would be easy to manipulate with your money?"

"What? God no, of course not!" He urges as he reaches for me. I take another healthy step away from him, and a hurt look flashes across his face before he pushes it aside. "I didn't bring it up because that's usually what people always see me as. I know you aren't like that. Hell, you are the opposite, honestly. That's why I like you so much, you want me...just me. Or well, you did."

I sigh before shoving his shoulder lightly. "Don't be stupid. I still like you. I just can't believe I didn't know that about you. Maybe I need to run a background check on you," I say with a weak smile.

His eyes flash with something I can't quite name before he gives me a small smirk.

"Don't do that. You'll find out about how I snuck into Veronica Johnson's house in the ninth grade and stole all of her underwear."

My eyebrows rise and I let out a surprised laugh. "Seriously?"

He nods. "It was a dare, supposed to be a joke. Her dad didn't think it was very funny. He called the cops. Thankfully, I got let off with a warning."

"Well, I'll be sure to watch my panty drawer closely from now on."

Declan laughs. "Good call, because she's got nothing on you." He is quiet for a minute before he looks at me. "Are we okay?"

"Yeah, I just... I feel like I know nothing about you, and you are already so embedded into my life. We talk every single day almost all day long, you and Tuck seem to already have a bond and here you are, a secret millionaire. It's kinda off-putting, you know? Like, what else don't I know?"

"I get it," he nods, hesitating slightly before he continues. "I have this gala thing for the organization that I need to go to. Any chance you'd like to be my date?".

"Oh, um. I don't know. Where is it?"

"Knoxville."

"Oh, wow. Uhm, when is this?"

"Next weekend."

I grimace. "There is no way that I can pull something like that off this last minute. Judy has only ever watched Tuck for one night before. I couldn't ask her to-"

"Tuck can come," he interrupts. "He should. I'd like to have you both come with me. My parents wanna meet you guys. We just have the gala Saturday night, the rest of our time we can do whatever you two want. I just," he pauses as he rubs the back of his neck almost nervously. "I'd love to show you where I came from, show you my home. I get it if you don't feel comfortable, though."

I don't know how to feel, honestly. Part of me wants to say yes just so I can put his nerves at ease, it's clear he wants me to go, well I guess me and Tucker. But it's not like I can afford to jet off to Tennessee with a week's notice. We'd have to pack, buy airline tickets, hotel. Oh god, there is just no way that we could pull something like this off. Not on this short of notice.

Shaking my head, I frown. "I'm sorry. I just don't think I could swing this with such short notice, you know, financially."

Declan shakes his head as he wraps his arm around me back and pulls me into him.

"Don't worry about it. It's on me."

"Declan," I grimace as he continues.

"No, really. I was planning on taking our plane and staying at my house since it's only a ten minute drive to the hotel where the gala is being held. You guys won't cost a dime more to come, honestly."

"Wait, you have a plane?" I gape.

He shrugs. "Well, yeah. Technically it's the company's."

I blink at him, unsure how to respond to all of this new information. Declan leans in closer, his hand going to cup my jaw as he speaks.

"Say you'll come, please. I want you to meet my family, even if my mama will embarrass the hell out of me. I want them to meet Tucker. I think you guys will like it and if you don't, we could always-"

"Declan," I say with a soft chuckle.

"Yeah?"

"Shut up and kiss me."

He nods with a smile as he leans down and presses his lips against mine. His tongue strokes against mine eagerly, like we haven't seen each other in ages. My hands go up to his shoulders, running up and down his neck as I grip the ends of his hair and deepen the kiss. His hand continues to hold my face firmly, while the other grazes the length of my body before settling on my ass, squeezing and pulling me closer to him.

He breaks the kiss and swears under his breath. "We should stop before we can't and then dinner will burn."

"Dinner?" I question as my eyes look through the glass doors at his spotless apartment.

Declan nods as he takes my hand and walks me inside, opening up the oven to reveal two take out containers warming in the oven. As soon as the door is open, the smell of oregano and basil swirl through the room. *Italian.*

"I picked it up from Giorgio's before I went to get you. Figured you might be hungry?"

"Starving. Thank you," I smile.

He nods and quickly grabs the warm dishes before setting them on some plates.

"Go sit," he gestures to the table.

I quietly walk over and sink down into the overstuffed chair. Oh my gosh, this seat is more comfortable than my couch. I guess that is the difference between a couch picked up at Goodwill versus furniture straight out of a magazine.

Declan sets a plate of spaghetti down in front of me as I smile at him gratefully. A couple of nights ago, I told him that spaghetti was my all-time favorite dinner. I swear, he really does remember everything I say.

We dig in, and my god, I think it's the best Italian I've ever had. I practically have a foodgasm with my first bite. Declan stops eating, his eyes becoming heated as I happily enjoy every bite.

"You can't make noises like that," he warns, his accent coming in thicker than usual.

"What?"

"If you wanna finish your dinner, you can't make those noises. I am one sexy moan away from throwing you over my shoulder and hauling you off into my bed."

A thrill runs through me as my eyes light up. I wipe my mouth with my napkin and push my plate away with a challenging look. He smirks and shakes his head.

"Eat," he orders as he takes a bite.

I pout for a moment before I take another bite. Dinner goes by relatively quickly as we idly chat about our days like this is totally normal. Like spending the evening in a multi-million dollar home eating dinner from an expensive Italian restaurant is just another Friday.

"Wanna watch a movie?" Declan asks when we finish eating.

I shrug and nod as he pushes up from the table to go over to the living room and turn on the TV. Before he can make it back to the dining room, I'm already washing the dishes. It's my biggest pet peeve, to have dirty dishes sitting in the sink and even if this isn't my house,

I know I won't be able to focus on anything if I don't do this. Plus, he went through the effort to feed me, I feel like it's the least I can do.

In no time, I have the dishes clean and drying on the counter. Declan walks in and gives the dishes a funny look before he smiles at me and wraps his hands around my hips.

"You know I have a dishwasher for a reason, baby," he purrs as his nose runs the length of my neck. Goosebumps breakout across my skin as I let out a breathy sigh, trying to focus on his words.

"Yeah, well they never do as good of a job as a hand wash."

"Hmmm," he hums as he nips at my ear before kissing where his teeth grazed. "Ready?"

"Uh-huh."

Honestly, I'm not even sure what I am agreeing to. I could have just agreed to move to South America or go streaking. As long as he keeps kissing and touching me like this, I really don't care. God, listen to me. If it wasn't obvious that I haven't gotten laid in years, it's blindingly apparent now.

Chapter Twenty-One

VI

We settle onto his couch as Declan plays some action movie before tucking me into his side, his large arm drapes around me making sure there isn't an inch of space separating us. I lean my head against his shoulder and wrap my arm around his ridiculously hard stomach. As the movie begins to play, I can't help but smile, everything is so easy with Declan, so comfortable.

Not even a quarter way through the movie one of Declan's hands starts tracing lines along my jean clad thighs. I smirk as each stroke gets a little higher until he grazes my hip bone. My face turns to him, and I see him watching me with a heated look.

Deciding to be bold, I sit up a little and swing my leg over his lap so that I'm straddling him. His hands instantly grip my hips tightly as I settle down on top of him. I wind my arms around him and bring my lips down to his. They move softly against mine, teasing me before he swipes his tongue past my lips. I welcome the contact and grind closer to him. He lets out a muffled groan as his lips move in rhythm with my hips.

Before I know what's happening, his hands grip my ass as he stands up. I quickly lock my feet around his lower back as he begins walking us deeper into his condo, never breaking our kiss. He carries me around like I weigh nothing, which I definitely know is not true.

I'm too focused on our kiss to look around us, but soon, my back is hitting a soft bed with Declan crawling on top of me. His lips seek mine again almost urgently as his hands run along my body greedily. Declan trails his lips down my neck and across my chest before he looks up at me.

"We can stop if you want," he offers.

I grab the hem of my blouse and whip it off my head, exposing my now bare chest to him in answer. One of his hands reaches up and cups one of my breasts, flicking his thumb against my nipple before pinching in a way that has my toes curling. I moan as my hands slide down his body and reach for the bottom of his t-shirt.

Declan reaches behind his neck and rips the shirt off with one hand, never pulling too far away from me. I look down appreciatively at his insanely ripped body that is currently hovering over me before I move my hands down to wander lower and begin working on his jeans. He helps me out and is quickly wriggling out of them. It is then that I notice he is also not wearing any boxers and he looks more than ready for me.

Declan's tongue draws a path across my stomach and down to the top of my jeans. He makes quick work of peeling them off of me, revealing my purple lace panties. His thumb brushes across the fabric gently at first before his large hand fists the material and rips them clean off my body.

"Hey, those were expensive!" I scold, though I couldn't really give a shit right now. Just the mental image of him literally ripping my panties off will come in handy for many nights to come.

"I'll buy you a thousand pairs if I get to tear them off your beautiful body every time. Now, be quiet and let me eat this pussy," he murmurs against my skin before his tongue laps at me eagerly.

"Shit," I curse under my breath as I dig my fingers into his thick hair.

I settle my thighs over his shoulders and his fingers grip my hips tightly, which will no doubt leave bruises by tomorrow. My back arches into him, which only gives him more access as he continues to devour me whole, his beard scraping against me as he does. I don't think I have ever been with a man who enjoyed going down on me so much. I've clearly been missing out. His teeth scrape against my clit, causing a shiver to run through my body. His eyes flick up to me, lust heavy in them as he does it again.

"Declan," I moan.

He pulls away slightly, his mouth glistening as he speaks.

"Say my name again, baby. I wanna hear you cry out my name while I drown in your cum."

My pussy pulses at his words before he burrows his head between my thighs once again and begins dragging his tongue through me back and forth, slow at first before picking up speed and flicking against my clit. My legs begin to quake as he picks up the pace faster and faster.

"Oh, shit. Dec, don't stop. Please, please," I beg as he gently nips at my clit, sending me off like a rocket.

"Declan!" I scream as I bury my hand into his hair and cum all over his face. I feel him lapping and sucking up my orgasm which has my pussy already pulsing with need again. When he pulls away, he looks at me, his eyes full of lust and his beard glistening with the remainder of my cum. Why is that so fucking hot?

Slowly, he reaches over to his bedside table, grabbing a foil packet before tearing it with his teeth and rolling it onto his hard cock with one hand. His eyes flick up to me quickly as he raises a questioning brow.

"Just say the word and we'll stop."

"Are you kidding me? If we stop, I think I'll die."

He smirks and lines himself up to me, slowly easing in one delicious inch at a time. It has been a long time, and he is huge compared to Tuck's dad, who was the only man I had ever slept with. As he sinks inside of me, it's a little uncomfortable, but I breathe through it as he pushes all the way in. I hear murmured curses under his breath as he looks down at where he is buried inside of me.

"God damn, baby. You are choking the life out of my cock."

"Yeah, probably because you are splitting me in two," I groan half in pleasure and the other half in pain.

His deep chuckle wraps around me as he comes up onto his elbows, hovering over me. "Hang on tight, baby girl. I'm gonna make sure you never forget whose pussy this is from now on."

I take a deep breath and blow it out as he begins thrusting slowly. It doesn't take long for the pain to fade away as intense pleasure overtakes me. We let out simultaneous moans, and I can't help but smile as he moves against me. Waves of pleasure spark through my stomach and across my body. It has never felt this good, ever. I'm not sure if Declan just knows what he's doing, or it is the emotional connection we have. Maybe it's both, but I'm too overwhelmed to care right now.

When my lower back lifts, he wraps a muscular arm underneath me and hauls me into his chest as he picks up his speed. His lips slant across mine in deep passionate kisses. I can taste myself on him and instead of being turned off like I thought I would, I feel myself get wetter. I lick the seam of his lips causing him to groan as our tongues tangle together. When he moves to my ear, he runs a hand through my hair gently as he whispers to me.

"You like that, baby? Does my dirty girl love tasting her pussy on my tongue?"

"Yes!" I gasp breathily.

"Fuck, that's hot. Look at you. You take my cock so good, sweetheart. This pussy was fucking made for me."

"For you, all yours," I babble as my eyes roll into the back of my head. Declan lifts us off the mattress and rests back on his heels, as he fucks me even deeper than before.

"Oh my god!" I moan, as he relentlessly pounds into me.

My head is facing the ceiling, and it takes me a moment to realize that there is a mirror on the ceiling. I should be questioning why he has one up there in the first place, but I'm way too turned on to see the way he is fucking me like a wild animal to bother. At this angle, it's like I'm watching a porno at home. The hottest, most realistic, best feeling porno ever.

Declan slips one of his hands behind my head, pushing our foreheads together as he continues to pound into me relentlessly.

"You are everything, Vi. Absolutely fucking everything. You are mine now, forever. You got it?"

"Mhmm," I agree quickly as his hold on me tightens, helping grind my clit against him.

"Words, baby, give them to me. Tell me you are all mine." His pace picks up even faster and I gasp out at the new spot he has just hit.

"Yes," I rasp.

"Yes what, Vi?"

"I'm yours!" I shout as he continues to hit that sweet spot over and over again. "I'm all yours, Declan."

"Good girl," he says as his hand reaches down to brush my throbbing clit. "Cum for me, baby."

The combined sensation of his touch and his words send me catapulting over the edge as I scream out my second orgasm of the night. My hands fist the deep blue silk sheets beneath me as my body clenches tightly around him, while he continues to chase his own orgasm. Only a few seconds later, he roars out his release as his body goes completely rigid above me. I can feel his cock throb inside of me as the condom swells with his release. He relaxes and drops us backwards until he is resting on top of me.

Our heavy breathing is the only noise in the room for a little while, as we try to come back down from our highs. Declan slowly rolls off me and stands up as he walks to what I assume is the master bath. He comes back wearing a pair of black boxers and drops onto his back, pulling my sweaty body with him until I'm tucked into his side. His lips brush against my temple as his arms tighten around me.

Smiling, he pulls my face up to him, holding my face in that treasuring way that he does. Declan presses his lips to mine in a way that is chaste yet passionate at the same time. When we break apart, he settles my head against his chest as I slip my leg in between his. He pulls the blankets over us until we are perfectly cocooned. Both of our breathing begins to even out eventually once we finally catch our breaths. I close my eyes and start to drift to sleep when I feel a soft kiss against my temple.

"I think I'm falling for you," Declan whispers against my temple.

Bam. Just like that, another crack forms in my walls, this one deeper and thicker than the last one. The fear is still there but the hope of what I think is to come outweighs it. I don't say anything, since I assume he thought I was asleep. Instead, I decide to let sleep creep in on me as I lay in the arms of an incredible man who thinks he is falling in love with me.

The next morning, I am woken up by scruffy kisses grazing the sensitive skin on my neck.

"Wake up, baby," Declan's smooth voice rumbles, his twang coming out extra thick this morning.

When my eyes fully focus, I see that he is standing in front of me with a plate in his hand and a blissful smile on his face.

"Don't you know it's rude to wake a woman up without coffee?" I say groggily.

He laughs. "I do, which is why I brought coffee and breakfast," he says gesturing to the mug on the bedside table and plate in his hands.

I sit up and accept the cup happily, taking a few generous gulps before I sigh and fully open my eyes.

"Breakfast, huh? You already got me into bed, what's this for?" I tease.

Declan smiles and chuckles as he kisses my lips gently before handing me a plate with eggs, weird looking bacon, and a piece of toast. I scrunch my nose up as I look at him. He seems to know what has me looking that way because he nods in understanding.

"Turkey bacon, way healthier than pork bacon."

I give him an incredulous look as I take a bite out of the toast.

"Way to take all the fun out of it. The best part of bacon is the grease."

A rough laugh rumbles through his chest as he drops down next to me and kisses my cheek. I smile as I swallow my toast.

"Thank you, this is really sweet. You didn't have to."

"When was the last time someone made you breakfast?" He questions. I shrug as I take a bite of the strange bacon, surprisingly not bad. "That's what I thought. You spend your whole life taking care of everyone and everything around you. You deserve to be taken care of too, you know?"

"I take care of myself," I say proudly.

"Well, now so do I," he grins.

His smile is infectious, and I can't help but return it. Last night changed something in me. It wasn't just the sex, which was absolutely mind blowing by the way, but we connected in a way I never have before. Not to mention he admitted to sleeping Vi that he was falling for her, but I'm not ready to broach that subject with him just yet.

"Deal," I smirk. "What time is it?"

"A little after eleven."

"Are you serious?" I ask wide eyed. "I can't remember the last time I slept in that late. Why didn't you wake me?"

"Why would I? You looked so peaceful, and you don't have work till five, right?"

"Well, yeah, but-"

"But nothing, Vi. Tuck is well taken care of with Judy, and you don't have to be home for hours. Relax, enjoy."

I look at him skeptically before I take another sip of coffee.

"You are kinda bossy in the mornings."

He laughs and shrugs but doesn't deny it.

"So, what do you wanna do today?"

"Honestly? Nothing. A hot shower and comfy clothes sound just about perfect."

"Coming right up, want some company," he asks as he wiggles his eyebrows.

I lick my lips seductively and smirk when I see the teasing look in his eyes leave as he watches the motion intently.

"Definitely," I whisper huskily.

Grabbing the breakfast plate from me gently, Declan sets it onto the bedside table before he scoops my naked body into his arms and practically sprints into the bathroom. I toss my head back and laugh the whole way.

After a very sudsy shower, I change into my extra clothes that I brought and brush my teeth before I pad out into the living room. I see Declan leaning up against the kitchen island in nothing but a baggy pair of sweatpants and damn if it isn't just about the best view I've ever seen. I sneak up behind him and slide my arms around his stomach as I shamelessly feel him up. His hand rests against mine to hold them in place instantly.

"Whatcha looking at?" I ask.

"Lunch. Anything sound good?" He asks as he shows me the takeout menus he is perusing.

"I just ate. I'm totally stuffed."

"You sure?" He asks as he spins around to face me.

"Totally. This really hot guy made me breakfast in bed. It was pretty awesome."

"Oh yeah?" he asks curiously, running his fingers through my wet hair. "You two serious?"

I shrug, doing my best to suppress my smile. He raises an eyebrow at me, very clearly unamused.

"Oh? Do you not remember what you promised last night?"

I don't respond again, causing Declan to practically growl at me as he wraps his arms around me tightly.

"You are mine, Violet Nielson. You agreed right before you came all over my cock. No take backs, deal with it, sweetheart."

"Fineee," I sigh dramatically, like it's such a hardship to be so wholly claimed by a man like Declan Daniels.

He gives me a mock glare before he swats the side of my ass and shakes his head. Stepping away from the island, he walks over to the fridge and pulls out some pre-packaged box thing.

"What's that?" I ask curiously.

"Lunch."

"You prepare all of your meals ahead of time?"

"Course not. I'm rich, remember? I pay people to do it."

I scoff and swat his arm. "Don't be a douche."

He chuckles as I walk over to the couch and drop down before grabbing a fluffy white blanket and wrapping it around myself. Declan joins me with his food in hand. He hands me the remote, and I browse through Netflix for a little before I click on a random comedy. I stretch my legs across his lap as he places a hand over them, softly running it up and down while he eats. My smile doesn't leave my face the whole day and only briefly disappears when we get to my door later that afternoon.

"I don't wanna say goodbye," he whispers against my lips.

"It's only until Monday," I remind.

He groans playfully and buries his head into the crook of my neck. "Toooo long."

"You'll be okay. I promise."

Suddenly, Judy's door opens, and Tucker bounds out excitedly.

"Declan!" He screeches as he runs up and hugs his leg excitedly.

"Hey, big man. How's it going?"

"Good! Grandma Judy let me eat a ton of candy, and we stayed up really late and watched Mickey Mouse all night!"

"Oh really?" I ask as I cross my arms and look accusingly at Judy as she steps into the doorway.

"Yes, really. I figured everyone deserved to have fun last night," she winks.

Oh my god. This woman, I swear.

My face flushes, and I shake my head as she laughs. Her smile fades as she clears her throat.

"Hey, Sweet Pea. I hate to do this to you, but I just got a call from my doctor, and they want me to come in right now. I tried to put it off but no go."

Panic sets in for a moment as I take a step closer.

"Is everything okay?"

"Oh yeah," she swats at the air. "You know how it is when you get to my age, things that aren't supposed to move do and things that should don't. They are just being dramatic, but I want them to stop calling me, so I'm just going to go in and take care of it."

"Okay, yeah. It's okay. Tuck can come with me to the diner. I'll set him up in a booth and he'll be fine."

"I'm sorry. I hate letting you down."

"No, no. Don't worry about it, take care of yourself and let me know what they say," I assure as I hug her.

She pats my cheek lovingly as she smiles. I don't know what I would if anything ever happened to her. Declan clears his throat as he watches me.

"I don't wanna overstep, but I could watch Tuck. If you are comfortable with that."

"YES!" Tucker exclaims before he darts into our apartment.

I let out a light chuckle at my kid's enthusiasm before I look up at Declan.

"That is so sweet to offer, but I don't want to put that on you."

He starts shaking his head before I've even finished my sentence.

"It's no trouble, really. I'd actually love to spend some time with him. But I totally get if you don't feel comfortable with that."

I bite my lip and tilt my head to the side. Usually, I am very particular of who I let watch Tuck. And by particular, I mean only Judy, Mindi and the girls at Tuck's daycare. I see the bond growing between Tucker and

Declan every time they see each other. Though I was worried about that at first, I can see that spending time with each other makes them both happy.

"Okay," I say softly. "As long as you're sure. He can be a bit of a handful and he has a hard time going to bed at night."

"Oh please, stop trying to scare the poor man. Tuck is an angel, and you two will be just fine," Judy butts in.

"I think I can handle it," Declan smiles before he steps into the apartment.

I turn back to Judy and cross my arms.

"Are you sure you are okay, Judy?"

"Oh, yeah. Don't you worry about me. So, things are going well with you two I take it?"

"Yeah, really well. He is so good to me, to Tuck too."

"He is a good one," she smiles approvingly.

"I think so too."

When I walk inside my apartment, I find Declan looking around the couch and then the kitchen.

"What are you looking for?" I ask with a smile.

"Tucker," he says with furrowed brows.

I laugh. "Hide and go seek?"

He gives a sharp nod. "The kid is pretty good."

I walk up to him and lean in close to his ear. "Check inside the bathtub, that's his favorite place to hide."

A wide smile stretches across his face before he gives me a quick peck.

"Thanks for the tip, baby." He turns on his heel and jogs down the hallway to the bathroom. Not two seconds later I hear Tucker groan.

"No fair! How did you find me?"

"Well, there are only so many places to hide, buddy."

They come down the hallway together both smiling, and it twists my heart in the best way.

"Yeah. Mommy says one day we will get a house with a big backyard. Then no one will ever find me."

"That sounds like a good plan," Declan nods as he looks up to me with a look full of promise. Promises he certainly can't keep.

Right?

"I gotta get dressed for work. I'll be right back," I say.

I only have about fifteen minutes before I have to leave so I quickly strip off my clothes and throw on my diner dress and white Converse before pulling my hair up into a high ponytail. When I step out into the living room, I see that Tuck has pulled out his coloring book and has already managed to string all fifty two individual crayons across the coffee table.

"Mickey is my favorite, but Minnie is my second favorite since she is Mickey's girlfriend," he explains to Declan as he points out all the characters.

"Oh yeah? I have always been a Goofy man myself."

Tuck nods in agreement like that is a solid choice. I smile as I watch them color together.

"Is Mommy your girlfriend?" Tucker asks.

I see Declan's face visibly pale as he sits up a little straighter and puts down the tiny crayon that was in his large hand.

"Would that be okay with you?" Declan asks carefully.

Tucker nods. "Yeah, Mommy smiles a lot around you. She didn't use to smile much."

A thoughtful look crosses Declan's face as he gives Tuck a small smile. "I smile a lot around her too."

"So, is she your girlfriend?"

"Yeah, buddy, she is."

"Good. That means you're gonna be my daddy one day, right?"

Now all the color has drained from his face as he shifts uncomfortably and grips the back of his neck.

"Not sure, big man."

"Well, when you know, will you tell me?" Tucker asks.

Declan lets out a rough chuckle. "You'll be the first to know."

I peek out from the hallway and walk out to the living room causing them both to look up at me. Tucker's smile is easy and carefree, Declan's is a little tight, and I can see his eyes are asking if I overheard all of that. I decide to play it off like I didn't and give him a casual smile.

"Well, I gotta get going. Tucker usually goes to bed around 7:30, but if he doesn't go down right then, don't worry about it. If he gets hungry, there are some things in the cabinets."

"We're good," Declan says as he stands to hug me. "Any allergies or things I should try to avoid?"

"Nah, he's pretty easy as long as you like Mickey Mouse and games."

"Love them," he smiles.

I glance over at Tucker before my eyes dart to Declan's lips, and I lean forward and give him a quick kiss. He kisses me back and then gives me a surprised look. I raise an eyebrow at him as I smile before walking over to kiss the top of Tucker's head.

"I love you sweetie. Be good for Declan, okay?"

"Okay, Mommy."

"Call me if you need anything, okay?" I tell Declan.

"We'll be fine. I was his age once, I got this."

"Okay, well thank you again. So much."

"Thank you," he smiles before kissing me one more time. "Now, get out of here."

"Alright, bye!"

I drive to work with a smile on my face the whole way. Tucker wants a dad so badly it breaks my heart. It isn't like I'm wanting Declan to fall into that role or anything, I just like the fact that Tucker has a man to spend time with. The older he gets, the less I'm sure he will want to spend time with me, which hurts but I get that it's a part of life.

My shift flies by, and before I know it, I'm back at my apartment complex and bounding up the stairs to my guys. *My guys.* I can't deny that the sound of that alone makes me giddy. When I open the door, almost all of the lights are off except for the hallway and the glow of the TV. Since I can't justify spending hundreds of dollars a month for cable, we only have a DVD player and the DVDs that we do have are mainly kid shows, so it doesn't surprise me to hear Cars playing.

Declan stands from the couch to greet me, wrapping me up into a hug before kissing me briefly.

"Hey, gorgeous. How was your night?"

"Good, how was yours?"

"Really good. We had a ton of fun. We ordered pizza and played *Operation* about a hundred times."

"And that is what you classify as a fun night?" I ask dubiously.

"Oh, yeah. I could have been a surgeon in another life." He nuzzles my neck before lowering his voice. "I mean, it didn't hold a candle to last night, but honestly, what could?"

I giggle and push him away. "Is that all you think about?"

"You have no idea," he smirks before capturing my lips with his. "I should go. I'll call you tomorrow."

"Okay. Hey, what is the dress code for this gala thing?" I ask.

"Dressy," he smiles.

I groan. "Great. Now I have to try to squeeze my mom bod into a Pre-Tucker dress."

Declan raises a challenging eyebrow as his hands trail down my sides, across my stomach and land on my ass.

"I love your 'mom bod.' Baby, you are like a damn wet dream in anything you wear."

"You have to say that because you are sleeping with me," I say with a scoff.

"Nah, but it's a big reason why I'm sleeping with you," he winks.

I scoff as he pulls me in for a kiss and dips me back slightly, stealing my breath away. When he pulls back, he smirks hovering just above my face.

"Goodnight, baby."

"Night," I say breathily as he stands us upright and kisses my hand before walking out the door.

When I lock the door, I walk down the hallway and slowly open Tuck's door to peek inside. I see him snuggled up with his favorite blanket and his Mickey stuffed animal as well as several books strewn around the room. I would bet anything Declan read every single one with him. I smile and close his door before I head to my room.

Once I get ready for bed, I crawl underneath my sheets and try to get settled. It feels extra lonely compared to last night. I won't be able to spend the night all the time, but I definitely want to do it as much as possible.

There is something about him. Something amazing and terrifying all at the same time. He is tearing down my previously impenetrable walls faster than I can build them. His words from last night play on a loop inside my head as I close my eyes. They have my chest swelling with hope and my stomach flipping in an equal amount of nerves and excitement. Not that I would admit it out loud just yet, but I think I'm falling for him too.

Chapter Twenty-Two

Declan

I pull out my phone and shoot Vi a quick text goodnight even if I just said goodnight not fifteen minutes ago. Ridiculous, I know. I've fallen for this girl way too hard way too fast, but I honestly don't think there is any way for me to stop it at this point. Not that I'd even wanna.

I had a ton of fun with Tuck tonight but fuck if I'm not ready for bed. We played hide and go seek, colored, and watched his Mickey Mouse DVD about a million times before I read him every single book they own. It was honestly a great night. Not as good as last night, but what could be?

When I step through the elevator and into my hallway, I instantly notice that the lights are on, and the TV is on. My brows furrow as I step deeper into the house. I know that I shut down the place before Vi and I left this morning.

Slowly, I reach over to the hall closet and grab the baseball bat that I keep in there. Gripping it with both hands, I carefully walk down the hallway until I crest the corner and into the living room. Instantly dropping the bat to the floor as I blow out a deep breath.

"Jesus fuck, Slater. You scared the shit out of me!" I bark.

My idiot friend turns away from the Mariners highlights to look back at me. His eyes drop down to the bat on the floor before he gives me a huge shit eating grin.

"What were you planning to do with that thing? You are a football player, bro, not baseball."

I scoff and roll my eyes as I walk over to the couch and drop down next to him.

"I don't need to play pro baseball to knock the shit out of a burglar."

Slater barks out a laugh as he nods.

"So, where you been, bro? I feel like I have to track your ass down these days."

I shrug. "I was watching my girl's son."

Slater's eyebrows shoot up his forehead as his eyes bug out.

"She has a kid?"

I can't help the smile that comes to my face when I think about Tuck.

"Yeah, man. His name is Tucker. He's four, and the funniest little guy. The kid is obsessed with Mickey Mouse, and swear to god, he ate more pizza than I did tonight. He's super sweet too. Vi has done such a good job raising him, especially on her own. It's fucking amazing really. She-"

I pause mid-sentence as I look at Slater who is staring at me with bug out eyes and his mouth slightly parted.

"What?" I ask.

Slater blinks and shakes his head slightly.

"Nothing, man. I've just never seen you like this."

"Like what?"

"I don't know...all...lovey, I guess. It's like a body snatcher took you in the middle of the night and I know that isn't true because it would take a whole fucking squadron to carry your ass away."

I scoff and shove him to the side but don't deny it. Lovey isn't exactly the word I would use but I couldn't tell you what word I would use, so I guess it works, for now.

"Where did you meet this girl again?" Slater asks.

"At a diner just outside of town. She's fucking incredible, Slater. I'm shit scared I'm about to mess it all up."

"Why?"

I blow out a breath as I lean forward and rest my forearms against my knees.

"Because I'm taking her to Knoxville, gonna try to break it to her easy."

Slater busts out laughing for several moments before he calms down enough to speak.

"You're shitting me, right? I don't care how chill this girl is, no one is going to react well to finding out that they have been lied to by their man in a room full of celebrity strangers. Are you even using that pea sized brain of yours or have you taken one too many hits to the head?"

"It's not going to be a room full. Just a few Buck players, you and Seb," I grumble.

"Hey, I'm not trying to tell you how to live your life, but I'm just saying, it isn't going to end well."

I shake my head at him as I lean back against the couch.

"No scenario will. I think I just gotta rip the band aid off."

"And you're a chickenshit," Slater adds.

I let out a humorless laugh as I nod.

"Yeah, that too."

We are quiet for a few moments when I cock my head to the side and look at Slater a little closer this time. We've been friends for a long time, and though it's been years since we've lived in the same area code, I know my best friend. His shoulders are slightly slumped, the mirth in his eyes is dulled, and the corners of his smile look forced, almost plastic.

"What's going on?" I ask.

Slater glances over to me, his smile tightening as if he is trying to reassure me.

"I'm good."

I give him a deadpanned look that has his smile slipping until he looks straight at the wall in front of us.

"Mom?" I question.

She's been in remission for a while, did that change? Is the cancer back?

Slater shakes his head softly but doesn't respond. Relief rushes through me as I nod.

"Football?" I ask next.

Another shake of his head.

"Nikki?"

Slater blows out a rough breath before leaning his head back against the couch and turning to look at me.

"I can't wait to meet your girl. I've never seen you look so happy, Mikey."

I nod softly, ignoring the deflection. He'll talk when he's ready, probably not to me but to his mom or Scarlett, his childhood friend.

"You'll love her," I say.

Truthfully, I've never felt so happy. I know I'm getting ahead of myself. I know I only just met this woman, and she comes with a son and probably a whole truck load of baggage that I haven't even begun to see, but I don't care. None of it matters. Vi is my endgame, and I'll do anything to make sure it stays that way.

Chapter Twenty-Three

Vi

Sunday morning, I'm woken up by a loud incessant pounding. At first, I think it's a hangover, but then I realize I didn't drink anything last night. Then the next noise I hear is Tucker squealing.

"Auntie Mindi!"

I sit up in bed and look around. Mindi is here? Before I can even get out of bed, my bedroom door is thrown open, and my best friend is climbing on top of me.

"Mindi, what are you doing here!" I shout excitedly.

"I missed your face, bitch! I'm in between jobs right now, so I thought I would come visit. You don't mind sharing your bed, right? Freelance photographers do not make enough to afford these Seattle hotels."

"What's mine is yours. Why didn't you call?"

"I like to keep you on your toes," she smiles.

"Okay, well, some of us have to work today. If you would have called, I could have shuffled some things around." I glance up at the clock and groan. "And if I want to keep my job, I gotta get my ass in the shower and Tucker to daycare in forty-five minutes."

"Don't you dare take my best bud away when I just got here! We'll hangout today. I'll take him to the children's museum or something."

I snort. "No, you won't. You guys will go to the store, fill my house with junk food, and then eat said junk food all day."

She points a finger gun at me as she sprawls out across my bed. "Bingo."

Laughing lightly, I shake my head as I crawl out of bed and start getting ready for work. I swear, I feel like that's all I do nowadays is work. Oh, wait, it is. Mindi comes into the bathroom and talks to me while I shower and get ready. She catches me up on what's new in her fabulous life, and I tell her briefly about Declan, to which she said, 'Thank God. I was starting to worry your vagina was going to be condemned.'

Once I'm dressed and ready to leave, I come out to see Mindi and Tucker eating a sugary cereal in front of the TV that definitely wasn't in our cabinets last night.

"Okay, kids. I'm off," I joke.

"Bye, Mom!" Mindi calls out.

I roll my eyes and go to walk out the door when I pause and turn.

"Oh, Mindi. I have to find a dress for that thing I was telling you about," I say as I glance at Tucker. I haven't told him yet, I'm sure he will be excited to be going on his first vacation.

"Want to come shopping with me after work?"

"Uh, hell yes! Where were you thinking?" Mindi asks.

"Ross? TJ Maxx?"

She scoffs and shakes her head. "Seriously? You are going to a swanky gala. Can't we go somewhere a *little* more high end?"

"Nope," I pop as I grab my purse.

"Fine."

"Alright. Love you guys!" I call out.

When I get to work, it is a total shit show. The bride for the Matheson wedding called and decided that she no longer wanted any roses at her wedding and wants carnations instead. The same wedding that I just finished all of the center pieces and bouquets for.

I don't know what it is about weddings that makes people go so crazy, but some days, I seriously can't handle it. If it were me getting married, I would prefer an extremely intimate wedding. I don't get why people feel the need to invite the person that they sat next to in high school biology class, but hey, not my problem.

Around one 'o'clock, Declan sends me a text.

Declan: Hey, beautiful. How's your day going?

Me: Work is a little crazy, but I woke up to an interesting surprise.

Declan: Oh yeah? I don't remember waking up in your bed this morning?

I huff out a laugh as I shake my head and respond.

Me: I said interesting, not heavenly.

Me: It's a good surprise. Mindi is in town! She's going to be staying with me for a little.

Declan: That's awesome. It's been a while since she has visited, right? I can't wait to meet her.

Me: Yes, you can. Trust me. She will give you the third degree. You may reconsider this entire relationship after you meet her.

His response comes almost instantly.

Declan: Nothing could make me reconsider this relationship.

My heart flutters at his words, and I slide my phone back into my pocket before getting back to work. Let's just hope to god that my best friend can control her word vomit for five minutes so she doesn't scare away the first man that I've liked in over six years. Hell, maybe ever.

When six o'clock rolls around, I let out an audible sigh of relief before I turn off the lights and lock the shop up. The drive home goes by pretty quick, and when I step inside, the house is littered with junk food boxes and wrappers literally everywhere.

"Mindi!" I shout.

She comes running out of Tucker's room with a guilty smile. "Shit, I thought you would be home later. I'll clean it all up, I promise."

"No, you won't," I grumble as I start picking up.

"I know, but doesn't it make you feel better when I say I will?"

"Not as good as if you helped."

"Fine," she sighs dramatically.

"Why are we friends again?"

"Because no one liked your cranky ass in high school except for me."

"Oh, that's right."

We both laugh as we pick up the house. Mindi and I have been as thick as thieves since sophomore year of high school. She was there for me when my parents died, when Tuck's dad pulled his shit, and everything in between. She may be a free spirit and drive me crazy most days, but she is my sister through and through.

Once the house is picked up, we load Tuck into the car and head to the mall. When I told Mindi that the party that I'm going to is kind of a date, she flat out refused to let me go to a discount department store. So, we compromised on the mall. Of course, once we get there, she drags me into the first high end dress shop we see.

"Mindi, I can't afford anything in here," I whine.

"We'll just use the five-finger discount like in high school," she teases.

"What's that?" Tucker asks.

"Oh," Mindi starts. "Five-finger discount means-"

"Mindi!" I snap as I give her a 'cut it out' motion.

She cackles as she browses through the racks before gasping and pulling out a glitzy red dress. It has a mermaid skirt and thin red straps that crisscross down the back until the fabric starts up again just above the ass. The dress is totally show stopping but not anything like I had in mind.

"Isn't it a little...flashy?" I ask.

"Duh. He told you dressy; this is dressy."

"It's also a little revealing," I say as I look over it critically.

She rolls her eyes. "Yeah. Just because he banged you once doesn't guarantee a repeat performance. You gotta put in the work, baby cakes."

My eyes bug out before I look back to see that Tucker is across the room walking around and, thankfully, out of hearing range. Looking back to Mindi, I tuck a piece of hair behind my ear as I lower my voice.

"Uh, yeah, it may have been the first time that we had sex, but it was definitely not the first time that we fooled around."

Her mouth drops and her eyes widen in surprise.

"You slut!" She gasps with a smile.

"Shut up. It isn't just sex. We really like each other. He's good to me."

"Uh huh, whatever. I need details tonight."

"Oh my god, no. We aren't in college anymore."

"Don't I know it? It's slim pickings out there nowadays. Anyways, stop being a hag and try this dress on."

"You know your nicknames for me aren't really common terms of endearment," I scoff as I take the dress to the dressing room.

"And yet, we have been friends for over ten years. No changing old habits now."

I let out a dry laugh as I wiggle into the dress. It fits surprisingly well, and when I look in the mirror, I let out a small gasp.

"What's wrong?" Mindi asks on the other side of the door.

Honestly, I'm kind of speechless. I was expecting to look trashy, like I'm trying too hard, but it looks...

"Stunning!" Mindi squeals as she thrusts the door open.

I turn to her and nod. "Right? I'm kind of in love with it."

"Well, duh. I have excellent taste. All you need is a nice red lipstick to give you some high speed DSLs and you are set!"

"DSLs?" I question.

"Dick sucking lips," she says, like it's something people say every day.

"Oh my god. Can you attempt to watch your mouth around Tucker, please. You are freaking horrible."

"Come on, you know I can keep it in check when I need to."

I raise an eyebrow at her, and she sighs.

"Well, I try."

I can't help but laugh as I shake my head at my best friend.

"C'mon," she whines. "Let's just get it and get out of here. Tucker and I want Dippin' Dots."

I pull at the tag to check the price and just about have a coronary. "Oh my god! Get it off! Get it off! And carefully!"

"What's wrong?" She asks as she glances at the tag.

When she looks at it, she just shrugs as she slowly helps me out of it. Clearly, she isn't in as much shock as I am.

"Mindi, the dress is $300. That's insane!"

She rolls her eyes and holds out her hand once I have carefully stepped out of the dress.

"Fine. Give it to me, and I'll put it back. Maybe you can wear something completely out of style from your closet."

"Gee, thanks," I snark.

I give her the dress and she rolls her eyes as she turns to walk away while I put my clothes back on. When I step out of the dressing room, I see Mindi and Tucker standing at the exit with a bag in her hand.

"What's that?" I ask.

"Oh, this?" She shrugs. "It's your dress. You were being too panicky and stingy for me, so I solved the problem and bought it."

"What! You can't buy me that! That thing was $300! Plus tax!"

"Just about. Now, let's go, I want ice cream!"

"Yeah!" Tucker joins in.

"Mindi, you have to return it right now. I don't need it."

She rolls her eyes. "Yes, you do. That dress was made for you, and you never do anything nice for yourself. So, I did something nice for you. I already ripped the tags off and threw them away so you couldn't return it. Just say thank you and buy me ice cream."

I let out a ragged sigh and run my fingers through my hair. Mindi raises an eyebrow expectantly, and I nod slowly as I take the bag from her.

"Thank you, Mindi."

"Of course, babe! Let's go," she says as she loops her arm through mine. "I know you would do the same if I had a hot date with some mystery millionaire. I'm still pissed you won't tell me his last name."

"I didn't tell you because you will internet stalk him within an inch of his life and probably order a full background check."

"Well, at least tell me you have done those things."

I shrug. "You know how anti-social media I am. No good ever comes of it. I really don't want to look him up and see pictures of him with an old girlfriend or worse a bunch of leggy models that make me look like a toad. Ignorance is bliss, you know?"

"No, I don't know," she scoffs. "Aren't you a teeny bit curious?"

"Not really."

I mean, I am, but like I said, I'm not sure I would like what I found. And the past is in the past. I just want to focus on the present.

We get ice cream before we leave the mall, and I make sure *both* of the kids eat theirs before we get into my car. When we get home, I tell Tucker that we are going on a trip to Tennessee with Declan, and he practically leaps to the ceiling. I'm so glad that he likes Declan as much as I do. Maybe more. Okay, not more.

Chapter Twenty-Four

Declan

"Mikey! How the fuck do you bench this much? You aren't even that big," Slater strains as he finishes his set. That's what he gets for stealing my bench mid workout.

I scoff as I look down at him. Slater isn't a small guy, but I have at least two inches on him and well over sixty pounds. He's a runner on the field, a receiver, and I'm the man responsible for breaking through walls, smashing them to pieces as I go after my target. We just aren't the same.

Seb comes over to take his place, adding thirty more pounds before beginning his set. Fucking show off.

"Are you guys sure you don't wanna fly with us? We are leaving tonight," I offer again.

Slater shakes his head. "Nah, I've got dinner with my mom tonight, and Nik isn't gonna make it."

I frown as I look down to see my best friend staring at his protein shake way too intensely before tipping it back. If it was just us, I'd probably say something about that but with a gym full of prying eyes and ears, I know to let Slate have his space.

"We're good," Seb grits through clenched teeth as he racks the bar and sits up. "Erica has an art show tonight downtown, so we are gonna leave in the morning. Rosie always has the hardest time with her ears when flying though, so that'll be fun," he grumbles as he re-does his man bun.

"Alright. I'm glad you're bringing the girls, Tucker is gonna love them."

Seb nods as he takes a sip of his water before moving over to the next machine.

"Have you prepped her at all?" Seb asks.

"What do you mean?"

He lets out a humorless laugh and shakes his head.

"I mean, you at least told her that there will be celebrity football players at the event right? She doesn't think it's just a bunch of rich people tossing money around. I mean, it is, but they also play ball, and from what you say, she doesn't exactly like us."

I shake my head. "It's not that. I just think she got burned, bad, by a football player and it just kinda puts her on edge." I run my hand through my hair to keep the sweat from my eyes. "It's gonna be fine. I'm going to tell her tomorrow, before we get to the auction. If I tell her before we leave, she might not come."

"And if you wait until you are in a room full of your teammates, new and old, and she finds out that way, she will dump your ass," Slater points out.

I grimace at his words. I hope that wouldn't be the case. I know she has a grudge or whatever, but what we have is special, real. She can feel it, I know she can. She wouldn't throw us away because I withheld what I actually do for a living. Right?

Once we wrap up our workouts, I take a long shower before glancing at the time. I still have hours before Vi gets off work. I should probably go home and start packing, but when I get in my truck, I find myself fifteen minutes later parked outside Blooming-Deals.

When I step inside, the first thing I see is a guy who looks to be in his late twenties, resting his arms against the counter as he leans into Vi. She is clearly uncomfortable, her normal smile nowhere to be seen as she observes the guy warily. I don't need to hear what he's saying to know that he's flirting with her. I can tell just from his body language, but his words have me crossing the room in three large steps.

"All I'm saying is nothing puts a smile on a woman's face like a good fuck."

Before Vi can respond, I'm behind the little shit, my hand cupping the back of his neck and shoving him face first against the counter. He squirms under my hold, but I keep him pinned easily as I lean down to speak in his ear, my eyes never leaving Vi's alarmed gaze.

"That is no way to speak to a lady. Whether she was interested, which I can guaran-fucking-tee she ain't, or not, you don't say shit like that to a woman. Ever."

The guy fights against my hold, but I only push down on him harder, causing him to whimper and snivel.

"Now, look up," I tell him. "Look at her."

The guy is shaking like a damn leaf under my hand as his head moves slightly to look at Vi, who is regarding him with a look of disdain, as she crosses her arms over her chest.

"You ever see her again, you walk the other way. You go to a new florist from now on. If I ever catch word of you near her again, I'll personally make sure you regret it."

"O-okay," the guy stutters as he continues to shake.

I yank him until he is standing before I shove him towards the door. He doesn't hesitate, scrambling out of the shop and running down the street presumably to his car. When I know he isn't coming back, I turn to face Vi before I make my way around the counter and cup her face in my hand.

"You okay, baby?"

"I'm fine," she nods. "Though I don't know how I'm going to explain that the Johnson wedding will no doubt be going with a new florist only three weeks before the wedding."

I raise a brow at her. "Was he the groom?"

Her lip curls up in disgust as she nods. *Fucking prick.*

"I'm glad you're safe," I say as I lift her head to look up at me fully.

"Yeah, it's easy when I have a huge personal bodyguard."

I bark out a laugh as I weave my fingers through her thick chocolate waves.

"I'll gladly guard your body every day of my life."

"Mmm what else would you want to do to my body every day?" She teases.

My cock already starts stiffening at her words as I close the distance between us and push my hard on against her stomach, causing her to gasp in surprise as I smirk.

"Every-fucking-thing."

Before she can respond, I capture her mouth, sucking and biting on her full lips, as my hands lower down to her ass. Wordlessly, I cup her ass cheeks through her sundress as she jumps and wraps her legs around my waist. Without breaking the kiss, I walk through the doors that lead to the back room before laying her down on the stainless steel work bench.

My hands go to the hem of her bright yellow dress as I make quick work of lifting it up and over her head before tossing it into a corner.

"Dec," she gasps. "I'm working! We can't."

I pause, my hand cupping her lace covered pussy as my eyes flick up to hers.

"Want me to stop?"

Desire is heavy in her eyes, and her teeth are sunk into her bottom lip like she is doing her best to suppress a moan. Slowly, I grind the heel of my palm against her clit, causing her to let out that moan she was holding in.

"Oh, fuck!"

"If you don't wanna go further, just say the word. Otherwise you better be prepared to get fucked good and hard."

She looks up at me, her eyes drunk on lust as she nods quickly.

"Please," she begs as she lifts her hips up slightly.

I smirk before leaning down to capture her lips with mine.

"Good girl," I praise before resuming my work, stripping off her panties and tossing them to the side.

My hands go to my pants, quickly undoing the belt before pushing them down enough to free my rock hard cock. I stroke it from base to a tip a few times as I look down at my woman. She's flushed and gorgeous, her legs spread open for me as she lays on top of an assortment of flowers on the table. She looks like a fucking goddess surrounded by all the colors of the rainbow with her pussy on full display practically begging me to sink into her, and I'm a gentleman after all, so how can I deny her?

I quickly grab a condom out of my wallet before rolling it on. When I line myself up to Vi's pussy, I glance up to see that she is already watching me, an impatient little pout on her face. So fucking sweet.

I don't take my eyes off her until I sink into her fully. I watch as her chest rises and falls in deep breaths, her eyes practically rolling into the back of her head as I bottom out. Her walls clench around me hard, so hard that I'm white knuckling the stainless steel edge of the table in an attempt to keep it together and not cum before I can even fuck my woman properly.

"Goddamn," I grit through clenched teeth. "You take me so good, baby. Too good. You're like a fucking drug," I say as I pull out almost fully before pushing back inside her.

Her back arches off the table, and I take advantage of it, slipping my arm underneath her, and yanking her closer to me as I begin thrusting faster. Her bra is still on and that is a damn shame because I know her beautiful tits would be bouncing away right now if not for the damn thing.

She reaches out almost blindly before her hands find my shoulders, her fingers curling into my muscle as she grinds her pussy against me.

"Dec, fuck. We shouldn't be doing this. Someone could walk in at any moment," she gasps.

My pace quickens as I hoist her up from the table and pin her against the wall right next to the door before I begin snapping my hips again.

"Then you better hurry up and cum, because there is no way in hell I'm leaving this shop until you cover my cock with your sweet cum."

Her pussy clenches at my words as she lets out a whimper. Her eyes are clenched tight as her face tightens, and I know that she's close.

"Eyes on me, beautiful," I demand.

Her hazel eyes fly open, clouded with want, pleasure, and something a little heavier. I watch, completely enraptured as her mouth falls open and her eyes widen just a bit as her body begins to shake, her pussy spasming, milking my cock like it's her fucking job.

"That's it, that's a good girl. Take what you need, baby."

Her head bobs in what looks like a nod as she wrings out the last of her pleasure from her orgasm. I continue thrusting into her, and I know that I'm not too far off either. That is until I feel a slender hand slip between us and cup my balls, rhythmically massaging them at just the right spot that has my orgasm taking over me. I fuck her through it, and she doesn't stop rubbing them until my legs are shaking and my thrusts stop. I blow out a long breath as I rest my head into her neck and inhale deeply.

When I pull back, I see her staring at me, an adoring look on her face. Leaning down, I brush a kiss against her lips before slowly lowering her to her feet. We both get dressed quickly, trading matching smirks as we do. Once Vi runs her hands through her hair, we walk out to the front to thankfully find the lobby empty.

"So, you're off at six, right?" I ask as Vi looks over the order she is working on next.

"Yep. I just have to run home and change, and then, we will be ready. I took Tuck to the store the other day and found the cutest little suit for him. He's so excited to wear it!"

I grin. "He's gonna be adorable. I can't wait to see what you are planning to wear."

Wrapping my arms around her, I haul her into me before grabbing the nape of her neck and pulling her in for another kiss. She sinks into me for a few seconds before she shoves at my chest, shaking her head and chuckling.

"You're insatiable, sir."

I lick my lips as I nod at her, causing her to laugh even harder.

"Oh my god. Leave! I'll see you at home."

My chest warms at that. Home. It's not my home, it's hers but the way she said it makes it sound different. It shakes loose a thought that maybe one day they will be one in the same. Can't say I hate the idea of waking up to Vi in my bed every morning. In fact, I fucking love it.

I give her a wink before heading out the door and going back to my place. It only takes me an hour to get everything together and after I run through some film that I was assigned to watch. I'm on my way to pick up the two people that are quickly becoming my favorites in the whole world.

Chapter Twenty-Five

Vi

A heavy knock comes from the front door while Mindi and I are in my bedroom talking and packing. We both lock eyes for one second before we are scrambling over each other to get out to the door first. Mindi literally shoves me to the ground before slamming the door shut and pushing something in front of it so the door won't open.

I bang on the door as I shout.

"Mindi Elizabeth Maxwell! Open this fucking door now!"

"No swearing, Mommy!" Tucker shouts from his room.

"Yeah!" Mindi laughs. "Be careful what you say. The walls are paper thin in this cracker box!"

"Gee, thanks. Feel free to leave said cracker box if it's not to your satisfaction."

"Nah, the food is free."

"I mean, it's not, but whatever. *Please* don't embarrass me."

"When have I ever done that?" She calls out as I hear her footsteps move towards the door.

"Every day of my life!" I shout.

"Well, hello handsome. Is it my lucky day or what?" I hear Mindi purr.

I push on the door hard a few times before whatever was put in front of the door gives. I'm able to slide my hand out to shove the large suitcase out of the way so that I can open the door fully. When I'm finally free, I step out into the hallway to see Declan shift uncomfortably as he looks down at Mindi and then over her head, probably looking for me.

"Uh, hi. You must be Mindi."

"And you must be my next hook up," she winks.

Declan's eyes widen, and he pulls at his white dress shirt nervously. She is clearly embarrassing him, and I can't hold back my chuckle. We used to do this shit to test a guy's worthiness back in high school. It was funny at the time and honestly weeded out more losers than you would think. But I'm not worried in the slightest about Declan, so I'm just gonna have to kill her for pulling this.

"No offense, but I ain't interested," he says with a hint of disgust. I have no doubt he thinks she is the shittiest friend alive right now.

Mindi nods thoughtfully before she smiles. "You passed test one, you may enter."

"What?" He asks cautiously as he steps inside.

"You have a couple more tests to pass before I deem you good enough to go out with my girl, but so far you are doing great. No pressure. Oh, and if you ever hurt her, I will chop your balls off and toss them in a blender."

Declan laughs uneasily as he scratches the back of his head.

"Are Vi and Tuck ready?"

"Yes, sorry. Ignore Mindi. She doesn't have an off switch, trust me. I've been looking for years."

Declan chuckles and nods as he leans down and brushes a semi-appropriate kiss against my lips. I say semi because he was clearly trying to keep it chaste in front of Mindi, but I'm still thinking about the way he fucked me against the table and wall at my work earlier and I can't help but nip at his lip, licking away the sting before tangling his tongue with mine.

A soft throat clears, and I blink out of the lust haze I was just so cozily wrapped up in to glance over at Mindi, who is smirking at us with raised eyebrows.

"No, no. Please, continue. You two are better than porn."

"What's porn, Mommy?" Tucker asks.

"Corn. Auntie Mindi said corn. She loves the stuff. Right, Mindi?"

"Yup, totally. It's my favorite vegetable."

I shake my head and roll my eyes as Declan chuckles.

"She is pretty crazy," he whispers lowly.

"Yeah, but she knows where I live, so there is no getting rid of her now. That's what I get for feeding the strays."

Declan lets out a laugh as Mindi smacks my ass before following me to my room. I grab my suitcase and Mindi grabs Tuck's as we make our way out into the living room. Declan quickly grabs the bags from us before running them out to the truck.

"I'm sorry I'm leaving. This is why it's good to call," I scold Mindi before wrapping her up in a hug.

"Please. You're sorry that you are jetting off cross country in a private plane with your millionaire boyfriend? The only thing you have to be sorry about is why you haven't set me up with one of his equally good looking and rich best friends."

I laugh and shrug. "Sorry. I've only met the one, and he is definitely married."

"That's not a deal breaker," she shrugs.

I scoff and roll my eyes at her. "Thank you for visiting and for the dress. I've missed you."

"I've missed you too, girl. Text me when you guys will land. I'm planning on being back here next summer so we will catch up then, okay?"

I nod. "Sounds good. Don't wreck my house before you leave, please," I say as Tucker hugs her goodbye before we head out the door.

"No promises," she sings as she waves goodbye to us.

We run into Declan on the stairs, and he smiles when he sees us.

"Oh, are y'all ready to go already?"

"Yeah, we're good."

"Let me just run in and say goodbye to Mindi," he says as he walks past me.

"Oh, you don't have to do that!" I say but he is already poking his head inside the door.

I can't hear what she is saying but from the way his face is flushed red as he comes back over to stand next to us, I'd bet it was embarrassing.

"Do I even wanna know?" I sigh.

Declan chuckles and shakes his head. "I don't think so."

When we get to the car, I watch as Declan opens up the rear passenger door where there is an identical car seat to mine installed. Declan lifts Tuck up into it as Tuck straps himself in.

I cock my head to the side as Declan opens my door.

"When did you get that?" I gesture towards the car seat.

"Oh, uh, just picked it up after the fishing trip," he says as he rubs the back of his neck. "I thought it would be easier than installing and uninstalling every time."

My heart clenches as I look up at this man before I raise onto my toes and press my lips against his.

"Thank you," I whisper.

His tongue runs along his bottom lip as he smiles and nods before helping me into his truck, not missing the chance to subtly squeeze my ass as he does. We get to a private airstrip in less than a half an hour, and when we step inside the plane, I'm in total shock.

The thing is huge and decked out in lavish gold and cream accents. The seats are at least twice the size of normal seats and are wrapped up in a buttery soft leather. Before I can comment on any of it, Tucker does the talking for me.

"Oh my GOSH! This is the coolest ever!" He shouts as he darts past me and begins running laps around the plane.

"Tucker! Stop running! Come here!" I scold while Declan chuckles and slips his arm around my shoulders.

"Let him play, baby. He's fine."

I watch as a stewardess comes out and smiles at Tucker before greeting us. She tells us that we are going to be taking off soon and to take a seat. She also asks if we want anything to drink. We all follow Tucker's lead and get a hot chocolate before picking our seats. The takeoff is smooth, and after about an hour or so, the shine of the whole thing wears off for Tucker and he begins playing the 'are we there yet' game. About three hours into the flight, he falls asleep in his seat, and Declan carries him into one of the bedrooms in the back. Yeah, a bedroom, on a plane. And not just one, but two!

Since there is a three hour time difference and it's about a six hour flight, we decide to do the same, taking what is considered the master bedroom before we pass out.

I wake up to featherlight kisses across my face and strong fingers running through my hair. When I blink my eyes open, I see Declan smiling down at me before he presses a quick kiss against my lips.

"Good morning, beautiful."

"Morning, what time is it?"

"Four in the morning local time."

I groan as I grab one of the pillows to cover my head.

"Why are you waking meeee?"

Declan chuckles as he presses a kiss to the back of my shoulder.

"Because we are landing in a few moments and a curious four year old came wandering in here a few minutes ago looking for his mama."

That has me shoving my pillow to the side and stepping out of the bed as I rub the sleep from my eyes.

"Shit. Okay, where is he? Did he say anything about us sleeping in the same bed? I can't believe I didn't think about him waking up before us."

"He's having breakfast upfront. He asked if we were having a sleep-over. I didn't know what to say, so I just kinda went with it," Declan says as he runs his fingers through his hair before standing next to me.

"What did he say to that?"

"That he wanted to be a part of the sleepover next time. I promised him we would build a fort in your living room when we got home and have one."

I smile at that and laugh. Well, okay then.

We step out of the back bedroom and to the front of the plane where Tuck is watching Mickey Mouse on the TV in the corner, eating a bowl of Fruit Loops as he does.

"Good morning, sweetie," I say as I kiss the top of Tucker's head before taking a seat next to him.

"Morning, Mommy! The nice lady over there said we are gonna be on the ground soon!"

"I heard, are you excited?"

"Uh huh! Declan said we could swim in the pool at his house today!"

"Oh, I'm sorry, baby. I don't know if we can do that. I didn't bring your floaties."

"I don't need them. I'm gonna be super brave like Declan."

Glancing out of the corner of my eye, I watch as Declan looks surprised for a moment before he nods and swallows.

"Thanks, big man."

We land a few minutes later and are immediately ushered into a black town car before we are pulling away from Tyson McGhee Airport and on our way to Declan's house. Since it's only four in the morning, technically one in the morning Seattle time, we all agreed we need more sleep. This time, I choose to fall asleep with Tuck in one of the guest beds. I'm glad that Tucker didn't freak out or get upset when he found Declan and I asleep in the same bed together, but I'm just not sure how comfortable I am with it yet. It's one thing to sleep with him and another to do it in front of my son. Maybe I'm overthinking this, but Declan said he more than understood, so I'm just grateful that above all else he gets it. Tuck comes first, always.

CHAPTER TWENTY-SIX

DECLAN

When I open my eyes, I'm a little confused at first. I've gotten so used to my condo in Seattle that for a second my bedroom in Knoxville seems almost foreign. It's only been a little over three months since I moved to Seattle, but it feels like a lifetime. From what I've seen, it's a pretty cool place, but from the moment we touched down in Tennessee, I realized how much I've missed feeling at home.

I wonder if Seattle will ever feel like home or if Knoxville will be the only place that gives me this feeling. Then again, maybe it wasn't the city and more the company I was with. Vi and Tuck seem to be changing everything for me. It may be too fast or too soon to say, but something in my gut tells me that wherever they are, that's home for me.

Glancing over to the empty side of my bed, I sigh. Vi and I have only slept in the same bed twice now, but it's enough to have me wanting it as much as I can get. I understood though when she said she didn't feel comfortable sleeping in the same bed in front of Tucker, at least until she talked with him more. I love how considerate she is of her son and his feelings. It makes her the best mom on top of being the best woman.

After a quick shower, I pad out to the kitchen in a pair of sweats, choosing to forego a shirt. I'm thankful I had the foresight to have the coffee machine brew a batch before we went to bed. It's already ten in the morning, but thankfully, the coffee is still warm.

I pour myself a cup as I walk over to the living room and turn on the TV. Sports center is the last channel I had it on, so it automatically pops up, going over last night's baseball game. Glancing around the room, I can't help but notice how empty the place looks. I messaged my housekeeper, who comes once a month to keep up on the place and told her to take down all of my football memorabilia in the house and put it in the garage. I asked my mama to do it, but she flat out refused and hung up on me. She said she didn't want any part in lying to Vi.

I'm not lying. Withholding some details, sure. But I'm not lying. And it's not for long. I have to tell her today, since the gala is tonight. Last night on the plane didn't seem like the right time since we were so tired, but I know I have to make time for it today. She's already in Tennessee now, probably best to rip the band aid off.

Soft footsteps echo through the hall before a sleep tussled Vi emerges. She's wearing a baggy shirt that looks to be about four sizes too big. It hits her mid-thigh and makes her look drop dead sexy. It takes a few seconds to realize that the shirt she is wearing my Brighton University t-shirt that I got freshman year.

"Morning," she says sleepily as she comes to sit next to me.

"Hey, baby. Were you able to fall back asleep?"

She nods her head as she runs a hand through her hair and cuddles up next to me.

"Yeah, Tuck and I were both out within a few minutes. I hope you don't mind, I wanted to change but didn't want to wake Tuck up by rifling through my suitcase for a shirt."

My eyes rake over her from head to toe as I smirk.

"Please, wear more of my shirts, take all of them. They've never looked this good on me."

She shakes her head and laughs as I chuckle and take a sip of my coffee. She eyes the cup like it's the holy grail.

"Let me grab a cup for you. What do you want in it? I had Amber pick up a bunch of different creamers and syrups and stuff so you could make it however you want," I say as I stand and make my way over to the coffee machine.

"Amber?" She asks stiffly.

My lips quirk up into an amused smile, though she wouldn't know it since my back is to her. I think about playing along, letting her stew over who Amber could be, but I don't have it in me to let her suffer, so I turn around and smile at her, leaning up against the counter while I do.

"My housekeeper."

Vi's narrowed eyes quickly soften before a faint blush creeps up her neck.

"Oh," she says softly.

Not being able to help myself, I cross the room and tilt her head up as I stand behind her and press my lips against hers.

"You have nothing to worry about, ever. There is only one woman on my mind, and she's sitting right in front of me looking sexy as fuck in my college shirt."

She bites her lower lip and nods before I press a kiss to her forehead and walk back over to resume my work on her coffee. Tucker wakes up a few minutes later, and since Tucker and Vi usually make Mickey Mouse waffles on Saturdays, we decided to make chocolate chip Mickey shaped pancakes. Tucker seemed to approve of the slight change since he scarfed down three the size of his face.

When we clean up breakfast, Tucker wants to go for a swim in the pool outback. We didn't have his floaties, but he didn't even need them. We stayed in the shallow end, and he swam back and forth from me to Vi until he was venturing out all by himself. I watched as Vi's eyes followed him like a hawk, and I made sure to subtly stay within arm's distance at all times just in case, but he didn't need it. I don't think I've ever been so proud in my whole damn life.

Around one in the afternoon, we are talking about going somewhere for lunch when my front door opens and shuts. I groan as my head sags before I straighten up to greet the intruders. There are only three people on this earth that have a key to my house and one of them is staying in New York for a case she couldn't get out of so that just leaves two others.

"There's my baby boy!" My mama exclaims as she rushes over to me and squeezes me into a bear hug before peppering me with kisses.

Her large blonde curls are tossed over her shoulder with a pair of large sunglasses pushed up on top of her head.

"Hi, Mama. It's great to see you, but I don't remember inviting you over for lunch," I say as I glance back behind me where Vi and Tuck are just out of sight. I still haven't had time to talk to Vi about, well, everything, and I know that if my mama is here my alone time possibilities have officially just ended.

"You didn't, baby. So, naturally, I was concerned why my son wouldn't want to spend time with his own mama, so here we are. Now, where is that beautiful girlfriend of yours," she says as she hustles past me.

I let out a sigh and shake my head as my dad comes over to me and claps my shoulder.

"How you doing, son?"

"I'm good. Be a lot better if Mama wasn't accosting my woman and her son in the next room over."

"Yeah," he sighs. "Can't help you there."

I laugh and nod as we follow after my mama. I see the moment my dad sees Vi. His eyes crinkle and a wide smile spreads across his face as he elbows me. A lot of people say that I'm a spitting image of my dad. The only difference is that I got Mama's golden eyes. Other than that, my hair, build, practically everything else is all dad.

"It's so nice to meet you, Violet! Declan has told us all about you and Tucker. We are just over the moon that y'all came out to be with us."

"It's Vi, Mama," I correct as I leave my dad's side to stand next to Vi, slipping my arm over her shoulder as I do.

She smiles up at me in what looks like thanks before turning towards my mama.

"It's really nice to meet you too, Mrs. Daniels. Declan has told me a lot about you guys as well."

"Oh, please," she says as she waves her hands at me. "Call me Mama or Nana or just about anything other than Mrs. Daniels. That's Rodney's mother, and she was the most horrid woman, God rest her soul."

"Mama," I groan.

"What?" She snaps as Vi laughs.

My mother peeks around Vi to see Tucker sitting at the kitchen island with a friendly smile.

"And you must be Tucker. Oh my goodness you are sweeter than a piece of pecan pie!"

"I love pie!" Tucker grins.

We all chuckle at that as Mama rushes over to him and wraps him up in a hug. He eagerly hugs her back and begins rambling on about what happened in the last episode of Mickey Mouse, and I watch as both my parents listen intently. My heart warms at the sight of almost all my favorite people in the world all in one room.

After my dad introduces himself to Vi and Tuck my mama pats the island like she usually does when we're in a loud house and she's trying to get everyone's attention.

"Alright. Vi, I have spa appointments for us in an hour if you want to change before we go. Or stay in your bathing suit if you'd like. They have a sauna that's to die for."

"You didn't," I deadpan. Why did I even ask? Of course, she did.

"What? I need a little girl time with my future daughter in law. You boys will have fun doing whatever y'all come up with, I'm sure. But we need to go and get ready for tonight. How do you expect us to be ready for a gala without a day at the spa? It's like I didn't even raise you," she tsks.

I shake my head as I look over to Vi.

"Please don't feel obligated to say yes. My overbearing mama doesn't understand when she oversteps. You don't have to do anything you don't want to."

Uncertainty flashes across her face only for a moment before she shrugs her shoulders.

"I don't mind. It sounds fun. But," she trails off as her eyes flick to Tucker.

"He can stay with us, we'll probably just go into town for some lunch, if you're comfortable with that? I had a car seat delivered here when you said you guys would come."

A sweet smile touches her face as she nods before turning to Tucker.

"What do you say, sweetie? You good to spend the day with Declan and his dad?"

"Yes! Guys day!" He cheers.

The room all breaks out into laughter as Vi, Tuck, and I go upstairs to change out of our swimming clothes. After hugs and a few kisses, we part ways, Vi and my mama getting into her car while my dad, Tuck, and I pile into my SUV in the garage. I love that my mama wants to get to know Vi, I just hope to god Mama will behave. Knowing Suzannah Daniel's though, the odds are definitely against me.

Chapter Twenty-Seven

Vi

I've learned three things about Suzannah Daniels over the last hour that I've known her.

Number one, she talks. A lot. About everything and nothing. She excitedly told me about the catering and decorations she picked out for the gala as well as the children's activities that she has set up in a smaller room down the hall. I guess she has several volunteers that play games with the kids, do crafts, and even has a little dance floor for them.

Number two, she loves her family, football, and good food. When we got to the spa and checked in for our appointments we were ushered back for massages where she talked about how the Tennessee Bucks, the local NFL team, were looking for this season. I guess Rodney and her are season ticket holders with their own private box. Makes sense since he used to play for the team, I guess.

Number three, I freaking love her. Her love for her children is so apparent, and the way she has instantly made Tucker and I feel so welcome is honestly amazing. Declan always spoke highly of her, and now, I get it.

I was honestly pretty nervous to meet Declan's parents at first. I didn't know what to expect. What if they didn't think that I was good enough for him? What if they thought I was just some gold digger? I'm sure they weren't expecting their golden boy to fall for a single mom, who works in a flower shop during the day and waitresses at a rundown diner at night. After spending just a few minutes with them though, I felt a little more at ease.

Suzannah and I are currently getting our nails painted. We've done massages, body wraps, and sat in the sauna. We've only been here for three hours, but it feels like we've spent all day getting pampered and waited on. It was a little strange at first, but I have to say, it's hands down one of the coolest experiences I've ever had. I see what the hype about it all is for now.

"So," she says as she turns to face me. "I have to be the protective mama bear for a moment. What exactly are your intentions with Declan?"

My eyebrows shoot up. "Excuse me?"

"Don't worry, sweetheart. I don't think you're with my son for his money or anything like that. But my son seems to have fallen for you, hard and fast. Do you feel the same?"

I clear my throat before I nod shyly. Suzannah smiles softly and pats my hand.

"Good. He just thinks the world of you and Tucker. You seem to be really good for him. There's no better feeling for a mother than to see your child happy. I'm sure you can relate to that."

"Definitely. Tuck's happiness is my first priority every day."

Suzannah nods. "It shows. You've done a wonderful job." She fidgets in her seat for a moment before she looks at me again.

"Declan says the father isn't in the picture?"

I hesitate for a second before I give a short nod. I didn't realize how much Declan had told his mother about me. Then again after meeting her she probably dragged it out of him after hours of interrogation.

"What's the story there, if you don't mind?"

I cringe slightly, wondering how much I should really reveal before I speak.

"I got pregnant in college. He didn't want to be a dad. End of story, really."

"He never contacted you or Tucker? Ever?" She asks with almost disbelief.

"No. It's best that way. He wasn't a very good man. I wouldn't want someone like that in my son's life or mine."

She nods. "I'm really sorry. That's just awful that he left you on your own like that. At least you had your family's support?" She questions cautiously.

I smile and shake my head. "My parents passed away when I was nineteen. My best friend has been like a surrogate aunt to Tuck though, and our neighbor is like his grandmother. Our family is small but wonderful."

She places her freshly manicured hand over her heart as she nods.

"Well now it's grown!" She says happily as she leans over the edge of her chair to reach me as she wraps me into a tearful side hug.

A laugh escapes me, and I hug her back this time. She is a lot, but she is completely sweet. If Declan and I did stay together, I could see Suzannah being a wonderful grandmother to Tuck.

We grabbed a quick lunch at the spa, and when we went to pay for everything, I tried to reach for my wallet, but Suzannah was already handing over a black credit card to the front desk. She shot me a conspiring wink before saying, "This is a write off. We can't be expected to attend an event for the foundation without being properly primped, right?"

I laughed and shook my head, insisting that I pay for my share, but she only waved me off before looping her arm through mine and walking me out of the building and into her car. When we get back to Declan's house, it doesn't take long for us to find the boys. They are in some rec room down the hall from the living room. Rodney is sipping a beer in the corner, watching Declan and Tucker with a smile as Declan helps Tucker hold a pool stick before striking a ball on the large pool table.

"Nice, big man!" Declan said before high-fiving Tuck.

I watch as my son jumps into the air and starts doing what looks like a victory dance before he sees me.

"Mommy!" He exclaims before running towards me and wrapping his arms around me.

I bend down to hug him before pulling back and running my fingers through his messy hair.

"Have you been having fun?" I ask.

"Uh huh! Declan and Papa took me to this place where we ate burgers on the river! Like the river was right under our feet! And then we came back here, and I've been learning how to play this game," he says as he points to the pool table. "I'm really good at it, Mommy!"

"I saw," I smile. "I'm so glad you had such a good day."

Standing back up, I see that Declan is only a step or two away from me, looking at me with a sweet smile before he leans down and places a brief kiss on my lips before leaning down into my ear.

"I missed you."

I smile as I lean back to look at him, keeping my voice low since I know Suzannah is doing her best to eavesdrop.

"It's only been a few hours."

"So? I wasn't planning on spending any hours away from you this trip. But my mama...well, you've met her. You get it."

I giggle softly as I toss Suzannah a small smile before nodding as I turn back to Declan.

"Oh, I get it. But I love her. She's sweet."

Declan nods as he snakes his arm around me.

"Do you think we could go for a walk? Mama, could you watch Tucker for a few minutes?"

"No," Suzannah says. "We only have a few hours until the gala and Vi told me that she isn't too well versed with hair and makeup so I'm gonna doll her up. You boys best be getting dressed too."

Declan blows out a breath as he shakes his head.

"Mama, we have four hours, not a few."

"You ever heard the saying 'beauty takes time'?" She sasses.

"Not for Vi it doesn't. It's effortless for her," he counters.

Rodney barks out a laugh as he raises his glass.

"Smooth talking son of a bitch. That's my boy!"

Suzannah smirks but shakes her head.

"Sorry, baby. You'll get her back when I'm all done with her," she says as she hooks her arm through mine once more and practically drags me out the door.

She steps outside before grabbing a dress bag and a beach bag as she makes her way up the stairs. I send Declan an apologetic look but follow his mom since I'm pretty sure there would be no way around it either way.

Suzannah pats a seat in front of a vanity mirror inside one of the spare bedrooms for me and the next few hours are a blur of hot irons, makeup, perfume, and lotions in between. I've never been so dressed up in all my life. Then again, I've never gone to a gala before, so I guess that makes sense.

When all is said and done, I'm slipped into the slinky red dress that Mindi bought me while Declan's mom is wearing a gorgeous glittery black gown that looks like it was made for her. We did long loose curls for my hair while she opted for an updo. As I swiped on my red lipstick,

Mindi's voice ran through my head about DSLs and I couldn't help but laugh at myself. I decided to snap a quick picture and send it to her.

Mindi: Damn, baby. Where have you been all my life? If I was into women, I'd be giving Declan a run for his money.

I snort as I respond.

Me: Yeah, that would never happen. One, you love dick way too much. Two, I love Declan way too much.

Mindi: Wait, what?

Mindi: LOVE?

Mindi: You LOVE him?

Shit. Why did I say that. I didn't mean it. Right? Right. It's way too soon to be even thinking that.

Me: I didn't mean it like that.

Mindi: Bullshit.

Me: I didn't!

Mindi: Okay Miss denial. Whatever. We both know what was typed. No going back.

Groaning, I lock my screen, ready to toss it to the side when my phone buzzes one more time.

Mindi: For the record, I love him for you.

I smile down at my phone before slipping it into the little clutch that Suzannah lent me before making my way out of the room to go find my boys. When I walk down the stairs, I find everyone huddled near the door, seemingly ready to go. When I lock eyes with Declan, my heart stutters, and if it wasn't for his hand railing, I would be on my face at the bottom of the stairs by now.

His eyes flick over me before he looks back to his dad, who he was talking to, before giving me a double take. His eyes widen to the size of saucers and his mouth literally drops. I swear it even looks like he stops breathing for a second. I know I have.

Declan is wearing a crisp black tux with matching black shoes. My god. This man in jeans and t-shirt is mouthwatering but all dressed up like this and he is basically sex on a stick.

When I'm close to the end of the stairs, he steps up to me and grabs my hands, holding them out for him to get a good look at me. I twirl slowly and laugh nervously when he doesn't say anything. Golden amber eyes snag my gaze when I turn back around, and total awe and adoration are clearly written across his face.

"You're..." he trails off as he shakes his head. "Absolutely breathtaking."

My heart skips and I bite my lip in an attempt to contain my grin. I hear a soft 'aww' coming his mom as I swallow and nod.

"You look amazing too."

Declan shakes his head, his eyes glittering with something I can't quite name before he leans in and brushes a soft kiss against my cheek. When he pulls away, the look in his eye hasn't faded, but his smile has grown as he looks at me before glancing down at Tucker who is standing at his side.

My heart melts as I see him in the little suit that I bought him, he looks so grown up, almost too grown up. Tears spring to my eyes as I hold out my arms for a hug. He wraps me up and gives me a quick kiss before standing back next to Declan. They exchange a glance before Declan leans down, whispering into his ear.

Tucker nods very seriously as he listens before he turns to me.

"You look real pretty, Mama," he says.

I smile down at him before sending a knowing look to Declan who just grins.

"Thank you, baby. You look extremely handsome. Think you would walk with me?" I ask, offering my arm.

He nods as he holds onto my hand as he begins leading us out of the house.

Rodney and Suzannah smile at us as they trail behind while Declan holds the door open for everyone. After a lot of begging and pleading from Tucker, I relent and let him ride with 'Nana and Papa.' Rodney promised me he would drive extra careful and that the large G-Wagon they are taking is plenty safe. I don't know how I feel about Tucker calling them Nana and Papa. Once again, Tucker seems to be getting a little too attached too quick. Who can blame him? It's really just been us, Judy, and occasionally Mindi his whole life. The poor thing is desperate for a family in any way he can get it. I just hope that this does end up being our family one day, I don't think Tucker or I could handle if it didn't work out at this point. We are both way too invested.

Chapter Twenty-Eight

Vi

Declan and I are in one of his sports cars, heading to the gala. I say one because the guy has seven vehicles. Seven. I don't know much about cars, so I couldn't really tell you what they are, but he has two trucks, an SUV, and four sports cars. Two of them look vintage while the other two are newer.

"With all the planning your mom has put into this night, I'm surprised we aren't taking a limo," I tease.

Declan looks over and gives me a tight smile before facing forward, his knee bouncing steadily as he drives. My smile slowly falls from my face as my brows furrow. I reach my hand out and rest it on his thigh. He tenses for a moment before he covers my hand with his.

"Are you okay, babe?"

"Yeah," he smiles, which looks a little forced. "You just look so beautiful I'm not looking forward to getting into fights all night just so I can keep the guys off you."

I laugh and shake my head, which causes his smile to grow a little more genuine.

"Yeah, I don't know what fantasy world you live in, but I'm not the kind of girl you need to worry about that kind of stuff happening with."

"Trust me, baby, you are *the* girl that kind of thing happens with. You just haven't had a jealous ass like me around, obviously."

I snort but don't say anything. He couldn't be more wrong. Tucker's dad was a jealous control freak. He was constantly causing a scene and freaking out on me for dressing like a 'slut.' Yet another moment where I'm reminded how lucky I feel to have found someone like Declan.

When we pull up to the hotel where the gala is being held, a valet runs over as Declan steps out of the car, he hands the kid the keys as he comes around my side to get my door. I place my hand into his as we step onto the sidewalk and up the steps where Tucker, Rodney, and Suzannah are already waiting for us. I go to take the first step when I pause. Declan is still standing at the bottom, looking conflicted before his eyes come up to meet mine.

"What's going on?" I ask.

He opens his mouth like he is about to speak before he shakes his head and swallows roughly, quickly wiping away any trace of unease from his face as he smiles.

"Nothing. Let's go inside, get this night over with so I can finally get you in my bed where you belong."

A blush rises up to my cheeks as we climb the stairs together. We all walk Tucker down to where the kids 'party' is being held. It's better than I could have imagined with kids of all varying ages dancing, playing games, and devouring the snack and candy bar that is the entire length of the room. I send an irritated look to Suzannah, who just snickers.

Tucker is practically vibrating with excitement at my side, and I can tell he wants to dart off and make some new friends.

"I love you, sweetie. If you need Mommy, just ask one of the grownups to come get me, okay?"

"Okay. Love you!"

"Rosalie! Daphne!" Declan calls out to two twin girls who look to be about three or four. They both turn and squeal before they tackle Declan.

"Uncle D! Uncle D!" They cheer.

He smiles as he looks at me. "Sebastian and Erica's girls."

I smile as I look down at them. One has gorgeous red curly hair while the other has dark black hair. I haven't met Erica, but I'm going to go out on a limb and guess that she is a red head.

"Tucker, this is Rosalie and Daphne. Why don't you show them that super cool trick you were working on today?"

"Okay!" Tucker says as he takes off running before doing some spastic jump and twirl in the air.

The girls squeal in celebration as they chase after him and attempt to do the same. I smirk as Declan smiles before slipping his arm around my waist, ushering us out of the room and down the hall. When we step inside the ballroom, my eyes widen as I take in the elegant décor. Everything is dripped in gold and creams, luxurious tablecloths, tall extravagant centerpieces, and three chandeliers hang from the ceiling. I turn around to give an impressed look to Suzannah, who smiles in delight as she greets a group of people.

"Want a drink?" Declan asks as he gestures towards one of the bars in the corner of the room.

"Yes, please."

Declan nods as we wait in line for a minute or so before grabbing two champagnes and walking around to find our seats.

"So, I didn't know Sebastian was going to be here? What does he do for the organization?"

Declan pauses before turning to look at me, that conflicted look passing across his face once again. His large hand comes up to cup the side of my face as he speaks.

"Baby, I've been wanting us to have some alone time to talk. I haven't known really how to say it, though."

Anxiety rises up inside me. No one likes to hear those words. Oh god, is he dumping me? Why would he take me all the way out to Tennessee, to meet his family only to dump me?

"Are you breaking up with me?" I blurt stupidly before I can even stop myself.

His eyes widen as he quickly shakes his head.

"What? Fuck no! Never. Why would you think that?"

"Well, usually when people talk the way you are, it's because they have bad news or want to break up or something."

"No, baby. Hell fucking no. You're mine, I told you that. I'm fucking keeping you," he promises as he lowers his head down and crushes his lips against mine in a kiss that is probably too passionate for public, but I'm too drunk on his lips to care.

"Aw, remember when we used to maul each other in public like the world was on fire?" A woman voice coos near us.

Declan and I break apart to see Sebastian and a stunning redhead wearing a cream dress on his arm. They are both grinning at us, well, the woman is. Sebastian seems to have what I would guess is a signature stoic look, but his lips are upturned in the corners slightly.

He looks down at who I'm assuming is Erica before his smile grows.

"Am I not accosting you enough in public, baby? Let's go find a dimly lit corner, and I'll change that right now."

She flushes at his words, but she doesn't shy away from him, if anything she looks ready to dare him to do so.

"Alright, easy troublemakers. Mama will have a fit if y'all start screwing in the corner," Declan says.

We all chuckle before he slides his arm behind my back and introduces us.

"Erica, this is my girlfriend, Vi. Vi, this is Seb's wife, Erica."

"It's so nice to meet you!" She smiles. "I've heard so much about you!"

"Really?" I ask, more than a little surprised.

"Yeah, really?" Declan asks as he narrows his eyes at Sebastian.

The giant of a man does his best to contain a smirk behind his glass of whiskey.

"Relax, Mikey," he rumbles with an eye roll.

I furrow my brows and smile as I look up at Declan.

"Mikey?"

Declan shrugs. "Old nickname."

I smile and nod. "I kinda like it."

We all chat for a little while. I learn that Declan, Erica, and Seb all went to college together and also played football together. Erica and I are talking about the kids and how fast they seemed to have become friends and how we should get them together soon.

Suddenly, a boisterous voice calls out from behind me as a large, tattooed hand clasps Declan's shoulder.

"What's up, man? Is this your girl?"

I turn around to introduce myself before I freeze.

"Slater?" I ask, completely stunned.

His smile slides off his face as his eyes widen. "Violet? Holy shit! What are you doing here?" He shouts as he wraps me in a tight bear hug.

"You know my girl?" Declan asks, sounding confused.

"Hell yeah. Violet and I were tight in college when I transferred up to the University of Seattle. She is the one who introduced me to Nikki."

"I go by Vi now, actually," I correct with a smile. "Wait, are you and Nikki still together?"

"Yeah," he smiles. "Put a ring on that shit and everything. We got married in Mexico three years ago.

"Oh my god, that is amazing! Congratulations! Is she here?" I ask as I look around the room.

"Nah she's on a girl's trip in Miami. When I got drafted, she dropped out of school and became a professional NFL wife," Slater teases with a wink.

"Ha! That's awesome. So, what are you doing here? You work with Declan too?"

"Hell yeah, best in the league girl!"

My smile slowly fades as confusion takes over.

"Wait, last I heard you were playing for the Crusaders?"

His eyes widen slightly before his smile becomes tight as he glances at Declan quickly before laughing lightly.

"Uh, yeah, I do."

"Wait. Wait," I say as I hold my hand up to get my bearings. My eyes flick over to Declan questioningly. He is watching me carefully, not giving anything away. Looking around the room my eyes catch on Darren Williams. I remember seeing something about him in the paper a few months ago. He is a cornerback for the Crusaders who got injured last season. And to the other corner of the room is the Bucks quarterback. I recognize him because Suzannah showed me a picture of him today, well, it was mainly pictures of his butt but still. I look back to Slater as everything starts to slowly fall into place.

Oh my god. How could I have been so stupid? Declan has always been so cagey about his job, never too specific. We never go in public and when we do, he's usually wearing a hat and sunglasses. Holy fuck. He didn't just play football in high school. I'd bet everything that I have that he is still playing too. *Professionally*. Holy FUCK.

"You're all professional football players, aren't you? You all play for the Crusaders? Is the whole team here tonight?"

Slater looks sympathetic for a moment before understanding flashes across his face, and he glances around the room before subtly shaking his head no. I blow out a breath, and give Declan a scathing look before I turn back to Slater.

"I gotta get out of here, now. It was nice seeing you. Tell Nikki I say hello."

I brush past him before he can say anything as I begin moving through the throngs of people.

"Wait, Vi. Please, wait. Baby, hear me out!" Declan calls out.

I'm so pissed at Declan right now. I can't believe he lied to me. He's a fucking NFL player? And for the fucking Crusaders? He is a fucking celebrity football player, and I was the idiot that didn't figure it out. But Declan is honestly the least of my worries right now.

"Vi!" I hear him shout again, but I don't turn around. My eyes are fully trained on the door, and I almost make it when I crash into a hard body. As a familiar sandalwood smell infiltrates my nose, my stomach instantly rolls out of instinct. *Oh god.*

"Easy, beautiful. Touch the wrong man like that, and he might have to do something about it."

"Get your hands off me," I snarl as I lift my head up to face the man in front of me, if you can even call him that.

His familiar green eyes round with recognition as his blond hair falls slightly in front of them as his mouth hangs open.

"Violet?" Chad balks, clearly shocked.

I take a wide step to move around him when his hand clasps my arm tightly.

"Where do you think you're going?"

"Let me go," I say evenly, the threat thick in my tone.

He yanks on me harder and jerks me closer to him, lowering his voice as he gets in my face. My arm is starting to hurt but I don't dare show him an ounce of weakness.

"I don't think so. It's been too long and you're looking pretty delicious tonight. Why don't we find somewhere a little more private?"

I attempt to free my arm again but with no luck when I hear Declan behind me.

"Vi! Baby, please. I'm so sorry. I didn't-"

He seems to instantly pick up on the tense air that surrounds Chad and I before his eyes flick down to Chad's iron grip on my arm. Declan stands up straighter, his voice lowering to an eerie sound.

"Brownstone, didn't know you were invited. Wanna explain why you're touching my girl?"

Chad's face darkens as he looks between Declan and me. His fingers flex slightly, and I can't help but blow out a soft breath as I try to hold the pain in. Declan notices my discomfort as he looks over at Chad again.

"Let her go. Now," his deep voice rumbles, his accent making him sound more dangerous than I thought this teddy bear of a man could be.

"Nah, I don't think so. You're actually interrupting something, so why don't you fuck off?" Chad says with a sinister smirk.

While he is in a standoff with Declan, I take advantage of the distraction and yank my arm free from his grasp. He reaches for me again but falls short as I practically leap away from him.

"Don't ever put your hands on me again, you stupid son of a bitch!" I shout, probably too loud, but I honestly couldn't care less right now.

"Come on, baby girl, don't be like that. There was a time when I was 'the love of your life,'" he mocks, tossing a smug smirk to Declan as he does.

"Wait. How do you two know each other?" Declan asks.

Chad's eyes fill with irritation, and he looks like he is about to say something, but I'm not sticking around for it. I take off running as fast as I can in my heels and out the door. My eyes frantically scan over the room and find him in no time. I run over to him, scooping him up into my arms as I continue running as fast as I can out of this place.

A few people call out to me, asking if I need help and Tucker keeps asking me what's wrong but I don't stop. I run like my life depends on it. It feels like it does right now. Thankfully there are several cabs just idling outside the hotel, and I jump into the first one I see before asking for them to take us to the airport.

My hands are trembling, and my breathing is labored as the world around me spins.

"Mommy? What's going on? I'm scared," Tucker says, his eyes wide with worry.

"We have to go home now, baby. We will get our stuff soon. We just have to go home," I say, unable to keep the shake out of my voice.

Tucker pouts but he doesn't argue because he's honestly the best fucking child. My clutch is vibrating like crazy, and I have no doubt that it's Declan trying to reach me. But I do not have the emotional capacity to deal with him right now. Running into my own personal nightmare is more than I'm able to deal with for one night.

CHAPTER TWENTY-NINE

DECLAN

"Vi! Shit. What the fuck, Brownstone? What are you even doing here?" I bark at him as I watch Vi run like her life depends on it out the ballroom.

"I was invited. I recently became one of your top donors. I thought it would be fun to fly out to bumfuck America and let you and your family kiss my ass just so I'd write a fat check."

I scoff as I roll my eyes. "First off, I mean this with all the disrespect in the world, fuck you. Second, how do you know Vi?"

Chad rolls his eyes at me as he crosses his arms over his chest.

"Violet and I went to school together, dated for a bit before I got drafted."

"Yeah, right," I scoff. There is no way in hell my Vi would ever date a piece of shit like Brownstone. I'm over letting this dipshit talk. Without another word, I turn and dart off in the direction that Vi went. I glance down the side halls before running into my mama.

"Mama! Have you seen Vi?" I pant.

Her brows furrow as she shakes her head.

"No. Why? What's going on?"

"She knows. She knows and I'm not the one who told her. She took off, and I need to find her. Explain. Apologize. Fuck, I don't know but I gotta find her," I say as I begin running my fingers through my hair.

My mother's face is full of disappointment, and she shakes her head.

"I love you, but you're an idiot. Let's see if she's grabbed Tucker yet," she says as she turns towards the hallway where the kids' room is.

"You think she would have left the entire event?" I ask, my eyes widening.

She sends me a side eye look as she hurries towards the door.

"Sweetheart, if it was me, I'd leave the whole *state*."

My stomach drops at her words as we step inside the room. My eyes scan over all the kids' heads, looking for that one blond head and huge hazel eyes that I've come to adore. A heaviness presses down on my chest when I come up empty, and I look to my see mama already talking to one of the volunteers, a pained look on her face.

"They're gone."

Her words hit me like a physical blow.

"I guess Vi ran in here, grabbed Tucker, and took off running. People were worried because she looked so scared. They also weren't sure if it was her kid so that is a relief."

Pulling out my phone, I hit call as I listen to the phone ring before it goes to Vi's voicemail. Fuck. I redial as I start making my way through the hotel and out front, my mama's heels clicking after me as I go. No answer. I call again as I give my valet stub to the kid at the booth.

"Fuck," I mutter before pulling my phone away from my ear.

"What are you going to do?" Mama asks.

I blow out a breath as I turn to her, giving her a tight hug before my car pulls up in front of us.

"I'm going after them."

Chapter Thirty

VI

When we got to the airport, we were lucky enough to catch a last-minute red eye flight to Seattle. It nearly maxed out my credit card, but I honestly didn't care. I just needed to get us out of there. Out of the state, away from *him*. Away from it all. Home. We had to go home.

I texted Mindi, asking her if she was still at our house. She said she planned on leaving tonight, but when I told her that I ran into Chad, she said that she canceled her flight and that she would be waiting for us. Tuck slept most of the way thankfully, but I couldn't get a second of sleep if I tried. I was too wired. On adrenaline or heartbreak, I wasn't quite sure.

He lied to me. He fucking lied. Was anything he ever told me true? Or was this all one big ruse? Did he know about Chad's and my past? Did Chad put him up to it?

The logical side of my brain knows that isn't the case. The logical side of me knows why he did what he did. I've been very transparent of my dislike of the sport, which is now very clearly his whole world. He liked me, he wanted a shot with me, so he hid the truth so that I'd give him a chance.

The illogical side of me. The emotional one. The one who feels like she has just had the rug ripped right from underneath her feet thinks that none of this was ever truly real. That I was the only one truly falling. That he was in it for the chase and now that he caught me, he didn't care if we imploded or not.

All of our stuff is still at his house. I don't know how or when we will ever get it back but if we don't then we don't. It's mainly just clothes, shoes and our toothbrushes. We'll live without it.

Tuck is still asleep in my arms as I struggle to climb the stairs with him. Gosh, when did my baby get so heavy? When I finally make it to my apartment, I don't even have to get out my keys before the door is being tossed open and Mindi is rushing towards me.

"Oh my god, babe! How are you? Are you okay?" She asks loudly before quickly lowering her voice when she sees a sleeping Tuck.

I wordlessly walk past her before laying him down in his bed, pressing a kiss against his forehead and silently slipping out of his room. When I turn around, I see Mindi with her arms crossed and a concerned look on her face as she watches me warily.

Blowing out a long shaky breath, I stare at her for a moment until she opens her arms for me. I crash into her, wrapping my arms around her as I begin to sob against her. She rubs her hand up and down my back as she slowly walks us to my room. When we make it to my bed, she lays next to me as she softly shushes me.

When I'm able to stop the tears from pouring down my face enough to talk, I wipe under my eyes, no doubt smearing Suzannah's handy work. God. I didn't even think about her. Her and Rodney obviously knew all along, neither said a thing. I don't know why their betrayal stings almost as bad as Declan's. Of course, they are going to side with their son.

"What happened, babe?" Mindi asks softly after a few moments.

"Declan is a pro football player."

Mindi's eyebrows shoot up to her hairline at that.

"For the Crusaders," I add.

Her mouth drops at that.

Yeah.

"I tried to get out of there when I figured out that other Crusader players were there. Who do you think I physically ran into on my way out though?" I ask dryly.

Mindi cringes. "Chad?"

"Chad."

A wave of chills runs through my body at just the mention of his name before I begin crying again.

"Why does he still affect me like this?" I ask, my voice shaking as I do.

"Shhh. It's okay, babe. He's a nasty son of a bitch. The man is completely evil. Of course, seeing him again is going to affect you."

"Everyone hurts me, Mindi. First Chad, now Declan. Why do I even fucking try?"

"Okay, knock that shit off right now. First off, everyone does not hurt you. Your parents never hurt you, I've never hurt you, Judy has never hurt you, and Tuck has never done anything but make you better. Second, do not ever compare Chad Brownstone to Declan ever again. They are not even on the same planet, and you know it. Declan lied, he fucked up, and I'm so pissed that he lied to you, but that man doesn't have a mean bone in his body, not towards you at least. I was around you two for three minutes and I could tell. That man is in love with you, Vi."

"He is not. If he loved me, he wouldn't have kept his entire life from me."

"Vi-"

"Can we just stop? Please, I don't want to talk anymore."

She bites her lip but doesn't say anything. Instead, she nods and lifts the blanket for us before turning the light off. I close my eyes and finally fall into a deep dreamless sleep.

A loud knock jolts me from my sleep. At first, I think I must have imagined it until it comes again. I glance over to the clock to see that it's six in the morning. We didn't get back to the apartment until a little after one, and I'm so thankful that I took the day off of both jobs today because I can't even imagine trying to pry myself out of this bed for anything more than making Tuck breakfast. My eyes flutter closed and I'm almost closed when I hear Declan's voice.

"Vi! Vi, open the door. We need to talk. Please, baby. Just let me know that you're safe!"

He begins knocking again, and I hear Mindi curse under her breath before she gets out of bed and storms through the house. I sigh before getting up, watching from my bedroom doorway as Mindi swings the door open. Declan's hair is disheveled, and he looks panicked and exhausted. I've never seen him look like such a mess. I'm sure the same could be said for me since I'm still wearing a glittery red evening gown and probably only a quarter of the makeup that was applied to my face.

"Go away," Mindi snaps before she swings the door shut.

Declan's foot sneaks in before it closes all the way, and he pushes it open again.

"Mindi, I need to talk to her."

"Yeah, well she doesn't want to talk to you right now. You fucked up, bud. Remember what I said I would do if you hurt her? Well, that girl is fucking hurt. She has had the worst night in a long ass time, and she seriously doesn't need your half-baked apology so just take your shit somewhere else unless you want me to get the blender out."

I watch as Declan absorbs her words, staying silent for a few moments. He lets out a rough sigh and laces his fingers behind his head.

"I know! I know I fucked up. But I also knew that I didn't have a choice."

Mindi puts her finger on her thumb as she looks up to the ceiling like she is thinking.

"Hm, I don't know. Maybe you could have tried not being a total tool and just been honest from the start?"

Declan gives her a deadpan look as he shakes his head at her.

"C'mon, be real with me. If I would have walked into that diner that night, told her that I was one of the top Middle Linebackers in the NFL and would love to take her out some time, do you think she would have said yes?"

Mindi stays quiet for a moment. "She didn't even say yes to you the first time."

"Exactly. Or the second or the third and that was all without her knowing what I do. I didn't get it at the time, but I've always thought that it was a football player that made her hate the sport and-"

"Yeah, no shit. And from what I hear, you know the asshole real well. You two buddy buddy and shit?" She snaps.

A dark look flashes across his face as he stares at her.

"I'd rather eat a bowl of rusty nails than be Chad Brownstone's fucking friend."

Some of the defense in Mindi's body language drops but she keeps her scowl in place.

"I can't let you in, Declan. I'm sorry but my loyalties don't lie with you."

He rakes his hands through his hair one more time before tugging at the strands as his arms drop to his sides and his entire body seems to deflate.

"Just...just tell her I'm sorry, okay?"

Mindi lifts her head higher but says nothing as he turns to leave. A pain settles inside my chest as the door thunks shut and the tears begin to pour more than ever before.

CHAPTER THIRTY-ONE

DECLAN

I blew it. I fucking blew it.

Everyone warned me, told me what a dumbass I was being, but I didn't listen. Now I'm here, paying the price. I sat on the ground outside of Vi's apartment for nearly three hours after Mindi wouldn't let me in yesterday. I was hoping that maybe she would change her mind, want to talk, yell at me, fucking anything. But to have her just shut me out like that hurt more than I could have imagined. Not that I didn't deserve it.

Fuck. I run my hands through my hair as I sit up in bed. I should have told her when I had the chance, I had so many of them, and I didn't take a single one because I'm a fucking chickenshit. I wouldn't blame her if she never spoke to me again, but fuck, I hope she does.

I'm tempted to text her. When I realized she left the gala I checked the security app at my house and saw that no one had been by. I knew she wasn't going to risk going back there so instead I headed straight for the airport. I missed the boarding for her flight back to Seattle by two minutes. Two fucking minutes. I tried to bribe the flight staff into opening the door, but they refused and threatened to call security if I didn't leave the terminal.

So I had the company plane fueled up and after a bullshit three hour delay, we were on our way back to Seattle. Back to my family. I wasn't surprised Mindi didn't let me in, she's a good friend like that, and on one hand, I love that Vi has someone like her in her corner; on the other, I wanted to shove her to the side before dropping onto my knees in front of Vi and beg for forgiveness.

Mindi was right though, I hurt Vi. I fucked up, and I don't have a good excuse for it besides being a selfish prick and wanting as much time with her on my terms as possible. Blowing out a breath I shake my head as I start getting ready for the day. Hopefully I can push Vi out of my head long enough to get through practice at least.

Unlikely.

When I get to the locker room, I get changed quickly before jogging onto the field. We go over a few things with our coaches before we split off into groups to start our warmups and start some drills.

About halfway through practice I'm getting some water when someone calls out my name. I turn around to see the king jockhole himself jogging towards me.

"Daniels, we need to talk," Chad says as he stands in front of me with his arms crossed and a serious look on his face.

I look him up and down and scoff. "Yeah, I'm good."

I go to step past him, but he steps in front of me, puffing up his chest.

"What's up with you and Violet?" He demands, causing my temper to raise to the surface instantly.

"Whatever goes on between *Vi* and me is none of your business, Brownstone," I emphasize Vi to get the point across that she isn't the same woman that he used to know.

"Whatever. I was just coming to tell you to be careful, man. Chick is a total psycho. She wanted to get married and have kids at like nineteen. When I broke it off with her, she faked being pregnant to try to keep me around. Lucky, I got outta that shit unscathed. I'd run fast if I were you."

What? Pretended to be...oh fuck. Nineteen? So, six years ago, minus nine months and...fuck. I don't know how this didn't cross my mind. I guess I was too busy freaking out over losing Vi that I didn't piece together everything from that night. So, Chad is the piece of shit that walked out on Vi, left her and Tuck to fend for themselves. Now I really wanna kick the shit out of the guy.

Something sticks out at me, though. Faked being pregnant? He doesn't know she was actually pregnant? He doesn't know about Tucker? Choosing not to share that information with him, I decide to just play along and nod.

"Crazy. Thanks for the tip, man."

"You got it," he says slapping my back before jogging off, tossing a look at me over his shoulder before he turns around.

I wonder if he would have stuck around if he knew that she wasn't lying? Probably not. He is still a piece of shit and a dumbass. Who the fuck would give up a chance to be with Vi? A fucking idiot, that's who.

When practice is over, I sling my bag over my shoulder as I make my way out the building. An arm swings around my neck and an obnoxious voice shouts in my ear.

"Dude, why didn't you tell me you were dating Violet Nielson?" Slater grins.

"Vi," I correct as my stomach bottoms out at the reminder that I don't think I am anymore.

Slater shrugs. "She will always be Violet to me. Shit, man, we were all super tight in college up here. When her and-". He pauses for a second and looks at me questioning. "You know she used to date Brownstone, right?"

I grit my teeth and give him a sharp nod. Yeah, put that together.

"Don't sweat it, man. It was a long time ago. They were hot and heavy for a while and then Chad got drafted and everything went to his head, and he turned into the guy we all know and hate. She took the breakup pretty hard. Girl dropped out of college and stopped returning our calls. Last night was the first time I have seen her in...damn, like six years. She is a good girl, though. Treat her right, yeah?"

"That's the plan," I nod, if I can get another shot with her.

He waves goodbye and I get into my car and head back to Vi's. As I'm driving, it occurs to me that Slater didn't mention anything about Vi being pregnant either, he didn't ask about Tuck or anything. Does he not know either?

Vi loves Tuck, he is her whole damn world. Why would she keep that hidden from everyone that she used to be so close with? Something isn't adding up, but we are definitely not in a place for me to be asking those kinds of questions, or any really. I think all I can do at this point is give her space and hope to hell that she will miss me as much as I'm already missing her. I'll give her some time but there is no way in hell I'm giving Violet Nielson up for good.

Chapter Thirty-Two

VI

It's been two weeks since Knoxville. Two weeks since I've heard from Declan or seen him. When he left my apartment that day it's like he disappeared from my life. No more calls or texts. No more drop in visits at the shop. It's almost like he never existed. Which is good, it's a good thing. I just wish it didn't hurt so damn bad.

Tucker has asked questions, questions I have no idea how to answer. He wants to know when we will see Declan again. How do I tell him never when the words are like stabbing a knife into my own chest?

Mindi left to head home to LA last week. She offered to take some time off work and shuffle some stuff around to stay with me, but I told her to go. The sooner things get back to normal, the better. Glancing down at my shoes my eyes hone in on the fading sharpied words.

Just Breathe.

"C'mon, Tuck. We gotta get going!" I call out as I open the front door.

When I take a step out to keep the door open, my foot kicks against something. Furrowing my brows, I look down to see a single red Dahlia and a plain white box on the floor. I look from side to side down the hall but see no one around.

Slowly reaching down, I pick up the flower first, noticing that there is a small tag attached to it.

Red.

I can't even look at this color without thinking of you. Without thinking about the first time that I saw you in your bright red shoes. You took my breath away.

My breath catches in my throat as I read over the words. The note isn't signed but it doesn't need to be. The thought that he was here, at my front door, and left this does something to me. I'm not sure if it's good or bad though because it fucking hurts.

Slowly, I lift open the white box to see a brand new pair of candy apple red Converse sneakers. They are beautiful. I pull one out of the tissue paper and lift it up, seeing almost immediately that they are my size. Of course, they are. When I reach for the other one my breathing stalls for a minute.

On the toe of the right shoe is a small heart drawn in black sharpie. A tear slips down my cheek before I even have time to stop it. Damn him. Does he think a pair of shoes and a flower will fix this mess?

"What's that, Mommy?" Tucker asks as he comes into the hallway.

I quickly stuff the shoes back into the box and shove it and the flower inside the door before shutting and locking it.

"Nothing, let's go."

"Hi, Grandma Judy!" Tucker greets.

My eyes flick up to see Judy watching me with a sad frown. I do my best to muster up a friendly smile, but I know it falls flat as I guide Tucker down the hallway and out to the car.

I thought that would be the end of it. But every day for the last six days I've had a new box and a different flower waiting on my doorstep.

On Tuesday, it was an orange pair of Converse with an orange Calla Lily.

Orange.

Like the first sunset we watched together on the boat. Such a perfect day.

Wednesday was a yellow pair with a Sunflower.

Yellow.

Like the sundress that you have. It's my favorite.

Thursday was a green pair of shoes with a green Rose.

Green.

Like the deepest flecks of green in your hazel eyes. I could get lost in them for days.

Friday was blue shoes and a blue Hydrangea.

Blue.

Like my sheets. I can't even look at them without thinking about how perfect you looked laying against them.

Saturday was a purple pair of shoes and a purple Orchid.

Purple.

Like the pair of panties you wore the first time we made love. I've never loved the color purple more than in that moment.

That last one was near my breaking point. Why is he doing this to me? When will he freaking stop? He's gone through the damn rainbow and guess what? I'm hurting more now than I was back in Tennessee when everything I thought I knew blew up in my face. I can tell this is hurting him too, which shouldn't bother me as much as it does. He needs to give this up, let me go, let me heal.

I've been scared to check my door today. I'm not sure if I'm more scared that something will be there or if something isn't. We have to go get some groceries tonight though, so I take in a deep breath and open the door. Unlike a single flower like all the other days there is a full bouquet laying at my feet. Filled with every flower that has been dropped off and a few more added in to make it one gorgeous rainbow blur. The card is simple.

I'll never stop caring for either of you.

I notice that the box is smaller than the others and when I open the lid, I gasp.

A small pair of rainbow tie-dyed high tops are sitting inside with a little heart on the right toe just like all the pairs he sent me. My fingers reach out to lift the lip and see that they are Tucker's exact size.

How?

"Are those for me?" Tucker asks excitedly.

I blink back the tears building in my eyes before I do my best to shake away the tears before I nod.

"I love them! Thanks, Mommy!"

I open my mouth to respond but come up short. I can't do this anymore. Enough is enough. Pulling out my phone from my pocket, I type out a quick and simple text.

Me: We need to talk.

His response comes almost immediately.

Declan: Anytime, anywhere. I'll be there.

My heart flips at his words, but I do my best to push it down.

Me: My place. Two hours.

Declan: I'll see you soon.

My head is telling me this is a terrible idea, that I should just keep ignoring him, that he will eventually give up. For some reason, I don't really believe that, though. So, at least he's coming on my turf, where I can kick him out when things undoubtedly get uncomfortable. It would be easier if we didn't have to meet at all, but this has all got to stop. I can't take much more of this.

Chapter Thirty-Three

Vi

When Tucker and I get back from the store, he helps me put away the groceries before I tell him to go watch a movie in his room. I rarely ever let him watch TV in his room outside of occasionally before bed, so he lit up like a Christmas tree before he darted off down the hall. Truthfully, I just didn't want him to see Declan here. He's been asking about him every day, and my stomach is already in knots just thinking about seeing Declan again. Good or bad knots, I'm not quite sure.

Two hours on the dot from when I texted him, a heavy yet cautious knock sounds from my door. My stomach flips and my heart begins pounding. I feel my palms begin to sweat as I set the bread down on the counter and cross the room, blowing out a slow breath as I open the door.

My eyes move up the wall of muscle in front of me until they land on a pair of golden amber eyes that are more dull than I've ever seen before. He gives me a tentative smile that quickly drops when I don't return it.

"Hi," he says softly.

I swallow down the massive lump that has suddenly blocked my throat before I nod.

"Hi."

Declan stands there silently, his hands in his jeans pockets as he watches me carefully, like he's nervous to move, to even breathe. Ugh, I hate this.

"C'mon," I say quietly as I gesture for him to come in.

He nods and wordlessly follows me in. When I shut the door, I turn to face him, crossing my arms like it will somehow make me stronger.

tougher. When it's clear he isn't going to speak first, I decide to rip the band aid off.

"The gifts have to stop, Declan. It's too much. The flowers, the shoes, the...notes," my voice cracks at the end, and I scold myself for being so weak. I close my eyes and shake my head, a new resolve settling over me.

"You didn't like them?" He asks, disappointment heavy in his features.

"Of course I did. That's not the point, though. You can't buy my forgiveness, Declan."

"I know. That's not what I was trying to do, Vi, I swear. I just..." He pauses as he runs a hand through his hair and shakes his head. "It wasn't supposed to go like this."

"Did you honestly think things could have turned out any different?" I ask as I drop my hands to my side in frustration.

"Did you?" I repeat.

He opens his mouth to speak, but nothing comes out. He gives me a hopeless look before he rubs the back of his neck as he glances at the floor.

"I don't know. I hoped."

"You hoped," I laugh bitterly. "You hoped that I would just fall at your feet because you're a hot shot athlete? That I would ignore the fact that you have been actively lying to me for three months-"

"Technically, I never lied. I-"

"Oh, cut the shit, Declan! Omission is the equivalent to lying. At least own that," I snap.

His jaw tenses as he hangs his head and swallows, nodding as he looks up at me, those amber eyes pinning me into place as he does.

"You're right. I fucked up. I lied. I should have told you sooner, a hell of a lot sooner. But I'm not sorry."

My brows furrow as I cross my arms over my chest.

"I'm not sorry, because if I would have done a single thing different, I wouldn't have had the best three months of my life with you and Tucker.

"I lied to you, and I'm so fucking sorry that I hurt you, but I'm not sorry that I lied. You know we would have never gotten to where we are now if I hadn't. I knew it was wrong, I knew I should have been honest. I couldn't, though. All it took was one taste from you, and I knew that I could never let you go. I swear to god, I fell in love with you from the very first moment that I laid my eyes on you!" He says, seemingly frustrated by the fact. Or maybe frustrated at the situation.

"I knew you were special. I knew I had to have you. You were very clear about how much you hated football. I wanted to be everything you wanted. I didn't want you to give yourself an excuse to not pursue this. I just wanted a shot with you, Vi."

He blows out a breath as he closes his eyes for a moment before opening them back up to look at me, a thick layer of emotion covering them as he speaks.

"You've changed my whole world. I'm sorry that I hurt you, but I'm not sorry that I lied. Given the chance, I'd do it again because it got me here. It gave me the opportunity to get to know you and Tuck, and to fall in love with both of you."

There it is. The final blow. The one that officially obliterates everything. My impenetrable walls are suddenly nothing but a pile of rubble and debris. The pain from my past that forged this mountain of a wall disintegrates before my eyes, allowing me to properly see for the first time what is right in front of me. I'm struck speechless. I stand there, mouth slightly agape, stunned.

"I don't know what to say," I whisper softly, not quite able to meet his gaze anymore.

He takes a small step closer, forcing my chin up so that I meet his eyes.

"Say that you love me too, say that you feel this between us just as strong as I do. Say that you don't want me to walk out that door. Say this isn't over between us," he practically begs as his hand holds my chin steadily.

"I don't," I respond.

His brows furrow but he doesn't speak. I lick my lips as I do my best to make sense of my thoughts.

"I don't want you to walk out the door. I don't want this to be over. I-I'm hurt and confused but I think...I think I'm in love with you too."

Slowly, his face softens as he nods gently before leaning down until his lips are just a hair's width away from mine.

"I love you so fucking much, Vi. These last three weeks have fucking killed me. I'll do anything to fix this between us, baby. Fucking anything."

I nod. "We aren't done talking."

His head nods in agreement before his eyes flick to my lips before coming up to meet my gaze, seemingly asking for permission. I give a subtle nod, and he closes the distance between us. It's sweet and tender, I can practically feel the emotion being poured into this kiss as his soft lips move against mine. God, has it really only been three weeks since I've felt his lips on mine? It feels like it's been years.

When he pulls away he rests his forehead against mine, his eyes still closed for a moment before he opens them and takes my hand in his.

"Whenever you're ready."

I silently lead him towards my room, glancing down the hall to make sure that Tuck is still in his room before we slip inside mine.

I move to sit on the bed and Declan hesitates for a moment before he follows me, leaving a few inches between us as he does. The room is thick with tension for a few moments before he speaks.

"So, Brownstone?" He asks.

I give him a sharp nod, causing him to bring a hand up to rub his beard as he watches me carefully.

"So, you two were really together?"

"Yeah."

"When?" He asks, his voice suddenly strained.

I can see in his eyes that he already knows the answer, he just wants to hear me say it.

"We broke up about six years ago when I got pregnant with Tucker. He walked out, never looked back."

Declan's jaw ticks as he looks away from me and gives me a terse nod. When he looks back, his eyes are clouded with something heavy and dangerous.

"So, he's never even met Tuck?" He asks.

I shake my head, causing his brows to dip slightly.

"I'm sorry. The guy is a piece of shit and if I'm being honest, it doesn't surprise me one bit, but it pisses me off that he bailed on you guys like that."

"He wasn't always the asshole he is now. When I knew him, he was just a loud-mouthed college guy that was extremely talented at football. Sure, he was kind of a douche, but he could be nice when he wanted to be. At least, I think so. Looking back, maybe he was just a good liar. It doesn't really matter either way, I haven't seen him since that day, and I was really hoping to keep it that way," I say as I play with the edge of my comforter.

He's quiet for a moment before he speaks again.

"I'm really sorry, Vi. I never meant to put you in an uncomfortable position. I kept putting off telling you, I was a chickenshit. I was so crazy about you. If I would have known, I never would have taken you."

I nod. "I promised myself I would never get involved with a guy like him again. No womanizers, no party boys, and definitely no football players. I never wanted to be hurt like that again."

"I would never walk out on you, Vi, you know that right?" He asks.

Giving him a tight smile, I nod. "I know."

It takes me a few more minutes to collect my thoughts. Honestly, it's pretty much the same two thoughts on repeat. *You lied. I love you. You lied. I love you.*

"You lied to me," I state again.

He nods solemnly.

"You hid things from me."

Again, he nods but doesn't speak.

"I don't even know you."

He reaches down and lifts up my hand, pressing it against his chest as he speaks.

"You know me, better than anyone in the world, I'd reckon. Everything was real, Vi. Everything. I misled you about my job-"

"You lied!" I correct.

He nods but doesn't speak. I feel my resolve weakening as I look into those pain drenched eyes, like me being upset with him physically hurts him

"Don't you have anything else to say?" I ask. "Maybe you want to grovel some more or something?"

Declan leans in until his nose brushes against mine as he closes his eyes.

"I love you," he says again.

My stomach does a cartwheel as my heart flip flops inside my chest.

"Not good enough," I grumble.

"I love you," he says again, pressing a feather light kiss against my cheek.

"So?" I counter as my arms move on their own accord to wrap around his neck.

I feel his mouth slightly smile against my skin as he nuzzles against my ear before placing another kiss there.

"I love you."

"You said that already," I say, not being able to keep my small smile locked down this time.

Pulling away, Declan looks down at me, all traces of humor gone as he looks down at me seriously.

"I'm so in love with you, Vi."

That right there is the nail in my coffin. He officially did me in with a single sentence. Smooth talking asshole.

"I love you too," I say softly.

Relief seems to wash across his face as he leans in to kiss me, but I put my hand up to his chest to stop him. "But I'm still pissed at you. I want the whole truth about everything and if you ever lie to me again, I will let Mindi put your balls into a blender."

He lets out a rough chuckle and gives me a breathtaking smile as he nods.

"What do you wanna know? I'll tell you anything. I don't want there to be any secrets between us."

I scoot over on the bed and lean back, gently patting the space next to me. Declan gives me a small smile before settling in next to me and lifting his arm. I lay my head on his chest as he holds me tightly.

"Is your name really Declan Daniels?"

He laughs softly. "Yes. Technically, Declan Derek Daniels."

"Damn. Guess your parents picked a letter and stuck with it, huh?"

"Seems like it," he smirks.

"And what do you do, just so we are clear?"

"I'm the starting Middle Linebacker for the Seattle Crusaders. I was drafted into the NFL my junior year of college by the Knoxville Bucks where I played for the last six years."

"And where do you live?"

He laughs like I'm being ridiculous. "Seattle, currently. In a condo downtown. I do have a house back in Knoxville, if you remember," he teases. "I'm having yours and Tuck's things shipped up here since I didn't have time to stop by the house."

I frown. "You didn't?"

He shakes his head. "I went straight to the airport. Once I knew you were leaving Tennessee, I came after you guys."

My heart flips at that. Fuck, why does this man have such a hold on me?

"Don't break my heart," I whisper.

"I promise," he says seriously. I lean in to kiss him again but this time he pulls away. "Don't break mine. You could do it easier than you think."

I run my fingers through his thick hair as my heart beats hard. It does something to me to hear that I have the same ability over him that he has over me. It makes me feel equal, like we are partners. My relationship with Chad was so one sided, so surface level. It only makes me realize what Declan and I have is so much more.

"I promise," I whisper against his lips.

He grabs my hips and pulls me on top to straddle him. I giggle at how easily he can swing me around. Declan grips the nape of my neck and pulls me down for a brutal kiss. I sigh against his lips as I begin trailing my fingers across his chest. He quickly pulls off his shirt with one hand, displaying his perfectly toned chest.

Without breaking the kiss, Declan grabs my top and whips it off of me so fast it damn near makes my head spin. We both make quick work of our pants, and he reaches into his pocket and rolls on a condom in record time.

He takes my hips in his large hands and lifts me up before lining me just above him and slowly lowers me down until we are flush. He lets out a satisfied groan and I whimper under my breath. I'm still getting used to how big he is, and this angle definitely makes it deeper. He seems to sense my discomfort and gives me a moment to adjust which I'm grateful for.

Soon, I start slowly rolling my hips against him as his hands tighten around me. I rest my hands on his wide shoulders as I pick up my pace, losing myself in his hypnotic eyes. Something is different tonight. It quickly becomes less about fucking and more about making love.

Normally, Declan fills the room with his dirty words and desires for what he wants to do to me. Not tonight, though. Tonight is about so much more, and I think we can both feel it. This right here is the start of my undoing. I can feel it deep in my soul.

He lets me control the pace, which is also a first, and I take full advantage of grinding my clit against his pelvis with every thrust. Declan lets out a rough groan of approval as I come almost all the way off him before sinking myself down again. Reaching behind myself, my fingers brush the back of his balls, making his hips buck in response. I smile down at him as I do it again, causing him to let out a groan.

I continue riding him while I massage his balls, and if his face is anything to go off, I'd say he doesn't have long. Chasing my own orgasm, I pick up the pace and ride him faster and harder than before. My thighs begin to tremble, and I feel my pussy begin to tighten.

"Vi," Declan groans almost reverently as he reaches a hand up to cup my face, his thumb brushing against my lower lip. My tongue darts out to it before I wrap my lips around him. I feel his toes curl against the bed. Without any warning, Declan lifts his hips up hard once and it seems to be all I need to fall apart.

My orgasm crashes over me fast and rough, and it takes me a moment to remember that I need to muffle my screams as I ride out the waves of pleasure. Declan is cursing as he follows right behind me, his legs shaking and chest heaving as his cock throbs inside of me. I collapse on top of his sweaty chest and take the moment to catch my breath. He brushes some of my hair off my forehead and kisses it gently.

"You are it for me, Vi," he whispers as his arms come around, to hold me in place.

Same.

Chapter Thirty-Four

Declan

I slowly stroke my fingers across Vi's creamy skin. She's so smooth, delicate. At least she seems like it, anyone who truly knows her knows that Vi is tough as nails and strong as hell. It feels good to have everything out in the open between us even if the last few weeks hurt like fucking hell.

Chad fucking Brownstone really is Tucker's father. My head is still reeling from that one. I mean, don't get me wrong. I can totally see him bailing on a chick that he knocked up, but it blows me away that Vi ever gave him the time of day, let alone dated him. She is way out of his league. Hell, she is way out of my league. I'm just thankful that she doesn't realize it yet.

I don't care who Tucker's real father is. There is a difference between fathering a child and being a dad. Chad doesn't have what it takes, nor does he deserve to be a dad to a great kid like Tuck. Not so sure I deserve it either, but I would like to think that one day I might.

I know the things I'm thinking are crazy, and the things that I'm feeling are even crazier, but I really don't give a shit. I've always been known to be kind of hardheaded. People have always labeled me as the strong silent type, and it's pretty accurate. I stay withdrawn making sure not to get too close to most, but I'm over that. I want Vi and Tuck for as long as they will have me.

I still can't fucking believe that she said she loves me too. I mean, maybe she said it because she felt like she had to. It's awkward when someone says that they love you and you don't say it back, right? For some reason, though, maybe my own delusion, I don't think that was it.

She gently stirs in my arms and lets out a peaceful sigh. I kiss her temple which rouses her enough to crack an eye open. She blinks quickly a few times before she wipes the sleep from her eyes.

"Morning," she rasps.

"Good morning, gorgeous."

"You been watching me, creeper?"

I shrug. "Only for a little."

"If you weren't so handsome that would be pretty off-putting," she says as she flings the blankets off and reaches for the cotton robe that is hanging next to her side of the bed.

"Good thing I'm handsome, I guess," I grin as I sit up.

"Mhmm."

She leans in to place a quick kiss before she walks out of her room and into the bathroom. After we made up last night, we went out to the kitchen and started making dinner. Vi got Tuck from his room, and when he saw me, he gave me the widest smile I've ever seen. I didn't realize until that moment how much I missed him. He jumped into my arms, and I scooped him up before carrying him through the apartment.

The night was spent with Tuck and I rough housing while Vi made dinner. I offered to help but she said it was help enough to keep Tuck entertained. I was going to head home when Vi offered to let me stay the night. I was surprised as hell but definitely wasn't going to argue.

When I step out of the room, I make my way down the hall to start a pot of coffee when I hear small footsteps down the hall, and I look over to see Tucker rub his eyes and look up at me. His little hazel eyes light up, and he smiles. I don't know how I missed it before but now that I know I see it, Tuck looks like a mini Chad. They have the same eyes, same hair, hell, even some of the same facial features. Doesn't make me love him any less, though.

"Declan! Did you and Mommy have another sleepover?" Tuck smiles.

I freeze, not sure how to answer his question when Vi pads into the room. Her wet hair drips onto her cotton t-shirt, and I can't help but admire how fucking beautiful she looks all the time.

"Yes, he did. That's okay right, sweetie?" She asks him.

"Uh huh! I wish he could spend the night every night."

My eyes find Vi's, and she gives me a small smile while she answers him.

"Maybe someday, Tuck."

My heart leaps at her insinuation. All she would have to do is say the word, and I'd have them moved out of this place in a minute. Maybe I'm getting a little ahead of myself, though. Twenty four hours ago I wasn't even sure that we were still together or if we would ever get back together. So, I push down my excitement about the idea and turn to face Tuck.

"Wanna get breakfast, big man?" I ask.

He jumps up and down and high fives me in excitement before Vi interrupts him.

"Sorry guys. I gotta get Tucker to daycare. Maybe another time."

We both frown as we look at her.

"But, Mommy, I want chocolate chip pancakes!" Tucker whines.

She sighs heavily and gives me an accusing glare. I hold my hands up in mock surrender as she shakes her head at me.

"I know, sweetie. But Mommy has to get to work, and Auntie Mindi is busy today."

"How about I take him for breakfast and then I can drop him off at daycare before I head to practice?"

"Practice?" Tucker asks with his head cocked to the side slightly.

"Oh, yeah. Declan, do you want to tell Tucker what your job is?" She asks with a raised eyebrow.

I nod and crouch down in front of him. Tucker looks at me intently and his serious expression makes me grin, he is too damn cute.

"I'm a professional football player."

His eyes round as he looks back and forth between his mama and me, like he is checking to see if I am messing with him.

"Really? Are you on TV?"

"Every Sunday during the season. A few Mondays too," I smile.

"That is so cool!" He bounces. "Can I come to a game? Please, please, pleaseeee?"

I ruffle his messy hair as I stand and laugh. "You better come to every home game. I have a feeling you're going to be my good luck charm."

Tucker beams at me, and I see Vi smiling as she watches us.

"That goes for you too," I smirk.

She continues to smile, but it doesn't quite reach her eyes. I didn't think about how anytime she ever comes to one of my games she will also be coming to one of Chad's games. Based on her reaction to him last night, I have a feeling their relationship was much more complicated than I had originally thought. I hope that him being there wouldn't stop her and Tuck from coming out to watch me play, but if it does, I'll get over it.

"Alright, sweetie. Go get dressed, and you and Declan can go have breakfast," Vi says with a soft smile.

Tucker pumps his arm in the air in celebration and races off to his bedroom. Vi chuckles as she looks at me and shrugs. I take a step closer to her and pull her into me.

"I promise to get him nice and sugared up before daycare."

"Great," she murmurs sarcastically.

I kiss the tip of her nose before I grin and lower my mouth to hers. Her head arches up to me, and I take full advantage. My hands lift to grip her head on either side as my tongue sweeps across hers teasingly. Fuck. I could devour this woman whole, and it still wouldn't be enough.

When we break apart, I rest my forehead against hers as I whisper to her softly.

"Are we okay?"

She pulls back and looks at me for a moment before she nods and leans on her toes to brush her lips across mine once more. I swear I could kiss her every minute of every day forever and never get tired of it. Vi sighs and steps away from me to grab her purse off the counter.

"Well, I got to get going. Thank you for taking Tucker to breakfast, in case you couldn't tell he is really excited. You are sweet."

"No problem. Maybe I can bring dinner over tonight?"

A small smile crosses her lips as she nods. I grin as I watch her head for the door. I swear I'm not a naturally smiley person, but ever since I met Vi Nielson, it's like I can't stop.

"Oh, and make sure to bring a bag. We are gonna have another 'sleepover,'" she winks before stepping out of the apartment and closing the door.

Can't fucking wait.

Only a minute after Vi has left, Tucker comes bounding out of his room in a pair of basketball shorts and a red t-shirt.

"Look, Declan! I look like a football player!" He beams.

I chuckle and nod, not having the heart to tell him that I think he's got the wrong sport.

"How about I get you a real jersey sometime, big man?"

"You can do that?" He asks excitedly.

"Of course. But I have one rule, you have to wear my number."

"Okay!"

I grin and high five him before we slip on his shoes. I help him into the brand-new car seat I bought for him and buckle him up before I fire the truck up. After realizing what a bitch they are to install, I thought it was best to just buy one and leave it until he doesn't need it anymore. I should be terrified at how quickly I'm slipping into this stepdad-like role, but fear isn't the first emotion that comes to mind.

We pull up to the diner Vi works at and Tucker chooses a booth in the back. Since it's Tuesday, it isn't overly busy but there are a few curious looks at me as I walk in, but not much else. True to his word, Tucker orders chocolate chip pancakes. I'm able to talk him into eating some eggs and sausage by telling him that he won't grow up big if he doesn't. He looked at me worriedly and practically inhaled his plate. That trick used to work for me as a kid too.

As I eat my omelet, I look around and take a better look at the diner. It's a pretty clean place but obviously very dated. There is only one waitress and that seems to be the norm since Vi is always the only one on shifts at nights as well. The place is small enough to get away with it, but I'm sure the staff would appreciate a second set of hands. I wish she didn't have to work two jobs. I hate seeing how exhausted she is every day. To know she is killing herself just to survive because Brownstone isn't man enough to own his responsibilities has me gripping my fork a little too tightly.

Technically, Vi doesn't need to work two jobs, though. If I'm being real, she doesn't need to work at all. I have more than enough to take care of her and Tuck, with a few million to spare. I know Vi pretty well by now, though, and there is no way in hell I'll risk the wrath that would follow a proposition like that. It's nice to finally be with a woman that couldn't care less how many zeros are in my bank account, but I wish she would let me help out, at least a little.

"Who is Chad?" Tucker asks out of the blue.

I freeze mid-bite and stare at him like a deer caught in headlights. There is no way in hell this is my conversation to have with Tucker. Unfortunately, the kid is as smart as a whip and persistent as hell, he won't let it go until I give him something.

"Just an acquaintance." His eyebrows furrow in question and I let out a short laugh and scrub my jaw. "Someone I know," I amend.

"And he is mommy's awaktence too?"

I smirk at his attempt and give him a soft nod as I take a sip of my coffee.

"Why do you ask, big man?"

"Mommy was crying when we got back from our trip. I heard her tell Auntie Mindi that she saw Chad and then she cried more. Is he mean?"

A pang of guilt runs through me. I've been beating myself up for weeks but hearing how even Tuck witnessed the fallout from my fuck up cuts deep. And is Chad Brownstone mean? Fuck yeah, he is. A mean fucking bastard, not that I'm going to say that out loud for little ears.

"Ah, don't worry about him, big man. Your mama is just fine."

"Okay," he shrugs as he takes one more bite before he pushes his plate back. "Can we go to the park?"

I smile and check my phone. "Sorry, Tuck. I gotta get to practice. Another day though, okay?"

He pouts but nods. I grab the bill and pay before we head out the door and get loaded up into the truck. I don't have any trouble dropping Tuck off. I guess Vi already called the woman and let her know I would be dropping him off. Just before he turns to run into the room, he wraps his little arms around one of my legs and squeezes.

"Bye, Declan. Thanks for the pancakes!" He calls out as he runs up to one of the other kids.

I rub my chest softly, trying to soothe the tight grip that just wrapped around my heart. This kid is something else. I wish I could spend the day with him instead of heading to practice. He seems to have already forgotten about me, though as he plays tag with some other little boy. Smiling, I turn around and head to my truck.

Before getting to the field, I stop by my place to grab my gear. I also grab a couple of things to take over to Vi's since I fully plan to take her up on her offer. There is something about her place that feels so comfortable, homelike. Sure, it is tiny as shit and pretty much the opposite of my place, but that's its charm, I guess. It's lived in, warm.

Not sure if my preference is the space itself or the people who live there, my bet is on the latter.

Chapter Thirty-Five

Vi

I'm walking up the stairs to my apartment after work, my feet dragging with every step. Today kicked my ass but knowing that Declan already picked Tucker up from daycare and they are both waiting inside for me has me moving faster than my feet want me to.

I'm up to the second level when a hand suddenly slaps my ass. I whip around startled to see a sleazy guy in his late thirties grinning at me with yellow teeth. His head is shaved, and his skin has pock marks all over.

"Hey, sexy. How's it going?" He asks as he takes a menacing step towards me.

I quickly back up but end up bumping into the railing behind me. As discreetly as I can, I slip my hand into my purse and wrap my hands around my pepper spray.

"Fuck off," I spit as I dart to the side in attempt to pass him.

"I'd rather fuck you, girly," he says as he grabs the arm that's in my purse.

Before I can pull the spray out, the guy is being ripped away from me before tumbling down the stairs. As soon as he lands on the bottom step, a huge guy stands over him and begins to rain down blow after blow. The sound of bone crunching echoes through the stairwell. I'm pretty sure I just saw a couple of yellow teeth bounce across the pavement from that last hit.

"Don't you dare touch her! You piece of fucking shit!" A familiar voice roars.

I lean to the side to see that it's Declan, who is beating the ever loving shit out of this guy. Instead of running up the stairs to my apartment, I rush down them to meet him at the bottom.

Declan kicks the guy in the stomach earning a pained groan from him. He kneels down in front of the guy and lowers his voice to a deathly level.

"If I ever see you here again, I *will* kill you."

Declan stands up and sees me standing just a few feet away from him. A dangerous look is plastered across his face that actually makes me take a step back before it softens. He makes short work of closing the distance between us as he wraps me up into his arms.

"Are you okay, baby?" He asks with concern pouring out of his eyes.

I nod and blow out a breath. "Yeah, fine. I was just about to mace his ass when you came."

"Come on," he nods as he picks up his duffle bag and what looks like a grocery bag before wrapping his arm around me.

We walk up the stairs in silence and open the front door. Muffled sounds of Tucker playing in his room hang in the air as we step inside. Declan shuts the door as I slip my purple shoes off and set my purse down. I let out a sigh and turn around to see Declan staring at me with his arms crossed.

"What?" I ask, already exhausted with this conversation.

"This place isn't safe. I don't feel comfortable with you and Tuck being here, especially by yourself most days."

I roll my eyes and cross my arms. "Okay, well what would you like me to do about it?"

"Move," he says simply.

I scoff as I move into the kitchen to get a glass of a water.

"How, Declan? Get a third job? There are no more hours in the day. I barely get six hours of sleep every night and work almost seven days a week while being a single mother. I can hardly afford this place as is and the only reason I can is because it's in a shit area!"

"Let me help you then."

My glare is filled with so much poison the tension in Declan's shoulders tighten as he blows out a rough breath before running a hand down his face.

"Vi, do you have any idea what could have happened to you if I wasn't there? What about if Tuck was with you? I just care about you guys, baby. I will go crazy never knowing if you are safe or not," he says as he takes a step closer and holds my hips in his hands.

I shrug and look away. He isn't wrong. I don't want to tell him that this isn't the first sleaze ball that has fucked with me since we moved here. It's cheap though, and the apartments are decent. That's more than you can say for most of Seattle. The housing market is so crazy expensive around here, what we really should do is move somewhere more affordable. But moving out of state or even moving in general costs more money that we do not have. Without meaning to, I break down and start sobbing.

Declan's arms wrap around me as he pulls me into his chest. He shushes me and rocks us back and forth gently. When I catch my breath, I look up at him through watery eyes.

"I try so fucking hard, Declan. I'm doing the best I can, but it isn't enough. That guy could have hurt me. He could have hurt Tuck! What kind of mother am I that I let myself or my son get put in a situation like that?" I sob.

Tears free fall, and I'm sure that my makeup is absolutely trashed by now, but I couldn't honestly care less at this point. Declan swipes each tear away with his thumbs as he gives me a sad look.

"Baby, you do so good. I admire the hell out of you, but you are human. I know you wanna take on the world but sometimes it's okay to ask for some help, especially from those that love you," he says the last part softly as he continues brushing his thumb against my cheek comfortingly.

I give him a watery smile before I look down. "I've never wanted to need someone else again."

"Everyone needs somebody, baby. Let me be that person for you."

I sigh. "I can't afford to move, and I won't take your money. I don't know what my options are."

Declan rests his forehead against mine for a moment before he speaks.

"You could always move in with me."

My brows dip as I look up at him. "You want me to move in with you?"

He smiles and nods. "And Tuck, of course. I have three bedrooms, plenty of room for both of you. Or we could get a house. Tuck could finally have that backyard he talks about. Whatever you want."

I shake my head. "We are not buying a house together. Are you crazy? We have been together for a little over three months!"

"Well, of course we won't buy a house together. I'll buy the house, and you and Tuck will live with me and make it home."

Oh my god, his words sound like they are from a damn hallmark card. How can this giant football superstar of a man be this sweet?

"No, Declan. I just can't. What if we don't work out? Then Tuck and I are left homeless and on the street?"

He takes a step back, hurt rippling across his face.

"Ouch."

"No, I don't mean it like that," I say as I reach for him. "I just...Tuck needs stability, you know?"

"Baby, I'm rock solid. I ain't going anywhere, ever. I know what I'm asking for. I know it's a lot to ask of you. So, this is me trying to convince you. When you're ready, say the word and I'll have you moved in an hour."

I let out a little laugh and shake my head. "You are so crazy."

A satisfied smile blooms across his face and he grips my face tightly as he kisses me.

"For my girl? Definitely."

Tuck comes out shortly after our little argument, and Declan makes some kind of sausage casserole with grits in it. It was surprisingly good. I asked him where he learned to make it and he said that his mom taught him. A man who is sweet, sexy and can cook? Sign me up. We all cram in at the dining table and spend the night playing board games and laughing as Tuck tells us elaborate stories that are one hundred percent made up but entertaining all the same.

We quickly fall into an easy routine of me going to work, Declan to practice and Tuck to daycare. On the days that Declan is done with football before I get off work, he picks Tuck up from the daycare, and they almost always either go to the park or get ice cream, or both. He spoils us rotten, but I can't deny that we eat every second of it up, especially Tuck.

It almost feels like we are a little family of three lately. Tuck loves having a man around to roughhouse with and talk about sports with, since Tuck's newest obsession is football. I love talking all night with Declan after multiple orgasms and then falling asleep in his arms every night.

Declan hasn't stayed the night at his house in over two weeks now, and we are enjoying every moment of time together that we can get. Tomorrow is Tuck's birthday, and I am having a bit of a rough day, mainly because all I have been able to get him is a football and a new board game. I haven't been able to get any dinner shifts lately because they hired someone full time that is able to work more flexible hours than I can. I try not to take it personally. They have done a lot for me that I am so grateful for, but it breaks my heart that I can't do something special for Tuck. I can't throw him a huge birthday party like he deserves.

"Do you think it's enough?" I ask nervously as I look at the two gifts I just finished wrapping and the cake that is freshly iced.

Declan smiles and nods. "I think he is going to love it, baby."

I feel his soft lips brush against my shoulder as his arms wrap around my middle.

"Well, I had an idea. A surprise for Tuck's birthday, and for you too, I guess."

"If it's a house, I'm going to punch you in the face," I scold.

A rough chuckle rumbles from his chest as he shakes his head. He has been relentless these last few weeks about us moving in together. He has been non-stop trying to 'convince me' to move in with him ever since. I just think it's too soon even if I secretly want to take that step with him.

"Not a house, I promise. Do you trust me?"

"I suppose," I say skeptically as I turn around to place a quick kiss against his lips.

He smiles. "I know you have tomorrow off. Any chance you could get off Sunday too?"

My face falls slightly and I shrug. "Yeah, actually. The new girl, Sarah, picked up my shift."

Declan smiles and kisses the tip of my nose before he gets on his phone.

"Perfect. Pack a bag for you and Tuck. Just for one night. Warm clothes."

Then he disappears down to the bathroom while he works some kind of magic no doubt.

In the middle of the night, Declan nudges me awake in bed.

"Hey, baby. Time to get up," he whispers as he places a soft kiss on my cheek.

"Are you high? It's..." I blink blearily as I glance up at my alarm clock. "4:30 in the morning. Go back to sleep."

"Can't do that. We have a special birthday surprise to give Tuck."

I lean up on my elbows and look at him a little more clearly. "Are you out of your mind, Declan Daniels?"

"Completely," he agrees as he bends down to kiss me.

I grumble for a few more moments before I get myself as ready as I can for 4AM. Declan said to pack and dress for warm weather, so I toss on a pair of jean shorts and a t-shirt before I slide on a sweatshirt for now. I grab my bags and go to wake up Tuck but find Declan already in his room scooping him up in his arms quietly. My heart flutters at seeing him cradle my baby so carefully. He winks at me when he sees me creeping on them.

We all walk out into the living room, and I notice that the cake and presents that I set out for him are missing. I give a panicked look and Declan comes closer to me to whisper into my ear, "They are in the truck already."

"Where are we going?" I ask.

He shrugs like he doesn't have a clue which causes me to scoff as I lock the place up and follow after them. The car ride is a quick one and soon we are pulling up to a private air strip with a huge plane sitting in the middle of the runway. I furrow my brows as I look over at Declan.

"We're flying? Again?"

Declan shrugs. "Guess we're about to find out."

I shove him and chuckle as he hops out of his side and opens my door before going back to grab Tuck. A few people come up to us and start grabbing our bags and taking them to the plane. Declan leads the way up the stairs and onto the plane.

"I can't believe that Tuck hasn't woken up yet," I say as Declan walks over to me and a stewardess comes over and wordlessly hands me a coffee. I take a sip and my eyes widen as I look over to Declan.

"You have Caramel Iced Coffee with extra caramel and whip ready for you on your private plane?"

"Only for you, baby girl," he smiles as he brushes his lips against mine and settles next to me.

"Seriously, Declan. Where are we going?"

He looks back down the hallway to see that Tucker is still passed out. A mischievous grin spreads across his face as he looks at me like a giddy little boy.

"Where would Tuck choose to go, if he could go anywhere in the world?"

"I don't know. Disneyland probably."

Declan has a proud smile and nods.

My eyes widen and I gasp as I swat his arm. "Shut up! You did not. Are you serious?"

"Think he will like it?" He asks.

"Like it? He is going to lose his fucking mind!"

I jump into his arms and cover him with kisses. Declan chuckles as his hands rest on my ass.

"You trying to become a member of the mile high club, Vi Nielson?" He rumbles lowly.

"With the man who whisked me and my son away for his birthday to Disneyland? You bet your ass," I smirk.

Heat fills his eyes and a thrill runs through me as his hold on me tightens.

Chapter Thirty-Six
Declan

"**Y**ou're gonna have to be quiet, baby. We can't have anyone knowing you're getting fucked thirty thousand feet in the air, can we?"

Vi bites her lower lip and shakes her head, lust swimming heavily in those beautiful hazel eyes.

"Good girl. Now, get those tiny shorts off before I shred them to pieces."

Excitement flashes across her face before she makes quick work of shimmying the shorts off and tossing them to the side as I pull my shorts down enough to get my dick out. She tosses a nervous glance over her shoulder where the cockpit is, but I steal her attention by pulling her down until she is straddling me. I waste no time pushing inside of her, and I swear to god my eyes roll into the back of my head at the feel of her.

Shit.

She is like fucking heaven. Her pussy is so warm and wet, it feels even better than usual.

"Condom," she gasps as I thrust up into her.

That explains it. I pause for a moment, waiting for her eyes to meet mine.

"I can stop. I have them packed in our bags up front."

Vi seems to think on it for a moment before she wraps a hand behind my neck and starts thrusting her hips.

"Fuck it," she murmurs before she presses her lips against mine.

That's all the permission I need. I adjust my hold on her hips so that I can lift her up farther and pull her down faster. When I'm inside this woman, I fucking drown in her, apparently, I also lose my damn mind because I never forget to wrap it up. That is step one. But I can't deny that fucking Vi raw has a new sense of need racing through me. The desperate need to take her, claim her, mark her as mine forever.

My pace quickens as thoughts of filling Vi up with my cum runs through my head. Fuck. Why the hell is that so hot?

"Oh god," she whimpers. "Just like that. Oh fuck, please, please, don't stop."

"No need to beg, baby. I couldn't stop if my life depended on it."

"Good!" She moans a little too loud.

I bring up a hand to cover her mouth as I continue pounding away at her.

"Shh, stay quiet, baby girl. We don't wanna get caught, do we?"

Her eyes roll into the back of her head, making me think maybe she likes the idea of being caught.

Interesting.

Turning my head to look behind me, I see that the bedroom door is still shut, and the seats are hiding us well from Tuck if he comes out, the same can't be said for the cockpit if anyone decided to come check on us. I think that's what has Vi all excited, though.

"Stand up, baby," I say before pressing my lips to hers briefly.

She furrows her brows nervously, but does as I ask as she stands in front of me. I stand up next, pulling my shorts all the way down before I spin her away from me and push on her lower back until she is bent over the seats in front of us.

"Hold on tight," I say before I push inside her once more.

I snake one of my hands around to cover her mouth as I begin fucking her deep and fast before I lower my lips to the shell of her ear.

"You see that, baby. If you look just ahead, that's the hallway that the stewardess could come out to check on us any moment now. She could see you getting bent over this seat like a dirty girl getting fucked from behind. Does that turn you on, Vi? You like the thought of getting caught?"

Her pussy throbs against my cock, practically squeezing the life out of me in response. I let out a rough chuckle, and I angle my hips a little lower before thrusting up, keeping them angled forward as I speak.

"That's so fucking hot. I love the idea of someone coming in here and seeing me claim what's mine. Because you are, Vi Nielson. All. Fucking. Mine," I say, punctuating my words with deeper and deeper thrusts.

She is practically laying against my chest as I lift her feet off the ground and fuck her into the air like a fuck doll. With the way her eyes are rolled into the back of her head, I'd say she is fucking loving it too.

Vi's pussy begins to constrict, her muffled moans growing louder against my hand as she cums all over my cock. My balls begin to draw up as I feel the familiar tingling sensation at the base of my spine. I quicken my thrusts as she begins to milk the orgasm right out of me. I let out a rough groan as I feel my cock twitch and pulse inside her, coating her walls with my cum.

"Fuck," I grit through clenched teeth. "That's a good girl. Take my cum. Every. Fucking. Drop!"

She moans her agreement as she nods rapidly. When my orgasm has faded, I slowly lower Vi onto her feet before carefully pulling out of her. When I do, I lower myself down to see my cum start to run from her sweet pussy and down her thigh.

That was reckless. I know that she's on birth control, but it's never a hundred percent effective. There is a slim chance that Vi could get pregnant. Fuck. Just the idea of that has blood rushing back to my cock and my finger trailing up her thigh, collecting the cum that has ran down her leg and shoving it back inside her.

Right where it belongs.

Looking up, I see Vi staring at me with parted lips and wide eyes. But instead of seeing panic or disgust, all I see is lust and want. Slowly, I stand and lower my face until my lips ghost just over hers. Her eyes flick over my face before she closes the distance between us and melts against me. Fuck. Have I said yet that this girl is going to be my undoing? Because I think I'm already undone.

When we break apart, Vi slips her shorts on and tells me that she is going to clean herself up, much to my annoyance. Now that I know what her pretty pussy looks like filled with my cum, I'd like to make it a permanent thing, but she disagreed. We'll revisit the topic later.

After I pulled my shorts back up and settled back in my seat, it didn't take long for Vi to come out of the bathroom and nuzzle up in my lap. I kissed the top of her head and wrapped her in my arms just as the stewardess came out to check on us. There was a slight blush to her cheeks, indicating that Vi and I were not nearly as quiet or stealthy as we thought.

Vi hid her face in the crook of my neck, and I just laughed it off. A few minutes later, a rustling sound comes from the back of the plane before a door opens. Both of our eyes light up with excitement as we scramble up to go get Tuck.

"Mommy?" Tuck asks hazily as he blinks rapidly, looking around. "Where are we?"

"Happy Birthday, baby!" Vi smiles, leaning down to kiss his cheek.

I stand behind Vi, smiling at Tuck as I nod.

"Happy birthday, big man."

"Thanks! Where are we?" He asks, confused.

"Well, Declan has a little surprise for you, sweetie," Vi says.

"We do," I correct quickly as I place a hand on her shoulder.

Vi shoots me a look, and I give her one right back. She needs to get the memo already, what's mine is hers and she better just get used to it.

"How would you feel about spending your birthday in Disneyland?" Vi says with a barely repressed smile.

"REALLY?!" Tuck screeches.

We chuckle as Vi and I nod. That seems to be all it takes to wake Tuck up fully. He springs up onto the bed and begins jumping up and down excitedly, screaming. "OH MY GOSH! OH MY GOSH! THANK YOU, THANK YOU!"

Before I know it, Tuck has launched himself into my arms and wraps his little arms around my neck. I'm a little surprised before I smile and wrap my arms tightly around him. There goes that tightness in my chest again. Before I met these two, I never knew that my heart could feel so damn full.

"You're so welcome, buddy," I say as I hold him tight.

When he pulls away, I gently set him down and he runs off, bouncing around the plane excitedly. I glance to the side to see Vi staring at me with a soft look on her face and a huge smile. She crosses the distance between us quickly and wraps her arms around my neck as she lifts up onto her toes and kisses me.

"I love you," she whispers softly.

I grin as I brush a piece of hair out of her face before cupping her jaw.

"I love you more."

CHAPTER THIRTY-SEVEN

VI

The rest of the flight went by quickly. Tuck decided he wanted to have his birthday cake for breakfast, and who was I to deny the birthday boy? We sang happy birthday to him as well as the flight crew which was really sweet. He opened his presents from me and was especially excited for the football. Declan also pulled out a few secret presents. A pair of Mickey Mouse ears and a Crusaders jersey with Declan's number. Tucker insisted on wearing the ears and the jersey immediately and bounced in his seat excitedly as we started to descend.

We were ushered into a car that was waiting for us and immediately taken to the front gates of Disneyland. Of course, Tuck was losing his mind with excitement, while Declan and I watched with big smiles on our faces.

The entire day was spent with Tuck pulling my arm out of its socket, while Declan trailed after us. We rode any and every ride in sight as well as took pictures with all of the characters. I thought Tuck was going to die when Mickey Mouse gave him a hug.

After a long day filled with too many treats and too many purchases from the park gift shops, at Declan's insistence, we are walking through the park towards the Disneyland Resort Hotel where Declan made our reservations. Tuck is crashed out, hanging onto Declan's neck, as we make our way through the giant suite and into one of the bedrooms. He sets Tuck down on the bed and pulls the blankets over him before leaning down and kissing his forehead.

When he looks up, he sees that I am watching him and a flush fills his cheeks.

"Ah, uh, sorry. I probably shouldn't have done that."

I smile softly and shake my head.

"No, it's okay. He loves you. You make him really happy."

"I love the little guy too," he whispers as he glances down at him before looking back at me.

Quietly, we make our way out of his room and into the master. After getting changed into pajamas, we get settled under the covers as Declan curls his arm around me.

"Thank you so much, for everything. This is all too much. You have officially spoiled him rotten. Both of us, really."

Declan smirks and brushes his lips against mine slowly.

"That was the master plan. Did you have fun today?"

I nod softly. "This has to be one of the best days of my life. I know it was by far the best day of Tuck's."

His blue eyes sparkle as he looks down at me, love and adoration shining brightly in them. "It was the second best of my life."

I quirk my head curiously. "What was the first?"

"Our first date. I was so fucking nervous, though. I thought I was gonna explode, and then I saw you and...that was all she wrote."

A wide smile spreads across my face as I kiss him one more time before settling back into his arms. He tightens them around me and kisses the top of my head like he wouldn't want to be anywhere else in the world.

The next day we spent another full day at Disneyland before we got on Declan's plane and headed home. I still can't believe my boyfriend has his own plane. Technically, he said it was the foundation's plane, but he is part owner of the foundation, so same difference.

We have been spending as much time together as possible lately since we know things are about to get really hectic. Their first pre-season game is this weekend, and we haven't really talked about how we will deal with the time apart. It isn't like he will be gone forever, but he will be traveling a lot now that the season is starting, so we will definitely be seeing less and less of each other.

I'm putting away the groceries when a knock comes from the front door. When I open it, I find a smiling Judy waiting in the doorway. She has still been acting weird lately. Every time I drop by, she says that she is busy or has an appointment. When I badgered her enough about what her original visit with the doctor was about, she finally relented and said it was just some high blood pressure, and now they have her on the right medicine. I'm really thankful it wasn't anything more serious because I don't know what I would do without her. I am not stupid though, I know she is keeping something from me, I'm just not quite sure what.

"Hey, Sweet Pea," Judy greets.

"Hey, Judy. What's up? Is everything okay?"

"Oh, didn't you know?" She says as she steps in the apartment and shuts the door. "I'm babysitting tonight."

"Oh yeah? Am I going somewhere or something?" I laugh.

"Yep!"

"Wait, what?"

"Mhmm. I am under explicit instructions to come over at 6:30 to babysit and make sure you wear that pretty dress that you wore to Declan's work party."

I cross my arms and raise my brows. "And where will I go in said dress?"

"Guess you will have to find out," she hums.

I laugh and I nod and head to my bedroom to get changed. Maybe I should have put up more of a fight. I usually hate being left out of plans, but I am way too excited to care right now. I have learned that Declan loves surprises and always seems to have a trick up his sleeve. I really shouldn't be surprised by anything at this point.

The dress slides on perfectly, and I pair it with my sparkly silver heels. I decide to go for an updo this time to really show off the dramatic back. My makeup is a lot simpler than when Suzannah did it, but considering I go most days with just a couple brushes of mascara, I would say it's an improvement.

Almost as soon as I'm finished, a knock comes at my bedroom door. I smile and open it to reveal Declan wearing a black suit with a white dress shirt and a red tie that matches my dress perfectly. In his hands is a beautiful bouquet of dahlias and hydrangeas. Every time he gets me flowers it is always a mix of the two, and I can't describe how much I love that he remembers my favorite flowers.

"Hey, beautiful. I was wondering if you wanna go on a date with me?"

"Wow. I would really love to, but I already have plans as you can see."

I gesture to myself, and he nods in appreciation as his eyes travel the length of my body. When they come up to meet mine, he gives me a challenging look that holds a small trace of amusement.

"Cancel them, you'll have more fun with me."

"Is that promise?" I muse.

"That is a guarantee, baby," he winks.

I laugh lightly and grab his lapels to pull him down against my lips. "Alright. But I don't put out on the first date," I tease.

"Well good thing this is like our twentieth," he says as he swats my ass.

I giggle as I take the flowers from him before slipping my arm through his as we walk down the hallway. When we reach the living room, Judy starts hooting at us.

"Whoa, look at you two. You guys look like you stepped out of a magazine. I tell you what, you two are going to make some beautiful babies one day."

"Mommy is having a baby?" Tucker asks.

I shout, "No!" at the same time Declan says, "Not yet."

My scowl finds Declan, and he doesn't look the least bit ashamed. Great, can't wait to explain that one to Tuck.

"Where are you kids off to?" Judy asks as she waggles her eyebrows.

"Just a night on the town," Declan says with an easy smile.

"Alright, well, have fun. Tuck and I have a hot date with Mickey and Minnie Mouse."

A laugh bubbles out of my chest, and I bend down to kiss Tuck's head. "Be good for Grandma Judy, sweetie. We will be home later."

"Okay," Tuck sings as he runs around the room.

We say our goodbyes before Declan walks me out the door with a hand resting on my lower back. He helps me up into his truck not missing the chance to squeeze my ass before walking around to his side.

"So where are we going?" I ask with an amused smirk.

"I was thinking we could have a nice dinner, just the two of us. Honestly, I just wanted to see you in this knockout dress again so whatever you want." My stomach grumbles audibly and we both chuckle. "Alright, dinner it is," he says as he puts the truck in drive.

Declan pulls up to a nice seafood restaurant that overlooks the water. When we step inside the lights are dimmed with candlelit tables around the room. The walls are a deep red, and the floors are an onyx-colored tile.

"I feel like I'm not rich enough to be in a place like this," I whisper as we are taken to our private table in the back.

"You aren't. But I am, so we're good," he teases.

I swat at him as he pulls out my seat. "Jerk."

He chuckles softly before ordering a bottle of wine for us. I scan through the menu and feel completely stumped as to what to get. They don't list any prices so that tells you just how outrageously priced everything probably is.

I decide to go with the shrimp scampi, and Declan orders the lobster tail. Once the waitress leaves, Declan takes my hand across the table and gives me a soft smile.

"So, what is the occasion?" I ask.

"Do we need an occasion to go on a date?"

"No, but I have a feeling there is more going on," I say with a raised eyebrow.

He tries to bite down a guilty smile as his thumb stokes the back of my hand.

"Well, I was hoping this would butter you up a bit." He pauses for a minute before he continues. "My parents are coming to town for my first game of the season. I would really like it if you and Tuck would come to my game."

My smile falls, and I pull my hand away from him as I sit back into my chair. I bite my lip as I think it over. I know Tuck would love to go. Honestly, I would really love to go to see Declan do what he does best and be there for him. Football is such a huge part of his life, and I want to support him. But I know who else will be there, and as much as I don't want to let him hold any power over me anymore, the idea of seeing him again makes me sick to my stomach.

"Before you say anything, you guys will have box seats, and you will be with my parents. I just, I would really like knowing my favorite people are in the stands watching me, cheering me on. But if it makes you too uncomfortable with Brownstone being there, I understand. I just don't want him to affect our relationship. Just because he's your past doesn't mean he needs to be dictating your future."

"You're right," I say softly.

"I am?" He asks, confused. Guess he was expecting more of a fight.

"Yeah. I have spent way too much time being upset about Chad. He is a blip from my past. The only good thing that came from that was Tuck, but there is no point in giving him a second more of my energy."

Declan smiles and reaches out to touch my hands again. "I agree. So, you'll come?"

I grin and nod before I lean across the table and kiss him probably a little too passionately for a swanky place like this. I can't help it, though. The man looks like a Greek God and is the biggest sweetheart that has ever lived. I'm so in love with him, and it scares the living shit out of me, but I have also never been so happy in my whole life.

Chapter Thirty-Eight

Vi

My hands are white knuckling the steering wheel as I pull into the designated parking area Declan told me to park in. He gave me this fancy pass that has me parked just outside of the back entrance of the stadium. We went over where to go and how to get to the family and friends' box that Tucker and I will be sitting in for the game. I told him I was starting to feel insulted that he felt the need to draw me a map and go over everything in such detail, but really, I thought it was cute.

Declan is really excited that we are coming to his game and so are we, especially Tuck. I glance back to see him bouncing excitedly in his seat, wearing his number fifty six jersey with Daniels scrawled across the back. He has hardly taken it off since Declan gave it to him. I'm just thankful he let me wash it before today's game.

"Alright, Tuck. You ready?" I ask.

"Yes!" He screeches.

I chuckle and get him out of his seat before taking his hand and walking across the road to enter the stadium. Some security staff stop us until we flash our fancy tickets at them, then they very helpfully point us in the right direction.

I glance down at my green Converse and grimace. Maybe I should have opted for something a little nicer. I could have thrown on a pair of flats or sandals or at least my black or white pair of Converse. I mean, I know I've already met Rodney and Suzannah, but I left in kind of a bad way. I don't know how much Declan told them, and I'm not really sure how to navigate all of this. Ah, shit. Now I'm nervous.

Just as we round the corner to make our way up to the private boxes, I notice Rodney, who honestly looks like what I picture Declan to look like in thirty years. Next to him is an excitable Suzannah, who starts pointing at Tuck and me as she bounces up and down clapping. She waves at us, and before I can even do anything in return, she is running towards us.

When she reaches us, she instantly wraps her arms around me and hugs me like she is trying to crack a rib. I awkwardly pat her back before she pulls away.

"Oh, my goodness! It's so good to see you again, sweetheart. I thought my knucklehead son was going to run off the best thing that ever happened to him," she says as she pulls away before looking at Tucker.

"I mean two best things!" She smiles as she scoops Tucker up into a hug.

"Hi, Nana!" He greets excitedly.

We all chuckle as Rodney steps over and gives me a hug and quick kiss on the cheek.

"I'm sorry for the part we played in it, darlin'. Truth be told, I didn't think Suzannah had it in her to play along. I thought for sure she was going to spill it all to you when y'all were at the spa."

"Lord knows I wanted to," Suzannah says with an eye roll.

I smile at both of them and nod. "Thank you, it's okay. We're good, better, even."

We make our way to the private boxes before Rodney opens a door allowing us all to file in. When we step inside, I look around and see that we are the only ones in here. The space is large with two rows of plush seats, a fully stocked bar in the back and two tables filled with food. Tucker immediately takes off running towards the large glass window that overlooks the stadium, pressing his face up against it like that will get him closer.

"Tucker!" I scold. "Don't touch the glass."

He steps back but only an inch or so. Rodney laughs as he comes up next to Tucker and squats down to his level as he starts pointing things out to him. Suzannah squeezes my hand.

"Don't worry about him, sweetheart. Let him play."

"I just don't want him to distract others when the game starts."

"Oh, there won't be anyone else. This is our private box."

My eyebrows raise as I glance around the room. "Oh, wow. It's very nice."

She smiles before she makes her way to the bar and pours two glasses of wine.

"We wanna try to come to every home game he has, and of course, any games he plays in Knoxville. You don't wanna sit in a room filled with the players' wives. They are catty and fake and vicious as hell, trust me."

I nod. Yeah, I don't think I could see myself getting along with women like that. Seb's wife seemed nice though, and I loved Nikki in college, but maybe they are the exception.

"Well, thank you both for letting us join. This is Tuck's first game, so he is really excited."

She smiles and nods as she hands me one of the wine glasses.

"Of course! Is this your first game as well?"

"First professional. I practically lived in the University stadium when I was in college."

"Oh really? So, you used to be a big football fan then?" She fishes with a curious look.

Okay, so clearly Declan didn't tell them everything.

My smile tightens as I shrug. "I guess so. One of my best friends from college is on the Crusaders actually, Slater Santos."

"Oh, I just adore him! He is such a cutie pie. He and Declan have been closer than fleas on a dog's back since college. Then Slater had to transfer up here to take care of-"

"His mom," I finish with a sad nod. "Do you know how she is? I haven't seen her in years."

"As far as I know, she's doing great. Been in remission for a few years, I think."

I smile at that. I always loved Slater's mom.

"That's so good to hear."

"It is. I'm glad the boys are all back together, Sebastian too. It makes dealing with some of the others tolerable for Declan."

"Oh? Does he have trouble with some of the guys?" I ask.

Declan and I haven't really talked about football too much yet, so this is news to me.

"Just one that he has told me about. I hear the quarterback is a bit of a pain."

Rodney scoffs as he walks by us to pour a scotch. "More than a pain. That kid is a grade A asshole," he stops and looks up to make sure Tucker is out of earshot before continuing. "Boy thinks he's un-touchable. He's talented, I'll give him that, but there is always someone bigger and better. His time will come. The coaches will drop him in a hot second because of his attitude as soon as he stops winning them championships."

I bite back a smirk as they perfectly depict Chad. He wasn't always like that. He was a little obnoxious and cocky in college, but he was a really good player, so it was well earned. But back then, he could still hangout in my dorm room and watch movies all night and be perfectly content. Once NFL teams started taking an interest in him, his ego inflated, and he thought he was better than everyone around him. Then when he was drafted, he wanted to break-up. I told him about Tucker, and… it didn't go well. Apparently, he only got worse with time.

"I'm so glad Declan has a good head on his shoulders. He has never let this lifestyle get in the way of what matters most. He is a good one, you know. Once he opens up enough to someone, he will love them forever," she says pointedly to me.

I smile and nod my agreement. That is exactly how Declan is. He is quiet and a bit reserved at times, but that man loves Tucker and me fiercely. You can see it plain as day.

The game starts soon after, and when Declan jogs out onto the field, Tucker goes crazy, shouting and cheering. I think he believes that if he yells loud enough, then Declan will hear him. They are playing the Boston Hawks, who Rodney tells me are a pretty formidable team, but they don't seem to be on their game tonight because the Crusaders have already scored two touchdowns in the first quarter.

Just before halftime, the Hawks snap the ball, and the quarterback looks around for an opening when Declan sacks him hard. The crowd is a mixture of groans and cheers. Declan jumps up and looks right at our box, even though I'm sure he can't see us. The jumbotron camera pans to him as he beats his chest a couple of times and points to what feels like is right at me. I wave like an idiot even though I know I probably look like a tiny ant up here.

"Did you see that! Declan waved at me!" Tucker shouts excitedly.

All of us chuckle softly as we watch Tucker bounce around cheering and shouting. I try to get him to calm down a little, but Rodney and

Suzannah tell me that he is fine. Once half-time starts the score is 14-0 as the teams disappear into the tunnel.

"How about we get some snacks, Tuck?" Rodney asks.

"Can we have nachos? Declan said you have to eat nachos at a football game, or you ain't doing it right."

I do my best to smother my laughter at Tucker's bad impersonation of Declan's accent. Rodney laughs too as he nods at Tuck.

"We could probably go scrounge some up if that's okay with you, Vi?"

"Tuck, you hate nachos. You never take more than one bite. Just eat something here," I argue with a sigh.

"Mommy, I'm not gonna get big like Declan if I don't eat like him," he whines.

I can't help but snort as I roll my eyes. My son idolizes that man a little too much. Sighing, I dig into my purse for some money, but Rodney shoos at me before putting his hand on Tuck's shoulder and steering him out into the hallway where a food stand is conveniently located.

Suzannah and I are sitting in the plush chairs when she turns to me.

"So," she draws out softly.

I cock a questioning brow at her because I've already been around her enough to know that she always has something to say.

"Sooo?"

She huffs and rolls her eyes before smiling. "I'm really sorry for how things turned out, sweetheart. Honestly, as soon as Declan told me that he hadn't told you his career, I told him he was an idiot. Bless his heart, he is a man, though, and as you know, most men are idiots a majority of the time."

I laugh and shrug. "It's okay, Suzannah. I appreciate it, but I'm glad that it's out there and we talked. And I'll deny it if you ever tell Declan, but I'm glad that he did what he did. Even though I hate that he lied to me, I wouldn't have given him the time of day if it hadn't worked out like that."

Her brows furrow as she leans into me closer. "But why, sweetheart?"

I bite my lower lip, contemplating how much I feel comfortable to reveal.

"Tucker's dad...he was a football player. It didn't end well between us, and I guess, in my head, I thought that if I stayed far away from athletes, I wouldn't be in that situation again."

Her face is sympathetic as she nods and pats my knee. Before we can say more, the door opens and Rodney and Tucker walk in, arms brimmed with snacks and treats. It's a funny sight, seeing this giant of a man trail after a bouncy five-year-old with a slushie, pretzel and nachos in his hands.

"Looks like you bought out the whole concession stand," I tease.

Rodney winks at me and Tuck shakes his head. "No, we left enough for other people. Look, Mommy! I got a fun cake!"

"A fun cake?" I question as he shows me the fried powdered sugar dough.

"Funnel cake," Rodney corrects.

"Yeah, that!" Tuck says.

I laugh and sigh. "Okay, well don't forget we are going to dinner after this, sweetie. Don't fill up on fun cake."

"Okay," Tucker agrees.

I shake my head knowing that I'm only wasting my breath. Tucker will most definitely not be eating at dinner tonight, but he looks way too happy for me to tell him no.

The teams come back on the field, and the game resumes quickly. The Hawks start to catch up, but the Crusader's defense continues to dominate. Declan ends up sacking the quarterback seven more times. Each time he hits his chest and points to our box.

During the game, Rodney loses his mind with each sack. Apparently, the league record for the most sacks in a game by one player is seven, and Declan has just become the new league record holder with his eight sacks.

"That's my boy!" Rodney booms as he claps loudly.

Suzannah bounces excitely and Tuck runs victory laps around the room as the clock runs out. The final score is 31-9, and the whole stadium erupts in cheers. The teams slowly make their way into the tunnel as Rodney and Suzannah gather their things up. I grab Tuck and my purse as we all make our way out the doors.

Rodney walks ahead of us, and we all link arms or hands, so we don't get separated in the crowds. Instead of following the flow, Rodney takes a weird turn, and we start heading down a set of stairs.

"Where are we going?" I ask.

"To go see Declan! This is the fastest way to the locker room. We'll wait for him in the hall."

My stomach drops and dread seeps in. I peek back at Tucker who is blissfully ignorant as we continue walking through the stadium. Chad has never seen Tucker and vice versa. Will he recognize him? I have to admit they bear a strong resemblance. Tuck has his eyes. Even some of the faces he makes reminds me of a young Chad.

I know I just told Declan that I'm not going to let Chad dictate my future, but that was when I thought I wouldn't have to directly face him again. Declan doesn't understand that Chad Brownstone is a living nightmare to me. Still, I don't want Declan's parents to think that there is something wrong, and I don't want to let Declan down. I decide to swallow my unease and lift my chin a little higher, mentally preparing myself for worst case scenarios.

Chapter Thirty-Nine

Declan

"Mr. Daniels, you just broke the record for most sacks in a game by one player. How do you feel right now?" The reporter asks as she thrusts the microphone into my face.

"Really good. The whole game was a team effort, and I feel really blessed to be a part of it."

She nods and smiles. "And what about your new celebration you did after every sack? Who was that to?"

Now I smile as I answer truthfully. "My family."

"Does that family include the woman that has been photographed with you lately?" She pushes.

"Could be," I muse before I gesture that the interview is over.

She sighs but nods as she turns and chases after Slater. I barely got dressed from my shower before the reporters started cornering me. I get it. I just broke a league record, and I'm riding a major high right now, but I'm too anxious knowing that my girl and my big guy are in the parking lot waiting for me.

Mine. They are definitely mine and calling them my family felt damn good. Granted, I was also referencing my folks too, but that isn't who I had in mind after each time I tackled the QB.

I pictured Tucker's proud grin and Vi's big smile. My biggest motivator, though? Picturing the Hawks' QB as Brownstone. I would love nothing more than to drill him into the ground. Even before I met Vi, I couldn't stand the guy. Now, I fucking hate him. I shake my anger off and latch on to my excitement as I make my way out of the locker room. I hope my mama wasn't overbearing. Who am I kidding, I know she was. But I know Vi is tough so hopefully Mama hasn't sent her running for the hills just yet.

When I turn the corner, I see Vi and Tuck standing across the hall from the locker room with my mama and dad behind them. Despite Vi's effort to hold Tuck back she is no match for his excitement. He comes tearing after me and jumps into my arms. I catch him mid-air and spin him around, earning an excited laugh.

"Hey, big man! Did you like the game?"

"Uh huh! You were so good! You jumped on that little guy so many times. I screamed really loud. Did you hear me?"

My eyes crinkle as I smile at him. "You bet I did. Why do you think I played so well?"

His proud smile clenches my heart, and I give him a hug before I go to set him down. Just as Tuck stands up a hand clasps my shoulder from behind. I turn around to see the last person I would prefer.

"Daniels, nice work today," Brownstone says, like paying a compliment to someone physically pains him.

I give him a short nod as I push Tuck slightly behind me. Not sure why I feel like I need to protect him from Chad, I just do.

"Thanks, you too."

He nods before his eyes flick down to Tuck.

"Who's this?" He nods. "I didn't know you had a kid."

"He isn't my daddy. He's my mommy's boyfriend," Tuck corrects.

I've never wanted Tucker to be quiet before, but right now, I really wish he would just fade into the background. Chad looks down at him before he looks up and sees Vi standing a few feet away. Vi steps quickly over to Tucker and grabs his hand, pulling him to stand behind her. Chad's eyes flick back and forth between Tucker and Vi several times before a look of realization passes across his face. He opens his mouth to say something but closes it quickly and shakes his head.

"See you around," he says to me, though his eyes never leave Vi.

The look he gives her doesn't sit well with me, and I see goosebumps breakout across Vi's skin as her eyes follow him. Once he steps out of the hallway, her shoulders instantly loosen. I bring my arm around her neck and pull her in for a tight hug. She melts into me and slips her arms around my waist.

"I got you, baby," I whisper into her ear.

She nods before she pulls back and smiles. "You did so good. You were absolutely incredible."

"Thanks. I told you that you guys would be my good luck charms," I wink.

She smiles and leans up to place a soft kiss on my lips that ends way too quickly for my liking. Then, I look over to see my mama and dad watching us questioningly. Guess they didn't miss the weird Chad interaction.

Mama shakes it off and produces a huge smile as she walks up and wraps her arms around me before kissing my cheek.

"I'm so proud of you, baby!" She beams.

"Thanks, Mama."

She grabs Vi's arm as Vi holds Tuck's hand, and they start heading toward the parking lot. My dad clasps his hand on my shoulder as we follow after them.

"You kicked ass, son!" Dad bellows proudly.

"Just doing what you taught me."

"No way. You had a fire under your ass like I've never seen before. You broke a record today. Don't be so modest."

I laugh and nod. "Well, thank you, I appreciate it. I feel pretty damn good."

He nods before he lowers his voice.

"So, what was all that with Brownstone?"

My eyes find Vi about twenty feet ahead of us, far enough to not be able to hear us. I look at my dad and shrug, trying to play it off even though I know he is too smart for that.

"They have a history," I say as I nod towards Vi. "Brownstone is Tuck's..."

Dad cringes and blows out a breath. "Brownstone has a problem with you two?"

I nod. "I think so. He came to me with some bullshit story about how she is crazy and to watch my back after he saw us together."

"Well, that's a tough one. This is your team and being with your QB's ex could cause you problems for the rest of your career."

"I know," I nod.

"But that girl," he says as he points to Vi. "She could be the rest of your life. If it comes down to it, the choice should be easy."

Not even a fucking contest. Dad squeezes my shoulder once more and we catch up to the girls and Tuck. My parents hop into their rental, and I ride with Vi and Tuck as we head to a nice steak house that I made reservations at.

"So, did my mama work you over too much?" I ask.

Vi looks over to me and nods. "A little but she is sweet. I like her a lot."

I grin. "Yeah, she is a bit much, but she means well. She was so excited when I told her that you were coming. I thought she was gonna hop a plane early."

She laughs and nods.

"I like your mom too, Declan!" Tucker chimes in. "And your dad bought me lots of snacks."

"What was your favorite snack?" I ask with a smile on my face.

"Oh, the fun cake!"

I give Vi a questioning look, and she shrugs. "He likes to call funnel cakes fun cakes."

"Yeah, because they're fun to eat!"

Tuck cracks me up. I laugh and nod. "Those are one of my favorites too, big man."

We pull up to the restaurant soon and are heading inside as Vi and I hold Tuck's hands and swing him through the parking lot. When we get to the maître d', he directs us to a table in the back where my parents are already seated. I pull out Vi's chair before sitting next to her. When I look up, I see my parents both watching us closely. My father with a smug grin, and my mother with an excited gleam in her eyes.

"So, how have things been, Dad?" I ask.

He nods as he takes a sip of his drink. "Good, busy as ever. We are looking for someone to help out with day-to-day operations full time, though."

My dad raises his eyebrows in suggestion. Nothing would make him happier than me retiring and coming to work for the foundation full time. Don't get me wrong, he is really proud of me, and he will tell you himself that his pro years are some of the best of his life, but it's a hard lifestyle sometimes and not long term by any means.

"You know I just signed a two-year contract," I remind him.

"I know, I know. I'm just saying you've had a nice long career. You're going to get burned out if you go for much longer, that is if you don't get injured first. Best to go out while you're on top."

"You are thinking of retiring?" Vi asks.

I shrug. "Maybe once my contract is over. Dad's right, I've had a good career. The travel can get to be a lot, and I have things that make me wanna stay in one place now," I say as I squeeze her thigh.

She smiles over her glass as a blush creeps up her neck. I hear my mother audibly *aw* at us as my father tries and fails to shush her. Tuck seems oblivious to what everyone else is talking about as he colors on the kid's menu.

We all order and talk about what my folks have been up to in Knoxville. Vi tells them about her jobs and how she hopes to open her own floral shop one day. The waiter takes away our dishes as my mama leans forward.

"Why not start your shop now, sweetheart?"

"Well, Seattle is pretty expensive. It's going to take me a while to start up my own business from scratch."

"Do you need an investor?" She asks.

I shoot a pointed look at my mama to drop it, but she isn't looking at me. Dad pats her leg to get her attention, but she isn't paying him any attention either. Vi flusters as she fiddles with the napkin in her lap.

"Oh, uh no. I'll get there, just takes time."

"Well, why wait? I've been looking for something to get involved in. I would love to invest in you, sweetheart."

"Mama," I warn.

"What?" She asks, irritated like I am the one stepping out of line.

I mouth at her to stop it, but she just rolls her eyes. She looks back at Vi who seems to be extremely uncomfortable. I put my hand on Vi's leg to show her that I'm on her side. My mama shrugs after a few moments as she takes a sip of her wine.

"Well, think about it at least?"

"Sure," Vi nods hesitantly. "That is very generous. Thank you."

My mama smiles sweetly at her before changing the subject and rambling on. After a few more minutes we all decide to head out for the night. My parents are staying at a hotel and then they are back on a plane tomorrow morning, so we say our goodbyes and promise to visit soon. They both tell me they are so proud of me and then both whisper to me how much they like Vi and Tuck. It makes me feel good to know that my family loves her as much as I do, not that their opinion could have changed that, though.

When we get to Vi's apartment, I look back to see Tuck is passed out in his car seat. Vi and I share a smile before I get out and scoop him up into my arms. He stirs slightly before he loops his arms around my neck and rests his head on my shoulder.

Vi walks ahead of us and unlocks the front door for me. I carry Tuck to his room and lay him in his bed as Vi comes in behind me. She pulls off his jeans but leaves him in his Daniels jersey. It makes me damn proud to see him wearing it.

I slip my arm over Vi's shoulder as we make our way out of his room and into hers. We both go through our typical nighttime routine before we settle into her bed. I can't remember the last time I slept at my condo, and I fucking love it. The place has always felt cold and empty. I don't miss it one bit.

"I don't know how I'm going to be able to sleep in hotel rooms this season when I know this is at home waiting for me," I murmur as I squeeze my arms that are wrapped around her.

"I'm sure you'll be just fine."

"Maybe my dad is right. If I made this my last season, then I wouldn't have to travel all around. I could be in this bed every single night," I say as I kiss the side of her head.

"Wouldn't you get penalized for breaking the contract?"

I shrug. "I would have to pay back some of the money from my signing bonus probably. It happens more often than you would think."

"Well, you shouldn't make a life changing decision based on the fact that you are bummed you have to sleep alone a handful of times a year."

"It's more than that. I like what we have going. I like that I know you and Tuck are here every night, that I don't go home to an empty house. I mean, I know it isn't like we are living together or anything but it kinda feels like we are, doesn't it?"

She nods. "We like having you here."

"Good, because you'd have a hard time getting rid of me now," I grin.

She chuckles and nuzzles into my chest before she closes her eyes and her breathing evens out. I place a kiss to her temple and whisper against her silky hair, "I'm gonna love you forever, baby."

Chapter Forty

Declan

It's Sunday. Game Day. We are in San Antonio ready to go up against the San Antonio Cobras, one of the top teams in the league, thanks to their star quarterback Trevor Michaels, who also happened to be a good friend of Slater, Seb, and mine in college. Well, maybe not Seb, but we won't get into that. This is one of the most exciting games of the year because we are so evenly matched with them. I should be pumped, excited, focused. Instead, all I can think about is what Vi and Tuck are up to.

Since It's Sunday, I'd bet anything Vi will probably make Tuck some chocolate chip pancakes after he begs her a million times and then they will watch that worn out Mickey Mouse DVD. Or she might find my present for Tucker that is a whole collection of DVDs I picked up online. Can't wait to catch hell over that one. Swear to god, never met a woman who hates being spoiled so much in my life. It's one of the things I love about her, even if it drives me batshit crazy some days.

Shit. I gotta stop thinking about her for five seconds and focus. We are receiving first so I line up in place as Trevor begins calling out players before he shouts, "Hike!" I barrel through the wall of linemen in front of me, keeping myself low enough to take them out and keep moving as I do. My legs stretch as I eat up the distance between me and one of my old best friends. He doesn't even see me coming, too busy reading the field to see where he is going to pitch the ball.

Nowhere, motherfucker.

Smiling behind my helmet, I plow into Trevor, taking him down to the ground hard. Being the good QB that he is, he manages to hold onto the ball through the tackle even if I can see stars spinning in his eyes.

"You good, Trey?" I laugh as I slowly stand up and offer a hand.

He blinks a few times before smirking himself.

"Fuck, Mikey. You can't do me like that. You got almost a hundred pounds on me. You could have fucked up my face, then how would I roll in pussy every night?"

I snort and shake my head. "You're Trevor Michaels, I'm sure you'd still roll in pussy, fucked up face or not."

"Oh, yeah," he smirks with a cocky wink before swaggering back to his team.

I love that guy, always will, but he's changed since college. When Seb and Erica got together, he fucking lost it, and he hasn't seemed to get it back since. Now he is just another notorious football playboy who is a little too full of himself, changes his women more than his sheets, and loves the attention that comes with being a professional QB1. He kinda cut everyone from his old life off once he got drafted his senior year, except Erica. Seb says that he still calls to check in on them sometimes, or should I say, her.

A few more plays go by, and the game is going much like how everyone predicted, they gain some yards, then so do we. They get a touchdown, so do we. I'm on the sidelines watching the game as Chad begins the play, stepping back to evaluate the field, he pitches it to Slater. The guy is one of the fastest running backs in the league, and he is proving it with the way he is moving right now. The throw is a little out of his reach but with a quick jump, Slater snatches the ball up and begins running again. He dodges a few Cobras before doing a spin around one guy like a fucking ballerina as he crosses over the line. Touchdown, in the most Slater way possible.

Slater begins doing his touchdown dance that really just involves him shaking his ass like he's in a rap video. We all give him shit for it, but the female fans I'm sure have nothing but good things to say about it. If it wasn't for Nikki, I have no doubt that Slater would be a huge heartbreaker still, just like in college.

Trev's O-line has really let him down today, mainly because this is the third time that I alone have sacked him today. Helping him to his feet, he shakes his head.

"Mikey, can you go do something else? Seriously." Trev scoffs before laughing self-deprecatingly.

"Trust me, Trev. I'd rather be somewhere else right now," I say as I jog off the field.

After one more play that ended in Seb taking the ball over sixty yards, the clock runs out with the score at 32-30. All of the Crusaders jump around and hype each other up while the Cobras look bummed. It's just the name of the game, though. Anyone can have an off day, and the game was damn close. If they tighten up that O-line, there is no way we would have won today.

Slater, Seb and me all made plans to meet up with Trev and grab some dinner and a drink. It's been too long. Dinner went by quick, but Slater had to bail soon after because Nikki called him screaming about her credit card being maxed out. Slater shook his head as he left, clapping our shoulders as he did.

Seb was the next to make his exit. Erica called because the twins are sick, and she is panicking all by herself back home. I didn't miss the way Trevor watched Seb walk away longingly, like he would do anything to be in his place. My heart hurts for the guy. He had Erica first, but he gave her up. Sometimes we have to live with our choices. I can promise, I'll never make a stupid fucking decision like that when it comes to Vi.

"Anything I can get you two gentlemen," a sultry voice asks to the side. I glance up to see that our waitress is practically standing against me as she leans in slightly, giving me a full view of her low-cut shirt. The excited gleam in her eye tells me that it isn't an accident, and she's more than ready to fulfill any request I might have. Unfortunately for her, nothing in the world sounds less appealing.

I do my best to remain polite but even I can hear the disdain in my tone.

"No, thank you. We'd appreciate privacy. Some space would be nice too," I say as I glance down to where her body is practically pressed against my arm.

Embarrassment quickly colors her cheeks as she shuffles back a few steps and drops her eyes to the ground. Trevor barks out a laugh as he shakes his head.

"Aw, baby girl, don't worry about him. He's no fun anyways. Make sure you're off when I'm ready to leave, and I'll show you a night you won't ever forget," he says as his eyes roam over her body, licking his lips slowly as he seems to be appraising her.

Some of her excitement returns as she stands up a little straighter, pushing her tits out a little more, and nodding quickly before hurrying past us to the back. Trevor's eyes follow her ass as she goes, causing me to roll my eyes as I glance down at my phone. I've been discreetly texting Vi throughout dinner. I tried to resist and focus on catching up with my friends, but I couldn't help myself. Trevor takes another sip of his drink before cocking his head at me.

"So, who is she?"

"Who's who?" I ask.

"The girl you've been pretending not to text all night," he says as he gestures to the phone in my lap.

Shrugging my shoulders, I set my phone onto the table as I take a sip of my beer.

"My girl," I say simply. I'll never get old of how that feels rolling off the tongue. Not as good as Vi rolling off my tongue, but still.

Trev raises a brow as he leans forward.

"No shit? Mikey settled down? What's her name?"

"Vi. I met her when I moved out to Seattle. She's fucking amazing man. And her son, Tucker, he is-"

"Whoa, whoa, whoa. She has a kid?"

I nod. "Yeah, he just turned five."

Trev's eyes are practically bugged out of his head as he looks at me like I just grew a third head.

"And you're just like, okay with that?"

I furrow my brows. "What do you mean?"

"Well, shit, man. All I'm saying is that sounds like a lot of fucking baggage. You're a football superstar, man. You could get any woman in this bar. You could get any woman in this country with a snap of your fingers. You want to trade that in for baby daddy drama and a woman who will no doubt drain your bank account before her and her kid skip to the next sucker?"

I bang my fist against the table, causing all of the plates and glasses to bounce. Trevor looks surprised but he shouldn't when he runs his mouth like a fucking idiot.

"Don't you fucking dare say another thing against my woman!" I bark. "You don't know what the hell you're talking about, Trev. So, I suggest you shut the fuck up. I love her, and if you talk any more shit, friend or not, I will beat the fucking piss out of you."

Instead of backpedaling like most would, he just shakes his head sorrily as he takes another sip of his drink.

"Love," he scoffs. "Hate to break it to you, Mikey, but love is bullshit. There will always be one person in a relationship that cares more than the other and then it's only a matter of time before the less interested person splits. Love is temporary, and it's a cruel bitch too."

I roll my eyes and shake my head.

"Like your love for Erica was so temporary?" I snap.

Trevor's eyes narrow at me slightly, but he doesn't say anything as I continue.

"Like you wouldn't drop everything, sell everything, get on your fucking knees and beg for Erica to be yours if you thought you stood a chance in hell against Seb?"

He rolls lips together but doesn't speak as he looks at me. Shaking my head, I stand up, throwing some cash on the table before pushing my seat back.

"You know, Trev, I know that you were hurt when they got together. But if you can't see how fucking perfect they are for each other, how in love they are, then you'll never be able to move on. And it's time, buddy. It's been nearly seven years. It's time to move on."

With that, I give him a stiff head nod and walk out of the restaurant, walking back to the hotel, which is just down the road as I pull out my phone and dial the one person that I know can turn my night around.

Smiling into the phone as she answers, I speak.

"Hey, baby."

Chapter Forty-One

Vi

The next few weeks pass by quickly. Unfortunately, Declan has had several away games and has been buried with practice and PT to keep himself in the best shape possible. I guess his position is a very physically demanding one, more so than others, so they have the team's PT specialist work with him regularly as a precautionary measure. Thankfully, we text nearly constantly, so it doesn't feel too bad.

Tucker's first day of kindergarten came and went. Declan called me the morning of and asked to talk to Tuck beforehand. When I tried to eavesdrop, Tuck told me to give him some privacy. I couldn't tell if I was offended or amused at his request for alone time with *my* boyfriend. I shed a few buckets worth of tears when I dropped him off, but I was so relieved when he came home and told me about all the friends he made and his really nice teacher.

Our home feels empty without Declan around. I know I'm guilty of being a little mopey since the last time he was able to make it over, but it isn't just me. Tuck asks me at least twice a day when we will see Declan again. My son has fallen in love, just like I have. I'm just so thankful that the man we fell for was waiting with open arms to catch us.

The Crusaders won the last three out of four games, and he is currently on his way back from South Carolina tonight. He promised that he would stop by after he dropped his bags off at his condo. I am hoping I can convince him to spend the night with me even if he does have to be up at four in the morning to start his day.

Right now, I'm busily making my famous meatloaf, which has become one of Declan's favorite meals. Even though he is supposed to be eating extremely lean and clean, he is constantly indulging with us whether it's a treat from the bakery or picking up some pizza. I have no idea how he keeps in such incredible shape while he continues to eat like a fourteen-year-old boy.

I check the clock for probably the fifteenth time tonight to see that it has only moved two minutes from the last time I checked. I audibly groan as I place the loaf pans into the oven and set the timer.

Just as I shut the oven door, a heavy knock sounds through the apartment. My stomach dips to the ground before sailing up to my chest. I bounce excitedly for a minute before I rush to answer the door. When I swing it open, the megawatt smile I have in place slides off and is quickly replaced with one of horror.

"Wh-what are you doing here?" I ask shakily.

Chad gives me a cocky smirk as he eats up the space between us and pushes his way into the apartment. I try to hold him at bay, but as always, he uses his sheer size to plow right through me. My hand rests on the open door, hoping I can somehow convince him to leave, and soon.

"Chad. You need to leave. Now," I order, my voice coming out more even this time.

His lips tip up and he gives me a look that tells me there is no chance in hell that he is leaving. Dread seeps in as my eyes scour the apartment. I need to call Declan or maybe the police. Tucker. Oh fuck, I need to get Tucker-

"Mommy?" Tucker's voice comes into the room as he looks at Chad warily.

Oh no.

"So, it's true," Chad says as his eyes flick back and forth between Tucker and me.

"Leave," I grit out through clenched teeth, hoping like hell he can't see the quivering in my jaw.

"Who are you?" Tucker asks.

"Chad," he says as he looks down at Tucker, seemingly assessing him. "What's your name?"

"Tucker," he says softly as he shuffles on his feet nervously.

"How old are you, Tucker?" He asks.

"Don't speak to my son!" I shout.

"Shut up, bitch!" Chad roars at me over his shoulder before turning back to face Tucker.

I abandon the door and rush past him to put myself in front of Tucker. Chad takes a menacing step towards me but seems to check himself.

"F-five," Tucker breathes softly behind me. His poor little body is quaking underneath my hands, obviously comprehending that this man in our apartment is not a friend.

"Hmm," Chad hums as his cold dead eyes lock on mine.

"Why are you here?" Tucker asks in a tone that I've never heard him use. It's almost like he is trying to be brave.

"Is it a crime to want to meet my son?" He asks with a sinister smile.

"Chad!" I seethe.

Tuck's eyebrows furrow as he looks around me at Chad. "Y-you're my daddy?"

"Looks like it," Chad shrugs.

I always wondered what Tucker's reaction would have been if he ever would have met his father. Would he be excited? Anxious? Upset? None of those reactions pass across Tucker's face, though. The one that does, surprises the hell out of me. Anger.

"I already have a daddy. Declan," he says proudly.

My heart twinges that he considers him to be his father figure. I know Declan would feel honored. But I know Chad all too well, and that was the worst possible thing Tuck could have said. Without hesitating, I grab Tucker's arm, quickly pulling him down the hallway with me before leading him into his door.

"Don't come out until I say, baby. Turn on the TV or something," I tell Tuck.

His wide hazel eyes look up to me in concern but unfortunately, I can't take the time to comfort him right now. I shut the door quickly and close my eyes before re-opening them, doing my best to shed the fear that has drilled its way down to my bones.

When I turn back to the living room, Chad's nostrils are flared, and his fists are balled at his sides. I slowly walk back into the room, while maintaining a healthy distance from him. My chin raises in faux confidence as my posture remains rigid.

"Leave or I will call the police and have you removed."

"You think you can have my kid and not tell me?" He snarls.

"You made it abundantly clear you didn't want a child. I did. You walked away from me, from us, and left me with more than a few parting marks, in case you don't remember."

He scoffs as he takes a step closer to me. Not wanting to look weak, I stand my ground. I can't let him know how truly terrified I am right now.

"Please, Violet. You always had a knack for theatrics. Don't try to pull me into your delusions."

"You beat the shit out of me, you stupid son of a bitch!" I seethe.

In my rage, I let my guard down for a moment too long, and before I can react, Chad shoves me with all of his strength to the ground. My hip catches the worst of it, sending a shooting pain through me. Slowly, like he has all the time in the world, Chad strolls over to me before bending down and grabbing a fistful of my hair, raising my face to meet his.

"Don't ever speak to me that way, you fucking whore. You were trying to trap me, ruin my career. You were nothing but a gold digging bitch!"

"You're a monster," I spit.

He gives me an evil smirk in response, one that I'm sure would make the devil himself shudder.

"I came here to talk. So, you better listen up. You will stay the fuck away from Declan Daniels. You will keep *our* son away from him too. I've already talked to my family's lawyers. They think they can spin this story to work in my favor, so here is how it's going to go," he fumes into my face.

"You got pregnant in college and never told me. We broke up when I was drafted, and I went off to play pro ball while you hid the knowledge of my own child from me for almost six years. Then when you started very casually dating a teammate of mine, I saw you and Travis and knew that he was mine."

"Tucker!" I interrupt. "His name is Tucker, you fucking asshole."

Chad's hold on my hair increases with a sharp yank as he continues.

"Then, we reconnected. Fell in love again and now we are one big fucking happy family. Coach has been all over my ass to settle down, or at least have the image of doing so. He's threatening to trade me if I don't do something to change my public image. This should work nicely. Any questions, Violet?" He sneers.

Despite the pain, I raise my chin so that I can look at him better. "And if I tell you to go to hell?"

Chad gives me that vile smirk again as he tilts his head to the side slightly as he leans in close, running his nose along the column of my neck before he speaks.

"Then, I'll take your precious son away from you. Let's be real, who will a court think is the more fit parent? A single mom working two jobs living in a rundown apartment in a nasty neighborhood? Or the well respected NFL player, who donates a few million every year to childrens' foundations and youth programs?"

Fear like I have never felt before overwhelms me. No one could possibly look at Chad and think he could be a better parent than me. No. He is bullshitting me. He doesn't want Tucker. He is just trying to manipulate me. Well, I'm done being manipulated by this asshole.

Shoving him as hard as I can, I manage to get a little distance between us until his grip tightens in my hair. I reach my hand up to his wrist and begin clawing and digging at him, and finally, he releases me before he stands and cradles his wrist.

"You stupid fucking cunt!" Chad roars as he glares down at me.

Suddenly, I hear the front door open and close as a dangerous air suddenly fills the room.

"What the hell are you doing here?" Declan asks.

I stand up quickly but don't rush to him, making sure I still keep myself in front of Tucker's door.

Chad turns to see Declan, looking him up and down before he turns back to me like he didn't even see him.

"I'll have a car come collect you two in the morning. If you don't come, then I'll take that as a sign that you want to go to court. Either way, I'll be seeing you *both* very soon."

With that, Chad turns to leave but doesn't get far when Declan grabs him by the throat and shoves him against the wall.

"What the *fuck* is that supposed to mean?" Declan practically growls.

To my surprise, Chad smirks even as I see Declan's hand tightening with every passing second.

"You'll see," he rasps with that evil fucking look in his eye.

"Just let him leave, please," I say.

My words crack at the end, and Declan must be able to hear the pain in them because he quickly releases Chad and steps to the side, glaring daggers at Chad until he is out the door. Declan quickly locks the door before crossing the room and wrapping me up in his arms. As soon as his warmth wraps around me, I fall apart.

I sob for what feels like hours before the door to my right opens.

"M-mommy?" Tucker asks shakily.

I look over to see his eyes filled with unshed tears and his lower lip quivering.

"Baby," I gasp as I drop to the ground and open my arms up for him.

Tucker runs for me and jumps into my arms as we both sob into each other.

"Don't let him take me, Mommy. I want to be with you," he cries.

My heart cracks at his words as I hold him tighter. He heard *everything*.

"Never, baby. You're my little guy. No one and nothing could keep Mommy away. You're safe, sweetie."

Suddenly, I feel thick arms wrap around us as Declan sits behind me and holds us both tight as he speaks roughly.

"Both of you are. I won't let anything happen to either of you."

I let out another choked sob as I nod and lean my head against his shoulder, still holding and rocking Tuck from side to side. Chad is fucking delusional if he thinks I will walk away from this man willingly; he is even crazier if he thinks he stands a chance in hell of taking my son away from me.

Chapter Forty-Two

Declan

I don't know how long we sat on the floor of Vi's apartment before the tears finally dried out. Once Vi and Tuck were able to calm down enough to speak, I told them that we were going to pack their bags and take them to my condo. They both agreed, and we quickly grabbed the essentials before getting out of there and driving over to my place.

I just put Tucker to bed in his new room. It's bare and plain, but we can do it up however he wants soon, because this is their home now. There is no chance in hell I'm gonna let them step foot back in that place. Not when anyone can have access to them.

Vi didn't tell me what was said between her and Chad, but it doesn't take a genius to figure it out. Based on Chad's words and Tucker's pleas, I know enough, but I need the full story. Chad wants to take Tucker from Vi. Fuck if I know why, but the why doesn't really matter. The son of a bitch isn't getting anywhere near my big man. I don't give a shit if Chad is his bio dad, that boy in there is all fucking mine.

Slowly, I step inside my room to find Vi sitting on the bed with her head in her hands. She's crying softly, and the sound alone shatters my fucking heart. Crouching down between her legs so she's gotta look at me, I tip her chin up softly, cupping her cheek and brushing away some of the fallen tears I speak.

"Baby, what happened? I'll fix this, whatever it is, I'll fix it. I just have to know how."

Vi blinks a few times before she blows out a choppy breath and swallows.

"Chad knocked on the door, I thought it was you, so I answered. He pushed his way inside and saw Tucker, put it together that he is his. Fucking told Tucker that he was his dad," she huffs before continuing.

"Tucker got...mad. I swear, I've never seen him so mad in all his life. He told Chad that he wasn't his father, that...well, that you were."

My chest seizes and my stomach flips at her words. What did I say? That kid is fucking mine.

"Chad got mad, so I put Tuck into his room. Then Chad told me he wanted me to break up with you. He thinks it makes him look bad that a teammate is with his ex and helping raise his son."

"It does, because he is a bad fucking guy," I scoff.

Vi nods. "I asked what would happen if I refused, and he said he w-would take Tuck. That the court would compare us and give Tuck to him. T-they wouldn't, right, Declan? They'd pick me, wouldn't they? The kids always stay with the mom unless it's something really b-bad, right? I-I'm not a bad mom. I try really hard. Th-hey won't take my baby from me, right?"

Anger rushes through me instantly. Are you fucking kidding me? What a fucking piece of shit! Who the hell threatens to take a woman's child away because he doesn't like that someone else stepped up. I'll kill the fucking bastard.

"No, baby," I insist steadily. "You're the best mama I know. No one is taking Tuck from you, and no one is taking you from me. If, and that's a big if because Chad Brownstone is a huge shit talker, he decides to take you to court, they will throw it out so fast."

"But I don't have the money like he does," Vi argues. "I can't afford fancy lawyers and-"

"I can, though. And I will. You will not lose Tucker. Do you understand me?"

Doubt flashes across her face, but I watch as it slowly starts to fade as she nods.

"Okay," she whispers.

I scoop Vi up into my arms and lay her down on the bed, pulling the blankets up over us. I can feel the moment she falls asleep. She needs it after the night she had. I was so excited to see her and Tuck after being gone for so long. I've been thinking about what I would do when I finally got back home to them, but tonight definitely didn't go as expected, not at all.

I don't know what Brownstone is trying to pull but I won't let him get away with this shit. He's hurt Vi and Tucker already enough to last a lifetime. Now that I'm here, no one will hurt them again. Especially not Chad fucking Brownstone.

Monday is a rest day but come Tuesday the team is having a light practice and I'm more than ready. Yesterday, I called my parents while Tucker was at school and Vi was at work. When I told them about what Chad threatened, my dad offered to fly out to Seattle and beat the shit out of Chad himself so that I won't lose my career over it. Then my mama offered to sneak Tuck out to Tennessee and hide him. I told her that as sweet as that is, it would not be looked at positively. She disagreed.

I park my truck and walk straight into the locker room with one person on my mind. When I round the corner, I see Chad standing there, laughing and bullshitting about god knows what. Not slowing down, I plow through the group of guys huddled around him as I step up to him until our noses brush. On instinct, Chad takes a step back until he hits the lockers before understanding flashes across his face.

"Have a nice rest day, Daniels?" He smirks.

"Stay the fuck away from them," I say lowly.

"No, I don't think I will. See, the thing is, that's my 'family'," he says using quotation marks with his hands. "If anyone should back off, I think it should be you. Pretty shitty to go after your QB's girl and son."

"Cut the shit!" I sneer as I take a step closer until our foreheads bump. "You and I both know you want fucking nothing to do with them. You wanna use them as a trophy, get Coach off your back, make sure you don't look like the piece of shit you are when your own teammate steps up where you should've. I don't know. I don't care either. They aren't some kind of prize that you can use to make the world think you aren't the shitty person you clearly are. Drop this bullshit or I will go after you and drag you through the fucking mud."

"Oh, yeah? What could you possibly do to me?" He laughs.

"Try me and find out," I promise, my stony expression unyielding.

"What's going on?" Slater asks as he pushes through the quickly building crowd.

"Nothing, Slate," Chad answers easily, keeping his eyes on me as he does. "Your boy here is just learning not to take things that aren't his."

"They aren't yours. Stay away from them!" I bark.

"Mikey," Slater says quietly as he grips my shoulder, attempting to pull me away, but I just shrug him off.

Chad gives me an amused look as he shakes his head.

"Not that I'm not thoroughly enjoying watching you make an ass out of yourself in front of the entire team, but it's done."

"Done? What the fuck do you mean done?"

Chad smirks at me as he speaks.

"I warned that bitch. I had a car sent to that shit hole yesterday. No one answered. I'd imagine she should be getting served," he pauses as he glances down at his watch. "Right about now."

My vision clouds over into a thick haze of red as I pull my head back and crack his nose with my forehead in one hit. Chad's nose explodes and sprays me and a few of the guys closest to us in the process. I rear my arm back to beat the shit out of this motherfucker when I feel a strong pair of arms wrap around me before literally dragging me backwards. I try to get out of the hold, but the grip only tightens.

"Calm the fuck down!" Sebastian barks as he continues yanking me backwards to the other side of the locker room as Slater follows with a half-amused smirk.

"I gotta say, I've been waiting for someone to hit that fucker for a long time, but you are definitely going to catch hell for that," Slater says.

"Like I give a fuck! Do you have any idea what is happening?" I roar.

"No," Sebastian says as he lets me go and shoves me against a bench before crossing his arms over his chest. "So, calm the fuck down and tell us."

My heart is practically beating out of my chest, and I can't seem to calm it down for the fucking life of me. It takes me several deep breaths before it evens out. Dropping my head into my hands, I shake it before looking back up at the guys.

"Chad's Tucker's father."

Sebastian's signature stoic look falls away as shock takes its place, and Slater's mouth literally hits the ground.

"Wait, what? That isn't possible. Violet and Chad broke up like..."

"Six years ago," I finish. "He knocked her up, and when she told him about it, he said that she was trying to trap him and dumped her."

Slater's shock quickly morphs to sadness.

"Why didn't she ever tell us? Nik and I tried to reach out to her for a while. She just...disappeared. We would have helped her. We would have...fuck, man."

"That's not all," I laugh bitterly. "Chad showed up at Vi's and told her that she needed to leave me and start playing house for his image. She told him to go to hell, and now he's gonna try to take Tucker from Vi."

"What? That's fucked up!" Slater says.

"I gotta get out of here, man. I need to go check on, Vi."

"Bro, you can't leave. The coaches are probably looking for you. Did you forget you just headbutted the fuck out of Chad? You're probably in deep shit."

"Then bailing out on practice shouldn't be a big deal," I say as I brush past the guys and head towards the exit.

"Daniels!" Coach Aberton shouts. "Get your fucking ass inside my office. Now!"

I don't respond, heading straight for the door. His voice keeps calling out to me, but he is the least of my concerns right now. I jump in my truck and head straight for Blooming-Deals, hoping like hell that Chad was bullshitting me. In my gut, though, I know he wasn't.

CHAPTER FORTY-THREE

VI

I've been trying not to think about the whole Chad incident. Declan's right, Chad is a huge shit talker, but when it comes down to it, will he really back it up? I don't think so. He doesn't want Tucker. He isn't that kind of guy, and after spending cumulatively fifteen minutes in his presence, I know that he hasn't changed since I've known him. If anything, he's worse.

I've been doing my best to just brush the whole thing to the side. Don't freak out unless there is a concrete reason to freak out, right? Right now, everything is just hypothetical threats. Like I said before, I will not let Chad Brownstone manipulate me ever again.

Once I finish up with a walk-in customer at the shop, I go to start working on the funeral order that is due tomorrow when the front door opens. A guy in his early twenties steps inside with a smile on his face.

"Hey, Violet Nielson?"

"Yeah?" I say curiously with a polite smile.

He nods as he pulls a manilla file folder up from his side and hands it to me.

"You've been served."

My smile stays frozen for a second before it slowly drops. The man is gone before I can even realize it, and when I flip open the folder, my stomach falls to the ground as an icy chill crawls up my spine. I stand stock still as my eyes trace over the words over and over again because I can't for the life of me understand them. Court summons. Chad Brownstone. Petitioning for *full* custody.

I can't breathe. I can't fucking breathe. My chest begins to heave as I desperately search for any oxygen in the room, but it's all gone. Every molecule of oxygen in this room has been sucked out, and I can't. Fucking. Breathe.

The sound of the door opening sounds through the shop, but I don't acknowledge it, I can't. I just stare at this piece of paper, and the signature from the devil himself at the bottom. This can't be happening. This can't be happening. He was supposed to be full of shit. It was supposed to be an empty threat.

Suddenly, two large hands cup my face and tilt me up until I meet the familiar golden amber gaze. His mouth is moving, but I can't hear his words. Everything is jumbled, and the only thing I seem to be able to hear in my head is full custody.

Full custody. Full custody. Full custody.

"Vi! Vi! Talk to me, baby!" Declan finally shouts.

"He actually did it," I croak with wide eyes.

Sympathy floods Declan's eyes, which tells me that he isn't nearly as caught off guard as I am about this.

"Listen to me, Vi."

"Full custody," I mumble. "He wants full custody."

"Vi!" Declan snaps.

I blink for a moment as I look at him, my eyes scanning over him frantically. He looks heartbroken but calm, not nearly as panicked and absolutely fucking terrified as I feel right now.

"Listen to me, he will not take Tucker. My sister is one of the best defense attorneys in New York. I've already called her, and she is packing her things right this second to be on a plane first thing tomorrow morning. You aren't alone in this. *No one* is taking your child from you, I promise."

His words don't do much to ease my fear, but it does loosen my panic a little. The panic of how I was going to come up with a lawyer, how I could possibly win something like this against someone like *him*. I don't have it in me to voice my gratitude, so instead, I just nod. Declan presses a chaste kiss against my forehead before lacing his fingers with mine.

"C'mon. Let's go home."

"I-I can't leave. It's the middle of the day."

The front door opens, and this time it's Margret. She gives me a pitying look as she walks past us without another word and into the back room. I glance up to Declan, who just nods as he begins ushering me out the door. I barely even have time to grab my purse before we are inside Declan's truck and heading to Tucker's school.

The rest of the day passes by in a blur. I pulled Tuck from school early, and we went back to Declan's condo and cuddled on the couch and ate ice cream for the rest of the night. Tucker asked what was wrong, but I can't even think about it without breaking down, let alone say it out loud. Despite the positive reassurances that Declan keeps giving me, a heavy dose of fear is alive and well inside of me, and no amount of comforting words eases that fear.

The next day, Margret insisted that I took the day off from work. Though I can't afford to miss a day at work, I also didn't have it in me to argue with her. The diner has pretty much all but fired me, so I found myself with an unusually free day. I wanted to keep Tucker home and hold him all day, but I knew that I had to send him to school. So, after I dropped him off with several hugs and kisses, I found myself driving around aimlessly in the city before I ended back up at Declan's condo.

I called Mindi on the drive and bawled my fucking eyes out. She's in the middle of a job in the Caribbean, but she promised me she would be up here for the court date, which is only two weeks away, December twenty third to be specific. What court handles custody cases during Christmas time?

When I step into the condo, I set my keys down on the kitchen island and make my way to the bedroom when a voice comes from the living room.

"You must be Vi."

I leap out of my skin as I whirl around to see a woman who looks to be in her early thirties with blonde hair and golden eyes. She is in an expensive looking pantsuit, and her hair is perfectly styled. She looks like she belongs on the cover of a business magazine.

"I am. Who are you?" I ask warily.

This has been one of the worst weeks of my life. I swear to god, if this woman says that she is Declan's wife or girlfriend or some bullshit, I will lose my shit.

"I'm Danielle Daniels, nice to meet you."

Danielle. Declan's sister. Definitely not a wife or girlfriend.

"Hi, crap. Sorry. I should have known. You look just like your mother, except for your eyes."

She smiles kindly and nods. "Yeah, all the kids got Daddy's eyes."

I nod and give her the best smile I can before an awkward silence descends over us. She seems to be patiently waiting me out, but I'm honestly not sure what to say. Seemingly out of patience, she cuts right to the chase.

"So, tell me everything you can about this Chad Brownstone."

She turns to her laptop case before opening it up and staring at me expectantly after only a minute or so. Gosh, right to it, I guess. Declan said his sister was a shark. I could use a shark in my corner right now. I feel more like a worm knowing that I'll be going up against Chad.

Slowly walking over to sit by her, I begin to tell her my entire story from the first day that I met Chad to the night that he left me bruised and bleeding on my dorm room floor. I feel a little uneasy telling her that part since I haven't told Declan about all of that. It's not something I like to talk about but if it helps us at all then I will tell the world.

Danielle remains completely professional and composed until I tell her about the injuries Chad left me with.

"Please tell me you went to the hospital?" She asks.

I shake my head.

"Filed a police report?"

I shake my head again.

Danielle blows out a breath as she shakes her head.

"Pictures?"

Glancing down at my lap I play with the edge of my shirt and shake my head.

"Well, shit. Scratch that part then. We'll have to go with another angle."

My head lifts. "Just because I didn't report him doesn't mean it didn't happen," I say softly.

She nods as she begins typing on her laptop.

"Very true but in the court's eyes, without proof of any kind, it's your word against his which will only end in finger pointing. It's not worth our time."

Shame like I haven't felt before burns through me. Maybe if I would have called the police or gone to the doctor none of this would be happening. I was scared, though. I didn't think anyone would believe golden boy Chad Brownstone would do something like that, and to be honest, I was embarrassed that I had fallen in love with such a monster. So, I buried it, I distanced myself from everyone except Mindi and tried to move on. Looking back, it seems that I made the wrong decision.

"I'm sorry," I whisper under my breath.

Danielle doesn't even look away from her screen as she continues typing.

"Don't be, it's in the past. Let's move forward."

Pausing for a moment, she glances up and sets the laptop to the side.

"Sorry, it's hard for me to turn work mode off sometimes. It's okay, Vi. After Dec called me, I did a little digging and Chad has been in trouble quite a bit over the last five years. He has DUI's, been nailed with possession on multiple occasions and even involved in a solicitation sting operation. Unfortunately, none of those charges ever came to much. Whether it was incompetent prosecutors or a lenient judge, he seems to have always slipped through the cracks with nothing more than some fines or community service. Probably at the help of his coach to tone things down so he doesn't get suspended.

"Let me tell you this, though. I can't sit here and promise you that things will work out, I can't promise that you have nothing to worry about. If you want false hope, then you need to go to my baby brother for that. I promise to always tell it like I see it. But I also want you to know something else, I do not lose."

Her honesty is strangely comforting. She is a little brash and serious, but it's honestly what I think I need. I know Declan thinks that he's helping when he acts like everything will be sunshine and rainbows, but I don't need false hope right now. I need to understand the situation I have found myself in and the realistic outcomes that are possible.

Clearing my throat, I nod at her as I give her a tight-lipped smile that feels more like a grimace.

"Thank you, I actually really appreciate that."

Danielle nods as she picks her laptop up and goes back to typing.

"I'm going to do everything in my power to not only make sure that you continue to have full custody of Tucker but also that Chad Brownstone won't be able to spit within one hundred yards of either of you ever again."

"That would be nice," I laugh hollowly.

Danielle smirks just as the front door opens. We both turn to see Declan stroll through the door, pausing when he sees us before smiling.

"Hey, baby. I didn't know you'd be home," he says as he walks over to me and places a kiss on top of my head.

"I'm doing well, thanks for asking. I'm not at all exhausted from the five AM flight I took to come out here. You're welcome, again," Danielle draws out sarcastically.

Declan chuckles before he walks over to her and messes up her hair.

"Yeah, yeah. Don't act like you did it for me. We both know mama would have kicked your ass six ways to Sunday if you didn't come. You should see her with Tucker. Total grandma mode."

Danielle smiles, probably the first genuine smile that I have seen from her as she nods.

"Good, lord knows she won't be getting a tiny gremlin out of me anytime soon."

"Or ever," Declan adds as he walks to the fridge to grab a protein shake.

"Preach," Danielle snorts as she finishes up on her laptop and shuts it, slipping it into her bag as she stands.

"I'm going to go get checked into my hotel. Vi, I'll be in touch soon. Little bro, always a pleasure."

Declan rolls his eyes and shakes his head at her.

"Mama and Dad are landing in a few hours. They wanna have dinner tonight," he calls out as Danielle makes her way to the elevator, not turning around as she speaks.

"It's nice to want things. Unfortunately, I have a custody battle to prepare for against a local celebrity vs a single mom with no evidence. I'm busy."

Pausing in the elevator doorway, she leans out to look at me, a suddenly sympathetic look spread across her face.

"Sorry, Vi. It's just been a week. Don't stress, let me do that, okay?"

I nod softly, and she gives me a stiff head nod before waving goodbye and stepping into the elevator. A heavy silence settles over us for a second before Declan speaks.

"So, that's Danielle."

I let out a soft chuckle and nod. "She is very no nonsense."

"That's one word for it," Declan laughs. "She is the most loyal person you'll ever meet. She is just a bit of a workaholic."

I nod. "Did practice finish early today?"

Declan takes a sip of his protein shake before setting it on the counter.

"Not exactly."

I furrow my brows and wait for him to explain.

He lets out a slow breath and rubs his jaw seemingly in thought before he answers.

"I kinda head butted Chad yesterday before practice and walked out to go find you."

My mouth parts as I stare at him in disbelief.

"Why are you just telling me this now? Why would you hit him? Are you in trouble?"

"I'm suspended for the rest of the season, and I have to pay some bullshit fine."

I frown as I stand to walk towards him.

"Why would you do that? You just threw away the rest of your season because of Chad?"

Declan turns to me and crosses his arms as he leans against the counter.

"I'd do it again in a fucking heartbeat given the chance. He's had it coming for weeks but him gloating about how he was gonna take Tucker away made me snap, okay?" He barks, harsher than he has ever spoken to me before.

So harsh, that I flinch in response before taking a step back. Declan's irritation quickly morphs into concern as he takes a step closer to me.

"Baby, I'm sorry. I didn't mean to spook you. I just...I'm so fucking mad that he's putting you through this, all of us, really. I can't help but wonder if," he pauses as wets his lips and looks over my head at the blank wall.

"If?"

Bringing his eyes back down to me he looks me straight in the eyes as he speaks.

"If you and Tuck would be better off if I wasn't in the picture. If I never would have met you, none of this would be happening right now. If I-"

I cut him off as I drag his head down to meet mine before I press my lips against his. He is stiff for a moment and doesn't reciprocate at first until he finally gives in and wraps his arms around me, kissing me like I may slip right through his fingers if he isn't careful. There is no way that'll happen. Ever.

Pulling away, I rest my forehead against his as I speak.

"Declan, we could never be better off not knowing you. You have changed our lives for the better. Danielle seems confident, and I could use some confidence myself right now. So, from now on, no more 'what if' talk. We are going to think positively and confidently. That son of a bitch is not going to take Tucker away from me...or away from you."

Something passes over Declan's face as he nods slowly.

"You're right. He's not. You guys are my family now, whether you like it or not. Protecting my family will always be my number one priority. Not football, not money. You, Vi Nielson. You and that boy. Always."

Chapter Forty-Four

Declan

My parents show up to my place shortly the next day, my mother with a harebrained scheme to bring a little joy to all our lives. So, my mama led us to the nearest Hobby Lobby where she proceeded to fill three shopping carts with Christmas decorations. I wish I was exaggerating but just ask my wallet, the woman went a little overboard, but she's always been a Christmas nut. If Tucker and Vi get a third of the amount of joy from it as my mother, then it'll be worth it.

We ordered some takeout before we literally spent hours decorating my condo. My mama ran the show while Dad and I lifted the heavy stuff and put things wherever she pointed. I think she just enjoyed bossing us around more than anything.

Red bows are tied in front of all my kitchen cabinets, green garland with lights and frosted berries are tacked around the perimeter of the entire condo. There are festive red rugs laid out in the hallway, living room, kitchen and bathrooms. Christmas trinkets and knick knacks are perched on top of any counter or ledge that my mother could possibly find. She even picked out three red velvet stockings, each with an embroidered letter on them. D, V, and T.

The last thing to tackle was the tree. I thought it would be fun to take Tucker to a Christmas Tree Farm and cut one down ourselves, but I also wanted everything to be decked out before Vi brought him home. So, we settled for a fake tree. Next year.

I look up at the ten-foot tree that with the angel on top barely fits inside my vaulted ceiling living room. My mother has just finished putting the final touches on it, and it is a blur of red, green, and silver. It looks like something straight out of Santa's workshop.

I smile to myself as I nod. Tuck is gonna love it.

Not five minutes go by before the elevator dings, and Vi and Tucker step out. The looks on their faces are instantly priceless. Vi's is one of shock and awe as her eyes swivel all around, her feet frozen in place. Tucker on the other hand has already done two laps around the whole place, shouting in excitement.

"Oh my gosh! Oh my gosh! Mommy, look! It's the North Pole! It's the North Pole!" He exclaims as he stands next to the red and white striped pole in the corner of the room that has a silver dome on top with a sign hanging off that says 'North Pole.' Another one of my mother's insisted purchases.

"What is all this?" Vi asks as her eyes scan over all the decorations, still stuck in front of the elevator.

Smiling, I walk over to her and cup her face before bending down to press my lips against hers. When I pull back, I smile down at her before lacing our fingers together and pulling her down the hallway. I watch as her head swivels, seemingly taking it all in before she pauses. I look over to see her eyes fixed on the stockings that are hanging above the fireplace. A glossy sheen takes over her eyes as she looks up to me. I squeeze her hand as I lead her over to where my parents are watching Tuck with wide smiles.

"This is amazing," Vi says as she shakes her head. "How did you do all of this in one day?"

"Suzannah is a slave driver," Dad says with an eyeroll as Mama smacks his arm and huffs.

"It's called delegation, Rodney. I made sure these two knuckleheads stayed busy. You're welcome."

I chuckle softly as I slip my arm around Vi's shoulders and nod.

"Thanks, Mama."

"Of course, baby," she says as she comes over and pats my cheek. "I'm gonna start on dinner now. Danielle should be by soon."

"How'd you manage that?" I ask with a smirk.

Mama raises her eyebrow at me as she holds back a grin.

"You think just because y'all are grown that you don't have to do what your mama says?"

I bark out a laugh as I shake my head.

"Can I help with dinner?" Vi asks.

"Oh, no, sweetie. You just got off work. Relax."

"I want to help," Vi insists as she smiles and nods.

Mama glances over to me, a pleased look in her eye before she nods at Vi and walks over into the kitchen. Vi turns to me and raises up on her toes to kiss me before leaning into my ear.

"Thank you. This is amazing. I'm begging you once again, though. Please stop spoiling him and me."

I pull back to look at her and smirk. "Never."

Vi rolls her eyes before turning to head towards the kitchen. I swat her ass making her squeal before I head over to where Tucker is watching the train that wraps around the bottom of the Christmas tree.

"What do you think, big guy?" I ask as I crouch down next to my dad and Tuck.

His big hazel eyes look up at me, filled with excitement.

"This is the coolest thing ever! Did Santa already come?"

I chuckle and shake my head. "Not yet, buddy. We still got a few weeks. What do you want Santa to bring you?"

Tucker seems to think about it for a while before he looks up at me.

"Can Santa make you my daddy?"

My eyes widen and my dad chokes before he has a coughing fit. It takes a few seconds of wide eyed staring before I'm able to respond. Scratching the back of my neck, I look at him awkwardly.

"Uh, I don't think Santa can make something like that happen, buddy. What about a toy?"

Tuck looks momentarily disappointed before he shrugs.

"I like Lego's."

"Can't go wrong with Lego's," my dad agrees before he sends me a wide-eyed look over Tucks head.

I nod as I pull Tuck into a side hug. We play with the train for a little while before Danielle comes in.

"I'm here, Mama. Now what is so important that you had to call me practically hysterical?" Danielle says before she stops. "Whoa, did a couple of elves throw a party in here or something?"

Tucker looks at me with wide eyes. "Did they!?"

I chuckle and shake my head. "No, Tuck."

"Oh, hi, baby," Mama greets. "Thanks for coming by. Dinner is almost ready."

"Dinner?" Danielle scoffs. "That was the big emergency?"

"You not seeing your mama when you're ten minutes down the road is the emergency. I know you're busy, and we appreciate you but sit your butt down at that table. We're gonna have dinner like a proper family."

Danielle blows out a breath and laughs as she shakes her head.

"Let me set the table," she grumbles.

"Why that would be so sweet, thank you, baby girl," Mama says.

Dad and I chuckle from the floor before we stand up and head over to the kitchen. Dinner is ready shortly after, and we all sit down around the table before digging in. Of course, it is a hell of a spread because my mama doesn't know how to do anything halfway. Covering nearly every inch of the table are plates of food. Fried chicken, green beans, fried taters and cornbread are littered in front of us like a feast.

"So, how did you have time to do all of this after practice?" Danielle asks as she gestures around the room.

My parents didn't think twice about it when I told them that I had the day off. I didn't wanna get into it with them because what's done is done. Shrugging, I dig at my food as I answer.

"Didn't have any today."

"Really?" She asks. "Because I ran into Slater at the coffee shop down the road. He was just getting back from practice. Said you are suspended."

I whip my head up and glare at her. Big sisters are a pain in the ass and apparently so are best friends. I'm gonna kill Slater and his big fucking mouth. News about my suspension wasn't supposed to be public knowledge until the end of this week at the least.

"Declan, what's she talking about?" Dad asks with a frown.

"It's nothing. Brownstone and I got into it in the locker room the other day. It's just until the end of the season."

"Declan," Mama admonishes. "What happened?"

My eyes flick over to Tuck before glancing at Vi. She nods, silently understanding me.

"Hey, sweetie. If you're done eating, can you go play in your room for a little?"

"Okay," Tucker says like the ridiculously good kid he is.

Scooting back his chair, he heads to his room. I wait until I hear the door shut before I start talking.

"Brownstone was talking shit about Vi. Saying that they were his family and that he was having her served with papers right then. I just fucking lost it. Slater and Seb pulled me away but then I didn't stick around to explain myself. I took off to find Vi. Coach suspended me for the rest of the season and said we would talk about next season later."

"Shit, Dec," Dad says with a shake of his head.

"He deserved it, and more. This is all a fucking game to him. A power play. He's a manipulative son of a bitch, and if I could hit him again, I would."

"You *hit* him? Like, physically struck him?" Danielle asks.

"Yeah, Dani. That's what hit means," I deadpan.

"Fuck, Dec!" She barks before dropping her fork against her plate. "Well, that angle is officially shot to hell."

"What angle?" I ask.

"Well, I just spent the entire day compiling evidence to display Chad as an abusive dangerous man. Without Vi having pictures or hospital records of the attack it was going to be challenging but not impossible. But now that you have physically assaulted, yes, that is the word they will no doubt use if the topic comes up, the biological father in a room full of witnesses, now you will be perceived as the dangerous one, not Brownstone."

Shit. I didn't think about how that would make me look. I was just...hold on. Attack?

"What attack?" I ask before my eyes flick over to Vi.

Vi's eyes are on her plate, steadily looking anywhere but at me.

"Vi?" I ask gently.

It takes a few seconds before she answers, still refusing to look at me.

"It was a long time ago," she whispers before dropping her head down to look at her lap.

Quickly pushing away from the table, I kneel in front of her as I tilt her chin up so she can face me.

"Baby, tell me he didn't hurt you. Tell me that he didn't lay his hands on you."

Tears quickly fill her eyes, and it's all the confirmation that I need. I should have known with the violent reaction she had to seeing Chad initially. Well, it's done now. He won't get the chance to take away Tuck or lay a hand on her again. He's fucking dead.

Pressing a kiss to Vi's forehead. I calmly stand up and walk over to grab my keys.

"Where are you going?" Vi asks, suddenly panicked.

"He doesn't deserve to breathe after laying his hands on you."

My dad is out of his seat and has me shoved against the wall before I can even reach the elevator. I push against him, the rage inside me slowly consuming every part of me. Despite my efforts, my dad keeps me pinned.

"Dec, think for a second. If you leave this place, you'll never see those two again."

I push against him again when my dad shoves me against the wall harder and turns my head to where a fear filled Vi is staring at me. Would it be so bad to go to jail if I knew that her and Tuck were safe from him? I don't think so. I'd do anything for them, fucking anything.

She must be able to read my thoughts or something because Vi quickly closes the distance between us, holding each side of my face as she begs me with her eyes.

"Please," she whispers softly. "I need you."

Slowly, the anger recedes as my chest untightens from her words. Blowing out a rough breath, I nod before my dad steps back and I wrap my arms around Vi.

"I'm sorry I never told you," she mumbles into my chest. "I hate talking about it. I don't talk about it. I just..."

"Shhh," I say against the crown of her head. "It's done. He'll never lay a hand on you again, and he sure as fuck will never get the chance to lay one on Tuck. We'll get through this together, okay?"

Letting out a choppy breath Vi nods and gives me a watery smile.

"Okay."

Chapter Forty-Five

Vi

Have you ever felt like time goes by extremely fast yet extremely slow at the same time? That's what the last few weeks have been like. I go to work and Tuck goes to school. Declan usually spends the morning working out, and since he is suspended, he has been helping remotely for the upcoming camps that the foundation has planned. In the afternoons, we have been doing all of the Christmas activities that Declan can come up with. We went ice skating last night, and I have the bruise on my ass to prove it. It's been wonderful and also painful at the same time.

No matter how hard I try to stay positive and confident, my stomach has been in undoable knots since that guy served me the papers. I can't stop the what ifs from running wild in my mind despite the fact that I have quickly learned firsthand that Danielle Daniels is a force to be reckoned with. She feels confident and so I should too, but this is my baby we are talking about. I can't just sit back and hope it all works out. It *has* to.

I haven't told Tucker about any of this yet. Mainly, because I don't think that there will be a reason for it. If the judge refuses to allow a change in custody, then nothing will change. If not...well, I'm not letting myself go down that rabbit trail right now.

It's been three weeks since we have stayed at my apartment, and Declan has asked me more than a few times if I wanted to send movers over there to have them clear the place and give notice. All times I have brushed off his offer. I love being here and so does Tuck, but we have only been together for a little over five months. It's terrifying to give up my backup plan if for some unfathomable reason Declan and I didn't work out.

I'm not working at the diner anymore. That position kinda fizzled out with the new girl taking pretty much all of my shifts, and I honestly wasn't too upset about it in the end. I've tried to pitch in around Declan's house, but he seems to always block my attempts. I even bought groceries the other day and then found the exact amount of money that I spent slipped into my purse the next day. The man is impossible, but he's mine.

It's Sunday, my day off, and I'm currently sitting at the island eating breakfast when the elevator opens. Declan went downstairs to use the gym about an hour ago so he shouldn't be done with his workout already. Before I know what's happening, I'm being tackled off the bar stool and falling backwards onto the ground. Pain stabs through my tailbone and races up my back at the impact of my body hitting the shiny floor.

"Ow, fuck. I thought you were gonna catch me," Mindi groans on top of me.

"You think you're hurt? You landed on me! Wait, Mindi?!" I shout. "What are you doing here!"

She rolls her eyes as she slowly leans up. "If you thought I was going to not be here for you, then you're seriously so dumb."

Despite my best effort to keep my brave face on, my eyes water and my lip trembles.

"You came all this way for me?"

"Of course, bitch. I love you and Tuck."

"We love you too," I sniffle.

"Duh, how could you not?" She teases as she plants a kiss onto my cheek before standing up and giving me her hand.

When I stand up, I see Declan standing there with a soft smile on his face.

"I'm assuming you're behind this surprise?" I ask.

He puts his hands up and shakes his head.

"Nope. This was all her, I was just informed when to be at the airport."

"Yep. Still mad I wasn't picked up in a limo or something. I mean, c'mon. You're a millionaire. What good is it that my best friend is riding a rich guy's dick if I don't reap the benefits."

"Mindi," I sigh heavily as I shake my head.

Declan barks out a laugh as he nods.

"Sorry about that. I'll try not to disappoint next time."

Mindi grins. "I knew I liked this guy."

I chuckle as I glance over to see Declan watching us with an easy smile.

Yeah, me too.

Tucker was just as excited as I was to see Mindi. When I told her that she came for Christmas he asked if she brought him any presents, which I scolded him for. Like the kid needs any more presents. From Declan's family alone, Tucker's gifts are practically taking up the entire living room under the ridiculously huge Christmas tree.

Tomorrow, we have court, and I couldn't be more nervous. Mindi talked me into having a glass of wine, which turned into two which turned into us sharing a bottle. No matter how much I drink though, I don't even feel buzzed or drunk, just nervous.

Mindi and I are sitting on the couch when Danielle comes over to sit with us. We have been going over how to handle tomorrow, who will be our character witnesses and what Danielle's plan is. Suzannah is going to stay here with Tucker while we are in court since Judy and Mindi are both going to be character witnesses for me. I can't even believe I'm in this situation in the first place. Where a judge has to look at me and wonder if I'm a good mother or not. It's fucking humiliating, to be honest.

"So, that about covers the planned points. Obviously, they could bring up something that I haven't thought of, unlikely, but still. Overall, I think we are well prepared," Danielle says with a head nod.

"Thank you, I really appreciate it," I say.

"You're practically family, Vi. Family always comes first for us."

I smile softly and nod as Mindi speaks.

"Sorry, I was just wondering, how can he even be pulling this shit in the first place without a paternity test? Vi, you didn't put him on the birth certificate, did you?" Mindi asks.

I shake my head as Dani speaks.

"Apparently, Chad obtained some hair follicles of Tucker through a PI and had the test run a few weeks ago. He submitted the positive paternity test with all of the filing paperwork."

A chill runs down my back, same as it did the first time Dani told me that. To think that Chad, or more likely a private investigator got so close to my son to get a hair sample is unnerving.

"Well, fuck," Mindi says on an exasperated breath. "Well, why aren't you bringing up the fact that Chad is an abusive piece of shit? He verbally put her down their entire relationship and then kicked the shit out of her when she was pregnant with Tuck. That should be brought up to the judge, right?"

Dani sighs and shakes her head.

"I'd love to bring it up, but we have no evidence, Mindi. No police reports, medical records, pictures-"

"I have pictures," she interrupts.

"You do?" Danielle and I ask at the same time.

Mindi rolls her eyes as she nods. "Duh. You weren't going to report him, which I still think is total bullshit, and I wanted you to have the option to go after him. Even if nothing could come of it, I wanted you to have proof that it happened. When you came over the next day and spent the night I may or may not have taken pictures of your face and arms while you slept."

"Creepy," I mutter.

Mindi rolls her eyes and Danielle is already standing, gathering up her things and walking out the door.

"Email me everything you have. I need to get this all put together. I'll meet you guys at the courthouse tomorrow. Be there at 8:45 on the dot."

"We will. Thank you, Dani," I call out as she throws a hand up in a wave.

Mindi quickly pulls out her phone and starts typing out an email to I'm assuming Danielle.

"Mommy?" Tucker calls out from his room.

I know Declan was in there reading him a bedtime story, but now that I think about it, he has been in there for well over a half an hour. When I step inside, I see dozens of books strung around Tuck's bed and a wide awake looking Tucker.

"Hey guys, what's going on in here?" I smile softly.

"Someone *really* wants to open a Christmas present before bed," Declan supplies with a smirk.

"Oh? And are we protesting sleep until we get our way?" I ask.

Tucker nods with a smile. "Please, Mommy. Just one!"

"Tuck, you have to wait until Christmas Eve to open at least one. It's the rules, babe."

He frowns and crosses his arms.

"What rules?"

I smile. He's got me there.

"Santa's," I reply.

His eyes go wide before he sags in defeat. "Fine," he grumbles before he lays down.

I lean over and kiss his forehead before brushing some hair out of his face.

"I love you, sweetheart."

"Love you too, Mommy," he says as he closes his eyes and rolls onto his side.

"Night, big guy," Declan says as he stands up from Tuck's bed.

"Love you, Declan," he murmurs before we sneak out the door.

When we get to the hallway, Declan has a look of surprise on his face before it melts into a smile. Leaning up onto my tippy toes, I brush my lips against Declan's. It's chaste at first but it doesn't stay that way for long.

My hands wrap around his neck as his arms band around my lower back. Declan's tongue flicks against mine as he deepens the kiss, causing a moan to slip out of me. His hands glide down my back, over my ass and to the back of my thighs before he lifts me straight into the air. I wrap them around his waist as he begins walking through the house, never once pulling away from the kiss.

"Yeah! She needs a good dicking. Bring your A-game big boy!" Mindi catcalls.

We both chuckle into the kiss but are too gone to care as Declan steps into our bedroom and kicks the door shut. Dropping me to my feet, Declan makes quick work of ripping my pants off. He stays crouched down before darting his tongue out to trace one long line through me. I gasp as I bury my fingers into his hair before he slips one of my legs over his shoulders. With my back against the wall, I push my pussy into his face as he continues devouring me.

I close my eyes and arch my back when I feel his hand grab my other thigh and wrap it around his other shoulder. Before I even know what's happening, I'm being lifted into the air, my back still against the wall, thighs hanging on Declan's shoulders and pussy in his face. There is something so fucking hot about the way this man tosses me around like a rag doll in the bedroom.

"Oh my god, Dec! Don't you dare drop me!" I warn before my words give way to a moan.

Declan pulls back for a second as he looks up at me, lips and chin glistening.

"And waste a drop of the finest thing I've ever eaten? Not on your life."

He goes back to work, licking and sucking just the right amount to have my body beginning to quake. I grind against his face harder this time, rubbing my clit against him in the process which has my pussy beginning to clench.

"Oh shit. Dec! I'm gonna-"

My words are cut off with Declan humming against my clit, the vibrations ripping the orgasm right out of me. I throw my hand up to cover my mouth, but I know that it doesn't muffle much as I scream my release. Declan doesn't slow down for a second as he licks and sucks every drop of my orgasm like it really is the finest tasting thing he has ever had.

When my legs stop shaking and my pussy stops pulsing, Declan slowly lowers me to my feet before he scoops me up once again and carries me over to the bed.

"You know, I can walk, right? I'm not an invalid," I tease.

"Maybe I just like carrying you," he smirks as he settles himself on top of me.

"You ready for me, baby?" He asks.

I bite my lower lip as I nod.

"Please, fuck me, Declan."

"No," he says with a shake of his head. "I just tongue fucked the shit out of your pussy, now, I'm going to make love to you."

I melt. Swear to all things holy, I melt right here in this bed as he slowly pushes inside me. I let out a satisfied groan when he bottoms out before he begins moving his hips in small rhythmic motions. I don't even realize that my eyes are closed until Declan speaks.

"Eyes on me, beautiful. I wanna look into them while I fill you full of my cum."

"Declan," I moan as my eyes roll into the back of my head.

"Look at me, baby," he commands a little more forceful this time.

When I do, he smiles softly as he brings a hand up to cup the side of my face.

"Good girl," he praises, making my heart a fluttering mess as he does.

His pace quickens as his muscles tighten. I feel the orgasm building inside me, and I can tell from the throbbing of his cock that he's close. Declan's slow rhythmic love making soon gives way to the passionate fucking I have come to crave. He leans down to kiss me as his hand slips between us, quickly rubbing tight circles over my clit that has me shattering apart.

Pulling away from the kiss, Declan looks down at me as his own orgasm takes over. I feel his cock throb and pulse inside of me as warmth suddenly fills me. He fucks me straight through his release, not stopping until the cum is running down my inner thighs.

When his hips stop thrusting, he stays still for a few moments, hovering over me as he brushes a piece of hair off my forehead.

"I'm gonna love you forever, Vi Nielson."

I smile, reaching up to cup his cheek much like he does to me.

"Same."

Chapter Forty-Six

Vi

With shaking hands, I put the finishing touches on my makeup before looking in the mirror. I'm wearing a pantsuit that I haven't worn since I first applied at Blooming-Deals. I decided to leave my hair down and go with natural looking makeup. Danielle said it would make me look more trustworthy, more motherly. What does that even mean?

Since the moment I opened my eyes this morning, my stomach has been in my throat. I've hardly spoken a word despite Declan's best efforts. I feel bad, but I'm not sure what to say—I'm not sure what to think.

Slowly, I walk out of the bathroom and into the kitchen where Tuck is happily munching on what looks like a stack of chocolate chip pancakes. Suzannah is at the stove cooking and greets me with a smile.

"Good morning, sweetheart," I say as I walk over and kiss the top of Tuck's head.

He looks up at me and smiles. "Morning, Mommy! Nana made pancakes. They're even better than yours!"

I huff out a short laugh as I ruffle his hair.

"Well, geeze, thanks. I'll have to remember that when Nana isn't around, and you beg for them."

Tuck happily ignores my threat as the sarcasm obviously rolls right over him. Declan walks into the room as well as Rodney and Mindi. They all stare at me expectantly. When I glance at the clock, I see that it's time to go already.

I'm not ready.

Crouching down to face Tucker, I twist his chair to face me, doing my best to keep my smile in place.

"Baby, I have to leave for a little bit. Nana is going to stay here with you, and I'll be back as soon as I can, okay?"

"Okay, Mommy! Then can we open presents?"

I let out a short laugh that comes across as more of a sob than anything as I nod and brush the hair out of his face.

"Sure, sweetie. I love you. You know that, right?"

"I know," Tucker says as he takes a bite of his food.

My eyes water as I wrap my arms around him and kiss the top of his head.

"So much," I whisper before pulling away, quickly dabbing at my eyes and smiling.

Suzannah walks over and hugs me tight before whispering into my ear.

"Everything will be great. My little girl knows what she's doing, and tonight, we will celebrate putting all of this behind us, okay?"

I nod as I pull away. "Sounds great."

Declan opens his arm for me, and I walk towards him until he is holding me into his side as we all walk out of the condo together. The drive goes by faster than I thought it would. But when we get to the courthouse, it's as if life begins crawling at a snail's pace.

The hollow clicking my heels make against the concrete stairs leading up to the looming building in front of me sounds more like the ticking of a clock than a pair of shoes. After twenty seven steps, Declan opens the door for us as we file into line at the security checkpoint. In the distance ahead, I catch sight of a crop of golden brown hair before it disappears into a room on the left. My stomach rolls as a cold sweat begins to break out over me. It's one thing to be questioned as a mother in front of a judge and god knows who else, it's another to sit in the room with the man who hurt me, abused me and abandoned Tuck, as he no doubt boasts about what a good person he is.

"Next," the aggravated security guard barks.

I jump slightly, before my eyes flick up to him apologetically, and I place my purse down, stepping through the metal detector as I do. He rolls his eyes at me but nods before turning his attention to Mindi.

When I pick up my purse, Declan is standing there with an understanding yet strained smile. I can tell that it's meant to bring me comfort, but right now, all I want to do is throw up. Wrapping an arm around my shoulders, Declan guides us down the hall towards that same door that Chad disappeared into not a few moments ago. Declan's strides are long and pace fast, at least it feels fast.

My steps slow until I'm standing frozen in place. Declan turns to look at me as Mindi, Judy, Dani, and Rodney do the same, all of their face's expectant but patient.

"I-I need a minute," I say softly.

Understanding looks are flashed at me simultaneously as each person gives me a passing hug or peck on the cheek before walking into the room. I stay stock still, trying, and failing, to control my breathing. I've got this. We've got this. Dani is a fantastic lawyer, and I'm a damn good mom. I've got this.

Blowing out a breath, I nod my head in determination, taking the final steps to two large wooden doors before I freeze once again. My heart instantly picks up, practically beating out of my chest as I raise a shaking hand to push against the worn wood. My palms are slick with a cold sweat as it presses against the rough surface. The overwhelming feeling to simultaneously pass out and throw up washes over me as the door opens and I take my first step inside.

An icy chill has come over me from the tips of my fingers to the ends of my toes as I begin walking through the room and over to the front. I feel all eyes on me the second I step inside. I told myself that I wouldn't look at Chad. I promised myself. And yet, the first place my eyes go to is his side.

I shouldn't be surprised at what I see. Chad is already staring at me, that evil fucking smirk that chills me to the bone plastered on his face. Like he is enjoying all of this, like he thrives on making my life hard. On making me hurt. He's dressed in a nice suit that probably cost him thousands with a fresh haircut that makes him look like the same prince charming that I thought I fell in love with. It took me way too long to realize that sometimes the prettiest packages hold the most vile contents.

Breaking eye contact with the devil himself, I look straight ahead before coming to sit next to Danielle. I don't have to look to know that Declan, Mindi, Judy, and Rodney are sitting just behind us. I can feel them there and it gives me the strength I need to keep it together.

The judge comes in only moments later before he asks Chad's lawyer to start.

"Your Honor, we are here to request that full custody of Tucker Nielson be transferred from Violet Nielson to Chad Brownstone due to child negligence and an unfit home."

Danielle makes a soft scoffing noise in the back of her throat that no one but me could probably hear. Her face is impassive and blank as she listens intently. Chad's lawyer goes off on this tangent about how our living situation is unfit and dangerous, how anyone could force their way inside.

Yeah, no shit. That's how Chad made it inside in the first place.

"Objection, your Honor. My client has already moved residences."

"Sustained."

Danielle nods as she jots something down and pats my leg. I think that's a good thing?

After Chad's lawyer finishes up, Danielle tells the judge that we are fighting to keep full custody with no visitation rights to Chad. She paints Chad perfectly. How he's been a playboy practically his whole life, ever the party animal with various misdemeanors against him that were all dismissed or diminished to a slap on the wrist due to his celebrity status or his well-known family.

After that, Mindi and Judy give their statements as character witnesses, stating what a good mother I am and how Tucker has always been well loved and cared for. Chad had a few guys from the football team be his witnesses, attesting to what a good guy he is and how good he is with their children, which I think is total bullshit.

Chad's lawyer also continues on as he talks about the locker room incident and Declan.

"My client is concerned for the wellbeing of his child due to the fact he is currently residing in the home of the man who on December second of this year assaulted my client."

The judge's brows furrow as he listens to Chad's lawyer continue.

"The assault was unprovoked, and we have multiple witness statements attesting to that. Due to the living situation that Miss Nielson has put herself and the child in question in, my client does not feel comfortable with her judgment or environment for the child."

Danielle's eyes crinkle in the corners just a bit but I can see that she is cringing. We expected this, she already told me it, but the look of concern in her eyes doesn't settle my already rattled nerves. Danielle doesn't comment, I guess she said that the more we would play into it the worse it would be since Declan did in fact assault Chad and to most, it would come across as unprovoked.

The judge asks if there is anything more to bring up when Danielle stands.

"Your Honor, if I could bring some last-minute evidence to your attention," she says as she pulls a poster board out with two enlarged photos of me six years ago.

Several gasps can be heard from around the room, one of them belonging to me. It was so long ago I almost forgot how bad it was. My lip is split and swollen, one of my eyes is black and blue and nearly swollen shut. I look practically unrecognizable with the swelling. The image beside it depicts finger shaped bruises on my bicep.

I chance a look behind me to see Rodney with his hand on Declan's shoulder, seemingly holding him in place. Declan isn't looking at me, though. He's staring straight at the pictures, a look of rage like I've never seen before across his face.

I try to catch his attention, to tell him it's alright but instead he turns his attention to Chad. I don't dare look at Chad so instead I just face forward. Danielle goes on to explain what led up to the pictures and the dates.

"Objection, your Honor, this is not sustainable evidence. These photos could be doctored to paint my client into a negative light," Chad's lawyer says.

"Do you have any other evidence to produce in support of this allegation, Miss Daniels?" The judge asks.

"We don't have any separate evidence, but if you will please look at the upper right-hand corner of the exhibit a, you will notice an alarm clock set to the time and calendar flipped to the month and year of the assault," Danielle says.

I lean forward and squint my eyes and sure enough, Mindi has a calendar and alarm clock that is visible. The judge examines it before nodding.

"Overruled."

Danielle nods. "With this in mind we are again asking for Violet Nielson to remain with full custody, and we are also asking at this time for a no contact order against Chad Brownstone for Violet Nielson as well as Tucker Nielson, your Honor."

"Lying bitch!" Chad shouts, a venomous glare pointed right at me.

Danielle's mouth drops as the judge pounds the gavel.

"Control your client or I will have him removed!"

Chad's lawyer quickly speaks to him, but Chad never takes his eyes off me. The look he gives sends a chill down my spine before I turn forward to face the judge.

"Is that all?" The judge asks.

Both lawyers nod, though Chad's lawyer is looking a little squeamish before giving Chad a scathing look.

"Very well, fifteen minute recess before ruling."

The judge disappears into the back room, and Chad and his lawyer begin furiously whispering to each other while Danielle turns to me, a smug smirk on her face for the first time today.

"What kind of dipshit lashes out like that? Especially when he's trying to prove that he isn't a violent piece of shit?" Danielle scoffs.

I turn back around to see Mindi and Judy giving me a thumbs up while Rodney nods encouragingly. Declan reaches his hand out for me, and I take it before he pulls it to his mouth and brushes his lips across it.

"Almost done, baby,"

I blow out a slow breath as I nod. Time goes by quickly and soon the judge is walking back in. My stomach is doing somersaults as my body shakes in anticipation.

"After reviewing all of the evidence and testimonies provided, a decision has been made. I award full custody of Tucker Nielson to Chad Brownstone effective immediately with no visitation rights to Violet Nielson until approved by a social worker."

The entire courtroom is completely still for three long seconds until a blood curdling wail of sorrow rips through the room. The sound is horrific and agonizing. It takes me a few moments to realize that the sound is coming from me. I drop from my chair to my knees as a pain like I have never felt before floods my soul, shredding me to pieces.

I can't breathe. I can't think. All I can do is hurt. All I can feel is this bone crippling pain that his words bring me. My mouth drops open in agony as I wait for another scream to fall from my lips, but my voice is gone, my breath is gone, and I sit there frozen in pain.

I lost him. I lost my baby.

Chapter Forty-Seven

Vi

My legs are too weak to stand, Declan literally has to scoop me up like a child and carry me out of the courtroom. I'm gasping for air, desperate for it but it's like the world has been sucked clean of oxygen and all that is left is carbon dioxide, poisoning my body and leaving it a tattered mess.

When Declan scooped me up, I saw Danielle's face, it was one of utter disbelief. Tears immediately filled her eyes as she apologized over and over again before she excused herself. Mindi was sobbing as we passed by, while Judy had a look full of sorrow as Rodney looked like he was just told that he was dying.

I sob for what feels like hours as Rodney drives the car. Declan and I are in the backseat and when my tears finally dry up, I slowly look over at him for the first time since the ruling. Tears are dripping from his eyes, but his face is stoic, like he can't believe this is really happening. This larger than life man has deflated and looks like a hollowed version of himself.

He glances over to see me watching him before he puts a reassuring hand on my back, but I don't want reassurance. I want my son. My baby. Oh my god. What in the living hell just happened?

Once we're at Declan's building, every step from the car to the condo feels like a thousand knives being stabbed into my chest at once. Every step brings me closer to saying goodbye and I know I won't survive it.

When I step through the door, I hear Tucker's laughter filling the space before Suzannah comes over to greet us. Her smile is wide, eyes so blissfully full of hope. As soon as she gets one good look at me, it all vanishes in the blink of an eye as she covers her mouth with her hand and shakes her head.

"No," she whispers hoarsely.

I don't respond to her, walking right past her as I make my way to Tucker. He glances over to see me and smiles wide before he runs over to hug me.

"Hi, Mommy! Nana and I were playing hide and go seek, and I won every time! She didn't find me once!"

I didn't know it was possible to cry anymore. I've cried what feels like gallons just in the last hour and yet tears build up in my eyes as I give him a watery smile.

"Of course, she couldn't. You're the best hide and seeker there is."

Tucker smiles happily before a tear falls down my cheek. His brows furrow as he cocks his head slightly.

"Don't be sad, Mommy. You can play too."

I let out a choked sob as I shake my head.

"It's not that, baby. I-I have to tell you something."

"Okay," he says, big hazel eyes full of concern.

My sweet little guy.

Taking a deep breath, I close my eyes for a moment before I sit on the couch and open my arms for Tuck. He quickly comes and sits on my lap, turning slightly to face me as I speak.

"I just got told that you have to go away for a little, baby. You have to go live with your father, Chad."

Tucker's eyes instantly widen with what looks like horror. "Why? You don't love me anymore?"

"NO!" I shout before another sob takes over me as I wrap my arms as tightly as I can around him. It takes me a few moments to pull myself together enough to speak again.

"Mommy loves you more than anything in this entire world, baby. You are the light of my life. I don't have a choice."

Tucker's eyes fill with tears as his lower lip trembles.

"I-is it because I don't clean my room good? I'll clean it every day forever. I'm sorry! Please don't get rid of me, Mommy!" He cries as he wraps his little arms around my neck and clings for dear life.

I thought my heart broke in that courtroom, but I was wrong. Right now, in this moment, my heart shatters into jagged irreparable pieces. We both hold each other and sob as we cling to each other like we are about to be ripped apart. Because we *are*.

Pulling back after a few minutes, I cup his wet cheeks as I look at him.

"You know that Mommy loves you, right?"

Tucker's face is pinched and twisted as he sobs, nodding softly.

"And I want you to know that if I could change this I would, in a heartbeat."

"I-Im s-scared, M-mommy," he stutters.

Me too.

"I know, baby. And it's okay to be scared, but you'll be safe."

Because if he isn't, neither the law nor the devil himself could stop me from murdering Chad Brownstone with my bare-fucking-hands.

"I just want to live here with you, Mommy, and Declan. I don't like Chad. I want Declan to be my daddy," he cries.

I don't have to look to know that Declan has crept into the living room. I can feel him there, so when he sits down next to us and wraps us both up in his arms it isn't surprising. We both lean against him as we all breakdown, Declan included.

"I love you, big guy, so much," Declan says as he looks at Tuck. "This isn't forever, I promise. We are going to get you back and get you home. This is just for a little, like sleep away camp," Declan says with a small convincing smile. So convincing, I almost believe his words. *Almost.*

"I've never been to camp," Tucker whispers hoarsely.

Declan nods. "You will one day and your mama and me will be there when that day comes, okay? We aren't going anywhere."

Suddenly, Declan's phone rings, cutting through the suddenly silent condo. He quickly fishes around in his slacks pocket before bringing the phone up and answering.

"Hello?"

He is silent for a few seconds before a dangerous glint flashes across his face. He stands up quickly and hangs up before leaning down and kissing the top of Tucker's and then my head.

"I'll be right back," he says as he moves quickly to the elevator and out of the condo.

Tucker and I continue to hold each other as I keep giving him the false promises that Declan started. Like how this won't last long, we'll all be together by Christmas, and that I'll never let anything bad happen to him. The last one I never thought would be a false promise, but with Chad Brownstone holding full custody over my child, I'm terrified that's a promise I can't keep.

"I love you, Mommy. You're the bestest Mommy in the whole world. Please don't get rid of me." Tucker says as he presses a kiss to my cheek.

I gasp for a breath but come up empty as tears tighten my throat like a vice.

"I love you, sweetheart. You are the best son a mother could ever ask for. I'm so lucky that I was picked to be your Mommy."

Chapter Forty-Eight

Declan

I couldn't fucking believe what George was telling me on the phone. As much as I wanted to stay with Vi and Tucker, I had to take care of the fucking prick currently in my lobby downstairs. Tearing out of the elevator, I storm up to the biggest piece of shit this world has known as I barrel right into him, shoving him against the wall as I grip his suit jacket in my fists.

"You couldn't give her a fucking hour with her son?!" I roar into his face.

Chad winces at the aggression in my voice before he quickly schools his face and attempts to shrug me off. I don't back up until the security guard standing next to the door clears his throat. Tossing a glare at him, I shove Chad against the wall once more before taking several steps away. I need space from him, or I may do something that I regret, like beat him to a bloody fucking pulp. Can't say I'd regret that too much, though.

"He's my son too, and I'd be careful about touching me from now on, Daniels. I've been nice enough not to press charges against your ass but all it will take is one little phone call and I'll have you rotting in a jail cell."

"You are a goddamn piece of shit!" I spit before I take a deep breath and look down at my balled fists, clenching and unclenching them as I think over our situation.

I'm still in fucking shock. I couldn't believe the words that came out of the judge's mouth, no one could really. I've never seen my sister look so caught off guard in her life, I haven't seen my father look that heartbroken since Donny's death, and I haven't felt this low since then.

I watched as the love of my life was destroyed with one singular sentence. I physically heard her heart splinter apart in front of everyone in that courtroom. Her excruciatingly painful sobs will haunt me for the rest of my days. Words were useless, so were actions. The only thing I knew to do was to scoop her up into my arms and get her the hell out of there. To get her to Tucker as fast as possible so that she could spend as much time as possible with him. And this motherfucker couldn't help but come straight here.

"We'll fight you. This isn't over," I promise.

Chad smirks. "And I'll win. Every. Fucking. Time. Honestly, Daniels, how are you surprised? You know who my family is, especially around here. You know what a little chunk of change can do in your favor. I'm only surprised you didn't use some of your own dough in the same way. Guess it really shows how much you care about them, huh?" He taunts.

Of-fucking-course he bought the judge off. That's the only thing that makes any sense. Dani had a solid case, any judge that wasn't corrupt would have seen what a wonderful mother Vi is and what a piece of shit he is. I bet anything the judge did see that and looked the other way anyways.

Judge McCarthy just got added to my shit list.

Our options are limited as of now. We are pretty much fucked, legally speaking. The only thing we can do at this point is fucking beg for Chad to give up this shit. Unfortunately, now that the court has been involved it will be more complicated than that, but it's a start.

The last thing that I wanna do is beg or be at the mercy of Chad Brownstone, but for Tucker, I'll do anything.

"What do you want?" I ask stiffly as I look up to him.

Chad has that stupid fucking condescending smile on his face as he cocks his head to the side slightly like he's clueless.

"What do you mean?"

"What do you want?" I practically seethe through clenched teeth. "What will it take for you to walk away from all of this, to walk away from them and forget any of this ever happened?"

Chad lets out a dry laugh as he shakes his head.

"It's too late."

"It's never too late," I argue. "Whatever you want, Chad, it's yours. I'll do fucking anything. Whatever you want, it's yours. Name your price. Please," I say earnestly.

Maybe I can appeal to the human side of him. There has to be one deep down in there somewhere, right?

Smirking, he lets out an amused noise as he crosses his arms over his chest.

"I like seeing you beg me for something. It's a good look for you. I know you're loaded, but so am I. I don't need money and you don't have anything that I want. Well, that's not true. I wouldn't mind having a go at Violet's tight pussy again but I'm more than a little irritated that she made me take it this far. Now I have custody of some little shit head all because she was being difficult."

Rage fills my body with his words, and I am walking towards him ready to throttle his ass, self-restraint be damned when the security guard steps between us and keeps me back.

"Mr. Daniels, I think it would be best if you went back upstairs."

"Yeah, Mr. Daniels," Chad snarks. "And tell Violet to get her sweet ass down here with my kid. I don't have all fucking night."

Nostrils flaring, I turn on my heel and walk towards the elevator, on my way to break the love of my life's heart some more.

When I step out of the elevator and into the hallway, I find Vi and Tuck right where I left them. Vi glances up to me and one look is all it takes for her to read me like a book. She begins to sob as her face contorts with pain.

Slowly, I walk over to her and crouch down to her level, resting a hand on her arm as I do.

"Already?" She asks on a broken sob.

I look to the ground and nod softly before looking back up at her.

"Can you-I c-can't pack-"

She doesn't need to finish her sentence before I am nodding my understanding and pressing a kiss to her temple as I make my way to Tucker's room. The tightening of my throat only worsens as I grab a duffel bag and begin packing away as many of his clothes and some of his favorite toys as I can.

This won't be forever. Dani will find a way around this.

She didn't come back with us, instead she went straight to the law office of a colleague of hers, and she promised my dad that she was going to get this thing overturned. *But who knows how long that could really take?*

I'm not sure where my parents, Mindi or Judy went, it's honestly the last thing on my mind right now. When Vi hugged Tucker like he was about to be ripped from her arms, my mama fell apart and my dad took her into the elevator. Maybe they went to the hotel, maybe they went for a walk. Either way, it's just us three in here, for now.

Blinking back the tears building in my eyes as I zip up the bag before slowly walking towards the door. I glance down at my feet to see Tuck's *Daniels* jersey there. Picking it up, I smile sadly before folding it on the bed. As much as I'd love to send it with him, knowing Chad, he'd probably burn it in front of Tuck just to get a reaction and there is no way in hell I will give that asshole any ammunition to hurt my big guy.

Fuck. I never thought that I would fall for a woman as fast and as hard as I did for Vi, but I really never thought that I would ever fall for a kid just the same. It's like Vi said in the beginning, they are a package deal, and I've wanted the whole fucking package from day one.

Anger washes over me once more as I shut Tuck's bedroom door a little too hard. This isn't over. Far fucking from. I will fight, steal and cheat anyone and everyone that I have to in order to get Tuck back for good and Brownstone behind bars for what he has done to Vi. I thought I was going to kill the motherfucker right then and there in the courtroom. Had it not been for my dad, I would have.

I glance up to see Vi and Tuck seemingly waiting for me by the elevator, their hands clasped tightly as tears run down both of their faces. Taking Tucker's other hand, we all step through the elevator. It's like we are a little family of three, or at least, we were. It takes me a few moments before I have enough courage to press the lobby button and even then, I regret it immediately. Desperation takes over me once again and I run through possibilities of how I can undo this shit show. How I can make it all go away.

When the elevator doors open, Vi takes a sharp breath when her eyes lock on Chad's. He watches her like a predator as we all slowly walk towards him. Tucker's hand is shaking like a leaf in my hand, and it breaks my fucking heart that he is so scared and there isn't a damn fucking thing I can do about it.

Chad's eyes flick down to where I'm holding Tucker's hand and his lip curls up in disgust. I don't want to give in to one damn thing this prick wants but if it helps our chances even a bit, I'll do it. Slowly, I let go of Tuck's hand and take a step to the side before laying Tucker's bag at Chad's feet. Chad looks semi pacified by the move, but Tucker looks up at me with hurt and confusion. Fuck. My heart would be in better shape if you tossed it into a blender before dumping it into the Sound.

Vi cautiously steps in front of Tucker, slightly pushing him behind her as she keeps her hands on him.

"Please," she begs on a hoarse whisper as she looks at Chad. "Please don't do this. He needs me."

Chad looks bored of Vi's pleas as he rolls his eyes.

"I warned you, Violet, you didn't take me seriously, and as you see, there are consequences," he scolds like she is a misbehaving child, and he is the disappointed parent.

What a fucking narcissist.

Vi nods shakily as she looks at him, seemingly desperate to do whatever it takes to stop all of this.

"I'll do anything, Chad. Whatever you want, just please," she says, the last part of her sentence breaking off on a sob.

Chad seems finally appeased as he looks down at her, a condescending smirk on his face as he takes a few steps until he is right in front of her. I have to stop myself from physically stepping between them as he leans down only a few inches away from her face as he speaks.

"You know what I want, Violet. But frankly, you being a disobedient bitch has pissed me off. So, let's see how a while away from your kid fixes that attitude of yours." He pauses for a minute before cocking his head slightly, his smirk growing. "Oh, I'm sorry. I meant *our* kid," he says as he reaches behind Vi and lands a hand on Tuck's shoulder, yanking him out from behind Vi.

"No! Stop! Please!" Vi shouts as she lunges for Tuck, but Chad gives her a challenging look that has her wrapping her arms around herself and shaking.

"Mommy?" Tucker questions frantically.

"I-it's okay, baby. Mommy will see you really soon, okay?"

Chad lets out a dry laugh as he shakes his head and takes a step back, grabbing Tuck's bag with him as he still has a firm hold on his shoulder.

"Don't count on it."

Turning on his heel, Chad pulls Tucker out the door and into the parked sports car in front of the condo, practically pushing Tucker into the front seat before walking around to the driver seat.

"H-his car seat," Vi says, almost to herself before she says it a little louder. "He's too little to be in the front seat! He needs his car seat!" She shouts as she runs towards the door.

Chad is already taking off though and the last thing that we see is Tucker's wide frantic eyes staring at us as the car drives away from us. Vi crumbles into a heap on the sidewalk as she screams 'no' and 'come back' over and over again.

I wish I could be stronger. I wish I could give her all these hopeful promises and tell her that everything is going to be okay. But I feel myself breaking on the inside, and all I have in me to do in this moment is sit on the ground behind Vi, pull her into my arms, and crumble right alongside her.

CHAPTER FORTY-NINE

VI

I don't know how long we stayed outside that night. It was long enough that the previously partly cloudy sky was swallowed whole with dark thunderous clouds before they opened up and let down a torrential downpour. Like the heavens were crying as hard as I was. Or maybe that's just me losing my fucking mind. Who knows.

I remember that my body began shaking from the bone chilling cold, and Declan finally stood us up and carried us upstairs. He wordlessly undressed me and carried us into the shower. I watched as he cranked it to the hottest possible setting, but the warmth never came. The water poured over my body, but comfort never came, relief didn't exist. It still doesn't.

It's been three days since my son was taken from me. My baby. Gone, in the hands of that monster, all alone, and as of now, I have no visitation rights. Danielle said that she is having a social worker squeeze me in as soon as possible for an evaluation so that I can at least have supervised visits. But even that won't be until after the new year.

I've spent practically every moment in these last three days laying in Tucker's bed. It's small and cramped, but it's not like I could get any sleep regardless. My appetite has vanished, my energy depleted. All I feel is utter heartbreak and defeat. Christmas came and went. Everyone gathered around the tree and after a lot of coaxing and desperate pleas from Declan, I emerged from Tuck's room for the first time to sit on the couch and stare at the dozens of unopened presents addressed to someone who wasn't there.

Tuck begged me to let him open a present early, and I refused him at every turn. Will he ever get to open the Lego set I bought him? Or the countless toys and new clothes that Declan got him? What would it have hurt to let him open one measly present, Vi? To watch the joy light up across his face as he revealed something brand new just for him. I'd give anything to see that right now. I'd give anything to have Tucker right now.

I should have listened to Chad. I should have walked away from Declan when he told me to. As much as it would have broken my heart, as much as I would have hated giving in so easily to Chad, I wish I could go back in time and change things. I know that sounds horrible because Declan is amazing. I am so desperately in love with him. He treats me like a goddess, but if I have to choose between my son and the man that I love...well, there really is no competition.

Nodding my head, it solidifies my decision, no matter how much it's going to fucking hurt. I step out of Tuck's bedroom and into the dining room where Suzannah, Rodney, and Declan are all gathered. They asked me if I wanted to have dinner with them about a half an hour ago, but I declined again.

When all eyes swing to meet mine, it's like understanding dawns on everyone at once. Suzannah and Rodney silently excuse themselves before heading for the door. Declan doesn't speak but he also doesn't look away from me. We stay there in silence for several moments before Declan stands and walks over to the kitchen cabinets, grabbing out a nearly full bottle of scotch and a glass. He pours it almost all the way to the top before taking a large sip. Pulling the glass away from his lips, he swirls it slowly, his eyes never leaving the amber colored liquid. When he speaks, his voice is rough and thick, like it pains him to speak.

"Tucker comes first, Vi."

His words equally relieve me and break me. He gets it, but I can see in the way he is trying not to show emotion, how much it kills him to understand.

"Always," I agree with a small head nod.

Declan's head nods as he takes a bigger sip this time before bringing his eyes up to look at me.

"I love you."

The way he says it, it's not like he is trying to sway my decision, like he is trying to convince me to stay. He says it in a way that comes off purely factual, like it's a certainty that is well known.

"I know," I rasp. "I love you."

Taking another sip of scotch, he nods again.

"I know."

Silently, I back away and move to my bedroom...I mean, Declan's bedroom, before grabbing a bag and quickly packing a few essentials. When I step out into the living room, I see that Declan is sitting at the couch, glass abandoned, as he drinks straight from the bottle. I pause next to him, to say something, do something maybe, but I'm not sure what. Declan keeps his eyes on the blank wall in front of him like I'm not even here. I'm thankful he isn't making it harder with desperate pleas and promises that we both know he can't keep, but is it so terrible that a tiny part of me wishes he was fighting for me?

Either way, the outcome would stay the same, and I'm sure he knows that. So, with one last look at him, I slowly turn, setting my key card onto the table and walk towards the elevator. As soon as the doors shut, I hear a loud crash that sounds like glass being shattered as other sounds of breaking and destruction ring throughout the condo. When the elevator starts moving the noises become muffled until they disappear altogether.

When the elevator doors open, I take it one step at a time until I am in the parking garage and stepping into my car. With a heavy heart, I start the car and drive away from the only man that I'll ever love, as I go after the only boy I'll ever need.

Chapter Fifty

Declan

The pounding in my head is the first thing that registers when I wake up the next morning. That and the dull ache in my hands and feet. Blinking my eyes open blearily, I realize that I'm on the living room floor.

Slowly pushing myself up to sit, I look around to see my apartment nearly unrecognizable. Last night flashes back in waves as I look at the shattered scotch bottle laying in remnants on the floor. I remember watching as it splintered apart against the wall, the dark amber liquid running down the wall like spilt blood.

From there it was like a blur, I had never felt so much anger inside myself at once, so much hurt. I don't even remember hurting this much over Donny. Maybe because the pain over him was a shock, it was quick and painful. But with Vi, I saw it coming from the moment the judge pounded his gavel. I just hoped that I would be wrong.

Every object near me was a casualty last night. The Christmas tree is flipped over, shattered ornaments broken across the floor, lamps smashed, chairs broken. It looks like there was a raid in here last night.

Glancing down at my hands, I see chunks of glass ornaments shoved inside them before peeking down to see the same of my feet. Guess I didn't really give a shit about the pain when I laid down in the mess and passed the fuck out last night.

The elevator door opens, and I know that it has to be my parents, Vi left her key last night and I'm not dumb enough to think that anything could bring her back to me. Nor would I want her to. She is where she needs to be. To keep Tucker safe and with her, she has to play a part and that part doesn't include me.

I hear my mama's soft gasp as she walks further into the room.

"Declan, what happened?"

I don't speak as she glances at my bloodied hands and feet before she rushes off to the bathroom. My father gives me a look full of pity and sorrow as he comes over to me, clasping my shoulder.

"We'll keep an eye on them, son. Don't worry. They'll be safe."

I wish I could believe him but knowing my girl and my big guy are living under the same roof as that piece of shit doesn't give me too much hope. He doesn't say anything else as he slowly starts picking up the broken pieces of my life. Well, the materialistic pieces at least.

I hate how much I've cried over the last week. I don't cry, ever, but tell that to my eyes because the fuckers have been leaking non-stop for what feels like ever. Sniffing back the tears that are beginning to build, I think over what last night really meant. What I just lost, what I'll never get back. It's getting harder to keep my shit together.

My mama is next to me in a flash, sitting beside me with a pair of tweezers as she slowly starts working on my hands. I don't stop her—don't have the energy to care. It can stay in there for the rest of my life, or it can come out. It doesn't fucking matter.

The elevator dings again before a familiar voice rings through.

"Oh my god! Dec! What happened?" Dani asks.

I look up at her with red rimmed eyes before disappointment colors her features, and she shakes her head, hanging it between her shoulders.

"I'm so sorry, Dec. I thought we had a stronger case. This is all my fault. I was confident. Too confident. I-"

"Not your fault," I rasp, cutting her off. "He bought off the judge. Bragged about it right to my face."

Understanding flashes across her face as she nods.

"I had a feeling, but I've been looking into this non-stop. We can appeal this and get a new judge. We are going to get Tucker back. Where is Vi? I want to-"

"Gone," I snap shortly, not having it in me to say more.

"Gone?" Dani asks, her brows pinched and confused.

She stares at me for a few moments before her eyes widen, and she covers her mouth with her hand.

"Dec, no."

I nod as mama starts pulling the glass out of the bottom of my feet. Dani slowly walks over to sit on my other side, leaning her head against my shoulder. We are silent for a few minutes before she speaks again.

"She was the one, wasn't she?"

I lick my lips before I speak, my chest squeezing painfully at her words.

"Yeah, she was."

Chapter Fifty-One

VI

I had never been as nervous as I was when I parked in Chad Brownstone's driveway and knocked on the door at nine o'clock at night. It took a few minutes for anyone to answer, I was convinced I had the wrong address until Chad answered the door in nothing but a pair of way too tight boxers.

He took one long look at me before he scoffed and walked back into the house.

"Took you long enough. The kid hasn't stopped crying since he got here."

I stepped inside, shutting the door, officially sealing my fate as I did.

"He has a name, Chad," I said with my arms crossed and expression purposefully blank.

"I don't doubt it," he said as he continued walking until he made it to the kitchen, grabbing a bottle of water as he spoke.

"So, how did lover boy take it? I assume you aren't stupid enough to try to keep shit up with him behind my back?"

"It's done," I bit off. "Is that what you want confirmed? I walked out, and he let me. Are you happy?"

He shrugged before walking out of the kitchen and down the hall. I assumed he wanted me to follow and so, to my disgust, I did. We stopped outside a large white door before he pushed it open, revealing Tuck who was laying in an oversized king bed.

Tucker's eyes went wide when he saw me before he squealed with delight, racing out of bed and over to me. I dropped to my knees and sobbed as I wrapped my arms around him, promising myself that I would do absolutely anything to never let him leave my side again.

"Keep it down, will ya?" Chad scoffed. "I've got company."

With that, he walked out of the room and upstairs.

"Are you here forever, Mommy? You won't leave me again?" Tuck asked.

I smiled at him through my tears as I nodded.

"Never again, baby. Everything is going to be okay now."

It's been two weeks since I walked out of Declan's life. Aside from having the occasional awkward dinner out with Chad where he encouraged us to act like a happy little family, we haven't seen him hardly at all. I have been going to the flower shop for work, and Tucker started going back to school once winter break was over. Life is, in a strange way, almost back to normal. Except it isn't at all.

I have this 6'3 hole cut out of my chest, and with every pump of my blood, my heart hurts a little more. I had to make a decision at the end of the day and as much as it hurt, being away from Tuck, not knowing if he was safe or not, that hurt more.

I'm currently in the back of the shop, working on a custom order that was just called in. They are apology flowers. I know that because the guy asked me to write on the card, 'She meant nothing, baby. You are everything to me.' I scoff to myself as I scribble down the empty words and bullshit apology before contacting the courier we use to deliver them.

The front door chimes, and I slowly make my way to the counter when I freeze. My heart squeezes and my stomach flips at the sight of him. Declan Daniels is standing just inside the door of the shop. Only, he doesn't look like the Declan I remember. Can someone change so much in just two weeks?

His shoulders are hunched, his posture slack like he is exhausted. His normally warm smile is vacant, instead a deep frown marring his gorgeous face. The normally golden honey eyes have dimmed into a dark brown accompanied by deep dark circles underneath.

Swallowing back the sudden emotion clogging my throat I do my best to straighten my posture as I look at him.

"What are you doing here?" I ask.

Declan licks his lips but doesn't speak for several moments before he rubs a hand down his face and takes a step closer.

"I just...I had to see you. Check on you. I've been worried."

I nod, doing my best to hide the love I feel for this man. Could he be any more perfect? Seriously, could he? I doubt it.

"I'm okay," I say softly.

Declan nods. "And Tuck?"

I smile as my heart twinges. The desperation in Declan's gaze speaks volumes. He cares about my son so much. I have no doubt he would walk through fire for my baby.

"He's okay too." I pause, wondering if I should say more before I add, "He misses you."

Declan's face crumbles in what seems like hurt before he nods and gives me an extremely forced smile.

"I miss him too. Will you tell him that?"

"Of course, I will."

We are both silent for several moments before he speaks again.

"Look, I understand why you left, and I'm glad you did. Tucker needed you and you needed him, but I don't like you guys under Chad's thumb. I don't trust him. What if he hurts Tuck?"

"He'll never get the chance," I say quickly with a shake of my head. "Besides, he mostly avoids us. We are more like roommates that hardly ever see each other. Since the Crusaders lost in the playoffs, he has been around a little more, but he usually pretends like we aren't there."

"And what if he hurts you?" Declan asks.

I give him a sad smile and a shrug.

"I hope that doesn't happen. He hasn't been aggressive towards either of us since I got there."

"If he hurts you, I'll kill him. You know that, right, Vi?"

Something like pre-meditated murder shouldn't melt me into a pile of goo like this and yet here I am.

I nod softly, making Declan nod too. As much as I don't want to say the next thing that comes out of my mouth, I have to.

"You need to leave, Declan."

His eyebrows furrow as he looks at me. "Do you want me to go?"

I shake my head. "It doesn't matter what I want. I *need* you to go."

"Chad isn't here," Declan argues as he looks around the empty shop. "It's just us, Vi. I missed you. I've been going crazy without you."

"I can't risk Chad finding out that we spoke. I haven't even gotten a lawyer to help me with getting legal visitation rights, let alone getting custody back."

"Lawyer? You have Dani."

I shake my head. "That's your family, Declan. Now that we aren't..." I trail off as he continues.

"Together?" He rasps.

I nod. "It isn't right to take up anymore of her time. I need to do this on my own and I will but it's going to take time. Time that I won't have if Chad finds out you stopped by and spoke to me. He'll take Tuck away, for good."

Declan shakes his head. "You aren't alone, Vi. You don't have to do this alone. I'm standing right fucking here-"

"I didn't ask you to be!" I snap before closing my eyes and cringing. When I blink them open, I see Declan standing there staring at me with confusion. "I'm sorry," I whisper. "I just...can you go? Please?"

He swallows roughly as he looks at me for a moment and nods.

"I never meant to do this, Vi. I never meant to come in and ruin everything. I just wanted to be a part of your life. Maybe it would have been better if I hadn't chased after you guys in that grocery store parking lot, though."

The verbal blow lands directly against my barely pumping heart, and I suck in a small breath at his words. His face is vulnerable, broken. His words don't come from a place of spite or malice. It's genuine, like he thinks he ruined my life by pursuing me. I'd like to tell him that I don't wish that, not for a second, but I just need him to leave, as much as it hurts.

Declan gives me a slow nod before meeting my eyes one more time as he turns and heads out the door. I don't realize that a tear has slid down my face until the door shuts. Wiping at my face quickly, I do my best to shake the interaction from my mind and move on with my day.

Fat fucking chance of that.

Chapter Fifty-Two

Declan

These last three weeks have been pure fucking hell. Without Tucker and Vi, my life feels empty, bland. Add in the fact that I don't even have football as an outlet, and I'm going fucking crazy. The only saving grace that I've had is Seb and Slater. They have tried to keep me busy, having me over for dinner, grabbing a drink or five when the nights are too fucking lonely, but it's not enough, not the same.

Slater is having a party at his place tonight to celebrate the end of the season, though there isn't much to celebrate. The Crusaders got annihilated by the San Antonio Cobras in the playoffs and the season kinda fizzled out. The only player on the Crusaders that had a decent game that day was Slater. Maybe that's why the crazy fucker is insistent on partying. Then again, the guy could never pass up an opportunity for a party regardless.

Chad's house is just down the road from Slater, and I was more than fucking tempted to drive by slowly, just in the slight chance that I could catch a glimpse of Vi or Tuck. Seeing her the other day did more bad than good. I thought that if I stopped by and checked on her, saw that she was doing good that I wouldn't feel so goddamn miserable, but it didn't help. Seeing her and not being able to wrap her in my arms and kiss her like the world was ending made it worse. So much fucking worse.

I don't even wanna be here. I haven't spoken to the coaches yet, but I'm done. I'm going to break my contract. I know they are probably expecting me to beg and plead to come off suspension for next year. They probably also want me to apologize to Chad. Hell will freeze over and give away free sno-cones before either of those things happen.

I thought I'd be sad when the time came to retire, and I am. But it doesn't have a damn thing to do with football and everything to do with the most addictive woman to ever exist.

And she isn't even mine. Not anymore, at least.

I step inside Slater's house, not bothering to knock because the fucker literally breaks into my house all the time. When I do, the first thing I hear is screaming coming from upstairs. Slater's house is all sleek and modern with a glass staircase and an open mezzanine on the second floor. I remember thinking it was ridiculous and gaudy when he sent me pictures, but Nikki fell in love with it and Slater fell in love with Nikki.

"I don't give a fuck if Stacy just got dumped. You do this shit to me all the time, and I'm fucking sick of it. If you aren't shopping you are jetting off on girl's trips, on my dime, remember? But you can't even find the time to show up to a fucking game or a party at your own goddamn house!" Slater shouts.

My eyebrows raise as I look to see Scarlett, Slater's childhood best friend helping the caterers set up food, because that's just who she is. She gives me an awkward smile as her eyes flick upstairs before she shakes her head.

Message received.

"I'm not going to sit here and let you talk to me this way!" Nikki screeches. "When you're done being a stupid fucking asshole, let me know!"

Nikki storms down the stairs, not even sparing me or Scarlett a glance before grabbing the packed suitcases next to the door and slamming the door shut on her way out.

Slater comes down right after her, shaking his head in what looks like disappointment and maybe a flash of hurt before he quickly masks it and tries to paste a smile on his face.

"Everything alright?" I ask with furrowed brows.

Slater and Nikki have been together forever, they always seemed rock solid. Maybe there is more beyond the surface, though.

"It's nothing, man. She'll spend a few grand out of spite, we'll fuck and be good as new. How are you?" Slater asks.

I shake my head, knowing that he definitely doesn't wanna talk about it, so I allow him to switch topics. Even if my life is currently a depressing as fuck topic.

"Been a lot better, that's for sure," I say.

"I'm sorry, man," Slater says as he claps my shoulder.

"Have you heard from her?" Scarlett asks as she comes to stand next to us.

I raise a brow at her before tossing Slater an accusing look who shrugs.

"It's Scar, man. Like I'm not gonna tell her everything. She's basically an extension of me. What I know, she knows," he says as he slings an arm around Scarlett's shoulders.

I don't miss the way Scarlett's cheeks slightly pink up as soon as Slater drags her closer into him, but I don't comment on it. I probably should have expected it. Especially with Scarlett becoming a part of the Crusader's physical therapy team, she and Slater are around each other more than ever, which means he blabs to her more than ever. Before I can give him shit for sharing my personal stuff with others, Seb and Erica walk in.

"Hey, Mikey," Erica smiles sadly before giving me a hug that lasts a little too long to be a simple greeting. This is a sympathy hug.

Holy shit. Does everyone know the ins and outs of my personal life? Erica pulls away, giving me a sad smile before walking over to Scarlett and hooking her arm with hers as they walk over to the kitchen, probably to gossip about me.

"You both fucking suck," I grumble as I turn to Seb and Slater.

"What the hell did I do?" Seb asks.

"You told your wife about my stuff with Vi, didn't you?"

Seb shrugs. "We don't keep shit from each other. Besides, she really liked her. She's been wanting us all to get together. It was gonna come up eventually."

"So, what's the latest?" Slater asks.

I shrug. "My folks went back to Knoxville after Vi left and Dani is working her ass off from New York since she had to get back for a case. My dad assured me that he would make sure that Vi and Tuck are safe. Not sure how he thinks he can do that, but I did see her last week at the shop. She looked okay, sad, but okay."

"So, just like you?" Seb asks.

"I don't look sad," I defend.

"No, you look like someone pissed in your Cheerios before running over your dog," Slater supplies, snickering slightly like this is a big fucking joke. Everything always is to him.

"Well, how the fuck would you like me to look when I lost fucking everything, Slater? Think about what it would be like to lose your career and Nikki all at once?"

Slater's eyebrows knit together as I continue.

"And then imagine losing Scar at the same time."

Now, all humor vanishes from his face completely.

"We get it, Mikey," Seb says. "I'm sorry. I wish we could do something."

I shake my head as I move to the fully stocked bar Slater has to the side and grab a beer.

"Forget it."

Slowly, people start showing up more and more until the house is brimming with players, coaches and gold diggers as far as the eye can see. Some are dancing, some are shooting the shit around the perimeter of the house and a group of guys are taking advantage of Slater's game room.

I'm sitting in the corner nursing a beer when in walks Chad. To my surprise though, he isn't alone. Vi comes into my line of sight a half a second later, her hand tucked into the crook of his elbow, a wide smile on her face as they greet people. The sight stings, and I have to physically look away for a minute before glancing back at her. Her smile is so goddamn beautiful.

I notice it doesn't reach her eyes, though. Her cheeks are tight, like she is consciously keeping her smile in place and her hands are white knuckling the fabric of Chad's dress shirt like she is angry.

She must be able to feel my eyes on her because in the next moment she turns and looks straight at me. When our eyes meet, the breath in my lungs is stolen as my chest tightens. Shit. How is she so beautiful? She is wearing a skintight blue dress that is a little more revealing than her usual taste, which tells me she didn't pick it out, which pisses me the fuck off.

I watch them carefully as they move through the party, Vi's eyes occasionally flicking to me before back to whoever they are mingling with. Chad is showing her off like the trophy she is. Except she isn't just some arm candy, she is so much more.

Slater comes up next to me, smiling until he sees where I'm looking. His smile falls away as he claps my shoulder.

"Let's get you a drink."

"I already got one," I say as I lift my drink, not taking my eyes off Vi as I do.

"Maybe another one?" Slater offers as Chad and Vi start making their way towards us.

"Hey, Slate. Nice party," Chad says before turning to me with a cocky smile, his arm now slipped around Vi's shoulder in a possessive hold.

"Daniels, I didn't know you were allowed at team functions being suspended and all."

I don't respond because that's exactly what he wants. Instead, I just stare at him, willing him to burst into flames right here and now. That would solve just about every problem in my life right now.

"Violet, always a pleasure," Slater says as he leans in and presses a kiss to her cheek.

"It's Vi, Slate," she corrects with a smile before Chad squeezes her shoulder tightly. "I mean, it was. I'm going by Violet again."

My stomach rolls at that. He won't even let her go by her chosen nickname? He is such a controlling piece of shit. He doesn't deserve to breathe the same air as Vi, let alone touch her skin.

Vi's eyes come to mine, just for a second but it's enough to send my heart racing. Chad must see it or hear my thumping heart because he speaks next.

"Baby girl, go get me a drink. I'll reward you well tonight for it," he says as he drags his nose up the length of her neck before nipping at her earlobe, the whole time keeping his eyes on me.

My grip tightens around my drink so much I'm sure it's close to breaking apart in my hand. I wait for fiery Vi to come up with some kind of snarky answer. To shove him away, call him a name, slap him, fucking anything. Instead, she cringes slightly before giving him a tight smile and nodding as she wades through the crowd in search of a drink.

Chad opens his mouth, no doubt to spew some more shit when some of the rowdier guys come in and greet Chad like he is their god. To be fair, these guys are young rooks, and the almighty Chad Brownstone is probably somewhat of a god to them. Chad drinks in their admiration and attention like a lush as they all wander off towards the game room. Slater watches them go with a shake of his head before looking at me and lowering his tone.

"Go get your girl. I'll keep watch."

I bump Slater's fist before quickly following in the direction of Vi. It doesn't take long to find her waiting behind a few people that are sitting at the bar. I don't waste a second, grabbing Vi's hand and pulling her with me through the kitchen and into the walk-in pantry. I don't look to see that she is following. Her hand latched onto mine almost immediately and that gave me enough hope to drag her in here and close the door before pushing her up against it.

Not wasting a second, I cup her face in my hands and dive down, capturing her lips with mine. She doesn't fight me even for a second as her tongue comes out, flicking against mine as she arches into my hold. My hands go everywhere at once. I start at her hands before trailing down her neck, over her breasts, down her torso and over her ass before I hike her dress up.

"I need you, baby. I need you so fucking bad," I say against her lips.

She nods. "Take me, I'm yours."

Pulling back slightly, I rest my forehead against hers.

"Do you really mean that?"

"For right now? In this moment? Yes."

It's not exactly the answer I wanted to hear but it'll do for now. Pulling her panties to the side I slip a finger inside her, letting out a groan as she whimpers when I sink all the way in.

"You're soaked, baby. Tell me it's all for me. Tell me I'm the only one that can make you wet like this," I rasp into her ear.

"Only you, Declan. Always you."

"Good girl," I say before nipping at her neck and pulling my finger out of her as I stroke my cock a few times before hooking her leg around my waist and thrusting into her.

Vi's mouth parts into a perfect o that has me desperate to shove my cock in it. Fuck. One quick fuck in a walk-in pantry isn't enough. I want it all with her. I *need* it all with her. But for now, this is all I get and I'm gonna savor every fucking minute of it.

Wrapping her other leg around me, I quickly lower my hands to her ass, lifting her into the air before pressing her back against the wall as I snap my hips rapidly. Her walls clench as she milks my cock like only she does. Being in her feels like coming home. Has it really been less than a month since the last time I've been inside her? It's a month too fucking long.

"Declan," she moans.

"Yeah, baby. Say my name. I want my name on your lips as you cum. Never forget who fucks you like this, who makes you feel this good."

"You," she whimpers as her hands go up to my shoulders, giving her better leverage to bounce on my cock like a fucking porn star. Goddamn, she is perfect.

Sounds of laughing and drinks clinking ring through the pantry. The party is getting louder, either that or people are getting closer. Vi sends me a panicked look, and she seems ready to bolt, but I don't let her. Tightening my grip on her, my fingers dig into her soft waist as I use our momentum to fuck her even harder.

"Dec," she moans softly. "We are going to get caught. I can't get caught. I-"

"Shh, baby," I soothe. "It's just you and me. Right now, right here. It's just us. Now be a good girl and cover my cock with your sweet cum."

Her eyes roll into the back of her head at my words as her pussy clenches down to me so hard that my balls instantly draw up. That's all it takes for me, I crush my lips against hers as my cock empties itself inside her, twitching and jerking as I coat her insides with my cum. If only it wasn't for her stupid fucking birth control. I'd do anything to see Vi get round with my baby. Even more so now that the possibility feels so fucking out of reach.

She cums only seconds behind me, her pussy squeezing the fucking life out of my cock as her body shakes and quakes until her body sags limply against me. Once we both catch our breath, she slowly unwinds her legs from around me as she stands on wobbly legs. I place a hand on her hip to stabilize her, lifting my other hand to cup her cheek as I stroke it gently.

"I love you, Vi," I whisper gently.

Tears gather in her eyes as she nods.

"I love you too."

"I can't stay away from you anymore, baby. It's breaking my fucking heart."

"I know," she says on a choked sob. "I can't risk losing Tuck, Declan. It hurts so bad to be away from you, but it fucking guts me to be away from him."

I nod my understanding. I fucking hate that I understand, but I do, and I love her that much more for being the type of mother that she is. Blowing out a breath, I look up at the ceiling before looking back down at her.

"Tuck comes first," I say.

"Always."

CHAPTER FIFTY-THREE

VI

After I snuck off to the bathroom to clean myself up, I found Chad and told him that I wasn't feeling well and was heading back to his house. He was playing some kind of drinking game with some of the guys and seemed too messed up to even realize what I was saying so I ordered a ride and quickly left. I had to get out of there. I knew that all it would take was one look at Declan and I together and everyone would know what we did. Not that I regret it. I've missed Declan more than I can say but it was reckless and stupid.

And hot. So fucking hot.

When I get back to Chad's mansion, I step inside to see Judy snooping through his office. Why he even has an office is beyond me. From what I've seen he spends a majority of his time in his bed, the kitchen or the pool, because he is a douche and has an indoor heated pool.

"Find anything good?" I ask with a smirk.

Judy nearly jumps out of her skin as she covers her heart with her hand.

"You scared the hell out of me, Violet Ann!"

I shrug. "Maybe you shouldn't snoop then."

Judy scoffs and rolls her eyes as she continues moving paperwork around.

"Well, Tucker already went to bed, and I had to find some way to pass the time. I figured digging up dirt on this son of a bitch was as good as any."

"He's too smart for that, Judy. Trust me, I've already tried."

Judy huffs as she crosses her arms.

"Well, what's the plan then? I hate you two being here. I'm worried sick every damn day."

I reach over and hug Judy tight to cut off her rambling.

"Thank you, Judy. Thank you for watching Tuck tonight. Thank you for being there for us over the years. You are the best surrogate grandmother I could have ever asked for."

"Well, you're welcome, sweetheart. I love you two so much, I just want you safe."

I nod. "We are okay for now, Judy. It'll take time. Besides Chad being a little handsy in front of Declan at the party tonight, he has barely glanced twice at me."

Judy raises an eyebrow and smirks.

"Declan was there?"

Biting back my smile, I nod.

"Andddd?"

"And what?"

"And how was the quickie you guys had in the bathroom?"

My eyes widen as I shake my head.

"Judy, the things that come out of your mouth, I swear."

"You gonna tell me I'm wrong?" She asks as she steps out of Chad's office and over to grab her purse.

"Yes, actually." I pause slightly. "It was the pantry," I murmur.

"Violet Ann, naughty minx," Judy snickers.

I scoff and shake my head as I wave goodbye while she heads to her car. Closing the door, I make my way to the kitchen to grab a drink of water before I head to bed when my phone vibrates. Picking it up, I open the text.

Declan: Where are you?

I bite my lip, wondering if it is a good idea to respond. I could always delete the thread later in case Chad decides to snoop.

Me: I left.

His response comes almost immediately.

Declan: Why?

Again, I pause. Should I be honest? I mean, when have I ever not been honest with him? He's always made it so easy to tell him every-thing.

Me: Because being around you and not being able to be with you is painful. It hurts me, and I know it hurts you too. Besides, there is no way anyone could look at us and not know what we just did.

His second response takes several minutes. I find myself sitting at Chad's island anxiously waiting for his text when it finally comes in.

Declan: I know, baby. But not even being able to see you hurts more. Can I see you again soon? Please. I know you have to keep up appearances with Chad but maybe we can find some time just for us?

Smiling at his words I bite my lip. God is that tempting. I know it would only come back to bite me in the ass, though. Chad Brownstone is a douchebag, he is entitled, selfish and an all-around horrible person, but he isn't stupid. He would catch us eventually. Then what?

Before I can respond, the front door opens, and I groan. I should have just gone upstairs when I had the chance. Now it's going to be nearly impossible to avoid Chad, and if I remember correctly, a drunk Chad is a very fucking annoying Chad.

Tiptoeing through the kitchen and down the hallway, I almost make it to Tucker's door when Chad calls out.

"There you are," he slurs slightly.

I freeze, turning around slowly to look at him. His gaze is unfocused, his hair disheveled as he sways slightly a few feet away from me.

"Me?"

He scoffs as he stumbles a bit as he comes closer to me.

"Yes, you. What other hot bitch do I have living under my roof?"

I scoff at his words as he closes the distance between us and wraps his arms around my waist as he brings me against his chest. Chad buries his face into my neck as he inhales deeply before murmuring against my skin.

"You smell so fucking good. Bet you taste just as good as I remember."

Trying to extract myself, I gently push Chad away but it's no use. His hold is too strong.

"I loved you back then, did you know that?" He drunkenly rambles on. "But I got drafted, and I knew that was going to open a lot of doors for me."

"You mean legs?" I snark.

Instead of getting mad, Chad barks out a laugh. "Pretty much. But I thought about you a lot over the years. You were by far the best tasting pussy I've ever had."

I wrinkle my nose up at his words as he speaks.

"Gee, thanks."

Chad begins running his nose up and down my neck before coming down to nuzzle my breasts.

"Chad, let me go, please," I say calm but firmly.

He stops nuzzling me for a second as he looks up at me, his eyes bouncing around as he does.

"I already did, I don't think I'm gonna again. This hasn't been too bad having you around, the kid either. You guys don't make too much noise, you look good on my arm. All that's left is one thing and this would be perfect," he murmurs as one of his arms comes around my front, cupping my pussy with a rough squeeze.

"Chad, stop!" I snap, causing irritation to flash across his face.

"Why should I? You're in my house, you're my girl-"

"I am not! You manipulated me and took my son from me. I'm here because of that little boy. Don't let some twisted delusion fool you, I can't fucking stand you."

I don't see the backhand coming, I should, but I don't. The force of his slap has me stumbling and then tripping in my heels. I fall to the ground, hitting my head against the cold floor with a hollow thunk. I see stars instantly and before I can gain my bearings Chad is straddling me before balling up his fists and delivering a blow to my left eye. I cry out in pain as one of his large hands grabs a chunk of my hair, lifting my head off the hardwood before slamming it back down.

He does it again and again and again until a warmth begins to run down my neck. Pain is ricocheting inside my head, but I'm so disoriented I can hardly do anything but scream.

"Mommy?!" Tucker suddenly shouts from his doorway.

"Go!" I cry out as Chad slaps me again. "Run, Tuck! Lock the door!" I scream.

Looking terrified, he starts to move towards me when I thrash.

"No, baby! Run! Hide! Mommy will be okay," I say even as Chad punches me in the nose, causing blood to spray us both in the process.

I hear the slamming of a door and pray to God that Tucker did what I said. I don't know if Chad will go after him too, he is so wasted he probably would, and I'd die before I let that happen. Hell, with the amount of blood collecting behind my neck I'd say I'm not too far from that as is.

"Had enough, bitch?" Chad shouts into my face. "Ready to spread those fucking legs for me yet!?"

The strong taste of iron gathers into my mouth from my nose or the repeated blows to the face, I don't know, but I don't waste a moment in spitting it all into Chad's face. Rage takes over him as he rears back and begins delivering blow after blow against my ribs. I hear several cracks as pain rips through me.

Twisting and jerking as best as I can, I'm able to get one arm out from his hold and I use it to hit him across the face. Unfortunately, it isn't nearly hard enough and seems to only piss him off. Chad's large hands are suddenly around my neck, squeezing with all of his might.

"You aren't even fucking worth the hassle! Just die, stupid bitch! DIE!" He shouts, his eyes wild and crazed.

I gasp for air, but nothing makes it through Chad's grip. My lungs are burning with need as a fuzziness begins to take over. The punishing grip on my neck only increases as Chad's arms shake with rage and strength. I'm clawing at his hands and arms desperately, but he is relentless as he squeezes harder and harder. My vision begins to double before the edges start clouding over.

Oh, God. This is it. Jesus, please protect my baby when I'm gone.

Chapter Fifty-Four

Declan

I stand there waiting for Vi's text as Slater's party begins to rage around me, I couldn't give a shit about all of that, though. Chad left a few minutes ago which means there is no way in hell I could sneak over there to see her and Tuck. I won't put everything in jeopardy just because I'm desperate to see her, to hold her again.

Suddenly, my phone rings. It's an unknown number but it's too late to be spam, so I answer.

"Hello?" I ask as I plug my other ear so I can hear better.

"Is this Declan?" A frantic man asks quickly.

"Yes. Who is this?"

"Frank Dalloway. Your dad told me to call you if I ever saw anything suspicious. I'm outside the Brownstone residence, and there is screaming. I think someone is being hurt. I called the police an-"

He doesn't even finish before I am running through the party and out the door. I don't even waste time getting into my car as I run the few blocks to where I know Chad's house is. Screaming? What kind of screaming? Fighting screaming? Painful screaming? Is it Vi? Tuck? Let's fucking hope it's Chad screaming.

I should have never let her walk out that door, two weeks ago or tonight. I let her walk into the arms of a monster. I should have found another way to get Tuck back. I should have done more, something, anything.

My body begins to sweat as my heart pumps harder, but I only push myself further. I have to get to them. I need to make sure my family is okay. I notice a blacked-out SUV parked out front of Chad's house, that must be the guy that called me. My dad hired a PI to watch over Vi. Of course, he did. Why didn't I think of that? I'll have to thank the fuck out of him later.

Tearing down Chad's driveway and up his stairs, I try the door handle and am so fucking thankful that the dumbass kept his door unlocked. Saves me time from having to break in. I throw open the door, frantically looking around the spacious house to see what's going on. The place is eerily quiet, except for a soft sobbing noise coming from the hallway.

"Vi? Tuck?!" I call out frantically as I follow the noise.

When I crest the corner, I'm not prepared for what I see. My legs give out, and I drop to my knees as I see Vi laying limp against the hardwood floor, a pool of blood surrounding her head and angry red fingerprints covering her slender neck. Her skin has an unnatural pale hue to it, and her chest is terrifyingly still. Oh my fucking god! NO! Baby.

Tucker is huddled over her, hugging and crying into her.

"Mommy, wake up! Mommy! I'm s-scared!"

Crawling over to them, I quickly feel Vi's neck, fear wrapping around me in a vise grip. It takes a second for me to recognize the slight thump of a heartbeat. I could fucking cry in relief right now. She has a pulse. It's fucking faint but it's there.

"Tuck," I say, but he doesn't look away from his mama. Tears are pouring down his face as he just stares at her face like he isn't all here.

"Tucker!" I bark, snapping him out of his trance.

"Declan?" He asks with wide eyes.

"I'm here, big guy, but we need to help your mama. The police are on their way, but we have to stop the bleeding. Can you go into the kitchen and grab a towel?"

Tucker nods as he shakily stands up before running around the corner and into the kitchen. Vi's face is absolutely beat to shit and something in me breaks. Her nose is very clearly broken with blood still slowly leaking out of it, her left eye is damn near swollen shut, and her lip is split several areas.

Brushing a piece of hair away from her face, my fingers gently graze against the small area of her skin that is left unmarked.

"Baby," I whisper hoarsely.

Tucker runs in next to me in the next moment with several small hand towels. Better than nothing. I take two of them and gently press them against the back of Vi's head where the majority of the blood is coming from. I don't wanna lift her head up in case her spine has been injured, but I know that there is way too much blood on the floor and that she can't afford to lose much more.

Looking around, I quickly survey the area but come up short.

"Tuck, where is Chad?"

He looks around before looking back at me.

"I-I don't know. He was here on top of Mommy, and now, he's gone."

He just left her. He left her for fucking dead, for her child to find her like this. I'm going to take a sick amount of pleasure in ending him.

In the next moment, the house is suddenly swarmed with several police officers, all shouting orders at each other and calling out.

"Over here!" I shout as I continue to hold pressure to Vi's head.

The first officer makes his way over to me, glancing down at Vi before pulling out his gun and holding it to me.

"Put your hands up!" He orders.

"I can't. She'll bleed out," I say calmly.

Tucker quickly darts in between us as he runs up to the cop.

"Don't shoot him! He saved my mommy. Chad hurt my mommy."

The cop looks at me warily for a moment as a few EMT's rush in.

"Jesus," the woman EMT breathes as she bends down next to Vi and begins pulling out supplies. "What happened?"

"I don't know. I just got here a few minutes ago. I found her like this, we've just been trying to stop the bleeding."

She nods, and I reluctantly step to the side as the other EMT replaces me. They quickly begin stabilizing Vi as the cop nods for us to leave the hallway. Reaching down, I scoop Tuck up into my arms as he curls into me.

"You're safe, buddy. You're safe," I whisper before pressing a kiss against the side of his head.

"So, what do you know about what happened?"

I give him the quick version of everything and how I got the phone call as a few other officers walk downstairs with a very drunk and belligerent Chad handcuffed. Rage washes over me as I see the blood splattered across his shirt and face, knowing it isn't his blood but Vi's. Setting Tuck down gently, I give him a look that says to stay there as I cross the room until I'm face to face with Chad.

Glancing at the officers holding Chad, I speak to them.

"I hope y'all can understand and forgive me."

Before they can ask what for, I wind back my arm and put every ounce of power I can into a punch to his jaw. I hear a sickening crunch and a snap. Wouldn't be surprised if I broke his jaw. Good. Goddamn motherfucker.

Chad cries out in pain but doesn't say anything, probably because he can't. Vi is being wheeled out on a stretcher, and the two cops glance at her, some of the color leaving their face before sharing a look with each other.

"You see anything, Skalsky?"

"Nope," the other answers. "We found him upstairs this way. That girl must pack a hell of a right hook."

"You can say that again," the first cop nods as they share a look with me and drag Chad out the front door and over to their police cruiser.

Walking over to Tucker, I pull him in for a hug again as his little arms latch around me. When he pulls back, I see that he's crying again.

"I'm sorry, Declan," he cries.

"Why, big guy?"

"I didn't protect Mommy. I tried but she yelled at me. She told me to run and hide. I tried to be brave but I can'tttt," he sobs as he hangs his head in disappointment.

My heart breaks for Tuck as I lift his head up so that he can look at me.

"You did so good, Tuck. You did exactly what you were supposed to do. Your mommy is going to be so proud of you. I'm so proud of you."

He cries a little harder before he nods.

"Is Mommy okay?"

"I don't know. Why don't we go find out?"

Tuck nods, and I pick him up before rushing outside. They are just closing the ambulance up when I get there.

"Wait, can we get a ride? My car is down the road."

The EMT looks at us before nodding. I blow out a breath before hopping up into the back and holding Vi's limp hand as we go down the road.

I don't know how long they will be able to keep Chad in jail for. His parents will probably have him bailed out in no time, unfortunately. But I'm going to spend every dime to my name to make sure that he rots in prison or in the ground until the end of time. I will do whatever it fucking takes to make sure that Chad Brownstone stays the fuck away from *my* family. Forever.

Chapter Fifty-Five

Vi

My eyes are so heavy, it's like they've been glued shut. It takes several tries but eventually I'm able to peel them open, well, one of them. For some reason, I can't see anything out of my left eye. The beeping of a machine is the first thing to clue me in. My head is fucking killing me.

Straining my right eye, I quickly glance above me to see that I am hooked up to a machine and definitely not inside Chad's house. I'm in the hospital.

"Baby," Declan breathes out beside me, relief heavy in his tone.

Glancing over, I see that he is cradling one of my hands in between his two large ones.

"Dec?"

"Thank god you're awake. I was beginning to lose my shit."

"What are you doing here? Where is Chad? Wait, where is Tuck? Did he hurt him? Oh my god, Declan. If Tuck got-"

"Shh, settle down, baby. It's okay. He's right there," Declan says as he points to the couch in the corner where Tucker is snuggled up underneath some hospital blankets fast asleep.

Blowing out a relieved breath, I wince in pain as my ribs begin to burn. Shit. He really fucked me up this time. I'm sure I don't even want to know what I look like right now.

"Thank you for being here. I don't even know how I got here or how you got here but I'll be okay. You have to go."

Declan watches me carefully as he lets me continue.

"If Chad finds out that you saw me in the hospital, he will probably do even worse than whatever he just did."

"He couldn't do much worse," Declan bites, a flash of anger passing over his face as he clenches his jaw. Shaking his head, he blows out a breath.

"He almost killed you, Vi. You had a major brain bleed. They had to take you in for surgery *yesterday*. It took so fucking long I was about ready to tear this hospital to pieces. Your nose is broken, three ribs are fractured, and your face has a lot of swelling."

I wince hearing the list of my injuries as I slowly reach a hand up and touch the bandage wrapped around my head. Well, that explains the headache.

"I found you unconscious, Tucker was laying on top of your limp body, crying his eyes out. I thought you were dead," he chokes out before gripping my hand a little tighter and bringing it up to his lips as he closes his eyes.

The mental image that he paints will haunt me for the rest of my life. My poor baby should have never seen any of that, no one should have.

"You found me?" I ask.

Declan nods. "My dad had a PI watching the house, just in case. He called me saying that he heard screams. I didn't let him finish before I was running to you from Slater's."

"You ran to me?" I parrot.

A soft look takes over Declan's face as he gently cups my cheek.

"I'd run to the end of the earth for you, baby."

My heart flip flops inside my chest as Declan leans forward and very gently ghosts his lips over mine. Butterflies soar through my stomach and up to my chest. I don't think I'll ever not get butterflies from this man.

When he pulls away, I blink my one good eye open as I look up at him.

"So, where is he?" I ask, scared to hear the answer.

Surprising me, Declan smirks. "In jail, waiting for a court date that Dani made sure won't happen for at least a few months."

I furrow my brows. "He didn't post bail?"

Declan smiles wider and shakes his head.

"He's being held with no bail. You and Tuck are safe. An emergency protective order was granted for you and Tucker against Chad. Once his hearing comes, we're gonna fucking ruin him, baby. Dani brought in a partner at her firm back in New York, and he is kicking ass and taking names. He got the court to grant you emergency custody after he dug up the financial records proving Chad transferred twenty-five thousand dollars into Judge McCarthy's bank account a day before we went to court. Chad will never see the light of day outside the prison yard again, let alone breathe in the same direction as you and Tuck."

"So," I ask, voice quaking softly. "It's done? We're free?"

"We're free, baby," he says with a nod. "So, do you still want me to leave? I can g-"

"Don't you dare!" I snap as I grab onto him desperately, hurting my ribs in the process.

I wince in pain, and Declan puts a reassuring hand on me as he chuckles lightly.

"Easy, baby. I was joking. You couldn't get rid of me if you tried. You're both stuck with me."

I smile softly as relief for so many reasons washes over me.

"Good, because if this last month has taught me anything, it's that Tuck and I can't live without you."

"You'll never have to again," he promises.

Declan and I talk for a little more before a soft knock comes from the door. The doctor comes in and checks me over, reiterating over and over again how lucky I am to be alive. I feel it. I thought for sure for a moment there that I was dead. I thought I was going to be ripped away from Tuck only when I had just got him back. It was by far the most terrifying thing that I've ever experienced.

The doctors said since I literally just had brain surgery, I'll be kept for observation for another few days. They also said though because I'm speaking and moving at least slightly, they are confident I will make a full recovery.

A few minutes after the doctors leave, Declan's parents, Judy, and Dani come in, along with a man in a pristine three-piece suit who looks to be in his early thirties.

"Violet Ann!" Judy says as she hustles over to me just before Suzannah does the same.

"Oh, sweetheart!"

"I'm okay," I say to them with the best smile that I can muster.

"Like hell you are! That man is going to rot in prison before he burns in fucking hell!" Suzannah promises, while Judy nods her agreement.

Rodney chuckles as he takes his wife by the shoulders and slowly pulls her away.

"Easy, honey. He'll get his."

"Yes, he will," interrupts the well-dressed man in the corner before he turns to address me.

"Violet, my name is Miles Greene. Dani and I have been working on your case, and I wanted to personally assure you that we will take this guy down."

"It's Danielle, asshole," Dani grumbles from the corner of the room.

I glance to see her practically sulking as she glares daggers at him. I don't know what the deal with that is, and I honestly don't have it in me to care. His words are music to my ears and for that, I'm grateful.

"Thank you, Miles. You have no idea what that means to me."

He nods, his eyes briefly flicking over me before his face tightens. I'm not sure if my injuries make him uncomfortable or angry. Maybe a little bit of both? He seems like the kind of guy that would probably expect women to always look prim and done up.

"My pleasure. Once you are on your feet, we will meet again and handle everything going forward. Dani and I have to get going back to New York for a case, but I wanted to personally let you know that we will take care of everything," he says as his eyes glance over to Tuck before coming back to me.

"It's Danielle. I know you aren't stupid because of that fancy Harvard degree in your office, so you must be deaf," Dani snaps.

"Danielle Daniels!" Suzannah admonishes.

Dani sends a withering look to her mom before shaking her head and practically shoving Miles out the door.

"C'mon, asshole," she grumbles before giving me a half of a smile and a nod. Miles gives her an amused smirk before looking back at me with a nod as they step out of the room.

"How are you feeling, Sweet Pea?" Judy asks, gently patting the back of my hand.

"I'm okay. How are you, Judy?"

She scoffs. "I'm fine. I'm not the one laid up in a hospital bed."

I chuckle lightly even though it hurts like hell.

"Touché."

"Mommy?" Tuck's sleepy voice asks.

I turn my head gently to see him sitting up on the couch, wiping the sleep from his eyes.

"Hey, baby. Did you sleep okay?"

His eyes widen as if he is now fully awake before he springs to hit feet and runs straight for me.

"Mommy!" He shouts before slamming into the side of my bed and burying his head into my chest.

I wince in pain but lift my arm up anyways to hold him close to me.

"Careful, big guy. Remember what we said?" Declan says.

Tuck eases off me slowly as he looks to Declan before me.

"Mommy has ouchies, and we have to be careful."

"'Atta boy," Declan smiles encouragingly.

"Are you okay, Mommy?" Tucker asks hopefully.

I glance around from Suzannah and Rodney's smiles to Judy's warm gaze, relief heavy in it before looking at Declan who is staring down at me like I'm his Sun and back to Tucker who looks at me like I'm everything to him. In reality, these people are everything to me. Yeah, I'm doing great.

EPILOGUE

DECLAN

It's crazy to think how much someone's life can change in one year. This time last year, I had just moved to Seattle from Knoxville. I was one of the top Middle Linebackers of the league. I had more money than I knew what to do with, an amazing set of parents, and a workaholic but loving older sister. I thought I had everything, until I met her, until I met *them*.

One year changed everything.

After Vi got out of the hospital and was all cleared by the doctors, true to Miles' word, Chad got his. Miles and Dani both represented Vi, and Chad was charged with first degree attempted murder, child endangerment, and bribing a public official. He may not rot in prison for the rest of his days, but he is definitely going to be in prison for the next fifteen years at least, so that will have to do for now.

On top of that, Miles went for the jugular and had all of Chad's possessions awarded to Vi as compensation not only for the attack but as a sort of back pay for child support over the years. I honestly don't know how he pulled it off because according to Dani, that isn't how things work, but everything was transferred into Vi's name just a month after the sentencing.

She didn't want any of it, though. Instead, she sold everything and had all the money donated to a non-profit that helps women get out of abusive relationships and also helps pay for lawyer fees in custody battles. She said it was time Chad's money went towards something good. I couldn't have agreed more.

We didn't stay in Seattle once all the court stuff was settled. There was nothing left for us there. I officially quit the team and paid the penalty fine for breaking my contract, much to the coaches' surprise, before we packed up our things and moved back home to Tennessee.

All it took was one weekend visit, and Vi and Tuck both fell in love with it. As soon as I saw Tucker running in the backyard of my home down there and Vi bent over in my walk-in shower, I knew that this was home for all of us. I'm just glad they agreed too.

Of course, we couldn't leave Judy behind. She didn't have any family outside of Tucker and Vi, and she didn't have much for her in Seattle either, so I had a moving company come over one day and pack all her stuff before we drug her onto the plane with us. She acted like she was mad about it for a day or two before she teared up and thanked me for not taking Vi and Tuck away from her.

My house has a guesthouse on the property, and I tried to convince her to move into it, but she refused so we compromised, and I bought her an apartment down the road. It was the least I could do for how well she took care of my family all those years before I found them. Plus, life without Grandma Judy sounds way too boring and way too appropriate for my liking.

Since I'm now officially a retired NFL player, I decided to take my knowledge and apply it to the foundation. My dad's been wanting to take a step back anyways and so I'm now heading up most of the day-to-day operations. I love that I still have football in my life without all the traveling away from my family.

When we moved down to Tennessee, I had a surprise for Vi. I took her to a cute shop on the main strip of downtown Knoxville where an empty business was sitting, waiting for her. I looked up everything I could about what it took to start a floral shop and had all the equipment bought and installed for her.

As soon as she stepped inside, she cried. She tried to tell me that she couldn't accept it, but it didn't take too much convincing for her to agree and thank me. We ended up christening the place in the backroom properly. I think that's by far my favorite spot of the shop. We were able to get it opened in no time, and all Vi had to handle was what kind of inventory and prices she wanted to have and choosing a name. She went with The Petal and The Stem, which I think everyone can agree is a hell of a lot more professional sounding and classic than Blooming-Deals.

I tried to hold out, but we had only been in Knoxville for twenty-four hours before I got down on one knee and proposed to Vi. I've been impulsive as hell from the first day I met this woman, so there really was no hope in this being any different. She sobbed, said that we were crazy and that it was too soon, even as she was hysterically nodding yes. Tucker cheered in celebration and ran laps around the house when we told him.

Vi wanted a small intimate wedding, and I couldn't have agreed more. We ended up just getting married in the backyard of our house with only our closest friends and family a month after I proposed. Slater, Nikki, Seb, and Erica were there. Even Trevor made it. He apologized for the shit he said and told me that he was happy for us. Mindi had to fly all the way from Spain to make the wedding on time, but she said that she wouldn't have missed seeing Vi in a big white ball gown for anything in the world.

As soon as Vi and I were officially married, I also filled out the paperwork to legally adopt Tuck. He is officially my son, not that I needed a piece of paper to tell me that. He loves his new last name and insists on introducing himself to damn near everyone he meets as Tucker Daniels.

It makes me grin like a damn idiot every time.

We're having a Sunday barbeque at our place today. The sun is shining as I flip some burgers while my dad and Tucker toss the football around. My mama is sitting by the pool with Vi, gossiping about lord knows what. Glancing out of the corner of my eye, I wonder if my mom has been able to see the bump yet.

Vi and I found out about six weeks ago that we are having a baby. It's been hell trying to keep it a secret because I want nothing more than to tell everyone and anyone in sight. Vi insisted though, until we got through the first trimester, she wanted to keep it a secret since miscarriages are very common in the beginning. But we are officially into the second trimester now and at our last doctor appointment, they were even able to see an early glimpse of the gender.

Smiling to myself, I shut the grill off and set the burgers onto the plate as I turn around to face my family. Mama is gonna lose her mind when she finds out that she is going to have a little granddaughter to spoil on top of her grandson.

A lot can change in one year, but Vi, she changed everything.

Thank you

Thank you so much for reading The Walls We Break! I hope you enjoyed these characters and this story as much as I did! (Well, everyone except Chad. He can get fucked.) The Hearts We Break, the third and final book in this series will be coming to you August 2023!

Pre-order your copy here! https://bit.ly/3Xt0Wyh

I'll be honest, this book took it out of me. It was a labor of love, exhaustion, frustration and many tears. Although it was a tough one to write, I felt like it was important. As a DV survivor, I've been there. I've felt the fear, the uncertainty, the hopelessness. If you or someone you know is in an abusive situation, know that it is not hopeless. There are so many resources for you, so many people here for you, an entire community, ready to support you.

Lean on others when you need the strength but don't forget to stand. You are stronger than your circumstances. I love every single one of you deeply.

National Domestic Violence Hotline – 1-800-799-SAFE(7233)

National Coalition Against Domestic Violence – https://ncadv.org/

If you enjoyed The Walls We Break it would mean the world to me if you could leave a review! Every single review makes the difference!

To keep up with the latest releases, giveaways and more make sure to sign up for my newsletter and follow me!

Newsletter – https://bit.ly/3q2s4px

Instagram – @katelyntaylorauthor

Tiktok – @katelyntaylorauthor

Facebook Reader Group – Katelyn's Twisted Readers

Facebook – https://bit.ly/3sIzXlE

Acknowledgments

First off, I have to as usual give the biggest shout out to my babe, Skarlet. You are my PA, my Alpha, my dream crusher, my brand manager (That still has a nice ring to it, right?) and one of my closest friends. If not for you, this book would never have seen the light of day. When I told you I couldn't do it, you told me to suck it up and get it done. When I called you bawling my eyes out writing the court scene, you were there for me (before you told me to suck it up and get it done). You make me better not only as an author but as a person. I am eternally grateful to know you and honored to call you my friend.

To my beta readers and advanced ARC readers, Jos, Dee, LJ, Cayla and Lynds. I love you guys. You all do more for me than I could ever express. I appreciate every single one of you for taking in the raw and gritty version of Vi and Declan and helping me make them who they are today. You all are superstars!

To my street team and ARC readers, you all are the backbone of this journey. My street team, you lovelies are there for me for every release and every single day in between. I appreciate your support and feel so honored to be hyped by such an amazing group of people. I'm so thankful for my ARC readers who take the time to read my books, review them and help spread the word. Without you, less (or possibly no) people would get the chance to experience couples like Vi and Declan (and I think that we can all agree anyone living a life without knowing Declan Daniels is only half a life.).